"Lisa. Don't go."

It wasn't a command. Instead Dave's voice held a hushed, pleading tone, and like some kind of invisible cord, it kept her from walking away more effectively than his grasp on her wrist ever could have. Then his grip relaxed, becoming more like a caress. Letting out a long, tortured breath, he slowly, slowly pulled her back around until she was standing in front of him. He looked up at her with a solemn gaze.

"Here's the truth. I kissed you downstairs because I wanted to. Because you looked so beautiful and we'd been sitting together all night and it seemed . . . God, Lisa." He exhaled. "Just looking at you has always done something to me I don't understand and I probably never will."

She held her breath, afraid to break whatever spell it was that kept the longing in his voice and the desire in his eyes. "And then you wanted more than a kiss."

His gaze played over her body, easing down over her breasts to her waist, then back up to her face again. His hands tightened against hers. "I still do."

By Jane Graves
Published by Ivy Books

I GOT YOU, BABE
WILD AT HEART

Flirting with Disaster

Jane Graves

IVY BOOKS • NEW YORK

An Ivy Book
Published by The Random House Publishing Group
Copyright © 2003 by Jane Graves

www.ballantinebooks.com

ISBN 0-345-458400

Manufactured in the United States of America

First Edition: November 2003

OPM   10   9   8   7   6   5   4   3   2   1

For my wonderful husband, Brian.
Thank you for giving me the wings to fly and a soft place to land. I'll love you forever.

chapter one

"You think I won't do it?" the man shouted. "Is that what you think? Well, you can damn well think again!"

Dave DeMarco bowed his head and let out a breath of frustration. This was not going well.

Five minutes ago, he'd pulled his patrol car onto Highway 4, heading back to the station after a particularly demanding shift, when the guy caught his attention. He was maybe fifty years old, sitting there in his immaculate suit, polished shoes, silk tie, and sixty-dollar haircut, just sitting there, as if he had nothing better to do than watch the world go by. And Dave might not have thought a thing about it, except for the fact that the place he'd chosen to sit was on a highway overpass, his legs dangling over rush hour traffic.

Dave had radioed the situation, asked for backup, then pulled his patrol car onto the overpass. He couldn't say for sure whether the guy was serious or not, but most of the time if potential jumpers chose a public venue they were just attention seekers, hoping for somebody to give a shit long enough to tell them not to take a dive. With luck, this guy was one of those.

Right now Dave stood ten feet from where the guy sat on the retaining wall, easing as close as he dared. He ticked off the procedures in his mind: *Get his name. Establish rapport. Keep him talking*.

He inched forward.

"Don't come any closer!" the guy shouted.

Dave held his ground, glancing down to the highway below, not surprised in the least to see that several cars had pulled over to the side of the road to watch the festivities. And already they'd been joined by a Channel Seven news van. Wonderful. An audience. This was going to be a regular dog and pony show.

"Hey, I'm warning you!" the guy shouted. "Back off, or I'm going over!"

Not likely. If he really did have a death wish, the coroner would be zipping the body bag right about now. But Dave still had to play by the numbers.

"What's your name?" Dave asked.

"Fuck off!"

"Now, something tells me that's not really your name. Try again for me, will you?"

Dave forced himself to remain calm. Patrol cops were taught to be patient problem solvers, and he'd always been damned good at his job. But right now, for some reason, he felt edgy and irritated, wishing the guy had chosen any overpass but this one on which to make his point. Maybe it had just been a very long day. Most days in recent memory had seemed like very long days.

Finally the guy's belligerent expression faded, and Dave saw a tiny window of communication creak open. "Frank," he said. "My name's Frank."

"Are you armed, Frank? Gun? Knife?"

"No. Of course not."

"Okay. Tell you what. It's a little dangerous on that wall where you're sitting, and I'm thinking maybe you ought to get off it. What do you think?"

"I'm thinking maybe I ought to stay right where I am."

"Okay, then. Tell me why you're doing this. What's the problem?"

"Like you give a shit about my problems?"

Dave didn't want to deal with this. He just didn't. He saw a couple of patrol cars lining up behind his on the overpass, and if he could have handed this one off to anyone else he'd have done it in a heartbeat.

"Just get down from there," Dave said, "and we can talk about whatever's bugging you."

"Yeah, right. Talk. Just how stupid do you think I am?"

Dave glanced at the gold band on the guy's left hand. "Tell me about your wife."

"What's to tell?"

"Got any kids?"

"Yeah. So what?"

"So maybe they'd like their father alive. You suppose?"

He made a scoffing noise. "Right now, I don't know anyone who gives a damn if I live or die."

"Now, Frank, you and I both know that's not true."

"You don't know shit about me. If you did, and you were me, you'd be up here on this wall, too."

Dave started to say it. He started to say, *You don't really want to do this, do you? Don't you know that suicide is a permanent solution to a temporary problem?*

But as the words ran through his mind, all at once they sounded like some stupid cliché that even the biggest idiot on the planet wouldn't buy. Lately he was having a hard time believing any of the bullshit he told people in his line of work: That if a husband and a wife would just calmly talk things out, they'd come to an understanding. That if a crackhead only went into rehab, he could kick that nasty habit and his life would be rosy. That suicide wasn't the answer, because it was a permanent solution to a temporary problem. Had there ever been a time when he'd believed any of that crap?

The truth was that anyone who even thought about committing suicide just might have a few problems that were going to stay with him pretty much through eternity. Dave would bet his last buck that within days of the obligatory psych consult Frank here would be back at it again one way or another, figuratively screaming at the world, trying desperately to make somebody else solve his problems because he sure as hell couldn't.

Well, Dave had news for the guy—bold-type, front-page, above-the-fold news: He couldn't solve them, either. Didn't want to solve them. Christ, he didn't even want to stand here and pretend that he did. And as he continued to stare at this man who thought nothing of displaying his mental malfunctions for the entire city of Tolosa, Texas, to see, something inside him snapped.

"So what's the deal here anyway, Frank?" Dave said. "Are you one of those corporate executives who played loose with the stock market and sent his company into the toilet?"

The guy gaped at Dave, his expensive silk tie fluttering in the breeze. "No! Of course not!"

"Find your wife cheating on you?"

"No!"

"Lose your life savings betting on the horses?"

"No! Nothing like that! I just—"

"To tell you the truth, Frank, I don't give a shit what you're doing here. And you're right. I don't know a damned thing about you, which means that for all I know, you might be on the right track."

The guy swallowed hard, his eyes as wide as searchlights. He looked down at the traffic whizzing by beneath him, then back at Dave. "What?"

Dave took one step closer and lowered his voice. "Jump."

"What?"

"Simplest thing in the world. Just jump the hell off this bridge and get it over with. Then maybe I can get the paperwork done in time to grab a beer and watch the Mavericks game."

"But . . . but I don't *want* to jump!"

Dave drew back with feigned surprise. "Oh, really? You don't want to jump? Then would you mind telling me why the hell you're sitting on this goddamned bridge during rush hour, screwing up traffic and dragging half the cops and paramedics in the city out here to deal with this?"

"Wh-what I mean," the guy said, "is that I don't want to jump, but I will. I will, if that's the only way—"

"The only way to do what, Frank? To show all those people who have been making your life hell that they shouldn't have? To show them that they never should have ignored you and all your problems? To show them the consequences of fucking you over? Is that what you're talking about?"

"No! Leave me alone! That's all I want you to do! Just leave me alone!"

"No," Dave said, taking another step forward. "You don't want to be left alone. If you'd wanted to be left alone, you'd have gone into the executive washroom, locked the door, and put a gun to your head. You wouldn't be sitting on this overpass, stopping traffic and providing the local press with a really juicy story for the evening news."

"No! That's not true!"

Dave inched closer. "If it bleeds, it leads, Frank. But you know that, don't you? You know that because you're sitting on this bridge, the press will gather around and the whole world will see all your pain in living color. Isn't that what you really want?"

"Shut up! Just *shut up*!" Frank clamped his hands onto the edge of the wall, his fingers turning white with the effort. "What kind of cop are you, anyway? I pay my taxes, and this is what I get?"

That really fried Dave. Like he was some kind of social worker or something? What in the hell did the guy expect? Day in and day out Dave dealt with this shit, playing Mr. Negotiator with wife-beating men, smart-ass kids, drug-addicted prostitutes, and other assorted users and abusers. And what he'd found out was that there was no solution to any of it. If the guy got up the nerve to jump, Dave could send somebody to pick up the pieces after the fact, but he couldn't fix what drove him out here in the first place, no matter how much tax money Citizen Frank poured into the city coffers. And speaking of tax money, far too much of it was being wasted right now.

Before the guy knew what was happening, Dave took one last step forward and wrapped his arm around Frank's upper chest. In one swift move, Dave pulled him backward off the wall, scraping his suit pants along the weather-pocked concrete and knocking the hide off the heels of his Bruno Maglis. Dave tried to cuff him, but the guy scuffled with him just long enough that his last thread of patience finally unraveled. Dave ordered him down on the ground in a tone that didn't leave any room for disobedience. Once he was licking asphalt, Dave yanked Frank's arms behind his back, clipped on the cuffs, then pulled him back to his feet.

"What's the matter with you?" Frank shouted. "Are you nuts?"

"Yeah, Frank. *I'm* nuts."

Frank's belligerent expression slowly crumpled, giving way to a look of total despair. As his eyes welled with tears, Dave walked him to his patrol car amid a smattering of applause and whistles from the road below. He opened the back door and deposited Frank inside.

As Dave was shutting the door, he saw his brother Alex approaching, walking with the self-assured gait and commanding manner of a police detective born to the job. Essence of cop oozed out of every pore in his body, but that wasn't surprising. Law enforcement was a profession as inherent to the DeMarco family as politics were to the Kennedys.

"Heard your radio call," Alex said. "Thought I'd come by and see what all the commotion was about. You okay?"

"Yeah."

"Nice work. Got here just in time to see you pull him back."

Yeah, he'd kept Frank from taking a dive today. But who was going to stop him next time? And there would be a next time.

There was *always* a next time.

"Pretty slick," Alex said. "So what did you say to the guy to get in close enough to grab him?"

Dave looked away, hating the admiration he saw in his brother's eyes. *I told him I didn't give a shit about his problems, that he could leap off that overpass right into a body bag for all I cared.*

"The usual. Got his name. Established rapport. Kept him talking. Told him that suicide is a permanent solution to a temporary problem. You know. Procedure."

He nearly choked on the word. He wasn't sure he was in the frame of mind to follow procedure again as long as he lived.

"I heard the lieutenant say once that they should loan you

out for the Middle East peace talks," Alex said. "In twenty-four hours the Arabs and Israelis would be one big happy family."

Dave faced his brother. "To tell you the truth, Alex, right about now I'd probably tell both sides to solve their own problems and leave me the hell out of it." He turned to get into his patrol car.

"Dave. Wait."

"I've got to get this guy to Tolosa Medical."

"Yeah, okay, but when you're finished, why don't we go for a couple of beers? I'll buy."

"I've got to get home."

"Aunt Louisa will keep Ashley a little while longer."

Dave turned back. "No. Not tonight. She's been having a little trouble at school, and—"

"Trouble?"

"Nothing big. Big to a five-year-old, I guess. I've got to get home."

Dave started to get into the patrol car again, and Alex caught his arm. "Then forget you. Think about me. I don't get a chance to go out very often, you know. Ever since Val and I got married, she's been keeping me on a pretty tight leash." Alex leaned closer and spoke confidentially. "She's got an evening surveillance tonight. If I play my cards right, she'll never know I stepped out for a drink or two."

That was as big a load of bullshit as Dave had ever heard. A private investigator, Val was hardly one of those women who expected their man front and center at the dinner table every evening at six o'clock. Dave heard what Alex was really saying.

Something's eating you. Have a beer or two. Forget about it, just for a little while.

Dave sighed with resignation. "Okay. I'll come by for a quick one."

Alex stepped away from the car. "I'll call John and tell him to come along."

Their brother, John, had also embraced the family business, which meant it had been a triple victory for their father,

Joseph DeMarco. Even years after being killed in the line of
duty, he was still a legend in the Tolosa Police Department.
Growing up in that kind of shadow, had any of them really
had a choice of occupation?

Alex pointed at Dave as he walked away. "The Onion. Six
o'clock. Be there."

Dave nodded and got into his car, refusing to acknowledge
the fact that Frank was sitting in his backseat, tears streaming
down his face and dripping onto his silk tie. And it wasn't until Dave was halfway to the hospital that his hands started to
shake and the realization of what he'd done smacked him like
a brick to the side of the head.

You told that poor bastard to jump.

And now all Dave could think about was, *What if he had?*

The Blue Onion was a grubby little beer joint and pool
hall, the hangout of choice for most of the cops who worked
the south side. Dave had never been able to figure out why.
Grime coated the tables, the rancid odor of stale smoke filled
the air, and the felt on the pool tables looked as if rats had
gnawed on it. It was just the kind of dirty, rowdy, in-your-face
establishment that he generally took great pains to avoid.
Among Tolosa cops, though, tradition died hard.

He met Alex at six o'clock, just as he said he would, intending to stay for a couple of drinks, watch a little of the
Mavericks game, then head out. They grabbed a table next to
the wall, and John joined them a few minutes later.

"About time you came out for a beer," John said as he
pulled out a chair and sat down. "I was beginning to think
you'd forgotten how to have a good time."

"I've been busy."

"You've been a hermit."

"Will you shut up? I'm here now, aren't I?"

John glanced at Alex with one of those "yep, something's
up with him" looks. Subtlety had never been one of John's
long suits.

"Heard you had a jumper today," John said as if he was just

making idle conversation. "Talked your way up to him, then grabbed him right off the ledge. That took balls."

Actually, balls hadn't been required. A eunuch could have pulled that one off, as long as the eunuch was a fed-up cop who didn't give a damn if he stepped over the line.

Way over.

As Dave was transporting Frank to the psych ward at Tolosa Medical Center, he kept picturing him sailing over that wall, his coat ballooning up behind him, his tie quivering in the wind, falling like a hawk taking a nosedive—right up to the moment when he wasn't falling anymore. Then somebody would have cleaned up the mess and everyone would have patted Dave on the back and told him that of course he'd done everything he could. That you couldn't win them all. Better luck next time.

"It was no big deal," Dave said to John. "He had no intention of jumping."

"Bullshit," John said. "You can never tell. You think you're dealing with rational people, but they're not rational. Not even close. Saw a cop talking a woman down once who swore she wasn't going to jump. He almost had his hands on her when she shifted gears and took a dive." He snapped his fingers. "Just like that."

Thank you, John, for making me feel so much better.

Dave drained his first beer, wondering how many more he'd have to drink before it took the edge off the way he felt right now. All he wanted to do was shove what had happened today to the back of his mind and pretend it had never happened.

"You said Ashley had a problem," Alex said. "What's up with that?"

Dave sighed heavily. "It's nothing. Some kid on the playground smacked her with a swing."

"So tell her to smack him back," Alex said.

"She sat down in the corner of the playground and cried."

"Well, that's not going to cut it," John said. "She needs to learn not to take any crap. Once the other kids know she'll stand up for herself, they won't bother her anymore."

"Come on, John. Can you really see Ashley hauling off and belting another kid?"

His brothers looked down at their beers.

Timidity was an unheard of characteristic in the DeMarco family, and it worried Dave that it seemed to dominate Ashley's personality. Then again, Ashley took after her mother far more than she took after him. She had none of the dark ruggedness of the DeMarco family, her face instead reflecting the tender features of her mother: sandy blond hair, brows fanning out in a gentle arch, ivory skin, delicate mouth. Even though Carla had been dead over four years now, barely a moment passed when he looked at his daughter that he didn't see his wife's face.

That night four years ago, Carla's car had sailed through the guardrail and off an icy bridge, plunging nose-first twenty feet down into the vast darkness of the frigid water below. What Dave had never told his brothers, never told anyone, was exactly what her death had done to him, and how he could live to be a thousand and still he wouldn't be able to put that night out of his mind.

"Maybe I need to go out on that playground," Dave said. "Grab the kid by the collar. Have a word with him."

"Yeah, and then his father's attorney will have a word with you," Alex said. "It's one thing for Ashley to beat up on a kid. It's another thing for her father to do the job."

"You're a cop," John said. "I can see the headlines now."

"Let her fight her own battles," Alex said. "Eventually she'll learn to kick some ass."

"Not that you can't teach her a move or two," John said, then turned to Alex. "But excuse me. If a boy hurts a girl, it's not his ass that needs kicking."

Dave shook his head with disgust. "Great. Next I'll be stashing a grenade in her Barbie lunch box, just in case something really big goes down."

"Barbie," John said, rolling his eyes. "Jesus, Dave. There's half your problem right there. Give her a role model with puffy blond hair and thirty-eight double-D boobs. I'll bet she takes all kinds of crap off Ken."

"A doll is not a role model."

"So get her a mother."

So get her a mother. As if it were that easy. "Yeah. I'll pick one up tomorrow on my way home from the station."

"At least date once in a while. When's the last time you even went out? You can't buy a thing if you don't go shopping."

He expected those kinds of questions from his sister, Sandy. That his brothers were starting in on him, too, told him his dateless status had reached crisis proportions.

"How long has it been since you got up close and personal with a woman?" Alex asked. "Maybe that would improve your disposition."

"There's nothing wrong with my disposition."

"Why don't you let Ashley stay with Renee and me one night?" John said. "That way you can invite a woman over. You know. Have a little privacy."

Privacy. Right. He might as well plaster a sign on his front door in big red letters: DAVE'S FINALLY GETTING SOME—DO NOT DISTURB. As if his family didn't already stick their noses into every other aspect of his life, they were moving in to take a ringside seat around his bed, too.

"I'll pass on that," Dave said. "But you know, the second I decide I want the whole world to know I'm getting laid, you'll be the first one I call."

"Hey, just trying to help, little brother."

His family. By the time they got through helping him, he really *did* need help.

Dave tried to turn his attention back to the game, but all at once he was struck by a monumental case of envy for what his brothers had that he didn't. Their wives moved in symbiosis with them, filling in their blanks. Renee was a calming influence over John, arresting his sometimes hotheaded nature, while Val was the only woman on earth who could kick Alex's ass and leave him with a smile on his face. Not that they didn't fight once in a while. Both couples could go at it like the WWF on a Saturday night. But their love for each other was never in question, and Dave wondered every day how he'd ended up the odd man out.

So get her a mother.

Everything came right back around to that, because, you know, after four years, he really ought to be getting on with things. After all, he'd taken Carla's death so well. That was Dave. He always made the best of things. Stuff rolled right off him, and then he moved on.

Yeah. Right.

There had been a time in his life when he'd felt sure of everything, but with every year that had passed since Carla's death he'd become more and more certain that he had no control over anything. Where Ashley was concerned, all he wanted to do was love and protect her, but sometimes he felt as if he was doing a really shitty job of being Mom and Dad all rolled into one. Hell, if he didn't have a clue what to do about her kindergarten playground problems, what was he going to do when things really got tough?

He knew what it was like to grow up without a mother. His had died when he was only six. So for Ashley's sake, he knew he needed to be thinking seriously about getting married again. And if he did, he would just keep on wearing that mask that said he had it all under control, that life was just wonderful, that he'd weathered the storm of his wife's death and gone on to find love and happiness a second time.

But he would always know the truth.

The Mavericks tied it up by halftime. During a news break, Dave pulled a ten from his wallet. It was time for him to hit the road.

"Hey, Dave!" John said. "Is that who I think it is?"

Dave turned his gaze back to the television. A cable news anchor was saying something about a plane crash. Something about the pilot being killed.

Then a photo flashed on the screen.

Dave froze, feeling as if the blood had thickened in his veins, slowing to a crawl, making him unable to move a muscle. Stabbed by recognition, long-buried emotion burst to the surface, and only by swallowing hard and grasping the edge of the table with tense fingers was he able to keep his face impassive.

"That's her, isn't it?" John asked. "Lisa Merrick?"

"Yeah," Dave said on a hushed breath. "It's her."

Out of the corner of his eye, he saw John and Alex gauging his reaction, but he couldn't tear his gaze away. After all this time, he was astonished to see Lisa's face and even more astonished that she looked nearly the same as she had in high school—strong features, short red-gold hair in a tangled, windblown style, and searing green eyes that radiated raw passion. In the dark of night sometimes he still thought about her, and when he did, this was the face he saw.

Beside Lisa's photo was one of a forty-something man, Dr. Adam Decker, who was with her at the time the plane went down. Then the report quoted Dr. Robert Douglas, who was the administrator of an organization that flew doctors into a remote area of Mexico to provide health care at a free clinic. He told reporters that on a volunteer mission Lisa took off near the town of Santa Rios yesterday evening, then crashed into a river. They didn't know the cause of the accident. There was speculation that the bodies might never be recovered.

"So Lisa Merrick became a pilot for a humanitarian organization?" John said. "Holy shit. Can you believe that?"

Yes. He could. John thought it was unbelievable only because he hadn't known her like Dave had. Nobody had. It didn't matter that she was a girl from the wrong side of the tracks, who apparently had nothing but a dead-end life ahead of her. All that mattered was that she'd wanted out of her situation. She'd wanted desperately to be a pilot, and it looked as if she'd accomplished that. She'd yanked herself up out of that quagmire loosely referred to as a family, gone after what she wanted, and gotten it. He felt a rush of admiration for what she'd accomplished. She'd lived her dream.

And now she was dead.

"Hey, Dave," Alex said. "Are you all right?"

Dave continued to stare at the screen.

"I guess it's kind of a shock," Alex said. "I mean, I know how you felt about her—"

"You don't have a clue how I felt about her."

Dave's relationship to Lisa had been a mystery to his brothers in high school. The physical attraction part they'd understood. After all, Lisa Merrick had been a well-endowed girl who dressed provocatively, who'd been the subject of more locker-room talk than any other girl in Tolosa South history. But trying to explain to John and Alex that he saw something in Lisa beyond her bad-girl reputation had been a losing proposition.

"So how *did* you feel about her?" Alex asked. "What really happened between you and Lisa Merrick?"

Dave gave his brother an icy stare. "I told you what happened. Nothing."

"Yeah, that's what you said back then. But this is now."

"Are you asking me if I slept with her?"

"You wouldn't have been the first guy to," John said. "Or the second."

"Or the tenth," Alex added.

"I was engaged to Carla! Do you really think I'd do that?"

"I can't imagine that you would," Alex said. "But I know what Lisa Merrick was like. Once she had a guy in her sights, it was all but over."

Dave leaned in and skewered his brother with an angry glare. "Look, Alex. I know what you thought of her. What everybody thought of her. But there was more to Lisa than you or anybody else ever knew. I don't expect you to understand that. But I do expect you to respect the fact that she's dead and shut the hell up about her." He shoved his chair back and stood up. "I've got to go."

"Aw, come on, Dave," John said. "We didn't mean to piss you off. Will you just sit down?"

Dave tossed another ten down on the table. "You guys have another beer on me. It appears you've got a lot more speculating to do."

Over his brothers' protests, he turned and walked out of the bar. By the time he reached his car, he felt a little shaky. He got into the driver's seat, closed the door, then stopped and leaned his head against the headrest, closing his eyes. Seeing Lisa's face on that television screen had awakened something hot and intense inside him, a reminder of the passion that had once oozed from her like hot lava.

She's dead. Lisa is dead.

The next hour passed in a daze. He picked up Ashley and brought her home, thinking he ought to have another word with her about standing up for herself with the swing smacker, but he couldn't think of a single useful thing to say. He gave her a bath, then tucked her and her stuffed rabbit into bed.

Pulling up a pillow, Dave sat down on the bed beside her, leaning against the headboard. She slid a bedtime book off her nightstand. Fortunately, she knew *Stellaluna* by heart and ended up reading it to him, so he could pretend to be listening when he couldn't have focused on the story if his life depended on it.

Ashley's voice was little more than white noise to him as the minutes passed. All he could think about was Lisa's plane going into that river in the Mexican wilderness and the tragic loss of a life that had clearly held more potential than even he'd been able to imagine. And he couldn't help wondering whether she'd forgotten him the moment they'd parted or carried his memory around inside her for the past eleven years, just as he'd carried hers.

Dave heard the phone ring in the kitchen. He turned to Ashley. "Back in a minute, honey. Flopsy can hold the place, okay?"

Dave grabbed one of her rabbit's floppy ears, laid it across the page, and closed the book. Ashley smiled up at him. He patted her on the arm, then rose from her bed, went down the hall to the kitchen, and caught the phone on the fourth ring.

"Hello?"

He heard a woman's voice. Soft. Grainy. Almost a whisper. "Dave?"

He pressed the phone more tightly to his ear. "Yes?"

"This is Lisa Merrick."

chapter two

For a few stunned moments, Dave's brain refused to engage. "What did you say?"

"Lisa Merrick."

Dave was speechless. All kinds of thoughts flew through his mind, none of them making any sense at all. Somebody had to be yanking him around. Big-time. Lisa Merrick was dead. That news report tonight hadn't left any room for interpretation.

"Look," he said sharply. "I don't know who this is, but it's not Lisa Merrick. It can't be. She's—"

"In the shop at school," she said on a harsh breath. "Three days before graduation—"

"Stop."

Dave felt a bone-deep sense of dread well up inside him. Either Lisa had told somebody what had happened that day and that person was playing one hell of a nasty joke, or . . .

Or this really was Lisa.

In that moment, he felt an irrational jolt of alarm that people who believed in ghosts might not be deluded after all.

"Where are you?" he asked. "What happened?"

"I'm in Mexico." Her voice sounded weak, disembodied. "My plane crashed."

"I know. There was a TV news report. That doctor, Robert Douglas, reported that you're dead."

"That's what he told everybody? That I died in the crash?"

"Yes. He said your plane went down right after takeoff. You need to call him. Tell him you're okay."

"No! I can't do that!"

"Why not?"

"Because he's the one who tried to kill me!"

Dave snapped to attention, a sinister shiver running all the way down his spine. "Wait a minute. Kill you? What do you mean? How?"

"My plane going down wasn't an accident," she said, a heavy, hushed quality to her voice. "It was sabotage. He thinks he killed me. And if he finds me now and realizes he failed, I'm dead."

"Where are you exactly?"

"Santa Rios. A couple hundred miles southeast of Monterrey."

Dave fumbled through a kitchen drawer for a pencil and scribbled the information on a pad beside the telephone.

"Lisa, listen to me. If you think somebody's out to kill you, you need to go to the authorities. Tell them what you suspect. Tell them—"

"No!"

"It's the only way. If you're in danger—"

"Don't you understand?" she said, panic lacing her voice. "They're in on it! The sheriff, probably, and God knows who else!"

Dave froze in utter disbelief. "Are you telling me there's a conspiracy to kill you?"

"Yes! Because I know about the counterfeit drugs! Robert Douglas is manufacturing them around here somewhere. Somehow he knew I found them, because he sabotaged my plane when I tried to take them back across the border. And then there were the men who came to make sure I died in the crash. The ones with the machine guns!"

"Machine guns?"

"My plane was hung up on the side of a ravine. They thought I was still in it, but I'd gotten out and moved to a ledge beside it. Then they shot at it. Over and over. It fell into the river. I fell, too, because I was still close to the plane. After I hit the water, I made it to the bank. Then I walked, oh, God, so far. All last night and all day today. I don't know how many miles. Finally I made it back to Santa Rios, to this phone—"

"Hold on. Slow down. Drugs? Machine guns? You're not making any sense."

"I'm telling you they're after me. They could be anywhere right now—I just don't know. If they see me, they'll kill me. Do you understand? They'll kill me!"

"You have to tell somebody down there what's happened to you. Find somebody—"

"No! I have no way of knowing who's in on it and who isn't! Robert Douglas for sure, but who else? I just don't know!"

None of this made any sense at all. It sounded like the ramblings of an insane woman. He'd heard conspiracy theories before, but this was ridiculous.

"Oh, God," she said with a weary breath. "My head . . . My head hurts so much. . . ."

"Your head? What happened?"

"I hit it on something when I crashed . . . the control panel maybe. . . ."

All at once, Dave understood. She sounded delirious. Delusional. She could have crawled away from the crash alive without anyone knowing it, trying not to be seen because of a head injury that had altered her cognition and induced paranoia. She was afraid, yes. But it could very well be that the thing she was afraid of existed only inside her mind.

He needed to find out exactly where she was, then get in touch with the law enforcement in Santa Rios or maybe even the doctor who thought she was dead. Get somebody down there to find her and get her to a hospital.

"Lisa," he said. "Listen to me. You need help."

"Yes," she said on a breath of relief. "Yes. I need help."

"Tell me exactly where you are."

"There's an abandoned silver-mining camp on the road leading southeast out of Santa Rios. It's about two miles out of town. I'm going to hide out there."

Hide out? Jesus. She *was* delusional. He scribbled down the information.

"Listen carefully," he said. "I'm going to send somebody.

Somebody to help you. A doctor. You've been injured, and you need—"

"No! Aren't you listening? The only doctor within a hundred miles wants me dead!"

How was he ever going to get through to her? "Lisa, you've been through a real trauma, so I understand how you might think you're in danger, but—"

"You think I'm crazy? Is that it? I got a bump on the head and went right off the deep end?"

"No, of course not. But sometimes head injuries—"

"Damn it, I'm not crazy! Robert Douglas is out to kill me!"

"Take it easy," he told her. "You're going to be all right."

"No, I'm not. I have no way out of here. I need help. I need . . ." She paused, her voice with a heavy, hushed quality. "I need you."

Dave felt a jolt of surprise. "Me? What do you mean?"

"I need you to come here."

"What?"

"Please."

He paced to the extent of the phone cord, then paced back. He couldn't believe this. Lisa Merrick was calling him with a story about smuggling and sabotage and attempted murder, and now she wanted him to come hundreds of miles to the backwoods of Mexico to foil a conspiracy to kill her?

"You told me once that if I ever needed you, I should call you." Lisa's voice slipped almost to a whisper. "I need you now."

Suddenly Dave remembered. Those were the last words he'd ever spoken to her, because after what had happened between them he'd wanted to do something for her. Anything. But all he could do was make a promise for the future, tell her that if something in her life ever became insurmountable, he'd try to help her.

How was he to know it would be something like this?

He should call the local authorities. After all, if she really was badly injured and somebody didn't get to her soon, she could die. Then again, if somebody really was out to kill her and he told them where to find her . . .

"Oh, no," Lisa whispered.

"What?"

"People are coming. Somebody might see me. I have to go."

"Lisa—"

"Help me, Dave. Please, *please* help me. . . ."

"Lisa!"

He heard the line click. Then a dial tone. Slowly he hung up the phone. As much as he tried to tell himself that she was injured and therefore deluded, he had no way to verify that.

You told me once that if I ever needed you . . .

He went to his computer and pulled up a map of Mexico. He located Santa Rios, a faint dot about two hundred miles southeast of Monterrey. He went to the Web site of Aero-Mexico and found a flight to Monterrey out of DFW in three hours. He could call the airline right now, make a reservation. Within the hour, he could be on the road to Dallas.

Tomorrow was Sunday, but he'd probably still need a few days off work. Since he rarely took time off, he was due. He could get his brothers to take care of Ashley, letting them know where he was going and when he planned to be back, just in case he encountered more trouble than he bargained for. Once in Monterrey, he could grab a rental car and drive to Santa Rios, where he could find Lisa and get to the bottom of this.

As he ticked off the plan in his mind, he kept telling himself that it was rational and logical to travel seven hundred miles to a town in the middle of nowhere, get Lisa wherever she needed to go, then get back home. Nothing crazy about that.

Who was he kidding? It sounded crazy as hell.

"Daddy?"

He jerked his gaze to the door. Ashley stood there in her fuzzy house slippers, her stuffed rabbit dangling from her hand.

"Come back. I didn't finish reading."

"Be there in a minute, honey."

She waited a moment more with one of those "your minutes are longer than my minutes" looks on her face, before turning and shuffling back to her room.

Damn. How could he even think of flying out of here only

hours from now? He should just call the station and find somebody who could get him a phone number for the sheriff's office in that little Mexican town, then call them and let them handle it. It could take a while to make a connection and get somebody out there, but nobody in his right mind would blame him for doing the rational thing, no matter what the outcome.

Even if Lisa was telling the truth and somebody really was out to kill her.

Dave dropped his head to his hands and rubbed his temples, knowing he had no business leaving his daughter and running off into the Mexican wilderness not really knowing what he was going to face when he got there. And he wasn't sure he was up to helping anyone with anything anymore. He'd gone to that well too many times in recent years, until barely a drop of water was left in it. The sick feeling he got every time he thought about what had happened on that bridge today made him wonder just how worthwhile he could be to anyone right about now.

But the very idea that Lisa might be alone and delirious, terrified, needing his help, sent a surge of adrenaline racing through him. He'd made her a promise once that he'd be there for her if she ever needed him, and it was a promise he had every intention of keeping. One phone call from her, and suddenly nothing else mattered.

He was going to Mexico.

In the woods adjoining the bunkhouse of the abandoned mining camp, Lisa sat against a tree on a bed of dead leaves still damp from the heavy rainstorm a few days before, surrounded by darkness so complete she could barely make out the road in the distance. In the scraggly woods around her she heard the occasional call of a bird or the scurry of various wildlife, but she didn't bother worrying about the snakes and wildcats and gargantuan spiders who undoubtedly called this place home. The enemy she was facing now made those look tame by comparison.

In one hand she gripped the handle of an old shovel she'd

found, because it vaguely resembled a weapon. The fingers of her other hand were looped around the strap of her backpack. Because the pills were in a plastic bag, they'd survived the trip through the river, and she was going to hold on to them no matter what. If she ever got out of here, she was going to make sure she had the evidence that could help take Robert Douglas down, along with every other person who had anything to do with the drug counterfeiting or the sabotage of her plane.

Then she thought about Adam.

At first she'd been so thankful he hadn't been on her plane when it went down, because he might not have survived. But now she realized that he could be in even bigger trouble than she was.

She didn't know if Robert Douglas knew that Adam had gotten called away at the last minute and told her to fly on to San Antonio without him. But just the fact that Adam knew about the drugs was enough to put him in danger the moment Robert found out that he was still alive. She wanted desperately to warn him, but she had no way to do it. Adam had traveled to a farm an hour from Santa Rios, and she didn't know the name of the woman whose baby he'd gone to deliver. She didn't know when he was going to return. And she was terrified to show her own face for fear that Robert would find out that she'd survived the crash and come after her again.

Adam, wherever you are, please be careful.

After slipping into Santa Rios and making that phone call, Lisa had come back out here, and now she'd spent most of the night hugging this tree, drifting in and out of sleep, waiting for whoever came up that road. Since it was a strong possibility that Dave had called the authorities, she couldn't go back inside the bunkhouse. She'd be a sitting duck. At least out here, if danger approached she could see it coming and have a fighting chance of getting away.

Right. Just her and her trusty shovel. The perfect weapon against men with machine guns. If only she had a real weapon. Unfortunately, Mexican officials didn't take kindly to anyone entering their country with firearms, so her Glock was currently sitting in her dresser drawer in her apartment in San Antonio.

Of course, she should have been miles away from here already. She should have found a different place to rest and recuperate before she formulated some kind of plan to get out of Santa Rios and back across the border. Instead, she'd come back here because she just couldn't shake the ridiculous fantasy that it wouldn't be corrupt Santa Rios officials who came up that road. It would be Dave.

How deluded had that been?

This was the place where she'd told him she'd be, so this was where she'd stayed. But she'd been crazy to believe, even for a second, that he'd drop everything and leave his little slice of middle-class heaven to come rescue her. Logically, she'd known that the minute she hung up the phone. Emotionally, she'd continued to hold on to a fragile thread of hope that kept her glued to this tree, watching and waiting.

Maybe he hadn't been able to leave town right away. Maybe he hadn't been able to get a flight out. Maybe he'd had car trouble.

And maybe he just didn't give a damn.

She was starting to face facts. She'd thought that Dave had only two options: send the authorities or come himself. Instead, he'd chosen to do nothing at all. She should have been happy about that, since it meant she was probably safe for the moment from the people who were trying to kill her. Instead, his indifference cut her right to the quick.

In the past eleven years, she'd adopted a string of policies that had served her well: Live for the moment. What you see is what you get. Don't count those chickens, because hatching is the exception, not the rule. Essentially, all a person could do was take every day as it came, stay on top, stay in control.

Right now, she had no control over anything.

Lisa closed her eyes, exhaustion overtaking her. The cover of darkness offered her the best opportunity to return to town, where she could try to find some means of transportation to get her back across the border. But the longer she sat by this tree, the worse she felt. Every time she tried to stand, pain shot through her head. With every hour that passed, her mind grew fuzzier, her body weaker. She'd run out of what little food and water she had hours ago, so her disorientation was only going to get worse, eventually edging into delirium. And just how delirious would she have to be before she lost her sense of self-preservation, before she just lay down and didn't get back up again?

You have to get out of here. Get up. Now.

Sluggish with fatigue, she forced herself to rise to her knees, but when she tried to stand, her legs wobbled dangerously. She fell to her knees again with a steadying hand against the tree trunk, telling herself that maybe she just needed to rest a little more, but in the back of her mind she had the most ominous feeling that if she didn't stand up now, she was never going to. A terrible vulnerability crept in, the same feeling she'd had when she'd seen those men coming at her, heard the shots, knowing that somebody meant to kill her.

Then she heard something.

She turned toward the road, and what she saw sent a surge of adrenaline racing through her, followed by a rush of cold, clammy fear.

Headlights.

chapter three

Lisa crawled sideways away from the tree where she'd been sitting, her palms and knees crunching against dead leaves, taking cover behind a large, prickly shrub. When she looked back at the road, it was so dark that she couldn't make out anything about the car. All she saw was the bright glare of headlights slicing through the night.

The car came to a halt. A man stepped out. He was nothing but a tall, dark silhouette, and she had a sudden flashback to the men who had stood at the top of that ravine and that moment of silence right before her plane had been blasted with machine-gun fire.

He stood behind the open car door for a moment, flipping on a flashlight. He directed the bright beam at the bunkhouse, then swept it toward the woods. Lisa ducked back behind the shrub just as the beam of light passed by her.

The car door slammed shut, the sound reverberating through the stillness of the night and searing her already raw nerves. She couldn't look around the bush again, just in case he was glancing her way. She just sat there, holding her breath, her whole body slick with sweat, praying she'd hear the bunkhouse door open and close behind him. If she did, she was going to run as far and as fast into the trees as her weary body would carry her.

Then the flashlight beam came back around, stopping a few feet to her right. Glancing over, she saw it had landed dead center on the backpack and shovel she'd left beside the tree.

Lisa put her hand over her mouth to stifle a gasp. She heard footsteps. Feet shuffling through dead leaves.

He was coming.

In a moment he would be right on top of her. He was undoubtedly armed, which meant she was a dead woman. Out here in the middle of nowhere, would anyone even hear the shot?

As the footsteps drew closer, she couldn't stand the tension any longer. She leapt to her feet. Fueled by adrenaline and driven by sheer terror, she started to run.

"Stop!"

His voice was deep and commanding, but still she ran. Behind her she heard the loud swish of his footsteps through the leaves as he ran to catch her, and he was closing in fast. A tree branch raked across her face. She slapped it aside, only to have her foot catch the edge of a sapling. She tripped, almost fell, then righted herself again and kept running.

"Stop!"

She braced herself for the bullet she knew was coming. She'd be dead before she hit the ground, but by God, she was going to die running.

But no shot came. Instead, he caught her arm. She screamed and tried to pull away, only to stumble and fall. In the struggle, he lost his footing and fell beside her. She flipped over and came up swinging, but he'd already risen to his knees. He caught her wrists and dragged her close to him. She twisted left and right, struggling in his grasp, desperate to pull away.

"Lisa! Stop it! *Stop it!*"

She froze, breathing hard. English. It suddenly dawned on her that he was speaking English. She focused on his face, blinking with disbelief. It couldn't be.

She had to have been shot after all. That was the only explanation. She was lying on the forest floor, drawing her last breath, her weak and fevered mind throwing her a bone in her last moments of life, making her believe something that couldn't possibly be. But she couldn't mistake those warm dark eyes she remembered from so long ago, eyes full of kindness and compassion and quiet strength that could soothe over even the most desperate of situations.

"You came," she whispered.

Dave's grip on her wrists relaxed at the same time his

brows drew together with intense concern. Suddenly her head felt light, and she started to weave.

"Lisa? Are you all right?"

All the tension and fear and pain of the past two days overtook her, and she lurched to one side, her muscles going limp. He caught her as she fell and swept her into his arms, and she was aware of nothing but the absolute assurance that because he was there, everything was going to be okay.

He carried her out of the woods and into the bunkhouse, lowering her to one of the beds. The mattress was brittle and cracked with age, but it was far softer than the ground where she'd spent the past several hours, and she sank into it as if it were a featherbed in a five-star hotel. He sat down beside her, the mattress dipping with his weight, then brushed the hair away from her forehead with his fingertips.

"Lisa? I need to know what's going on here. Can you talk to me?"

She blinked her eyes open. He'd rested the flashlight on the floor on its end, its beam reflecting off the ceiling, casting a dim glow around the room. She opened her mouth to speak, but her throat felt dry as dust.

"Do you have any water?" he asked.

"Had some in my backpack," she croaked. "When my plane went down. It's gone."

"When's the last time you ate something?"

She slid her hand to her stomach. "I don't remember."

"I'm going to go to the car. Get some food and water. Okay?"

She nodded. He slipped out the door, returning a moment later carrying a large canvas bag. He sat down beside her again, unzipped the bag, and pulled out a bottle of water. He helped her sit up, then cradled her in his arms as he put the bottle to her lips. She took several swallows, then turned away.

"More," he said.

He brought the bottle to her lips again, encouraging her to drink until her stomach felt sloshy. Then, with a steadying arm around her shoulders, he lowered her gently back down to the bed.

"Are you hungry?" he asked.

She put her hand to her stomach. "Don't . . . Don't think I could eat."

"Does anything else hurt besides your head?"

She felt so weak and sleepy she could barely speak. "Pretty much everything."

He wrapped his hands around her thigh, squeezing gently. She flinched with surprise at his touch.

"Just checking to see if anything's sprained or broken," he said.

He ran his hands all the way down to her ankle, squeezing softly as he went, then did the same to her other leg, bypassing a place at her calf where her jeans were ripped, with a cut beneath.

"Any pain?" he asked.

Pain? God, no. His touch felt like heaven, so warm and gentle and protective, relaxing her muscles when they'd been wound so tightly for the past two days that she'd barely been able to breathe. It was all so unbelievable. Never in her wildest dreams could she fathom a scenario like this, a situation that would bring Dave DeMarco seven hundred miles to the backwoods of Mexico to touch her one more time.

"No. Nothing hurts. Not like anything's broken."

He gave her arms and fingers the same treatment, then placed his palms against her rib cage, pressing gently. "How about here? Anything hurt?"

"No. Just sore. Bruises and stuff."

"The plane crash."

"Yes."

"Have you gotten much sleep?"

"No," she said. "Couldn't sleep."

"Because they're after you?" he asked.

"Yes," she murmured, then felt a jolt of panic. She thought she heard a lilt of disbelief in his voice, a patronizing tone that told her he still wasn't completely sure she was in possession of all her marbles. She grasped his arm.

"You haven't told anyone where I am, have you?"

"Only my brothers, and they're not telling anyone. You're safe. But sooner or later you probably need to get to a doctor."

She sat up suddenly, every muscle screaming with pain. "Didn't you hear what I told you on the phone? He's out to kill me!"

"Take it easy, okay?" he said, easing her back down again. "I hear you. We're not going anywhere right now. Are there any other doctors in Santa Rios besides Douglas?"

"No. The clinic is all there is. That's why it's here. Because this is the place that needed it the most. But Robert Douglas is not what he seems to be. I swear he's not. You have to believe me. If he knows I'm alive, he'll kill me!"

She wanted to shout, but her voice came out in a raspy whisper. She sounded crazy. He was going to think she was delusional. He was going to drag her into town, take her to the clinic, and if he did . . .

"They already shot at me after the crash." She dug her fingers into his arm. "They had machine guns. Machine guns!"

She was rambling like a madwoman, her voice slurring worse than the time she'd done a dozen tequila shots in high school and passed out. She tried to clear her throat, but she coughed instead. Weakness overtook her and she could barely muster up the energy to talk again. Did he understand? Did he understand how much danger she was in?

"Just go to sleep," he told her.

"No. I can't sleep. I can't."

"You need sleep, Lisa. We'll talk again when you wake up."

"Promise me," she said weakly. "Promise me you won't tell anyone that I'm alive."

"Lisa—"

"Promise."

"Of course. I promise."

"But if they come—"

"I'll protect you. Just sleep."

She stared up at him, still amazed that he was here. In spite of the chaos that ruled her mind right now, still she remembered with startling clarity that day so long ago that she'd looked into those dark eyes and imagined a thousand more tomorrows filled with the sight of him.

"Just sleep," he repeated.

His voice was quiet, hypnotic, and suddenly she felt as if a hundred pounds of pressure were being exerted on each of her eyelids. She had no doubt that she was only one step away from a well-placed bullet if Robert should find out she was still alive, so she should still be afraid, still be on her guard. Every shred of her being was geared toward standing up for herself, taking no crap, defending her own life. She felt driven to stay awake. *Needed* to stay awake. But with Dave here . . .

I'll protect you.

For the first time since this whole thing began, her pulse returned to normal, her muscles relaxed, and her jangled nerves quieted to a sleepy lull. He told her she was safe, and she believed him.

And she slept.

When Dave passed through the distasteful little community of Santa Rios, swerving his way up the potholed road to the abandoned mining camp, he'd had a hunch the situation wasn't going to be pretty, but he hadn't expected this.

He hadn't expected to find Lisa hiding out in the trees, then running from him like a cornered animal. He hadn't expected the crazed expression of fear in her eyes. And he hadn't expected her to look as if she'd been to hell and back through a sewer pipe. Three times.

He sat on the bunk across from her, his back against the wall, shining the flashlight in such a way that allowed him to watch her but didn't disturb her sleep. She wore a pair of jeans, boots, and a white sweatshirt with a Dallas Cowboys logo over the left breast. All were splattered with mud and grime, as if she'd gotten wet, then rolled around in the dirt. Her reddish-blond hair stuck out in ten different directions like a stray kitten caught in the rain. Various minor scrapes and cuts marred her arms and face, and on her forehead was a bruise that spanned two or three inches and wrapped around to her temple, black and purple in the middle, ringed by pale yellow, with a deep scrape in the center crusted with dried blood.

The good news was that he'd seen her pupils reacting equally to light. His meager emergency medical training told him that was a good sign in favor of no neurological damage and probably no internal bleeding resulting from her bump on the head. Considering she'd been in a plane crash, she'd come away relatively unscathed.

It had taken her approximately three seconds to fall asleep once she closed her eyes. No wonder. It was probably the first real sleep she'd had since the accident. Since she didn't seem to have any significant injuries outside of the whack she'd taken to the forehead, he guessed that she was just completely exhausted from lack of food and water and from the effort it took to crawl away from that crash, along with the tension that came from believing that somebody was out to kill her.

That was the question he'd pay a thousand dollars for an answer to right about now. Did somebody actually want her dead?

He knew for a fact that if circumstances were right, the human mind could take some strange detours. He'd once helped pull a guy out of a wrecked 18-wheeler who had a bump on his head and thought he was being abducted by aliens. Dave had been reasonably sure that no aliens had been spotted in the area. He'd once cornered an escaped psych patient in the produce section of a grocery store who was absolutely certain he was Jesus Christ, and Dave hadn't been the least bit inclined to phone the pope to alert him of the Second Coming. Why, then, would he take this outlandish story of hers seriously?

Trouble was, no matter how outlandish it seemed, he just didn't know the truth, and he had no intention of going anywhere until he did. But he was unlikely to get the truth by continuing to question her when she was half out of her mind from lack of sleep. Until she woke, he hoped with a newly acquired grip on herself, he was stuck here.

He grabbed a bottle of water out of his bag and took a drink, then smacked the lid down again, thinking about how

Alex and John had gone berserk when he told them he was coming here. Dave had ended up telling them that they could flip out all they wanted to, but when the dust settled he was still going to Mexico. Eventually they'd backed off. John had taken Ashley, and Dave had hit the road for Dallas, barely catching a 10:15 flight out of DFW to Monterrey.

It did feel more than a little surreal that he'd ended up in this godforsaken place, staring at a woman he'd thought he'd never see again. A woman he'd thought was dead. A woman who, even though she was a wreck right now, he couldn't take his eyes off of. Lisa Merrick was imprinted on his brain to represent all things hot, sexy, and dangerous. Even now, just looking at her made his heart pick up its pace and his mouth go dry.

At age eighteen, she'd been a volatile, defensive, hard-edged girl who'd seen more of the seamy side of life than a woman three times her age ever should have. At maybe five-foot-four, there wasn't much of her, but he pitied the poor person who underestimated her.

She'd matured physically, her shapely girl's body becoming lush and womanly. She wasn't dressed nearly as provocatively as she'd been known to back then, but still her sweatshirt outlined her breasts in a way that dared him to stare. They rose and fell rhythmically with every breath she took, and for a long time he held the flashlight steady, not even bothering to try to drag his gaze away.

He remembered a time in high school when he'd seen her on the back of Derek Brody's motorcycle, wearing a crop top so short that a simple lift of her arms left little to the imagination. And as she rode that motorcycle behind that spike-haired, leather-clad, silver-studded son of a bitch she called a boyfriend, she'd looped her arms around his waist and pressed those breasts against his back, and to this day Dave still remembered the stark envy that had rolled through him at that moment.

Consequently, when Lisa slid into the seat beside him the first day of shop class in the second semester of their senior year his brain had instantly fallen to his crotch and stayed there for the remainder of the hour. Right off the bat, she gave him a blatant, protracted, up-and-down stare, as if she was picturing what he looked like naked, then spent most of the class period crossing and uncrossing her legs, displayed at their most spectacular in a pair of cutoff shorts that couldn't possibly have passed the dress code. But few people messed with Lisa Merrick, including Mr. Pennington, the vice principal. Once Dave had seen her walk past him, and Pennington's gaze had slid right down the curve of her back and landed dead center on her ass. Looking back over her shoulder, Lisa had winked at him. One wink, and the poor bastard had fallen apart. His squinty little eyes had flown wide open, his pasty face had turned six shades of red, and he'd stumbled back to his office as if he'd been kicked in the groin.

As the teacher droned on and on about engine overhaul, Dave leaned away from Lisa, trying to put as much distance between them as he could. But still he could feel her next to him, shifting and breathing and running the eraser of her pencil back and forth across her lower lip. He pretended to focus on what the teacher was saying, all the while thinking about Lisa's lips and just how adept she might be in the use of them. Then he thought about how Carla would be waiting for him after class. If she'd had any idea what was going on in his mind right then, she'd have broken down and cried.

At the end of the hour, the teacher told them to pair up for a project they were starting the next day, and Dave hadn't moved quickly enough. When the shuffle was over, only two people were left without partners.

Shit.

Lisa turned and looked him right in the eye. "Well, De-Marco, looks like you're stuck with me. You got a problem with that?"

She might as well have drawn a line across the greasy shop floor and dared him to step over it.

"Of course not. What makes you think I'd have a problem with it?"

"Body language, baby. If you lean any farther away from me, you're going to fall right out of that chair."

He instantly sat up straight, only to have her turn away with an amused shake of her head. She stood up and slid her backpack over her shoulder, giving him another one of those brazen up-and-down stares, accompanied by a mocking smile.

"I'll be counting the hours until tomorrow," she murmured, with a sexual lilt to her voice that would have put Madonna to shame. She walked away, her backpack bouncing against her hip. After half a dozen strides, she glanced back over her shoulder and caught him watching her. She smiled knowingly, then slipped out the door.

Damn. Pennington wasn't the only idiot around there who couldn't keep his eyeballs in his head. Why couldn't he have been looking at anything else at that moment besides Lisa Merrick's ass?

Because trying to take his eyes off her was like trying to stop an avalanche from rolling down a mountainside.

For the first several days they worked on that project together, she'd gone out of her way to dress provocatively, bombarding him with so much sexual innuendo that he couldn't even apply a screwdriver to something without her finding all kinds of meaning in it.

Then one day she'd been sitting in a chair next to the workbench, twisted around in such a way that he could barely look at her without having an unobstructed line of sight right down the front of her shirt, and of course she wasn't wearing anything underneath that shirt that might get in the way of his view. It had taken a significant amount of orchestration for her to reach that pose, and in the beginning it would have rattled him. But slowly his perception shifted, and instead of letting it intimidate him, he started to see it for the attempted manipulation it was.

"Lisa?" he said, unscrewing a bolt and removing it, dropping it to the workbench with a soft clatter. "Why don't you just go ahead and take off your shirt? I can see everything you've got anyway. But then, you know that, don't you?"

A self-satisfied smile crossed her lips. "So do you like what you see?"

"I'm not interested."

"Oh, you're interested, all right. You're just too whipped by that prissy little girlfriend of yours to consider taking a walk on the wild side."

"We're getting married this summer."

"Yeah? Well, I was thinking about all the fun we could have in the meantime. You're not bad-looking, DeMarco. A girl could do a lot worse."

He tossed the wrench down on the workbench, then turned and leaned over the chair where she sat, putting a hand on either arm. He stared down at her.

"Let's get something straight, Lisa. I don't think much of girls who hand out sex like candy. The truth is, though, that you don't think much of yourself, either, or you wouldn't dress like a slut and go after anything in pants."

Lisa met his gaze evenly. "Am I to take that as a no?"

"Someday you'll figure out that you've got a lot more to offer than just your body. As soon as that happens, maybe some decent guy will have you."

"Decent," she said, rolling her eyes. "You mean boring."

"I said exactly what I meant."

As he returned to his task, she gave him yet one more of her patented "go to hell" looks, and he was sure that all he'd accomplished was to piss her off to the point that the remainder of the semester was destined to be one gigantic confrontational nightmare. Then she'd shown up for class the next day, and he couldn't believe his eyes.

She wore a pair of jeans topped by a solid blue T-shirt that, if anything, was a size too big. She'd pulled on a pair of worn Reeboks. Her short reddish-blond hair was free of the gel she used to spike it, fluttering in soft curls around her face. She still wore makeup, but she'd toned it down considerably. It was so unlike the in-your-face fashion statement she usually made that he couldn't take his eyes off her. The longer he watched her, though, the more defensive her expression became.

"What are you looking at?" she asked.

"Nothing," he said, but he couldn't stop staring. "I don't know. Your hair, I guess."

"Yeah. My hair." She ran her fingers through it, then gave him an offhand shrug. "I didn't have time to do anything with it this morning."

"It's pretty. I like it that way."

She blinked with surprise. "You do?"

"Yeah."

She looked away self-consciously, stroking her fingers through it again. "Like I said. I ran out of time."

In spite of her explanation, he was sure he saw a blush rise on her cheeks. In that moment, something tripped inside him, an awareness he hadn't felt before.

She did it for you. Because of what you said. She cares what you think.

That realization astonished him. It was as if a window opened up and he began to see inside her, revealing tiny fragments of a vulnerability he'd never imagined. And it fascinated him.

For the next hour, she talked to him only about pistons and carburetors and other engine-related topics without a hint of the sexual suggestiveness that had filled practically every word she'd spoken to him up to that point. Still, every glance they exchanged seemed to take on new meaning, and when the bell rang to signal the end of the class period he actually felt a rush of disappointment.

As the weeks passed, instead of the verbal sparring that had characterized their first few days together, they started to have actual conversations, and soon Dave found himself coming up with reasons to drag their shop class projects into after-school time. Because Carla would have flipped out if he'd shown Lisa any attention at all, he rarely talked to her if their paths crossed in the hall. But looking back, he thought Carla must have sensed just how many of his waking moments were spent with Lisa on his mind.

Dave flicked off the flashlight and leaned his head against the wall of the bunkhouse with a heavy sigh. He thought about getting some sleep himself, then decided maybe he'd better stay awake on the off chance that Mexican marauders with machine guns stormed the place.

God, that sounded loony, like some kind of B movie playing at two o'clock in the morning.

He thinks he killed me. If he finds me now and realizes he failed, I'm dead.

B movie all over again.

With luck, she'd wake in a few hours completely lucid, feeling a little silly for going so far off the deep end tonight. Then he could get her to a doctor or anywhere else she needed to go. His duty would be discharged, his promise fulfilled. He'd return to his real life, she'd return to hers, and that would be that.

Wouldn't it?

He froze as those words played through his mind, then settled back against the wall, telling himself how crazy that sounded. Fate had been a real bitch to him in recent years, taking him places he'd never wanted to go. But now he couldn't fight the sense of inevitability he felt, as if the past eleven years had existed only to get him to this place at this moment to see Lisa one more time.

chapter four

As Adam Decker navigated the rugged rain-furrowed road on his way back to Santa Rios, every muscle in his body ached, and he felt as if he hadn't slept in a week. When he finally saw the city lights through the darkness ahead, he breathed a sigh of relief, but not just because he was so eager to hit the sack and get some sleep.

He hated driving at night. He hated it even more when he was forced to navigate a dark, deserted road like this one that seemed to twist and turn right into the middle of nowhere. The quiet unnerved him. The isolation made him tense and edgy. His fingers throbbed from gripping the steering wheel so tightly, and he shook them alternately to release the tension.

He took a single deep breath and let it out slowly, focusing on the lights in the distance, telling himself again, as he had repeatedly for the past hour, that he needed to get a grip. Sunrise would be coming soon, and that always worked wonders for him, clearing away the tension that fogged his mind at times like this.

He couldn't believe that he'd been within ten minutes of flying out of Santa Rios with Lisa when the woman's husband came to the clinic. Adam had wanted so badly just to turn his back and leave, particularly since he needed to be with Lisa to hand over those pills to U.S. Customs agents and tell them what they'd discovered.

Instead, he'd traveled an hour to a farm where he helped the woman through nearly two days of grueling on again, off again labor, followed by a delivery that had been one for the record books. At age forty-three, pulling all-nighters was starting to become a real chore for him. It would be a relief when he left his practice in San Antonio in two weeks and moved to Chicago to take over as head of Greenbriar Medical Center. Not many chiefs of staff were called out to deliver babies in the middle of the night, and from now on that was just the way he wanted it. In Chicago he could begin again. Leave bad memories behind. Start a new life.

Even if it meant he'd never see Sera again.

No. He couldn't think about that now. He couldn't think about how beautiful she was, or how every moment he spent with her was singular and special, or how he'd lain awake nights sometimes wishing their friendship could evolve into something more intimate. But he knew that any relationship between them would only end up breaking her heart as well as his, so leaving now was the best thing for both of them.

No matter how much he was going to miss her.

A few minutes later he passed the clinic, a simple modular building that was more functional than attractive. It contained a waiting room, three exam rooms, a small kitchen, an administrative office, and a storage room. Next door, a cramped, aging, four-unit apartment building had been renovated for volunteers to stay in when they were in Santa Rios. Right now all he wanted was to go back to one of those apartments and sleep for about twenty-four hours straight.

After that, he'd have to deal with Robert.

By now Lisa had put the physical evidence into the hands of U.S. Customs officials and told the story of how they'd found the counterfeit drugs Robert had tried to smuggle aboard Lisa's plane. Adam had no doubt that the moment the man crossed the border back to the U.S. he'd be put in jail.

Since Adam had been gone for a few days now, he had no way of knowing what had happened since Friday. But if Robert was still down here, he would have no idea that Lisa had tipped off the U.S. officials. Adam could simply pretend nothing at all had happened until he could get Lisa to swing down here again and fly him back to Texas.

A minute later, Adam opened the front door of the apartment building and went inside, heading for the first door on the right. He dropped his keys as he was pulling them out of his pocket, and they clattered against the floor. As he was picking them up, a door across the hall opened. Robert appeared in the doorway.

Robert Douglas was a tall, imposing man who wore a permanent frown intended to intimidate anyone in his presence—friends, patients, and colleagues alike. On first glance he was a handsome man, but a second look easily picked up the arrogance and insensitivity he exuded with every breath. But right now there was another dimension to his expression Adam hadn't anticipated: complete and utter shock.

"Decker? What in the *hell* are you doing here?"

"What do you mean?"

"The plane. You were on that plane with Lisa."

"No, I wasn't. Something came up at the last minute."

Robert's eyes shifted with suspicion. "Where have you been for the past few days?"

"A patient went into labor before I could leave," Adam said. "Selina Victoro. I had to go there."

"Did you come straight back here?"

"Yeah."

"See anybody along the way?"

Adam paused. "No. It's five in the morning."

"Come in here."

Robert's voice had escalated, with a commanding tone that went beyond his usual authoritative manner, and Adam felt a shot of apprehension. "I'm pretty tired, Robert. I need to get some sleep."

"Come in here now."

Something's wrong. Something's very, very wrong.

Adam followed Robert into the living room of his apartment. Robert closed the door, then turned to face Adam. "Looks like I've got a little problem here, doesn't it?"

Adam stood stock-still. "Problem?"

"You're certainly acting ignorant for a man who discovered a hundred thousand dollars' worth of counterfeit drugs."

Adam was so startled by Robert's out-and-out admission that for a moment he was speechless.

"That's right, Decker. It's just as you suspected. I'm the guilty party. But then, you're not really surprised by that, are you?"

Robert nonchalantly opened a box on the top of the desk and extracted a cigar, dragging it under his nose and inhaling with pleasure. "Did you know it's a crime to import Cuban cigars into the U.S.? A *crime*. Most asinine thing I've ever heard of." He put the cigar to his lips and lit it. He puffed on it, then blew out the smoke. "That's what I like about Mexico: no rules. You'd be shocked at how simple it is to manufacture counterfeit pills that look like the real thing. Why more people aren't taking advantage of the opportunity I'll never know."

Adam couldn't believe this. It was as if Robert were talking about a legitimate enterprise he'd had the foresight to invest in.

"It's a lucrative business, Decker. I'm talking millions. Not hard to amass that kind of money when a single phony Lasotrex is worth up to ten bucks on the U.S. retail market." He gave Adam a sly smile. "I might even consider giving you a piece of the action if you're interested."

Adam felt a surge of pure disgust. "I work for a living, Robert. That's something you know nothing about."

"Oh, yeah? I know nothing about work? As if I haven't spent hours at a time elbow-deep inside the body cavity of some seventy-year-old man who's one foot in the grave already? Put up with whining, lawsuit-happy relatives? Dealt with all that insurance company bullshit?" He dragged on the cigar. "I know all about that kind of work. I prefer something a little more . . . entrepreneurial."

"Entrepreneurial?" Adam said, his voice escalating. "How about illegal? Unethical? Immoral?"

"Easy, Decker. You're starting to hurt my feelings."

"How did you know we found the drugs?"

"Lisa was being watched."

"Watched?"

"I don't leave anything to chance. I wanted to make sure the defibrillator got onto that plane. Lisa transports medical equipment all the time, so there was no reason for her to suspect anything. I told her to fly the device to San Antonio because it needed service, and my contact was going to pick it up from her. Should have gone like clockwork." He shook his head with disgust. "But clumsiness? She *dropped* the damned thing. How the hell was I supposed to prepare for something like that?"

Adam remembered how they'd been hurrying to beat the storm and get off the ground, only to have lightning explode a short distance away. Startled at the sudden noise, Lisa had dropped the defibrillator onto the runway. The plastic casing had cracked wide open, and a huge bag of tiny blue pills had spilled out. They'd both been stunned at the sight and even more stunned when Adam scratched the surface of one of the pills to discover that they were counterfeit. But neither one of them had been surprised in the least when they realized who must be at the heart of the operation.

"You should have known Lisa would eventually find out," Adam said. "Why did you have to involve her?"

"I didn't intend to. Not for the long haul, anyway. It was a short-term fix. My usual supply line broke down, and my distributors were crawling up my ass for me to get the product to them. I've got customers to satisfy."

"Customers to satisfy? *Customers?*" Adam took a threatening step forward. "Shut it down, Robert. Shut the whole operation down. Now!"

"Kill the goose that lays the golden eggs? I don't think so."

"How can you do this to your father?"

Robert's eyes narrowed. "My father has nothing to do with this."

"The hell he doesn't," Adam said hotly. "He started this clinic. You're running it only because he's in bad health and he's got this idea that maybe someday you'll care about it as much as he does. When he finds out you're using it as a front for a counterfeit drug operation, it's going to kill him."

"What my old man doesn't know won't hurt him."

"Oh, he's going to know, all right. It's only a matter of time. Lisa's in the States right now with the drugs in hand, telling the authorities everything. You haven't got a prayer of getting out of this!"

"I'm afraid Lisa can't tell anyone much of anything right about now."

"What?"

"Lisa is dead."

Adam froze. "What did you say?"

Robert flicked his cigar into a nearby ashtray. "Her plane went down shortly after takeoff, nose-first into the river. She didn't survive."

Adam's knees buckled. He stumbled away, one step, two, placing his palm on the back of the sofa to steady himself, his head swimming with horrified disbelief. It couldn't be. Not Lisa. *No.*

"But how? What happened?"

"Seems she had water in her fuel tanks."

"What?"

"The fuel is pale blue," Robert said. "If water is tinted blue and mixed with the fuel, a pilot just might miss that on a pre-flight. Especially if she's in a hurry to leave."

It took a moment for Adam to absorb what Robert was telling him, for one wicked word to form in his mind.

Sabotage.

A surge of pure hatred ripped through him. "You son of a bitch! You goddamned son of a *bitch*! You *killed* her!"

Adam started back across the room, intending to wrap his hands around Robert's neck and squeeze until there wasn't a breath left in the man's body. At the same time, Robert yanked open a nearby desk drawer and hauled out a gun. Adam stopped short as Robert leveled the weapon at him.

"Don't take another step, Decker. Right now, everyone thinks you were on that plane. You're presumed dead. If I made it a reality, no one would ever know the difference."

Adam stared at the gun incredulously. "You won't shoot me. You might be able to sabotage a plane, but killing a man in cold blood—"

"Do you really want to take that chance? I don't have to

account for a damned thing down here. Up to and including murder."

"Why? Because you have the entire Santa Rios sheriff's department in your hip pocket?"

Robert smiled. "Good call."

Adam had been fishing with that accusation, and it disgusted him to find out how right he was.

"So what are you going to do?" Adam said. "Are you going to shoot me?"

"Not unless I have to."

Still holding the gun on Adam, Robert stepped over to an end table, picked up the phone, and dialed. After a moment, he spoke in Spanish in a hushed but commanding tone, telling the person on the other end of the phone that Adam was standing in front of him right now. And telling him to come and fix what he'd screwed up so badly.

He hung up the phone. "Sit down."

"What's going on here?"

"Just shut up and sit."

It wasn't long before Adam heard a car engine and, after a moment, the sound of the outside door of the building opening. A few seconds later, two men came into the apartment whom Adam recognized immediately as frequent patrons of Esmerelda's, a local bar. Enrique Rojos and Ivan Ramirez were men who'd always seemed to be just one foot inside the law, and now Adam knew why.

They stood with their backs to the wall, their faces impassive, like soldiers awaiting orders. And, like soldiers, both men were armed. The precise moment Adam realized why, he felt as if a cold wind blew through him right to the bone.

He turned to Robert, swallowing hard, an indescribable sensation of dread nearly paralyzing his voice. "The woman whose baby I delivered. She and her husband know I wasn't on that plane."

"They're ignorant farm people with no communications. They're lucky if they even know they're in the twenty-first century. And even if they start thinking that maybe the time line isn't right, I'll simply tell them they must be mistaken. Do you really expect them to argue with me?"

Adam stared at the men's weapons, the desperation of a condemned man washing over him like a cold river. He turned back to Robert, searching his face for some kind of humanity.

Nothing. He saw nothing. Robert just stared at him evenly, as if the magnitude of his actions had failed to touch any part of his brain that might relay a little remorse.

"You're actually going to do this, aren't you?" Adam said, his voice hushed and disbelieving.

"Believe it or not, Decker, I always liked you. But I'm not a man who lets his personal feelings get in the way of business." He strode to the window and stared out into the night. "Do it quickly. One shot. And make sure the body's not found."

Gabrio Ramirez lay with his head propped up on a pillow, the lit end of his cigarette glowing red in the darkness of his bedroom. The radio was on low, but it sounded like nothing but noise to him. The stale, hot air in his room choked him, making it hard to breathe. He just lay there, staring at the cracked ceiling, wishing to God he could go to sleep, but there was no way. No way was he ever going to sleep worth a damn again as long as he lived.

What the hell had he done?

Watch her, Gabrio. That's your job. Make sure she puts those drugs on the plane.

That was what his brother, Ivan, had told him to do, and that was what he'd done. When Lisa dropped the heart machine thing and the drugs had spilled out, he knew they'd found out.

He'd actually felt excited. Excited that he had important information to pass along to Ivan, who'd then pass it on to Dr. Douglas. He figured they'd shut things down for a while, then reopen once the heat was off. That had to be worth a few points in his favor, he thought, him being smart enough to see that something was up and report back. And pretty soon if he was smart like that, he'd be somebody important in the scheme of things, somebody other than just Ivan's kid brother. Then he found out that this was more than shoplifting or burglary or stealing car stereos.

This was murder.

They'd killed Lisa and Adam. Both of them were dead because of the information he'd passed on. He should have known. He should have *known* what was going to happen. How could he have been so stupid?

Once, when he was hanging around the airfield, just playing it cool like he always did, Lisa had asked him if he wanted to go up in her plane with her. He couldn't believe it. He'd acted like it was no big deal, but when that plane took off, inside he'd felt so excited he almost couldn't stand it. She'd been nice to him like that. Taking him flying.

And now she was dead.

Gabrio ground out his cigarette, then swung his legs around the edge of the bed and sat up. Sweat trickled down his temples, and his stomach churned. He felt so hungry, but the only time he'd tried to eat, he'd thrown up, and he wondered if he might eventually just starve to death.

Maybe that would be for the best.

He fingered the silver crucifix that hung just beneath his collarbone, the one his mother had given him six years ago right before she died. If he closed his eyes and thought really hard, her face came back to him—so warm and pretty and smiling. To his ten-year-old eyes she'd looked like the Blessed Mother herself.

Then the phone rang.

Gabrio jumped at the sudden noise. He let it ring once, twice. Finally he walked to the kitchen, picked it up, and heard his brother's voice.

"Gabrio?"

"Yeah?"

"Meet us out on the humpback road north of town. We've got work to do."

Gabrio's heart jolted hard. Then the line clicked, and a dial tone droned in his ear.

As he slid the phone back to its cradle, his hands were already shaking. Nothing good happened under the cover of darkness, away from town, where nobody could be a witness. Nothing.

He bowed his head and took a deep breath, trying to think of any way he could say no. He wanted to stay right here and pretend that Ivan hadn't called him. But then he thought about how his brother had always looked back at him, waiting for him to follow in his footsteps, clapping him on the shoulder when he did as he was told and smacking the hell out of him when he didn't. Disobedience was something his brother didn't put up with, and the people he associated with didn't, either.

Gabrio fingered the crucifix again and mumbled bits and pieces of a Bible verse his mother had taught him, something about the valley of the shadow of death and fearing no evil. It didn't help, though, because the truth was that Gabrio feared evil. He feared it a lot. Because now, when he looked into his brother's eyes, that was exactly what he saw.

Adam lay in the backseat of Enrique's car, pulling against the rope that bound his hands behind his back, a subdued but frantic resistance to what he knew was coming. The rope ground into his wrists, but still he fought it, reaching for a miracle, praying for deliverance, even as he was filled with the sickening knowledge that these were his last few minutes on earth.

The car slowed. Stopped. Enrique killed the engine. In the sudden quiet, Adam could hear the pulse of blood racing through his veins and echoing in his ears.

Ivan got out and yanked the back door open. Enrique came around, and together they grabbed Adam's arms and pulled him from the car. Enrique opened the trunk, extracted a rifle, and lobbed it to Ivan.

Another car approached, headlights ripping through the night. For a moment, Adam was filled with hope. Then he saw who got out of the car.

Gabrio approached, his eyes widening when he saw Adam. "What the hell is he doing here? I thought—"

"Slight miscalculation," Enrique said. "Seems he wasn't on the plane."

"But since everybody already thinks he's dead," Ivan added, "we're going to make sure that happens."

Every word they spoke sent waves of sickening disbelief through Adam. Was Gabrio a possible ally, or was he as ruthless as his brother?

"This is murder, Gabrio," Adam said. "You're crossing a line here, and you can't go back. Just by being here, you're guilty, too. You know that, don't you?"

"Shut up," Ivan said.

"How can you drag him into this?" Adam shouted. "He's just a kid!"

"Yeah, and all kids got to grow up, don't they?" Ivan turned to Gabrio. "You got any problem with this?"

"Course not," Gabrio said.

Ivan looked back at Adam. "Turn around and start walking."

"What are you doing?" Gabrio said.

Ivan grabbed Adam by the arm, spun him around, and gave him a shove. "Blood spatters."

Adam walked about ten feet to the edge of the road, stopping at the point where the shoulder took a steep dive down a hillside. He turned back to face the garish glow of the headlights.

"Turn around!" Ivan shouted.

Of all the ways Adam thought he might die, this was beyond his comprehension. Tremors of fear raced through him, the cold, dark terror that came from looking straight into death. He refused to give in to it. Instead, he met Ivan's gaze.

"No. If you're going to pull that trigger, you're going to have to look me in the eye when you do it."

"You think that's a problem for me or something?"

"Shit, man," Enrique said. "Shoot him, or I'm going to."

Adam glanced at Gabrio. The kid stood stock-still, his eyes wide, not moving a muscle.

"You're not like them, Gabrio," Adam called out to him. "You don't have to be like them. Don't ruin your life. Do you hear me?"

"Shut up!" Ivan said.

"Go to Sera. She'll help you. Just go to Sera—"

Ivan raised his rifle to his shoulder, and a shot exploded. Adam flinched at the last moment, but the bullet struck him in the chest and spun him around. The momentum sent him tumbling down the steep hillside, his head whacking hard on a protruding rock. It felt as if he fell forever before finally coming to rest at the bottom of the hill, his body twisted, his hands still bound tightly behind his back.

Oddly, he felt nothing. No pain. Nothing. Instead, he had the strangest feeling of floating, as if he were evaporating from the earth. A light appeared, a bright, stunning light that seemed to fill his mind. And in it, hovering like an apparition, was Sera's face, that sweet, beautiful face he wished to God he could see just one more time.

Even in these last moments of life, she was all he could think about, the only woman since Ellen who had stirred something inside him, the one woman who'd made him think about finding again what he'd lost that terrible night three years ago.

It was his last thought before he plunged into darkness.

Gabrio stared down the hillside, feeling the reverberation of the gunshot slice its way right through his heart, echoing forever through the stillness of the night. His breath came in short spurts, and he held it for a moment, trying to get it under control, even as the anguish he felt nearly knocked him to his knees.

"Gabrio," Ivan said.

Gabrio whipped around and met his brother's challenging stare. Ivan tossed him a flashlight.

"Go down there and make sure he's dead."

Gabrio fought desperately not to let his horror show on his face. No emotion. That was the goal. In his brother's world, if you felt anything you were weak. You couldn't even pause. Delay equals fear, and you never show fear.

"What's the matter, kid?" Enrique said with a mocking grin. "Afraid to touch a dead body? Huh? Afraid his ghost will come back to haunt you or something?"

"He's not afraid," Ivan said sharply, then turned to Gabrio. "Are you?"

"Course not," Gabrio said.

"Go," Ivan said.

In a daze, Gabrio eased down the hillside, sidestepping protruding rocks, fighting the nausea that welled up in his stomach. He only hoped he could keep from falling to his knees and throwing up.

He came to a halt beside the body, shining his flashlight on the man's face. Blood. Jesus *Christ*, there was so much blood, pouring from a wound in his upper chest. And his head. He'd hit his head, and blood was spilling out there, too.

Tears burned in Gabrio's eyes, and he swiped his eyes with his sleeve, hoping it would just look like he was wiping sweat off his face. The man was still as death.

Crouching down, Gabrio reached out his hand, paused, then rested two fingers beneath Adam's jawline along the big artery there. He told himself he had to hold them there for only a few seconds, only until he was sure, but the shock of what he felt made his heart lurch.

A pulse.

Mary, Mother of God. He's still alive.

"Gabrio!" Ivan called out.

His brother's voice jangled his nerves. His brain grew foggy, and he couldn't think. He just couldn't *think*. All he could do was feel—the terrible burning sensation in the back of his throat, that feeling of horror that slid along every nerve.

If he was going to be loyal to Ivan, he had to go back up that hill and tell him the job wasn't finished yet. But he knew what would happen then. One more gunshot. Close range. And then it really would be over.

You're not like them, Gabrio. You don't have to be like them. Don't ruin your life.

Gabrio stood up and walked back up the hill. He stopped in front of Ivan, slipped a cigarette from his pocket, and lit it.

"Dead?" Ivan asked.

Gabrio dragged on the cigarette, then blew out the smoke. "Dead."

Ivan clapped him on the shoulder. His brother's touch revolted him, almost as much as the pride he saw on his face. *Pride.*

"Let's get rid of the body," Enrique said, starting down the hillside.

Gabrio stepped in front of him. "I'll do it."

Enrique laughed. "You? No way, kid. We have to make sure this one isn't found."

"He can handle it," Ivan said sharply. "Can't you, Gabrio?"

Gabrio's mouth went dry as dust. "Handle it?" He took a nonchalant drag on his cigarette, hoping they couldn't see his hands shaking. "Get rid of a body out here in the middle of nowhere? You think I can't handle a chickenshit job like that?"

"Sure you can," Ivan said, then turned to glare at Enrique.

Gabrio continued to stare at Enrique with a disdainful expression, forcing himself to not so much as blink.

Finally Enrique turned away. "Fine. Do it. Just don't fuck it up."

Ivan glared at Enrique. "He's not going to fuck up anything."

"Yeah. Well, maybe we'd better stick around just to make sure."

"We don't need to stick around. If my brother says he'll handle it, he'll handle it."

"I'm just not sure about the kid. That's all."

"Hey!" Ivan said. "Who do you think fingered the two of them in the first place? Huh? Without Gabrio, they'd be across the border by now."

And Lisa would be alive. And Adam wouldn't be bleeding to death. Jesus Christ—what had he done?

Finally Enrique went to the trunk of his car, grabbed a shovel, and stabbed it into the ground in front of Gabrio. "On second thought, it won't be a problem. I mean, you know the penalty for fucking this up, don't you, kid?"

He did. No mercy. If anyone found out Adam was alive, he was dead. And nothing Ivan could say would stop that. Hell, right now he wasn't completely sure his own brother wouldn't be the one to pull the trigger.

Ivan turned to Gabrio. "Come back to the house when you're through. We'll have a couple of beers, huh?"

He clapped Gabrio on the shoulder one more time, and then he and Enrique turned and walked toward the car. Gabrio forced himself to wait until the car disappeared down the road, then turned and raced back down the hillside. He knelt beside Adam.

"Dr. Decker. Hey, man. Can you hear me?"

The man stirred slightly but didn't respond. Gabrio yanked off his shirt, jerking it hard until it tore. He wadded up part of the shirt and pressed it hard against the wound, then ripped a couple of strips from it and tied it around the man's chest to hold the pack in place. But it wasn't working. By the faint light of the rising sun Gabrio saw blood still coming out. And the doctor's head was still bleeding, too. What the hell was he going to do now?

"I'm sorry," he said, tears clouding his eyes. "I'm so sorry. . . ."

The man needed a doctor. Unfortunately, the only one in Santa Rios wanted him dead. And the second Gabrio's brother found out what he'd done . . .

Then he remembered Adam's last words: *Go to Sera. She'll help you. Just go to Sera—*

Right now, she was the only person on this earth that he thought he just might be able to trust.

For the past two days, Serafina Cordero had sat in the upstairs bedroom of her rambling farmhouse, sleeping only when she couldn't keep her eyes open any longer. She didn't remember the last time she'd eaten. She felt like crying, but she didn't have a tear inside her left to shed.

Adam was dead.

She leaned back in the rocking chair where she sat, dropping her head against it and closing her eyes. She'd always thought of herself as a strong, resilient person who could take whatever life threw at her. But not this. Not this.

During the two years Adam had come to Santa Rios to volunteer at the clinic, their interaction—long conversations, shared moments of laughter, eyes meeting in prolonged glances—had slowly become as intimate as if they were lovers. But whenever it looked as if their relationship might move toward a physical acknowledgment, he'd kept her at arm's length. Yes, she'd been younger than him. At twenty-seven, much younger. And the death of his wife only three years before had surely affected the way he felt about other women. But the connection between them had been so strong and so real that she knew he had to feel it, too. He had to feel how much she loved him.

But still he'd left her.

It had crushed her when Adam told her he was moving to Chicago and wouldn't be back. But even though he would have been hundreds of miles away, she could have had hope. She could have hoped that somewhere down the road their lives would intersect again and she'd have the future with him she'd always dreamed of.

But now he was gone forever.

She looked out the window to see the sun coming up—a stunning orange and red display that would have put a smile on her face under any other circumstances. But now she merely stared at it blankly, wondering how many more sunrises she'd have to see before a moment of her life would pass that wasn't consumed by grief.

Suddenly she heard a knock at her front door, three times in quick succession. She sat up suddenly, startled at the noise, even as heartache dulled her senses.

No. Go away. Please just go away.

The knocking persisted.

It had to be a woman in labor. Nobody came to her house at the crack of dawn for anything else. As a nurse-midwife, she was used to getting dragged away at all hours, because babies never came on schedule.

Somebody needs you. They're counting on you.

That thought was what finally drove her to stand up, her head pounding, and walk out of her bedroom. She trudged down the hall to the stairs, every step feeling as if she were moving through quicksand.

The knocking continued, loud and harsh.

She descended the stairs and stopped at the bottom, clutching the banister. In the past five years since she'd gotten her degree and returned from the U.S. to live in Santa Rios, she'd seen scores of babies born. But suddenly it felt so hopeless. How was she going to face bringing another life into this world when the man she loved had so recently left it?

Taking a deep breath, she forced herself to go to the door, throw the lock, and swing it open. And what she saw shocked her.

Gabrio Ramirez stood on her front porch. He wore no shirt. Blood streaked his chest and right arm, and an unmistakable look of panic filled his eyes.

"Gabrio? My God! What happened?"

"I-it's not me," he said.

"You're bleeding! Come inside!"

"No! Just come with me! You have to come with me!"

He turned and trotted down the porch steps.

"Is there a woman in labor?"

"No!"

"Gabrio!"

He turned around, walking backward as he talked. "Please! Just come to my car! *Now!*"

Her heart beating apprehensively, she slipped out the door and followed Gabrio to his rusted-out Chevy Impala. He opened the back door. She came around it, peered into the backseat, and let out a gasp of pure agony.

Adam's body.

He lay on the seat, broken and bleeding, one arm dragging on the floorboard, his hair matted with blood.

"Oh, God." She turned away instantly, bowing her head, sobs immediately choking her voice. "Oh, God, *no.*"

She stumbled away from the car, her stomach grinding with nausea, feeling so light-headed that she was afraid she was going to pass out.

The plane crash. Somehow Gabrio had recovered Adam's body from the plane crash and brought him to her. It was the only explanation.

Gabrio grabbed her by the arm and spun her back around. "Please do something!" he implored, his eyes filling with tears. *"Please!"*

"Do something? But I can't. I—"

"Yes, you can! You're a nurse! *Do something!*"

Sera recoiled at the boy's outburst. She didn't know what to say. What to do. *He's dead. I can't raise the dead. Is that what you expect me to do?*

Taking a deep breath, she forced herself to step back toward the car and peer into the backseat again. Her gaze traveled hesitantly up Adam's legs to his waist, and then to his chest. It was covered in blood, but . . .

She blinked. It couldn't be. For the first time she realized . . . Fresh blood?

Then she saw something else, and she was so shocked that she had to grab hold of the car door to keep from collapsing. In the faint morning light she could just make out Adam's chest rising and falling with short, shallow respirations.

He was alive.

chapter five

Eerie shafts of late morning sunlight streaked through the grime-crusted windows of the bunkhouse, weakly illuminating Lisa's pale, bruised face. Dave had dozed on and off for the past several hours, but she'd slept like the dead. He watched as she stirred now, turned over, lifted her head, and, after wearing a confused expression for several seconds, closed her eyes and dropped her head back down to the mattress.

She moved her legs over the side of the bed and sat up with a muffled groan. "What time is it?"

"Ten after eleven."

Dave hoped that the next words out of her mouth would be something like *Boy, I must have been out of my mind before,* or *I bet you thought I was a little nuts, huh?* or maybe just *Gee, Dave, false alarm. Sorry for dragging you all the way down here for nothing.*

Instead, she looked toward the door, then craned her neck to peer out the window. "Nobody came looking for me, did they?"

Dave sighed. Yeah, he still had a problem here. It remained to be seen whether that problem had to do with injury-induced paranoia or something straight out of an action-adventure movie.

"How are you feeling?" he asked.

"Like I got hit by a truck."

"Do you think you could eat something?"

"Maybe in a minute."

Dave dug through the bag he'd brought and pulled out a

bottle of water. Sliding off the bed, he came over to sit beside her. She took the bottle, drank, then bowed her head, expelling a long, weary breath.

"You need water. Drink more."

She did.

"You were a little out of it when I got here."

She glanced at him, then looked away. "If you'd been through what I'd been through, you'd have been a little loopy yourself."

"Does your head feel better now?"

She looked at him warily. "Yeah."

"Are you thinking a little clearer?"

Her eyes narrowed. "Are you asking me if I've gotten over the silly notion that somebody is trying to kill me?"

"Take it easy, Lisa. I just need to know what's going on here. That's all."

"I told you what's going on here. Drugs. Sabotage. Plane crash. Men with machine guns. How much clearer do I have to make it?"

"Are you sure that's what happened?"

"Stop patronizing me."

"I only want to know—"

"Damn it, will you listen to me? I'm not crazy! Somebody is trying to kill me! I found the drugs. My plane went down. They came after me—" She let out a breath of disgust. "Forget it. You're not going to believe it until you see it."

She stood up, wobbling a little. She righted herself, then strode toward the door of the bunkhouse.

"Where are you going?" he asked.

She ignored him and walked outside.

"Lisa!"

He went to the door and watched as she stepped toward the edge of the woods, looking left and right the whole time as if she expected somebody to leap out of the bushes and grab her. She reached the place where he'd found her sitting last night and picked something up off the ground. As she walked back, he realized it was her backpack.

She came back through the door, slapping the backpack

against his chest. He grabbed it in a reflex action, and she
stalked on past him and sat back down on the bunk with a
weary sigh.

"Open it," she said.

He walked back over to the bunk where he'd been sitting,
tossed the backpack down, and unzipped it. Inside was a
thick plastic bag. He pulled it out.

Holy shit.

Pills. Thousands of them. Tens of thousands. What the
hell . . . ?

"They're made to look like Lasotrex," Lisa said. "A
vasodilator."

Dave knew that counterfeit pharmaceutical operations
went on all over the world, and Mexico was definitely a hot
spot. If she'd found something she wasn't supposed to, somebody could very well want her dead. If so, the moment she
showed her face . . .

Damn. His mission to get medical help for a delusional
woman had just turned into something potentially more
treacherous.

"So what do you think now?" Lisa said. "Still think I'm
imagining things?"

"I think," he said, "that we need to talk."

Lisa's mind still felt fuzzy and disoriented, but maybe the
sleep she'd had meant she'd be able to put a few consecutive
thoughts together and tell Dave exactly why she'd asked him
to come seven hundred miles into the middle of the Mexican
wilderness.

He sat down on the opposite bunk, his elbows on his knees,
his hands clasped in front of him. He wore faded jeans, boots,
and a denim shirt with the sleeves rolled to his elbows. He
still had the same tall, well-developed body he'd had in high
school, though the leanness he'd shown back then had given
way to a more substantial build that made him look even
more powerful. He had the kind of face women dream
about—strikingly handsome, with strong features, deep, dark
eyes and a sharp, mesmerizing gaze. His face was marred

only by a few age lines, and the congregation of those lines at the corners of his eyes and around his mouth told her he smiled a lot.

He wasn't smiling now.

"Give me the whole story," he said, "and don't leave anything out."

The whole story. Good God. It felt as if she'd lived a lifetime in the past couple of days. She sat up a little more, releasing a weary breath, her throat dry and scratchy.

"It started," she said, "when Adam Decker and I were getting ready to fly out of here on Friday afternoon. He's one of the doctors who volunteer at the clinic. The clinic is closed on weekends except for emergencies, and that's when we swap out the staff. I was going to take Adam back to San Antonio, then bring another doctor down here."

"San Antonio?"

"I live there now. Adam does, too. The organization is based out of there."

Dave nodded for her to go on.

"A storm was approaching, so Adam and I were hurrying to take off before it hit. Before we left the clinic, Robert gave me a defibrillator to get serviced in San Antonio."

"A device that shocks hearts back into action."

"Right. It was a portable unit, about the size of a small suitcase. I take a lot of medical equipment back and forth, so I didn't think anything about it. Adam and I were hurrying toward the plane, trying to beat the storm, when lightning struck only about fifty yards away. Scared the hell out of me. I recoiled from the flash and dropped the defibrillator. The plastic casing cracked wide open. And guess what was inside." She nodded toward the pills. "Adam said they looked like Lasotrex. But then he scratched the surface of one with a pocketknife. The blue exterior gave way to a white interior. He said if it was really Lasotrex, it would be blue all the way through."

"So they're definitely counterfeit."

"Yes. Apparently this kind of thing goes on all over the world. Mexico, South America, the Orient, the Middle East.

They manufacture fake pills for pennies, then transport them to other areas and sell them at retail prices. Adam estimated that there had to be least a hundred thousand dollars' worth of them in that one bag."

"You say Douglas is the culprit. But what's his motive? He's a doctor. A guy like that has to have all kinds of money. What does he need with more?"

"Actually, he doesn't have a lot of money. He botched an appendectomy a few years ago that ended up killing a guy. He got hit with a multimillion-dollar malpractice suit that cleaned him out. Rumor has it that he was so negligent and the award was so big that nobody will insure him to practice medicine in the U.S."

"So how did he end up down here running a humanitarian organization?"

"It's not his baby. It's his father's. Bernard James Douglas is a respected heart surgeon. He began the clinic a few years ago, and then his health began to fail. So he put his son in charge."

"He doesn't know what Robert is like?"

"I think deep down he does. He just refuses to believe it. I think he's hoping that someday his son will grow a heart." She made a scoffing noise. "He's got a long wait."

"I can't imagine that a man like Robert would put up with being sequestered in a tiny Mexican town for very long."

"Are you kidding? He thrives on it."

"How so?"

"People look up to him here. It's as if God himself had dropped down from heaven to diagnose their illness or pre-scribe a drug. He tosses enough money around that shop, owners are happy to see him walk through the door. He plays poker with the sheriff and a couple of other guys every Friday night and usually comes out on the winning end, which means he probably cheats. And he has his pick of the local women for all kinds of recreational activities. Throw in a profitable counterfeiting operation, and he's in paradise."

"Sounds like a real asshole."

"Actually, I haven't had any problem dealing with Robert."

"Oh?"

"Yeah. I told him once when we were cruising at ten thousand feet that either he could lose his condescending attitude or he could land in Santa Rios the hard way."

"How's that?"

"Without a plane."

For the first time, Dave cracked a tiny smile. "I see you haven't changed a bit."

She raised an eyebrow. "Is that a good thing or a bad thing?"

"Oh, it's a good thing," he told her, a smile still playing on his lips.

Suddenly she had the strangest feeling, as if eleven years hadn't passed at all and she was basking in his approval all over again.

No. She didn't need that. She wasn't that lost, lonely kid anymore, the one who'd have sold her soul for a kind word from anyone. But still, there was something about the way he looked at her, as if he could see right inside her. At least in that way, he hadn't changed a bit, either.

"Tell me more about Robert's connection to local law enforcement," Dave said.

"Well, as I told you, he's really chummy with the sheriff, but there's more. In a place like this, the moment anyone shows up with anything shiny and new, it has a way of disappearing. Participating in burglary and theft and carjacking is just an alternative lifestyle. That means the clinic should be ripe for the picking where drugs and equipment are concerned. Nobody touches it. In this town, I think the people who enforce the law and break the law are pretty much one and the same. And Robert's probably got them all on his payroll."

"Which means he can run a counterfeiting operation with no interference."

"Exactly."

"How do you think Robert found out that you and Adam discovered the drugs?"

"I don't know. But there's a possibility we were being watched."

"Watched?"

"Yes. By Gabrio Ramirez. He's a sixteen-year-old kid, maybe part of a local gang. His car was parked near the airfield when we were leaving."

"Were you suspicious of him at the time?"

"No. Not really. He hangs out at the airfield a lot. I took him flying once. You should have seen his face when I gunned it down the runway, then pulled back and started to soar. He loved it. That day he even spoke English to me, when he pretends most of the time that he doesn't know how. Ever since then, he shows up just about every time I take off or land. I think maybe he was hanging out just because he likes flying."

"Or he was keeping an eye on you."

She sighed. "Maybe. But I'd like to think that he's just a good kid who needs a break. From what I hear, his mother moved to the U.S. with him when he was just a baby. She died when he was ten. His only living relative was his brother, Ivan, so he came back here to live with him. Ivan's got no obvious means of support but always has wads of cash. Around here, that spells *gang*."

"Which Gabrio could be part of."

Lisa sighed again. "Maybe."

"Did he see you find the drugs?" Dave asked.

"I don't know. He could have."

But she still didn't want to believe that Gabrio had anything to do with the sabotage of her plane. Most of the time, he had the look of a boy with nothing but a dead-end life ahead of him, who despised where he was but wouldn't admit it in a thousand years. She knew that look, because she'd worn it herself once. But she'd discovered that there was something about leaving the earth and climbing into the clouds that made just about anything seem possible. She'd thought maybe Gabrio had felt that, too. Now she wasn't so sure.

"So what did you and Adam do once you realized what was going on?"

"We knew we didn't want to deal with any Mexican officials, so we decided to take the drugs back across the border and hand them over to the customs officers at the commuter airport in San Antonio and tell them what we suspected. Since Robert was trying to smuggle them into the U.S., his network clearly extends there, so U.S. authorities would definitely get involved. But in the meantime, the storm hit, and we had to wait it out. Then right as it was clearing off, somebody showed up at the clinic. A man whose wife was in labor. Adam's an obstetrician. There's a midwife in town, but the patient was supposedly high-risk and in premature labor. Adam insisted she needed him, so he took me to the airstrip, told me to go on without him, then went to deliver the baby."

"How long did you have to wait for him?" Dave asked.

"I didn't wait. Adam said the woman lived at least an hour away and that he had no idea how long he'd be. He insisted that I take off for San Antonio without him."

Dave blinked with surprise. "But he was on that plane with you when it went down."

"No. He wasn't."

"Douglas reported him dead right along with you."

For several moments Lisa just stared at Dave, dumbfounded. "But he's not dead. He was never even on the plane."

"I imagine Robert knows that by now."

Lisa knew what that meant, and she felt a shot of apprehension. "I didn't know the name of the woman he went to help. I had no way to warn him."

"This is Sunday morning. He left for that woman's house on Friday afternoon. The chances of him still being there are slim. One way or another, something has already happened."

"What do you mean?

"Maybe he came back, heard about your plane going down, speculated that it wasn't an accident, and got out of town. That's the best possible scenario."

"And the worst?"

"He had no idea what was going on. And if Robert saw him and realized he was still alive, he was in big trouble." Dave sighed. "Robert missed him the first time. You can bet he won't make the same mistake twice."

Oh, God.

Lisa felt a rush of total despair as the enormity of the situation crashed down on her. *No.* This couldn't be happening. Not to Adam. Tears gathered behind her eyes, making them feel hot and tight.

"Do you know this was his last trip down here?" she said. "In two weeks he was taking a chief of staff position at a hospital in Chicago." She paused, feeling a choking tightness in her throat. "And now this."

Adam's wife had died a few years ago under circumstances that would crush any man, but time had passed. He'd picked up the pieces and moved on. Why he'd chosen to give up the thing he did best and move to Chicago to take an administrative job she didn't know. She only knew that she was going to miss him. These past two years, he'd been almost like an older brother to her, a person she could talk to, laugh with, confide in. Throughout her life, those kinds of people had always been in very short supply.

And now she might be missing him forever.

"Are you all right?" Dave asked.

"Yes," she said, fighting to hold her voice steady. "Of course."

"Lisa?" he said gently. "Was he somebody special to you?"

"He was a friend."

"A good friend?"

"I guess we'd gotten to know each other pretty well."

That was all she could say. If she told Dave just how much Adam meant to her, she was going to lose it. She turned away, gritting her teeth. *Damn it.* What force in the universe was it that dangled people in front of her like some kind of emotional bait and, as soon as she started to care about them, yanked them back and watched her crumble? Well, whatever it was could get its kicks somewhere else, because she wasn't going to fall apart. She *wasn't.*

"It's still possible he got out of here," Dave said. "If so, then maybe he's still alive."

Lisa nodded, knowing Dave didn't really believe that. No matter how unlikely it was, though, she was going to be praying for it, on the off chance that there really was a God out there and he really did give a damn.

"Where exactly did you crash-land?" Dave asked. "They said your plane went into a river."

"It got caught up on the side of a ravine. I made it out of the plane to a ledge beside it. That's when the guys with machine guns showed up to obliterate what was left of my plane. It went into the river. Unfortunately, I ended up falling right along with it."

"But you hung on to your backpack."

"Yes. But not the parts of the defibrillator. I really wish I had those, too, but there was only so much I could grab on my way out of that cockpit."

"Then you found your way back to town to call me."

"Yes."

"Do you think anyone saw you?"

"No. I don't think so."

Dave sat back. "Okay. The best thing we can do is get out of here and get back across the border. You're going to show customs agents these drugs and tell them your story. I'm going to flash my badge and back you up. After that, I guarantee you they'll be all over Robert the minute he steps foot back in the U.S."

"But as soon as I show myself, I'll be a target. Robert still wants me dead."

"Once the story is out, he'll be forced to leave you alone. If you end up dead, he'll be suspect number one. He doesn't dare risk that."

She breathed a sigh of relief. "That's the best news I've had since this whole mess came down."

"But we do have a problem. We can't take a commercial flight, because we'd have to smuggle the pills through security at the Monterrey airport. That's too risky."

"So what do you suggest we do? Cross the border by car?"

"I'd rather hand the drugs over to San Antonio customs agents, just as you'd planned to. That would put us well within the U.S. border, and we'll be talking to agents you're familiar with."

"But that means we need to fly back," Lisa said. "Unfortunately, my plane is at the bottom of the Mercado River."

"Can you rent a plane in Monterrey?"

"There's a commuter airport there. A couple of aviation companies. Rentals should be available."

"Then that's our plan." Dave checked his watch. "It's nearly noon. We can be in Monterrey by three or three-thirty. With luck, somebody will have a plane available and we can head out right away." He stood up, tossing his bag over his shoulder. "One quick stop in Santa Rios, and we'll be on the road."

"Why do we have to stop?"

"The car's nearly out of gas, and there's next to nothing between here and Monterrey."

"What if the wrong person spots me in town? Not likely, but Santa Rios isn't all that big."

"No problem. You can ride in the trunk."

Lisa felt a surge of dread. "No. No way. Not the trunk."

"Just until we get out of town."

"Nope. I don't do small, closed-in spaces."

"It's the safest place for you."

"I'm serious, Dave. I'm not getting in that trunk."

Finally he sighed with resignation. "Okay. The floorboard of the backseat, then. Covered up with this." He picked up an old moth-eaten blanket off one of the bunks and gave it a shake.

Lisa didn't really like the sound of that, either, but riding under a blanket in the backseat beat feeling as if she were sealed inside a moving coffin.

She stood up and grabbed her backpack. When she wobbled a little, Dave took it from her, lowered it back to the ground, then placed his hands against her shoulders.

"Hey, take it easy, okay?"

"I'm fine."

But for a moment she wasn't. As the events of the past few days overwhelmed her, she bowed her head and took a deep, steadying breath.

"Everything's going to be okay, Lisa. I'm going to get you

out of here. And then I'm going to do everything I can to make sure Robert pays for what he did to you."

"He attempted murder in Mexico. How can he be prosecuted for that in the U.S.?"

"If a crime is committed by one U.S. citizen against another in connection with a conspiracy that began in the U.S., the law allows for prosecution even if the crime was committed on Mexican soil."

"So all we have to do is tie him to the counterfeiting conspiracy and they can go after him for attempted murder?"

"Yes. We'll get him, Lisa. I promise you."

The expression of determination on his face amazed her. That he was making her problem his problem amazed her even more. Suddenly she was swept away by the same force that had drawn her to him all those years ago, that steady, anchored feeling she had whenever she was around him, as if he was the foundation that could calm all the turbulence in her life.

She remembered lying on the bank of that river after her plane went down, wet and exhausted, staring up at the starry sky and feeling more alone than she ever had in her life. Sure, she had friends, but they were people she wouldn't even impose upon to help her move from one apartment to another, much less get her out of a situation like this. And her family. She would rather die a slow death in the Mexican wilderness than speak to any of them ever again.

Then she'd thought about Dave.

Just call me if you need me.

His words had stayed in the back of her mind for years, like a promissory note in a dusty file just waiting to be uncovered. They were what had moved her to stand up on the bank of that river, exhausted, her head throbbing, and begin the long walk back toward Santa Rios, driven to put one foot in front of the other because she knew that if only she could talk to him somehow everything would be all right. Now that she felt more lucid, she realized what a slender thread that had been to hold on to. How could she have thought that he'd come seven hundred miles into the middle of nowhere to help her?

And yet he had.

Still, she knew why. Dave DeMarco was the kind of man who would sooner lose a limb than go back on a promise, no matter how ill-advised that promise might have been. And as he stood here with her now, dead tired and undoubtedly counting the miles they were going to have to travel before he could get back home again, she had to believe he had a few regrets about that.

"Maybe now you wish you hadn't made that promise to me back then," she said. "It was a pretty unfortunate thing to say at the last moment, wasn't it?"

"Unfortunate?"

"Look, I know you're here only because you felt obligated. You made me a promise, and you feel as if you have to fulfill it. It's just the way you are." She paused. "The way you've always been."

"Yes. Which is why I'm careful about the promises I make."

"It was a long time ago."

"Did I mention anything about an expiration date?"

"No. But we were kids, Dave. Kids don't always do smart things."

"I knew exactly what I was doing then." He slung her backpack over his shoulder, his gaze never leaving hers. "And I know exactly what I'm doing now."

He wrapped his arm around her shoulders and guided her toward the door, and she resisted the urge to slip her arm around his waist and lean into him. No matter how much Dave was helping her now, she'd discovered that at the end of the day there was only one person she could depend on, and she had only to go to the nearest mirror to find her. He was here now because of a promise he'd made, and soon he'd be out of her life again just as quickly as he'd arrived.

The sooner she could rely on herself again, the safer and more secure she was going to feel.

As Dave drove into the outskirts of Santa Rios, he was struck once again by just what a crappy little town it was. Aged storefronts lined the main drag, and the windows of every one of them could have benefited from an economy-sized bottle of Windex and a supersize roll of paper towels. A couple of kids raced down the sidewalk on skateboards, while shiftless men hovered around the street corners, smoking, scratching, and spitting. Hell, no wonder nobody wanted to set up an actual medical practice here. There wasn't a country club, a golf course, or a five-star restaurant in sight.

He saw the gas station in the distance, a tired cinder-block building that might have last been painted sometime around the turn of the century. The nineteenth century.

"Lisa, we're getting close to the gas station. Get under that blanket."

"I will."

"And don't move an eyelash."

"I hear you."

"I still say the trunk would be better than the backseat."

"Yeah, and all the screaming just might tip somebody off that I was in there."

"Just how claustrophobic are you?"

"You mean, how closed in do I have to be before I start sobbing uncontrollably?"

"Yeah."

"I'm not doing too great with this blanket over my face. Does that tell you anything?"

"And you fly private planes? Aren't the cockpits a little small?"

"Yeah, but there's all that sky out there beyond it. Not a problem."

Dave swung the car into the gas station lot, then pulled up next to one of two pumps.

"We're there. I'll have us out of here in a couple of minutes."

He reached under the dash, flicked open the gas tank cover. He stepped out of the car and had just pulled the nozzle off the pump when he was greeted by a stubby little Mexican man wearing a greasy denim shirt. The name *Fernando* was embroidered just above the pocket.

"Buenos días," he said with a gregarious smile, taking the

gas nozzle from Dave's hand. "No es necesario hacer nada. Esta es una gasolinera de servicio completo."

While Dave's command of Spanish was somewhat conversational, most of the time it was limited to *Yes, you were speeding* and *Drop the weapon and put your hands behind your head,* so he wasn't exactly making out what the guy was saying.

"No hablo espa´nol," he told Fernando.

"Ah, you are American," he said, smiling even more broadly and talking a little louder, as if Dave had a hearing problem to go with his language barrier. Fernando eased the gas nozzle out of Dave's hand. "What I say is that I am happy to do. I will put gasoline in the car."

Customer service? Dave hadn't counted on that. Then again, Fernando's enthusiasm probably stemmed from the fact that Dave was driving a sporty late-model car. Such vehicles seemed to be a rarity in Santa Rios. Fernando probably assumed Dave had a few more pesos than his average customer and a tip might be on the horizon, a tip that would grow in proportion to how much he engaged in chatty conversation.

"The car, she is *very* good," Fernando said, parking the nozzle in the gas tank with a soft clatter. "A Mustang, yes?"

"Yes," Dave said. "It's a Mustang."

Fernando left the nozzle in the tank, then ran his fingertip back and forth over the side panel of the car. "She is red. That is very hot. A red car is like a sexy woman. She moves so good, and the eyes—they fall on her and you cannot remove them."

Or he couldn't take his eyes off it. Something like that. Unfortunately, Fernando was loaded with bad English and wasn't afraid to use it.

His gaze lingered over the side panels, then slid along the downward curve of the hood. Then he lowered his head to glance through the driver's side window. "The seats? Leather?"

"Yeah," Dave said, moving in front of the window. "Leather." *Just be still, Lisa. Be very, very still.*

"Ah," Fernando said, breathing deeply to make his point, "leather smells like perfume. The perfume of a sexy woman."

Right. Eau de Cowhide. Sexiest scent south of the Rio Grande.

Fernando circled to the back of the car, teasing his fingertips over the rear spoiler, wearing an expression of sheer bliss. He compared cars to women. Dave wondered if he told women that they reminded him of cars. He glanced at the man's left hand. No wedding ring.

Probably.

Fernando walked around to the opposite side of the car, then bent over a rear fender, spending an inordinate amount of time admiring one of the tires. Apparently Firestones were as sexy to this guy as high arches in stiletto heels.

The gas pump clicked off. Fernando came back around the car to extract the nozzle from the tank, moving slowly, regretfully. A drop of gasoline fell onto the car and slithered downward. He removed a handkerchief from his pocket and gently wiped the gasoline away, then flipped the hankie over and buffed the paint with a slow, circular polish. Now, if only he could refrain from lighting two cigarettes and handing one of them to the car, maybe they could get the hell out of here.

"Much fortunate man you are to have this car," Fernando said, his smile positively orgasmic. "Much, much fortunate."

Dave noted the outrageous price of the gasoline and pulled enough money from his wallet to cover it. Fernando went into the station, and after a few minutes he returned with Dave's change. Dave gave him a few extra pesos for his trouble. Fernando thanked him profusely for his generosity and started back toward the building. But just as Dave was getting back into the car, the man stopped by the right rear tire, a look of horror on his face.

"Señor!" he called out. "Come! A problem!"

Shit. What now?

Dave circled around to the right rear fender. Fernando pointed at the tire, and Dave stared in disbelief.

A flat tire? How in the hell had that happened?

"A beautiful tire," Fernando said with a sorrowful sigh. "And now she is dead." Then a smile popped back onto his face. "No problem. I will fix."

God, no. If he let the Metaphor Man jack up this gorgeous red vehicle and fondle her tires, they'd be here all day.

"No, that's okay," Dave said. "I can change it myself."

"But, señor, I can—"

"No," Dave said. "I can handle it."

Fernando looked longingly at the car for a moment more, with the dejected expression of a dorky guy who'd been turned down for a date with a gorgeous woman. Finally he turned and walked back toward the station.

Dave slid into the driver's seat, putting his wallet into the glove compartment so he could clue Lisa in on what had happened.

"We'll be here a minute more," he said quietly. "We've got a flat tire."

"A flat? How did that happen?"

"Given the road we drove down here on, I guess I'm surprised the other three aren't in the same condition."

"I'm suffocating under this blanket."

"I know. I'll get the tire changed as fast as I can and we'll be out of here."

Aside from a man who had parked near the building and gone inside for a Coke or a pack of cigarettes, the station wasn't busy, so Dave popped the trunk and removed the jack and the spare with the car still sitting at the pump. He changed the tire in record time.

Then, a few minutes later, as he was tossing the flat tire into the trunk, he spotted the problem. He hadn't picked up a nail or run over a sharp rock that had penetrated the tread.

The tire had been slashed.

Dave was in the process of putting two and two together, but he hadn't quite reached four when he felt something cold and hard just beneath his left ear.

A gun.

chapter six

Dave's attacker slammed him down on the trunk of the car, the spoiler jamming him in the ribs and knocking the wind out of him. The guy reached into Dave's pocket, grabbed the car keys, then gave him a hard shove sideways. He stumbled a yard or two and went down hard, whacking his shoulder on the pavement.

What the *hell* was going on?

Dave instantly leapt to his feet, but not before his attacker slid into the driver's seat of the Mustang and slammed the door.

Carjacking?

Shit. Lisa was in the backseat.

Dave raced around the car just as the guy flicked the door locks and started the engine. Dave grabbed the nozzle off the gas pump, spun around, and smacked it through the driver's window. The glass shattered and sprayed. Dave had just flipped the door lock when Lisa flew up out of the backseat and wrapped the blanket around the guy's head, pulled him back hard, and pinned him against the headrest. Dave flung the door open and yanked the gun out of the guy's hand. Grabbing him by the wrist, Dave hauled him out of the car and threw him onto the ground.

The guy swatted the blanket away and started to rise, but Dave gave him a smack across the face that sent him tumbling backward onto the pavement. Dave leapt into the car, tossed the gun into the passenger seat beside him, jammed the Mustang into gear, and took off.

"Lisa?" he said, breathing hard, searching for her face in the rearview mirror. "You okay?"

She looked up from her sprawled-out position in the backseat. "Yeah. Sure. Plane crash, carjacking—I'm doing just great."

"Nice move with the blanket."

"It was all I had. I had to improvise. Problem, though."

"What?"

"I know our carjacker. Ivan Ramirez."

"The guy you talked about earlier? The one who's part of a local gang?"

"Yeah. That's the one."

"Does he know who you are?"

"Yeah. He knows."

"Did he get a good look at you?"

"Eye to eye as we were pulling away."

Shit. "Do his criminal skills go beyond carjacking? Say, to drug counterfeiting?"

"This isn't a very big town. I'm betting he's into everything illegal he can get his hands on. But even if he's not involved with the counterfeiting, all he's got to do is tell somebody that I'm alive and it'll eventually get back to Robert."

"Then we need to hotfoot it to Monterrey. And I still want you to stay down. No need to push what little luck we have left."

Lisa slid onto the floor of the backseat. "Speaking of lack of luck, what are the odds of Ivan coming into that station and grabbing the car we're trying to get out of town in?"

"Pretty good, since the flat was no accident."

"What?"

"The tire was slashed."

"What?"

"Nice system they've got going. Fernando spots a nice late-model car. He flattens the tire, then phones his partner. During the time it takes to change it, the other guy gets there. He grabs the car, and Fernando gets a cut of the profit."

"And since Ivan is into all things criminal—"

"Guess who showed up." Dave shook his head. "Unfortunately, I didn't spot the scam until I saw the tire. By then it was too late."

Dave braked at a stoplight, an antsy feeling crawling up the back of his neck. Pedestrians crossed the street in front of them. He found himself searching every face for anyone who looked a little shady, which was pointless. Hell, right about now, everybody in this town looked like a criminal.

He hit the gas again. Before long they approached the northern edge of town. One more stop sign, and nothing but open road lay ahead. As Dave brought his car to a halt, another car pulled up to the stop sign on the cross street.

A patrol car.

"Lisa, we may have a problem."

"What?"

"Just stay down. No matter what happens, just stay down."

Dave began to pull away from the stop sign, only to have the cop on the cross street hit the gas hard, wheeling his car in their direction.

"Damn it!"

"What?" Lisa said.

"Just stay down!"

The patrol car cut in front of Dave, screeching to a halt only inches from his front bumper. A cop leapt out, his weapon drawn.

"¡Salga del carro!" he shouted. "¡Manos arriba!"

Dave understood that loud and clear, but he had no intention of getting out of his car and putting his hands up, now or anytime in the near future.

He threw the car into reverse, swung it around 180 degrees, then hit the gas, tires shrieking against asphalt. In his rearview mirror he saw the cop get back into his car. He took off after them, lights flashing and siren wailing.

"What the hell is happening?" Lisa shouted.

"We've got a cop after us."

"You're kidding."

"Tell me this is how they treat traffic offenders in this town. Tell me he's not chasing us because Ivan made a phone call."

"I think Ivan made a phone call."

Shit.

Dave sped down the street, heading back into town, but traffic thickened, slowing them down. When he came to a stop sign, he wheeled around the car in front of him, barely missing another car coming across the intersection from his right. Tightening his grip on the steering wheel, he stomped the gas pedal to the floor. A shot exploded, blasting the rear window of the car, showering glass on both of them.

"Stay down!" Dave shouted.

The moment the traffic cleared on the opposite side of the road, Dave hit the brake and wheeled hard to the left, spinning the Mustang around in a one-eighty to head back north. When he passed the police car still traveling south, the cop took another shot. The bullet narrowly missed them, taking out a storefront window instead in an explosion of glass. In his rearview mirror Dave saw the cop pull the same one-eighty he had, and within seconds he was half a dozen car lengths behind them again.

"Damn it!" Dave said. "I can't shake him!"

"Any cars between us and him?"

"Nope. He's coming right up behind us."

"Is that gun up there loaded?"

"I have no idea."

"Let's find out."

Suddenly Lisa rose from the backseat, leaned over into the front seat, and grabbed the gun. Before Dave knew what was happening, she'd spun around and pointed the gun out the back window. Three shots exploded in quick succession.

"What the hell are you doing?" he shouted. *"Get down!"*

A second later, Dave heard a crash behind them. Looking into his side mirror, he saw that the police car had crossed traffic, jumped the curb, and smashed into a lamppost.

"Bingo," Lisa said, turning back around and slumping wearily in the seat. "Got his tire. And his radiator for good measure." She was breathing hard, still clinging to the gun. "Adrenaline. Amazing stuff."

"Give me that!" Dave reached over the seat and yanked the gun out of her hand. "You could have gotten your head blown off!"

"It was that or have him chase us all the way to Monterrey. I prefer a leisurely drive, thank you."

Unbelievable.

Dave floated the next stop sign, wheeling the car hard to the left to avoid hitting vehicles crossing the intersection, then stomped the gas again.

"Well, since my cover's blown," Lisa said, climbing into the front passenger seat and plopping down with a weary sigh, "I might as well ride shotgun."

"From now on, you'd better mean that figuratively."

"I took out the bad guy and you're complaining?"

Dave couldn't believe this. On a normal day, he'd be back in Tolosa, stopping speeders and breaking up domestic disputes. Instead, he was playing car chase with crooked Mexican lawmen who were just dying to blow his head off, partnered with a woman who made Bonnie Parker look like a kid with a water pistol.

"Where the hell did you learn to shoot like that?" he asked.

"When I'm home in San Antonio, I go to the shooting range once a week."

"Oh, yeah?"

"Yeah. I have a license to carry concealed in Texas. But they're funny about you bringing guns into Mexico. Drugs, they get a little pissed. Guns, they toss you in jail and throw away the key. Makes no sense, but there you go. I feel downright naked without my Glock."

"So why the handgun proficiency?"

"A girl's gotta protect herself."

"So you can hit a paper target at a shooting range. Who taught you to how to blast away at the bad guys?"

"Bruce Willis. Arnold Schwarzenegger. Sylvester Stallone."

"Yes, and they go home at the end of the day no matter

how many times they've been shot. Stick to chick flicks, will you?"

She gave him a look of total disgust. "Are you really that sexist?"

"No, I'm really that rational."

"Chick flicks. Right. I can learn how to sit around a dining room table with four other women and whine about my boyfriend. Or bitch about my boss. Or, of all things, *find* myself."

Dave just shook his head.

After a few more minutes, when no other Santa Rios lawmen seemed inclined to take out after them, Dave unwound a little. A little.

"Robert is going to be surprised to find out that I'm alive," Lisa said.

"I imagine he is. But once we get back across the border and you go to the authorities, there isn't anything he can do about it."

"Will we run into any trouble in Monterrey?"

"They have no clue who I am or where I came from," Dave said, "so they have no way of knowing where we intend to go. Unless Douglas has the ability to cast a very large net, he'll never be able to find us."

"Do you think they'll try to follow us there?"

Dave glanced into the rearview mirror for the hundredth time. "Haven't so far. We may have shaken them for good."

"So I guess Robert and his partners in crime really do have an in with the local cops."

"I'd say that's a safe bet."

"Then it's nice that we're getting the hell out of here." Lisa looked around the interior of the Mustang. "And in such a hot car, too. Too bad it stood out in Santa Rios like a peacock in a flock of buzzards."

"This was all they had left at the rental place. Well, this or a fifteen-passenger van. I actually thought this would be less conspicuous."

"Can't think of better bait if you want to catch a carjacker."

"And if I'd had any idea that carjacking was going to be an issue, I could have bought a junker for what this one cost to rent." Dave circled his gaze around the car. "What am I saying? This one just became a junker."

It had one shattered back window, one blown-out driver's side window, and a few bullet holes here and there for good measure.

"They're going to love getting this one back at the car rental company," Lisa said. "What are you going to tell them?"

"I won't be telling them anything. If anyone caught our license plate number, they could have somebody waiting for us there. We're not going to take that chance. We'll just leave the car on airport property. They'll find it sooner or later, and the insurance I took out will cover the damage. Then we'll pick up a cab to the commuter airport."

"Will they check the small aviation companies? Maybe wonder whether we're going to rent a plane?"

"I doubt that. I think one of two things will happen. They'll check the plate number, realize it's a rental car, and ambush us there, or they'll assume I own the car, in which case they'll think we're going to drive back across the border. Doesn't mean I won't be keeping my eyes open, though."

Dave stepped harder on the gas, then had a thought that made him step on the brake. "Damn it."

"What?" Lisa asked.

"The spare tire. It's one of those undersized ones meant for emergencies only. You're supposed to drive only forty miles an hour with one of them. At that rate, it'll take us at least five hours to get to Monterrey."

"Can't you push it any harder than that?"

"If that tire blows, we'll be stuck out in the middle of nowhere."

"The later it gets, the more unlikely we are to get a plane today."

"I know. I'll move it as fast as I can."

Lisa settled back in her seat with a heavy sigh. Dave glanced over at her. "You okay?"

"Yeah. I'm fine." She paused. "Still a little tired, I guess. Hadn't counted on a shoot-out with the bad guys."

"Don't you *ever* do anything like that again."

"Sorry. Can't promise that." She turned to look at him, her head resting wearily against the back of the seat. "See, Dave, there are only two kinds of people out here in the wilds of Mexico. The quick"—she dropped her voice dramatically— "and the dead."

He started to chastise her again, but when a teasing smile played over her lips his heart just wasn't in it.

"Wake me when we're halfway there," she said, "and I'll drive the rest of the way so you can get a little sleep."

"You need rest more than I do. I can take us all the way to Monterrey."

"I said wake me at the halfway point. It's not fair for you to have to drive the whole way."

She put one booted foot against the dashboard and folded her arms, then took a deep breath and let it out slowly, her eyes drifting closed. He took the opportunity to steal long glances at her, which confirmed what he'd discovered the moment he'd lain eyes on her again. The years hadn't begun to diminish the attraction he felt for her.

In spite of the fact that he'd ripped into her for grabbing that gun and blasting away at the bad guys, the fact that she'd actually done it filled him with feelings he hadn't counted on. Admiration. Awe. Respect. He thought about Carla, how sensitive she'd been, like a fragile porcelain figurine always poised to slip right out of his hands. But Lisa was tough and unbreakable, with a shell so thick a sledgehammer couldn't blast through it. Hell, she hadn't needed him to come here. All she needed was a vehicle and a weapon and she could have taken on the entire Mexican army. And the very thought of having a woman like that . . .

No. He had to get a grip here. He knew that emotionally charged situations did this to people, and apparently he wasn't immune. Given the circumstances they were dealing with, his attraction to Lisa should have been the furthest thing from his mind.

Oh, hell. Who was he kidding? With a few hundred miles of open road stretching ahead of him and nothing else to occupy his mind, it was the only thing he was going to be able to think about.

chapter seven

Lisa closed her eyes, but as tired as she was, she didn't sleep right away. The low hum of the Mustang's engine was hypnotic, relaxing her, drawing her back through memories of the last few times she'd seen Dave, memories that had grown hazy with age. But with him sitting beside her now, they seemed sharper, more focused, and she found herself remembering details she thought she'd long forgotten.

Throughout high school, she'd watched him from a distance, because no girl on the planet would be immune to those good looks. No matter how attractive Dave had been, though, it had been a generally known fact that he belonged to Carla and always would. But what Dave had seen in Carla Lisa had never understood. In high school, she'd seen Carla as one of those silly little fools who exuded a helpless kind of delicacy, who begged to be taken care of by a man at every glance. What the hell was the attraction in that?

Consequently, Lisa had told herself that Dave was no different from all the other swaggering jocks at Tolosa South who dated prom queens and daddy's girls, whose only interest in a girl like her would be in getting her naked behind the stadium bleachers. So when she'd ended up as his partner in that shop class, she'd baited him, teased him, telling herself that hot or not, he was just one more guy who looked down his nose at girls like her, so why not have a little fun?

For several days, he took everything she dished out. He stoically put up with it, offering little in the way of a comeback.

Then he decided he'd had enough.

Someday you'll figure out that you've got a lot more to of-

fer than just your body. As soon as that happens, maybe some decent guy will have you.

The moment those words left his mouth, she felt as if he'd slapped her. From the time that she was thirteen years old, the only attention she'd ever gotten from guys was because of her body and the way she dressed. To suddenly have one suggest that he was disgusted by her appearance sent her into a tailspin. When she got home that day, she looked at herself in the mirror.

Really looked.

And she hated what she saw.

With Dave's words still playing inside her head the next morning, she toned her appearance down. Way down. So much so that she felt self-conscious, as if everyone were looking at her and wondering what the hell was up. Then she'd gone to shop class.

She remembered how Dave had stared at her and she'd almost slipped back into her cloak of defiance, hiding behind the "I don't give a damn" role she'd played for so long. Then he said something about her hair.

It's pretty. I like it that way.

Such a stupid little thing. But to this day she remembered the swell of elation she'd felt, the one that had made her heart beat like crazy.

From then on, she put aside the smart-ass remarks and the sexual come-ons and they started to talk. Really talk. No matter how chaotic the rest of her life was, she could come into that class, put it all behind her, and spend an hour being herself. The relief of that was like a weight had been lifted from her chest, a way to finally breathe. Dave was the same from day to day, greeting her with a comfortable smile, cutting up with her behind their teacher's back, and deferring to her enough times on the project they were working on that she knew he respected her opinion. Unlike the dark, sullen, angry guys she tended to date, Dave was open and friendly, with an understated sense of humor that had her captivated. They barely talked to each other outside of class, but even if he was with Carla, he'd look at Lisa sometimes for a few seconds, and it felt to her as if the two of them shared a bond that nobody else would ever understand.

The semester passed quickly. Then one day, less than a week before school was out, they were alone in the shop, putting in some after-school time to finish up a cylinder head overhaul. While they were working, their discussion drifted around to their impending graduation and their plans that followed. Dave told her that of course he and Carla were getting married and he'd be going to college in the fall and eventually become a cop like virtually every other member of his family. Then he asked her what her plans were.

"I'm going to get a job," she told him.

"That's good. Doing what?"

"I don't know. It doesn't matter."

"Doesn't matter?"

"I just need to save some money."

"What for?"

For years she'd had a dream boiling inside her like a volcano on the verge of erupting, something she wanted as much as she wanted her next breath. But now she hesitated to say it. Dave's opinion had come to matter so much to her that she couldn't have stood it if he'd laughed.

"Tell me," he said. "What are you planning to do?"

Finally she faced him. "I'm going to take flying lessons. I want to be a pilot."

A look of surprise had crossed his face, which she instantly read as disbelief that somebody like her could ever achieve so lofty a goal. She drew herself up defensively, even as her heart was breaking.

"Go ahead. Say it. You think I'm crazy."

"Crazy? Why would I think that?"

"Because it takes money and brains to fly a plane, of course. I'm broke, and I've barely got the grades to graduate. That's what you're thinking, isn't it?"

"No. That's not what I'm thinking. You already told me you're going to get a job and save money. And as far as intelligence goes, your grades have nothing to do with that. You chose to screw off and skip class. Are you going to show up for your flying lessons?"

"Of course."

"Then I'd say you're as good as in the air."

She searched his face for any indication that he was patronizing her. Teasing her. Lying to her. But he just continued to look back at her with a matter-of-fact expression, as if achieving her dream was a foregone conclusion if she wanted it badly enough.

"I know it costs a lot of money," she said. "It's almost five thousand dollars to get a pilot's license. But I figure if I can save two hundred dollars a month, in two years I'll have it. That's not such a long time. Not really. I swear I'll quit eating and live on a park bench if that's what it takes."

And because he just stood there listening to her, she kept talking. She told him that she was going to become a charter pilot and that someday she was going to buy a plane of her own. Maybe even start her own aviation company. She remembered a tiny smile crossing his lips at that point, and she knew she'd said too much.

"I know you think I'm dreaming," she said. "But I can do it. Every bit of it. You just stand back and watch me."

"Of course you can do it," he said, his smile growing. "I'd just hate to be the person who got in your way. Bruises, bloody nose, broken bones. It wouldn't be pretty."

Slowly she smiled back at him, the most wonderful glow of warmth spreading through her. She could do it. She knew she could.

And Dave thought so, too.

Suddenly that meant everything to her. His approving gaze exhilarated her beyond words, making her feel strong and capable and in control of her life. Making her feel as if she was only one step away from taking right off into the clouds.

Then his smile faded. "I don't think you're crazy. But somebody does. Who told you that you'd never have the money or the brains to fly?"

She turned away. "Nobody."

"No. There was somebody. Who?"

Her stomach clenched with the memory, but she managed an indifferent shrug. "My father."

"Your father?"

"He saw a copy of *Plane & Pilot* magazine in my room a few months ago. He asked me why I had it. I told him I wanted to learn to fly."

"What did he say?"

"He told me that flying was expensive and I sure wasn't going to be able to count on him for any financial help. He told me that it took somebody really smart to fly a plane, so that left me out, too. Then he told me to get my head out of the clouds and go buy him a couple of six-packs and a carton of cigarettes."

"What about your mother?" Dave asked. "How does she feel about it?"

"She'd have to stay sober long enough to give me an opinion. But you know what? If I were married to my father, I'd stay drunk most of the time, too."

"Yeah. I know what you mean. My father's not the easiest guy in the world to live with, either."

"I'll trade you any day."

"You haven't met my father. You might think twice about that."

"Oh, yeah? Look at you. Your brothers. You've got it all. Just how bad could things be around your house? Does your father live on unemployment because he keeps getting fired? Leave for days at a time and not tell you where he's been? Wave a gun around and threaten anyone who pisses him off?"

"No."

"Then I'll trade you. Just say the word."

Dave sighed. "Yeah, my old man can be pretty demanding. But I've got other relatives. Aunts and uncles and grandparents who live nearby. If things get bad around the house, there's always somewhere else to go."

He might as well have been speaking a foreign language. She had no sense at all of what it would be like to have other people she could depend on when things got tough.

"Don't you have an older brother?" Dave asked. "What about him? Will he help you?"

"Lenny?" She shook her head. "He moved to San Antonio. I haven't talked to him in years. With luck, he's quit dealing drugs and actually made something of himself. But I really wouldn't know."

"So you have to deal with your parents all by yourself."

She shrugged. "No big deal. I'm used to it."

"Are you really?"

She started to say that of course she was. After all, she'd lived with it for the last eighteen years, hadn't she?

Then those years raced through her mind like a horror movie flashback, reminding her of the desolation, the desperation, the feeling that she was alone in the world with nobody to turn to. She was so ashamed of where she came from that she'd never told anyone what her life was really like, but Dave kept staring at her as if he actually gave a damn, and suddenly she couldn't do anything but tell the truth.

"No," she said, her voice a harsh whisper. "I'm not used to it. I'll never get used to it. I never know what I'm going to find when I go home."

"Like what?"

She let out a shaky breath. "My parents screaming at each other. My mother bruised and bloody because my father can't keep his fists to himself and she doesn't have the guts to leave him. My mother sitting in the kitchen, emptying a fifth of bourbon and passing out."

"That's terrible," Dave said.

It was. And it seemed even worse when she said it out loud. Her hands started to shake. God, why were her hands shaking?

"The trailer where we live is small," she went on. "There's no place to go to get away from it. Sometimes I feel as if the walls are closing in on me, like I'm sealed inside a coffin, screaming to get out, but nobody's listening." She paused, taking a deep, unsteady breath. "On the north shore of Stillman Creek, there's this little clearing surrounded by pine trees. Sometimes I go there and lie on my back in the grass. I stare up at the sky and take deep breaths of fresh air that I'm not sharing with anyone else. And I can watch the planes fly over. I just lie there and imagine taking off and soaring into the clouds and never coming back again."

"You don't ever want to come back here?"

"That's right. My parents can go to hell for all I care."

Dave shook his head slowly. "That's too bad."

"It's just the way it is. I just wish I could have left sooner."

"What?"

"From the time I was about thirteen, I've thought about running away. About a thousand times. But I was just a kid. . . ." She shrugged helplessly, her eyes filling with tears. "I didn't have anywhere else to go."

She felt Dave staring at her, but she couldn't look at him. Not after she'd just given him a perfect picture of just how horrible her life really was.

"Lisa? Does your father ever hurt you?"

"Mostly I just stay out of his way."

"You can't possibly do that all the time."

"I can take care of myself."

"I know you can," he said gently. "You just shouldn't have to."

She turned to look at Dave, and the compassion in his eyes was like a beacon drawing her to him. All at once she realized how close he was standing and that he showed no inclination to back away.

"You can't help how you grew up," he told her. "It doesn't mean you're like them."

"Everybody assumes I am."

"You don't go out of your way to convince them otherwise."

He was right. She thought about the way she dressed most of the time, the way she acted, and she felt sick to her stomach. It had been her way of saying to hell with everybody who assumed she was trash just because of where she came from. Then she'd looked at herself through Dave's eyes, and it had opened hers in a way she'd never expected.

"Why do you date guys like Derek?" Dave asked.

She shrugged weakly. "You said it yourself. A decent guy wouldn't have me."

He closed his eyes. "I'm sorry, Lisa. It's not true. I mean it. It's not."

When he opened his eyes again, he stared at her with such empathy that she couldn't look away. She blinked, and a tear slid down her cheek.

"Please forget I said that," he murmured.

"It was no big deal."

"Yes, it was." He eased closer to her. "I'm sorry about that. And I'm sorry about your parents, too. About how you've had to live. What you've had to deal with. I'm sorry about . . . everything."

The regret she heard in his voice made it even harder to fight the tears. She opened her mouth to say something, but suddenly she couldn't talk anymore. A silent sob choked her, and she put her hand over her mouth.

"God, Lisa. . . ."

She squeezed her eyes closed, and a moment later she bowed her head and began to cry. Before she knew what was happening, Dave had taken a step forward and pulled her into his arms.

For a moment she felt disoriented, unable to comprehend what he was doing. But when he slid his hand to the back of her neck she leaned into him and rested her head against his shoulder. He felt so strong and steady, sustaining her when she couldn't bear one more thought about the sordid life she lived, filling her with a sense of warmth and security unlike anything she'd felt before. As close as they'd become in recent weeks, she would never have imagined him touching her like this, acting as if he would hold on to her forever if that was what she needed. She wrapped her arms around him, tears streaming down her face, and the wall of invincibility she'd spent her whole life trying so hard to maintain crumbled into dust.

"I hate them," she said, clinging to him, sobs filling her voice. "I hate them both. But I'm not going to be like them. I swear to God I'm going to be better than that. I'm going to take control of my life. I'm going to fly. You'll see."

"I know," he said, stroking her hair. "I know."

He held her for a long time, whispering calming words to her, letting all her tears come out. When her sobs finally faded, he eased away from her, still cradling her in his arms. She wiped her eyes with the back of her hand, then slowly turned her gaze up to meet his. He brushed a strand of hair away from her temple, his eyes never leaving hers. A second passed, then two. Lisa saw his intent, but it wasn't until he lowered his head and dropped his lips against hers that she allowed herself to believe that it was happening.

Dave was kissing her.

He splayed his fingers against the back of her neck, urging her closer, and suddenly blood was pumping wildly through her veins even as her muscles went weak. When he slipped his tongue into her mouth and stroked it against hers, it felt so warm and sweet and intimate that she almost collapsed in ecstasy. She loved the clean, masculine smell of him, the smooth skin of his neck beneath her hands, the soft groan that rose in his throat as she shifted slightly and deepened their kiss even more. She clung to him desperately, kissing him back with all her heart, feeling as if thunderclouds had parted and sun was shining through. He was the light in all her darkness, the one person who could make her forget the terrible place she'd come from and believe that tomorrow could be better than today.

She hadn't dared even to think it before, but now she wanted to shout it. She loved him. Loved him with an intensity that bordered on insanity, and for the first time, she allowed herself to hope that maybe he felt it, too. Other guys might kiss a girl and have it mean nothing, but not Dave. Not him. Not when he was engaged to somebody else.

"You're not going to marry Carla," she whispered against his lips. "Tell me you're not going to marry her."

He slowly eased away, looking a little dazed, as if he was waking from a dream and hadn't fully regained consciousness.

"Oh, God," he said on a harsh breath. "What am I doing?"

"No," she said, holding him tightly. "Don't stop. *Please* don't stop."

He pulled away again, disengaging her hands. "No. I shouldn't be doing this. I shouldn't be—"

"Don't say that! You want it. Just as much as I do. We've both wanted it for a long time."

"But Carla—"

"Forget Carla! She's nothing but a pampered little rich girl who's going to make your life miserable. You can't possibly love somebody like her. You can't!"

"Of course I love her! I'm *marrying* her, for God's sake!"

His words struck Lisa like a hammer blow. This had meant nothing to him. Nothing. All he could think about right now was his precious Carla and how she'd perish at the very thought of him kissing another girl.

Especially another girl like her.

"I mean it, Lisa," he warned. "I don't want Carla knowing about this. She can't know. She *can't*."

Lisa felt as if she was being swallowed in darkness when only seconds ago nothing but light had filled her mind. For those few moments when he was kissing her, she'd held out hope that maybe . . .

Maybe what? That maybe he'd actually want her? When she'd just stood there and told him just how shitty her life really was? The kind of family she came from? How was he supposed to look at her now as if she was a decent girl, one a decent guy might actually want?

A decent guy like him.

Stop it. Who the hell are you kidding? Like there was ever a chance of that? Ever?

"Don't worry," Lisa said, swiping the tears off her face. "Your secret is safe with me. I wouldn't think of breaking up such a perfect couple."

"I'm sorry, Lisa. I'm so sorry if I made you think—"

"You didn't make me think a damned thing." She stuffed a notebook into her backpack.

"Lisa. Don't go."

"We're done."

"No, we're not. If we don't finish this engine—"

"What? We'll get a lousy grade? What makes you think I give a damn about that?"

"This was my fault," he said. "I'm the one to blame."

"Oh, for God's sake. It was just a stupid kiss!"

"But you were upset. I never should have—"

"Will you just forget about it? Carla will never know. Isn't that all you really care about?" She slung her backpack over her shoulder.

"Lisa. Wait."

She stopped and turned back, glaring at him.

He turned his palms up. "We're friends at least, aren't we?"

"Oh, my *God*. The oldest line in the book? Save it, Dave. I've heard that one about a hundred times."

"It's not a line. Not when I really mean it."

"Friends. Right. Once you and Carla are married, I'll come on over to your house for dinner some night. How would that be?"

He bowed his head, letting out a harsh breath.

"Maybe we're friends in here," she said. "But out there, you act as if you barely know me. Isn't that true?"

He looked up at her again, and she saw regret in his eyes. "Yeah. I guess that's the way it's been. And that's my fault, too."

He put his hand against her arm, then slid it down until he circled her wrist with his fingers. "I know we'll be going our separate ways. But if there's ever anything you need, if I can help you somehow, I want you to call me. Okay?"

She glared at him. "And if your wife answers the phone, am I supposed to hang up?"

"Just call me if you need me. I mean that, Lisa."

His dark eyes focused on hers, sealing his offer with an expression of total sincerity. She knew he meant what he said, and it only made her want him that much more.

"I won't be needing you," she told him. "You, or anyone else."

She jerked her arm from his grasp and left the shop. He called after her, but she walked faster, then started to run. She circled the school building until she reached a secluded alcove where a pair of Dumpsters sat.

She slid down the wall, letting her backpack fall on the ground beside her. She rested on her heels, hugging herself, nausea overtaking her, tears flowing down her face. She bowed her head, still sensing the warmth of his arms around her and heartbroken at the thought that she'd never feel it again. Not once in her short, pitiful life had she ever gotten a damn thing she wanted. Ever. So she'd stopped wanting.

Until Dave.

To have something she'd wished for so desperately dangled in front of her, then jerked away, was simply more than she could bear.

Lesson learned.

She feigned sickness so she didn't have to go to school those last three days of her senior year. She couldn't have endured seeing Dave again. She couldn't have tolerated sitting next to him in class or watching him walk down the hall with Carla. And above all, she couldn't have tolerated the pity she was sure to see in his eyes. Or maybe he would have acted as if he didn't even know her, and that would have been the worst blow of all.

Two weeks later, Dave married Carla in a ceremony at the First Methodist Church of Tolosa in front of two hundred friends and family members. The last thing Lisa did before leaving town was stand near a cluster of azalea bushes across the street from the church, waiting until the bells rang and the doors opened. Dave and Carla came out, all smiles, Dave looking so handsome it made Lisa's heart ache. Carla wore a dazzling gown with yards and yards of lace and a train so long that it took two bridesmaids just to haul it around for her. For all the terrible things Lisa had said about Carla, she would have sold her soul to be just like her at that moment. The kind of woman Dave would want to marry.

But then she realized that he'd done her a favor. She didn't really love him. After all, Carla was his ideal woman, a silly, dependent little fool who barely had a brain in her head or the ambition to do anything but play house. Lisa knew that any man who would want a woman like Carla would only make her miserable.

She was going to do more with her life. Much more. Flying meant freedom. Adventure. A life full of excitement. Full of the respect that low-life people in east Texas trailer parks couldn't possibly hope to have.

Eleven years later, she'd accomplished all that, and more. But still she'd never forgotten Dave.

As the Mustang sped along the deserted Mexican highway, Lisa turned her head a little and blinked her weary eyes open just enough that she could see him sitting beside her. He'd slipped on a pair of sunglasses against the bright sunlight and kicked back in the driver's seat, his forearm resting along the driver's door and his wrist looped over the top of the steering wheel, looking every bit as gorgeous as he had as a teenager. As much as she'd been drawn to the high school version of Dave, it didn't begin to approach the way he looked now—tall, strong, handsome, and in control.

Thank God he'd come. If he hadn't, where would she be?

She knew where she'd be. She'd still be sitting out in those woods, getting progressively weaker, more delirious, losing strength, slowly going out of her mind. . . .

She didn't even want to think about it.

Still, this was nothing more than a detour in her life. A momentary setback. Yes, she needed Dave now, but once they got to San Antonio and all this was nothing but a bad memory, she'd be on her own again.

And that was just the way she wanted it.

chapter eight

"Lisa? Time to wake up. We're almost there."

Dave watched as Lisa opened her eyes, blinking against the sharp sunlight of late afternoon that streaked through the windshield of the Mustang.

"What time is it?"

"Five-fifteen."

"I slept five hours?" she said. "I told you to wake me up. It wasn't fair for you to have to drive the whole way."

"I told you I don't mind driving. But I can't say that I won't welcome a decent bed and about twelve hours of uninterrupted sleep."

Yeah, he was ready to be there, all right. He'd turned the radio on low, more to help him stay awake than because he had a fondness for Latino music, but still his eyes were growing heavy. He nodded ahead. "Monterrey coming up."

Lisa stretched a little and sat up, looking ahead at the city sprawled against the backdrop of the Sierra Madres.

"Should we worry about anyone following us?"

"I haven't seen any indication of it, but I'm keeping my eyes open until we can get lost inside the city."

Ten minutes later they hit the city limits. At first glance, Monterrey didn't seem much different from Dallas or Houston, with multilane highways, plenty of modern buildings intermingled with older ones, and familiar fast-food franchises.

Dave pulled into a grocery store parking lot and parked near a bank of pay phones. He grabbed a jacket out of his bag and put it on, then took the gun he'd appropriated from Ivan, stuck it in his jeans, and pulled the jacket over it. They got out of the car.

Dave stood next to Lisa as she contacted three aviation companies at the commuter airport. Unfortunately, because they'd hit the city so late, she discovered that the soonest they could get a rental plane would be tomorrow morning. She reserved it, then hung up.

"A plane will be available at ten-thirty tomorrow morning," she told Dave. "That's the best I can do."

"So we're stuck here overnight."

"Looks that way."

"Ever been to Monterrey?" he asked.

"Yeah."

"Know of a place we can stay?"

"There's a little mom-and-pop place on the east side. It's cheap." Lisa turned back to the phone. "I need to make another call."

"Where?"

"Adam's office in San Antonio. He's in practice with two other doctors. Hopefully somebody will still be there."

Lisa spoke offhandedly, but Dave knew the emotion hidden behind her words. She wanted to know for sure what had happened to Adam. If the people in his office still thought he'd gone down in the plane crash, that meant he hadn't surfaced, which meant there was little chance that he was still alive.

This had to be hard for her, not knowing Adam's fate and knowing that she'd escaped death herself by the slimmest of margins. She'd had a hell of a time the past couple of days, and it wasn't over yet. Dave held his breath, hoping for good news.

A moment later, he saw Lisa snap to attention as if somebody had come on the line. Without identifying herself, she merely asked if a memorial service was being planned for Adam. Dave could tell from the look on her face that the news wasn't good.

She hung up the phone but held on to the receiver, her head bowed.

"Lisa?"

She took a deep breath, then raised her head again, her jaw tight. She turned and walked back to the car. He followed, and once they were inside, Dave turned to her.

"What did they tell you?"

She stared at the dashboard, but still he could see her eyes glistening. "His memorial service is scheduled for Thursday morning at ten o'clock."

She spoke matter-of-factly, but Dave heard the tremor in her voice.

"This doesn't mean he's dead," he told her. "We just don't know yet, okay?"

"You and I both know that's not true. If he were alive he'd have told somebody by now."

"We can't be sure about that. He may have found out what was going on. He may be trying to get out of Mexico without being spotted, just as you are. Had you considered that?"

She turned to him, a glimmer of hope on her face. "Do you really think so?"

"It's possible."

She stared at him a moment longer, then turned away again. He didn't want to give her false hope, but until they found out for sure what had happened to Adam there was still a chance he was alive, no matter how small. And even false hope was better than no hope when she was facing a situation like this.

Dave started the car. "Are you hungry?"

"Yeah. Starving."

"McDonald's okay?" he said, pointing up the street. "Not exactly gourmet food, but it's fast."

"Fast is good."

They grabbed Big Macs and fries and Cokes, and both of them were hungry enough to eat on the spot as they drove to the hotel.

"Take it easy," he told Lisa. "You haven't eaten much in the past few days."

"Don't worry," she said, popping a couple of fries into her mouth. "I've got an iron stomach."

Why did that not surprise him?

At Lisa's direction, Dave drove to the part of town where the hotel was, and slowly everything took a turn toward the historic. And the festive. The entire area was an explosion of color, with street vendors selling bread and fruit and flowers and various kinds of artwork, along with big, gory-looking skull masks.

"What's with all this stuff?" Dave asked.

"What day is today?"

"November first."

"Ah. El Dia de los Muertos."

"Huh?"

"The Day of the Dead. It's actually two days, November first and second. It's when Mexicans honor the dead, only it's not a downer. They decorate everything, and some of them even go out to the grave sites and eat and drink and dance."

"Okay. I've heard of that. It's like a great big party."

"Right." She took a sip of Coke. "Not all Mexicans celebrate, though, particularly in the big cities like Monterrey. Some of them even go the Halloween route with pumpkins and witches and all that. But some people still like to uphold tradition."

"And some people just like to party."

"Yeah. It's kind of like Christmas. Some people celebrate with three masses. Others just eat themselves sick and watch a couple of ball games."

Finally Dave pulled up to the hotel, a two-story structure with heavily stuccoed walls stained by decades of rainwater, tattered awnings, and a rusted wrought-iron gate leading to a courtyard, which the native flora had pretty much overtaken.

Lisa pointed to an alley that ran beside the hotel. "This car is conspicuous. There's a parking lot in the back. Wouldn't hurt to pull back there."

Dave swung the car around to park in the rear. He got out of the car, tossed their trash into a nearby trash can, then grabbed both of their bags from the trunk. A minute later they stepped inside the clay-tiled entry of the hotel, which soared two stories to a balcony above and was lit by a huge wrought-iron chandelier. The foliage explosion in the courtyard had made its way indoors, filling every corner with greenery and sending ivy crawling up the roughly textured walls. In a large gathering room beyond the entry, several people scurried around, carrying food and drinks as if they were preparing for some kind of celebration.

"Day of the Dead?" Dave asked.

Lisa nodded. "Looks like it."

In a parlorlike room to their right sat a large table dressed with a mustard-yellow cloth. Spread out on it were baskets of bread and fruit and sweets, along with vases of marigolds and a parade of framed photographs. A large crucifix hung on the wall behind it.

"What's that?" he asked Lisa.

"A family altar."

"Huh?"

"Has to do with Dia de los Muertos."

Before Dave could ask exactly *what* it had to do with it, a slender middle-aged man looked out from the gathering room and hurried to the desk. He raised a dark bushy eyebrow when he saw Lisa's dirty clothes, messy hair, and bruised forehead, then introduced himself as Manuel Lozano.

"Do you have any vacancies?" Dave asked. "We need to stay one night."

"I'm sorry," Manuel said. "The front door should be locked. For Dia de los Muertos, only family and friends are in the hotel."

Lisa slumped with dismay. Dave could see how tired she was, her shoulders drooping, her eyes heavy and bloodshot. In spite of the sleep she'd had last night, she was coming off a huge deficit and could use a whole lot more in an actual bed. And she definitely needed a shower. He wouldn't mind a little of those things himself.

Lisa gave the man a look of utter helplessness. "So you're telling me there's no room at the inn for a couple of weary travelers?"

"No room at the inn?" The man raised that same bushy eyebrow again, seemingly amused by the reference. "No, there is not. Unless, of course, one of those travelers is having a baby."

Dave blinked. "Baby?"

"Why, yes, I am," Lisa said, suddenly coming to life. "I'm going to have a baby. Maybe tonight, even." She leaned across the desk, smiling at Manuel. "Now, you wouldn't want to be an innkeeper who turns away a poor pregnant woman, would you?"

Manuel gave her a sly smile. "Hmm. How did you arrive at my inn?"

"By donkey, of course," Lisa said. "Not an easy way to travel, let me tell you."

Manuel nodded thoughtfully. "And for what purpose are you in Monterrey?"

"Why, to pay our taxes."

"And three wise men will come from the east?"

Lisa gave him a plaintive look. "Will that help us get a room?"

The man smiled. "Perhaps."

"Donkey, taxes, wise men, and a big old star. I swear."

"Christmas falls on El Dia de los Muertos?"

"Amazing, isn't it?"

The man gave her a pseudostern look. "As I said, only friends and family for these two days."

Lisa let her head fall against the desk.

"But you are now my friends. I have one room available. You may stay."

Lisa jerked her head back up. "Oh, thank you!" Then she gave him a wary look. "Now, you're not putting us out in the stable, are you?"

"Why, certainly not. But your donkey will be comfortable there."

Dave didn't like this. Staying in the same room with Lisa was undoubtedly going to make his mind go places where his body shouldn't. He had no business complicating this situation until they could get the hell out of Mexico and everything was back to normal.

But right now, staying at this hotel was the path of least resistance, and he'd had more than enough resistance for one day. And in the end, he had to admit it would be safer. Even though there was no indication that anyone was on their trail, the one-gun-equals-one-room formula was probably a good one to follow.

"And of course you will join us this night for our Dia de los Muertos celebration," the man went on. "We have much food and drink."

"I'm afraid we can't," Dave said. "We're both ready to drop."

"When you hear the music, you will change your mind."

"Thanks, but all we're looking for is sleep right about now."

Manuel gave them the key to room 203 and wished them a pleasant stay. Dave and Lisa climbed the stairs and went into the room, where he was nearly blown over backward by the decor.

Color. Everywhere there was color. From pumpkin orange to pea-soup green to Kool-Aid purple—this room had it all. The bedspread. The oil paintings. The draperies. Everything was awash in a cataclysm of hues so bright that Dave could have stared straight into a solar eclipse and not done his eyes as much damage.

"I think I'll go back to the car for my sunglasses," Dave said.

Lisa blinked with disbelief. "I don't care how tired we are. This room's going to keep us awake all night." She walked across the room and pulled the draperies open, revealing glass doors leading out to a secluded balcony. "Okay. Check this out. It'll give your eyes a rest."

Dave came up behind her. Through a break in the foliage that enclosed the balcony he saw the Sierra Madres towering in the distance. A rattan sofa with a padded vinyl-covered cushion afforded a nice place to sit to enjoy the view.

"Pretty slick how you talked that guy into giving us the room."

"I just played the Catholic card."

"He did it because he liked you."

She turned and gave him a crafty smile. "I have a way with men."

He sure as hell couldn't argue with that. Lisa had some obvious physical attributes a man would have to be in a coma to miss, and Manuel had been fully conscious.

"Problem," Lisa said.

"What's that?"

"I need a shower, but I haven't got anything clean to put on. My suitcase went down with the plane, and everything in my backpack has been through the Mercado River. Can you help me out?"

Dave reached into his bag, pulled out a shirt, and handed it to her.

"Don't suppose you have a pair of women's panties in there, do you?" she said.

"Nope. I had to pack light. Left the recreational stuff at home."

"I'll be stuck with my dirty jeans when we leave here, but for now I can just wear this."

Lisa disappeared into the bathroom. He sprawled out on the sofa with a weary sigh. He'd left Dallas only yesterday, but it seemed as if he'd been gone a month.

The white noise of the shower running lulled him until he almost fell asleep. A few minutes later, the bathroom door opened and Lisa came out. He sat up. Stared. Even when she'd been a mess before, she'd commanded his attention, but now he'd be lucky to pry his eyes away with a crowbar.

Her cheeks were flushed pink from the hot shower, giving her face a warm glow. She wore the sleeves of his pale blue shirt rolled to her elbows. The tail of the shirt hit mid-thigh along her bare legs. Even with several bruises marring them . . . good God. What a sight.

She tossed her dirty clothes onto the floor of the closet, and when she stood again her back was to the patio door. With the evening sun filtering in behind her, the cotton fabric of his shirt suddenly seemed gauzy and translucent, revealing every hill, valley, and curve of her body beneath it. Her short, still-wet hair was a tangle of dark reddish gold that reflected her personality far more than a sleeker style could ever have. She combed both her hands through it, and the movement made the shirt rise up on her thighs, inching closer to revealing a part of her he had no business thinking about, much less looking at.

She's got nothing on under that shirt.

As those words pounded at his brain, which currently was minus most of the blood that kept it in working order, she ducked into the bathroom again, returning with a sample-sized lotion that must have been provided by the management. She sat down on the bed, pulled up one leg, and placed the sole of her foot on the bed, the tail of the shirt barely covering the private parts he was having such a hard time keeping his mind off of. She opened the lotion and sniffed it, making a face of disgust.

"Damn. Floral. I *hate* floral stuff."

With a sigh of resignation, she poured some of it into her hand. Starting at her ankle, she smoothed it up to her knee, then back down again, moving slowly and thoroughly, avoiding a healing cut on the outside of her calf that was pink-edged from the heat of the shower. Then she tucked that leg and pulled up her other one, giving it the same treatment. There was nothing deliberately sensuous about it, but suddenly it was as if every atom in the room had become electrified and all of the energy was coming straight from Lisa.

He grabbed clean clothes from his bag and headed for the bathroom. It was nearing seven o'clock. They were both exhausted, which meant an early bedtime. In the same bed. Together.

What had he been thinking? He should have insisted on finding a hotel with a room for each of them, no matter how tired they were.

He was going to take a shower. A long one. And maybe by the time he got out she'd be under the covers. On the other side of the bed. Asleep.

Half-naked.

Make that a long, *cold* shower.

chapter nine

Lisa pulled back the covers and climbed into the king-size bed. The hot shower had lulled her senses, making a pleasant feeling of relaxation flow through her. She laid her head on the pillow and pulled the covers over her, blinking wearily.

In just a few minutes, Dave would be joining her. That she was in the same room with him after all this time was astonishing enough. That she was sleeping in the same bed with him was beyond belief.

That he'd come to Mexico to help her was unfathomable.

Downstairs in the Lozano household, music started to play, an upbeat Latino number that tapped softly, rhythmically, through Lisa's mind, soothing her to sleep. But when the bathroom door opened and Dave came out, she opened her eyes again. And what a sight she saw.

He wore nothing but a pair of jeans. He had a towel draped over his shoulders, but it did little to hide the part of his body that was currently naked. Strong, sculpted shoulders, a broad, powerful chest, and a rock-solid set of abs all merged together to take her breath away.

Dave pulled the towel from around his neck and tossed it aside, then went to the desk and picked up the phone. "I need to call my brother."

Lisa nodded sleepily. Dave went a few rounds with whoever was acting as hotel operator in the Lozano household, then dialed several numbers. He sat down in the chair to wait for the call to go through. He stared out the patio doors, and she stared at him. A lot had happened to him in eleven years. He'd grown up, become a cop, had a child.

Lost a wife.

Lisa had been shocked to read the newspaper account of Carla's death, a dramatic accident on an icy bridge that had left Dave alone with a nine-month-old daughter to raise. As jealous as she'd been of Carla, she never would have wished that kind of misfortune on either of them. It was the kind of tragedy that could age a man fast, making him cynical and hard-edged, giving him the kind of attitude about life that would fuel any resentment he felt at having to play knight in shining armor to a woman he probably never thought he'd see again. But Dave didn't seem resentful at all. Merely determined to get the job done.

Dave pressed the phone closer to his ear. "Hey, John," he said, then listened for a moment. "Yeah. Everything's fine. We're staying tonight in Monterrey, and I'll be home tomorrow. I'll tell you all about it when I get there." He listened for a moment more, his expression growing irritated. "Would you stop worrying? I'm telling you everything's okay." He turned away and lowered his voice, but Lisa could still hear him. "We're renting a plane to fly into San Antonio tomorrow morning, and I'll be heading back to Dallas soon after that. . . . Yes. I already told you. Everything's fine. I'll fill you in on the rest later."

Dave glanced at Lisa. She looked away quickly, pretending she wasn't listening to every word he spoke.

"Yeah," Dave said. "Put her on." After a moment, he smiled, and Lisa could tell by the conversation that he was talking to a child. He said something about a rabbit named Flopsy and some other kid stuff Lisa couldn't quite decipher.

"Yeah, I love you, too, baby," Dave said finally. "Put Uncle John back on, okay?" Pause. "John? It's getting late. Why isn't she in bed?" Dave listened for a moment, and suddenly his eyebrows flew up. "She's *what*? Jesus, John, will you guys quit spoiling the hell out of her? She's going to expect that every night. . . . Oh, yes, she will! And then I'll have to play the bad guy and tell her she can't do all that crap at home." He stood and paced to the end of the phone cord and back again. "Oh, you think it's funny? Wait until you guys have kids. I've got one hell of a long memory, big brother, and payback's a *bitch*."

Dave looked over at Lisa and rolled his eyes. He listened for a while longer, then sighed with resignation. "Okay, fine. Whatever. Buy her a pony. Take her to Disney World for a month. Hey, why don't you pay for her college education while you're at it? That I can use."

He exhaled with disgust, shaking his head. He listened for a moment more, and then his tone grew more somber. "Will you stop with the questions? I told you I'm fine. I'll be home tomorrow evening. Give Ashley a kiss for me, will you? . . . Yeah. I'll see you then. Good night."

He hung up the phone. "My family. Good God."

"How old is your daughter?" Lisa asked.

"Five."

"So what's your brother doing?"

"Get this. He and his wife have her stuck between them in bed, feeding her fudge and popcorn and letting her stay up past her bedtime watching *Cinderella*. Renee gave her the remote and told her she could rewind the good parts all she wanted to, which means an hour-and-a-half movie turns into three hours. All that sugar means she won't sleep worth a damn, even if she has a chance to sleep after staying up so late." He shook his head with disgust. "Wait until they have kids. I'm going to teach them to sling oatmeal across the room and run naked down the street. And any other bad habits I can think up."

In spite of his feigned anger, Lisa could feel the love radiating from Dave as he talked about his family, and suddenly she was struck by an image of just how idyllic his daughter's life must be in that alternate universe, the one where little girls ate fudge and popcorn and watched *Cinderella* while snuggled up next to people who loved them. And because Dave worried about dumb things like that, she knew what a good father he must be—kind and gentle and always, always there.

"So you never spoil her," Lisa said.

"Of course not."

"Liar."

"Not like that I don't!"

He glared at her. She stared at him pointedly, and after a moment he rolled his eyes. "Okay. Maybe a little. But only a little."

"Let them spoil her, too," Lisa said. "It won't hurt her a bit."

"Oh, yeah?" He pulled down the covers on his side of the bed and slid beneath them. "Wait until you have kids. You'll eat those words."

"Me? Please. I won't be having any kids."

"Why not?"

Lisa laughed, but it sounded hollow. "Come on, Dave. With the gene pool I'm drowning in, I'd be doing the world a favor if I sterilized myself."

"Don't say that."

She looked away. "You know where I come from."

"I don't care. Don't talk like that."

"I have no desire for kids. Or a husband, for that matter. Family obligates you."

"Yes, in some ways it does."

"Well, I can't deal with that. I fly charter, which means I have to be ready to take off at a moment's notice if some oil company executive needs to be in Galveston pronto, or some widow with more money than sense decides to head to Jamaica for the weekend with a couple of friends to play in the sun. Thing is, if I go there, I get to play, too, until they're ready to fly back. I never thought I'd have that kind of freedom, and I love it. I don't want to depend on anyone, and I don't want anyone depending on me."

"I bet you've met a lot of people," Dave said. "Seen a lot of places."

"Yes. And it's been wonderful."

Dave flipped out the light and relaxed against the pillow with a weary sigh. Downstairs, the music grew louder, as if the Lozanos were gearing up for one hell of a party.

"Where family's concerned," he told her, "you have to think of it as trading one good thing for another."

"What do you mean?"

"You trade a little of your freedom to have people to come home to who love you. People who'll stand by you no matter what. People who worry about you."

"Yeah, it starts with worry," she said. "Then they ask where you are. What you're doing. Who you're with. When you'll be home. In my case, it's, 'Why do you have to spend so much time flying?' And pretty soon, if that keeps up, I'm not flying anymore."

"Who's done that to you?"

"Men. Always."

"So you resent the fact that they expect you to cut back on your schedule to spend more time with them."

"Yes."

Dave shifted, tucking his arm behind his head. "Maybe they just weren't the right men."

Lisa thought about that, wondering if it was true. "Let's put it this way. I have yet to find a man who makes coming down out of the clouds as exciting as going up."

Several moments passed during which the only sound in the room was the reverberation of the music downstairs. Then Dave turned to look at her, his face barely more than a silhouette in the moonlit room.

"Someday," he said, "you will."

His voice was softer now, slipping down into a lower register, like a lover's in the dark, and the very sound of it made her heart rush. In the few months after she left Tolosa, she'd had the most irrational daydreams, her mind making up a hundred wonderful fairy-tale scenarios that might bring him back into her life again. Not for a moment, though, had she actually believed that it would happen, and most certainly she'd never conceived of it happening like this.

Suddenly, even in the king-size bed, she was acutely aware of Dave lying next to her. She thought she could even feel the heat of his body, hear his soft breathing. She didn't want commitment. She didn't want forever. She didn't even want tomorrow. She just wanted this moment to edge into something more. She imagined him reaching for her, here in the darkness of this hotel room where they were a million miles away from their real lives. He would pull her into his arms, say sweet, intimate things to her, and then—

"Good night, Lisa."

He shifted. Turned away. He took a deep breath, exhaled softly, and was still.

Oh, you are such a fool.

She let out a silent sigh, reminding herself once again why childish fantasies were dangerous things.

"Good night, Dave."

Thirty minutes later, Dave's eyes were still open.

Wide open.

He thought he was so tired he could sleep through anything, but not this. No way could anyone sleep through this. He swore he could feel the bed bouncing in rhythm with the undulating bass of the music downstairs. Not three minutes after he and Lisa stopped talking and started trying to sleep, the Lozanos kicked their party into overdrive.

Dave and Lisa lay on their backs, staring at the ceiling, listening to one explosive song after another.

"What the hell is going on down there?" Lisa asked. "Did Ricky Martin stop by with three thousand of his biggest fans?"

"No. That would be tame compared to this."

Lisa flipped to her side, buried one ear in her pillow, and put her palm over the other one. "I know what it is. Before the dead can come back, they've got to *wake* the dead."

A few more minutes passed. Another song began.

"Oh, God, no. 'The Macarena'?" Lisa threw the pillow aside and sat up on the edge of the bed. "Where's the gun? Gimme the gun."

"No, Lisa," Dave said. "No homicide."

"Why not? It's the Day of the freakin' *Dead*, isn't it?"

"Not that you couldn't get away with it. With that noise, nobody would even hear the gunshots."

Lisa fell to her back on the bed and pulled the pillow over

her face. "I'm going to have permanent hearing loss. I swear I am."

Dave sat up with a weary sigh. "I'll go down there and see if I can get them to drop the noise level a few thousand decibels."

"Now, wait," she said, sitting up again. "I know I was talking about hauling out the firearms, but really, you have to be diplomatic. Manuel was nice enough to give us this room, you know."

"Of course I'll be diplomatic. I'm a cop. I handle this kind of thing all the time." He stood up and shrugged into a shirt, buttoning it half-assed and not bothering to tuck in the tail. "I'll only be a minute."

He ran a hand through his hair a few times, thought about putting shoes on, then decided what the hell and simply left the room. He trotted down the stairs and rounded the corner into the huge gathering room, astonished at what he saw.

Twenty or thirty people were dancing and tossing down alcohol as if this were the 1920s and prohibition had moved south of the border. Husbands, wives, boyfriends, girlfriends, cousins, aunts, uncles, grandparents, friends, acquaintances, total strangers—hell, he didn't have a clue who all these people were, but boy, did they like to party.

In the next room, Dave saw the bluish glimmer of a big-screen TV. He couldn't see the screen itself, only the glow of it on the faces of a dozen drunk and disorderly people sprawled on the chairs and sofas around it. The only exception to the frivolity was an old woman sitting in a rocking chair in the corner of the room, holding what looked like a photograph. Just rocking back and forth and staring at it, as if the party of the century wasn't going on all around her.

Manuel came up beside him. "Hello! Good party, yes?"

Oh, hell, yes. These people made Mardi Gras look like a church picnic.

"Actually, I was just wondering if maybe you could hold the noise down just a little. The music. It's a little loud."

"Eh?"

"The noise!" Dave shouted. "Could you knock it down just a little bit?"

"Oh!" Manuel said. "It is loud?"

"Yes," Dave said, thrilled to have finally broken the sound barrier. "But just a little."

Manuel waved his hand. "Ah. This is not a problem. Come with me!"

Dave wondered what was up, but he followed Manuel across the room to a table, on top of which resided a bottle of just about every kind of alcohol known to man, alongside a gigantic plastic bin filled with ice and beer bottles. Manuel reached into the bin, extracted a Dos Equis, and popped the top off. He held it out to Dave.

"Celebrate with us," he said with a big grin, "and the music is just right!"

Dave slumped with frustration. He held up his palm. "No. Really. I can't. We were just trying to get some sleep, and—"

A sudden roar went up from the next room where people were huddled around the television. Shouts. Whistles. Beers were held up, then drained.

"Ah!" Manuel said. "Touchdown! Cowboys sixteen, Redskins zero."

"Cowboys?" Dave said. "The Dallas Cowboys?"

"There is a different Cowboys?"

"How do you get the games down here?"

Manuel grinned. "Satellite. A miracle, yes?"

"What quarter is it?"

"Second. You will watch?"

He thought about Lisa up there in that room, trying to sleep. *Damn.* He had a problem he had to take care of here. He'd promised her.

But really, though, when he thought about it, going back up to the room was probably the worst thing he could do. What if she'd fallen asleep? As tired as she'd been, she'd probably dozed off the minute he left. If he went back up there now, he'd just wake her up all over again, wouldn't he?

Of course he didn't want to do that.

And thinking a little more about it, if it weren't for her calling him to come down here to Mexico, right now he'd be planted on his sofa at home, watching this very game with John or Alex and having a Dos Equis right out of his own fridge. That entitled him to watch at least a few downs, didn't it?

He grabbed the beer from Manuel's hand. "Maybe for just a minute," he said, and followed him to the television.

chapter ten

Lisa looked at the clock on the nightstand. Dave had left the room fifteen minutes ago, and the music was as loud now as it had been the moment he walked out the door. So loud, in fact, that it had apparently paralyzed his nerve endings, leaving him unable to stumble back up the stairs.

It better have, anyway.

Lisa tossed off the covers, grabbed the only jeans she had—her dirty ones—and pulled them on. She yanked the door open, trudged down the stairs, and came around the corner to find the room filled with smoke and laughter and bodies moving with the music. She saw Dave across the room, his back to her, standing beside an ice-filled barrel. Unbelievably, he was popping the top on a bottle of beer.

As he tipped the beer up and took a long drink, she came up behind him. "Dave!"

He choked hard, coughing, then spun around. "Lisa?"

"What in the *hell* do you think you're doing?"

He opened his mouth to speak, but nothing came out. Finally he shrugged weakly. "I'm . . . uh . . . just, you know, having a beer, I guess."

"You're having a beer, you guess? While I'm up there trying to *sleep*? Is that what you've been doing all this time?"

"Come on, Lisa! It's only been, like, five minutes!"

"Try fifteen!"

"No," he said, shaking his head. "Now, it couldn't have been that long. No way."

"Oh, yeah? I watched the digital clock click by, Dave. *Fifteen times!*"

"Oh," he said sheepishly.

"Did you talk to them about the noise?"

"Yes. Now, I did do that. I mean, I tried, but—"

"But they stuck a beer in your hand and you forgot all about why you came down here? I thought you were an expert at handling this kind of thing!"

"I am, but—"

"When you break up loud teenage parties do you let them bribe you with alcohol?"

"Oh, all right!" Dave gave her a look of total disgust. "The Cowboys are playing, and I wanted to see the game. Which, of course, I'd be watching right now if I were at home. But I'm not at home, am I? See, I got this phone call late one night. There was this woman on the other end, wanting me to come to Mexico—"

"What did you say?"

Dave stopped short. "Uh . . . which part?"

"You said the Cowboys are playing? Is it the Redskins game?"

"Yeah."

Lisa glanced toward the TV. "Which quarter?"

"Second."

"Is there room for one more in there?"

"You want to watch the game?"

Was he kidding? If she hadn't gotten stuck in Mexico, she'd be planted on her sofa in her apartment in San Antonio, watching this very game alongside a couple of friends from her apartment complex, having a Dos Equis right out of her own fridge.

"Maybe for just a minute," she said, hauling a beer out of the barrel. When she turned back, Dave was smiling, a broad, brilliant smile that made her heart lurch.

Suddenly she didn't feel the least bit tired after all.

A couple of hours and a couple of beers later, Dave wondered why in the world he'd wanted to sleep in the first place. The music was loud. The beer was good. The game was better. And when the refs made a bad call Dave got to learn a whole bunch of Spanish expletives he'd never heard before. Outside of his family, he'd had very little social life lately, and he was surprised at how good it felt just to relax with a bunch of people who were hell-bent on nothing more than having a good time.

And sitting next to Lisa wasn't half-bad, either.

Ever since he'd seen her come out of that bathroom earlier wearing his shirt, he hadn't been able to think about much else. Now they were sitting on a sofa populated by a couple more people than it was really designed for, which had shoved him and Lisa right up next to each other. Knee to knee. Thigh to thigh. Hip to hip.

She'd pulled her dirty jeans back on, which was all she had, but that didn't matter to him in the least. Not one woman since Carla's death, no matter how sexy she dressed, how beautiful she smelled, how clear she'd been about her intentions to move to the bedroom, had affected him the way Lisa did right now. All he could think about was touching her anywhere he could get away with in polite company, then leading her back upstairs to move his hands into places polite company would never allow.

The final two minutes of the game ticked off, and with every second that passed Dave grew more restless. Pretty soon they were going back up to that room. Did he really want to draw a line down the center of that bed?

In the last seconds of the game, the local Cowboys fans let loose with a barrage of cheers that the Cowboys themselves probably heard all the way back in Dallas.

Manuel, who'd been sitting in a chair beside the sofa, leaned over and spoke to Dave and Lisa: "A victory. Time to celebrate!"

Before Dave could do a lot of pondering on what that might mean, everyone was getting up and he found himself being dragged into the middle of a group of men moving into the other room to the table full of alcohol bottles. Lisa was likewise being herded along with the women to a spot about ten feet away beside a table. On it sat a bowl of lime slices and a saltshaker. This family was so nuts that squirrels had to be circling the house, so God only knew what was coming next.

"What's going on?" he asked Manuel.

"Tequila shots," Manuel said with a big grin. "Lozano style."

To Dave's utter amazement, a woman grabbed a lime out of the bowl, then gyrated forward in time to the music. She tilted her head to the left, simultaneously squeezing a slice of lime over the side of her neck. Another woman picked up the salt-shaker and sprinkled it over the spot where the lime juice was. Then all the women turned in unison and zeroed in on a man standing next to Dave. The wedding ring he wore said he was probably the first woman's husband, or at least Dave hoped he was. The man's grin grew bigger with every second that passed.

Manuel grabbed a shot glass from the table, filled it with tequila, and handed it to the man. With a big, provocative smile, he started walking toward the woman. She smiled back at him, making little "come on over here" signs of invitation with her fingertips. When he reached her, he dipped his head and licked the salt and lime off her neck. Then he put the shot glass to his lips, downed the tequila, dropped the glass to the floor, and kissed his wife long and hard amid an explosion of rowdy whistles and cheers.

Dave just stood there, gaping at the spectacle. *Animal House,* Mexican style.

He glanced at Lisa, and she was wearing one of those "what in the hell have we gotten ourselves into?" looks. His sentiments exactly.

Another woman limed and salted herself, and the group enticed her partner to step forward. He licked, drank, and kissed. The crowd went wild.

Then, as that couple stepped aside, a woman moved up behind Lisa and squeezed a lime slice over her neck. Lisa spun around, brushing her hand against her neck, shaking her head wildly. The women laughed. A second or two passed during which Dave actually wondered what these people had in mind.

Then Manuel held out a shot of tequila in front of Dave.

He glanced back at Lisa. The moment their eyes met, she stopped all the neck brushing and stood frozen in place. The women around her giggled. One grabbed another lime slice and dribbled it over the curve between Lisa's neck and shoulder to replace what she'd swept away, the open collar of his shirt leaving plenty of bare skin for the lime juice to slither over. The woman followed with a sprinkle of salt.

Through it all, Lisa didn't move. Didn't even flinch. All she did was stand there, motionless, speechless, watching Dave watching her, as if she couldn't believe that he would even consider doing anything as outrageous as this.

He couldn't believe it, either.

Just being around Lisa set him on fire, which meant that right about now he ought to be running for a fire extinguisher. Instead, all he wanted to do was crank up the heat.

He took the shot glass and started toward her.

He moved slowly, deliberately, his gaze never leaving hers, her green eyes widening more with every step he took. The noise level around him shot completely off the scale with the crowd egging him on, tossing out provocative comments, as if this were the best entertainment they'd had in ages.

Finally he stopped in front of her, standing so close that he could see the rise and fall of her chest with every breath she took. Glancing down, he saw a drop of lime juice slither down her neck onto her collarbone, dragging a few granules of salt along with it.

As he leaned in, her eyes drifted closed. He placed his hand on her shoulder, and when he caught that single droplet of lime juice with the tip of his tongue every muscle in her body seemed to contract. He moved upward to the hollow between her neck and shoulder, found the salty spot, closed his mouth over it with a soft, sucking motion of his lips and tongue. Beneath the rough texture of the salt, her skin felt satin smooth.

With one last sweep of his tongue, he rose again, put the shot glass to his lips, and downed its contents in a single swallow. He dropped the glass, tucked his hand around the back of Lisa's neck, tilted her face up, and kissed her.

The moment he dropped his lips against hers, he sensed her surprise, but only a second elapsed before she wrapped her arms around his neck and kissed him back. The tequila tasted like fire, but her mouth seemed hotter still.

Hot tequila. Hot kiss. Hot woman. *Damn,* this was good.

He slid his arm around her back and pulled her right up next to him, her breasts crushed against his chest, as he continued to kiss her with an enthusiasm that made the crowd go wild. He had the fleeting thought that if his family could have seen him, they would have known for sure that he'd slipped right off the deep end. Dave, the ultimate conformist. Nice, normal, dependable Dave, who wouldn't even think of pulling a stunt best left to drunk frat boys.

Maybe that was why it felt so good to do it.

When he finally pulled away and looked down at Lisa, her eyes were dazed and heavy-lidded, seemingly unable to tear themselves away from his. After another round of applause, the family's attention turned to the next woman, who doused herself with lime juice and salt and moved forward. Lisa snapped out of her daze and moved aside. Dave moved right along with her, and the action shifted away from them onto the next couple. Then Lisa looked back at him.

It had been a long time since he'd felt a woman's touch and an even longer time since the heat of a woman's body had warmed his own, and he knew for a fact that he'd never had a woman look up at him with the desire he saw in Lisa's eyes right now.

He slid his hand along her neck, leaned over, and put his lips next to her ear. "Let's go back to our room."

She turned her head, her cheek grazing his, and he felt her breath against the side of his neck. "I can take the stairs two at a time. Can you?"

Dave nearly jumped out of his skin. Hell, yes, he could, with her slung over his shoulder if he had to.

But just as they had turned to leave, the music suddenly stopped. Dave turned back, surprised to see all the motion in the room come to a halt. The sudden silence, after the raucous music all evening, was almost painful. Glancing around, he saw the old woman rise from her rocking chair. She turned and gave a roundhouse stare to all the people present. As if she'd spoken a command out loud, everyone set their glasses down and scurried toward the parlor, many of them dragging chairs along with them.

"What's going on?" Dave asked Manuel.

"It is ten o'clock."

"That's significant?"

"Twelve years ago, my father died at ten o'clock on El Dia de los Muertos. My mother believes that is a sign. She believes he gathers our dead relatives at that hour and returns with them to visit. We must prepare to greet them."

Oh, no. No way. Dave had no intention of greeting anyone, dead or alive, because he'd just made an appointment with Lisa he was going to keep. "Maybe we'll just go back up to our room—"

"No! You must stay! This is what everyone is waiting for!"

Dave shot a glance at Lisa. Her cheeks were still flushed, and she was looking at him in a way that said the minute they stepped back into their room clothes were coming off at the speed of light.

"It's a family thing," Dave said. "And close friends. We don't want to interrupt."

"No interruption," Manuel said. "Come. I will tell you about it."

To Dave's dismay, Manuel swept them both into the parlor and right up to the altar, where the perfumey smell of the flowers and the candles about knocked Dave over backward. Manuel pointed to one of the photographs.

"My great-uncle Sergio. He died in the Spanish-American War." He pointed to a grainy photo of a young woman. "My great-grandmother Antonia. She died of rheumatic fever at age twenty-nine. And this is my father, Benecio. He was killed in a train accident near Cuernavaca."

Manuel continued through his family tree, which had more branches than a hundred-year-old oak. Unfortunately, their host's generosity pretty much obligated them to stand there and listen until their host chose to shut up.

"One candle is lit for every relative who has died," Manuel went on. "If a candle is not lit for a person, his soul must light a finger to guide him back."

Sounds painful. By all means, keep those candles lit. Can we go now?

Lisa was standing beside Dave, and all at once he felt her palm against his shoulder. She slid it slowly downward until it rested at the small of his back, and something inside him liquefied at her touch. All this talk about dead people was going in one ear and out the other. He couldn't smell the flowers or candles anymore. He could scarcely hear Manuel's voice. He was having a tough time even making his eyes comprehend the photographs the man was so lovingly pointing out. All he knew was that Lisa was touching him, and he was overcome with the compulsion to touch her back.

"I told you about our family," Manuel said, after what seemed like an hour. "Now tell me about yours. Is there someone you wish to remember?"

"What?" Dave said.

"A relative who has died."

Dave froze, staring at Manuel. In contrast to the tumultuous noise level of only a moment ago, the room was eerily quiet. He glanced back at the altar, and for the first time he actually looked at the photographs there, at each one individually. There were dozens of them, old and new—men, women, a few children. These people had been here once. Now they were gone.

The dead.

A blurry, out-of-focus image of Carla swept through Dave's mind. Suddenly he became aware that not a single Lozano was speaking and that everyone's attention was focused squarely on him.

He shook his head. "No. No one."

"Do you have a photograph? You may put it with these on the altar—"

"No," he said sharply. "I don't have any photographs."

That was a lie. He still carried Carla's photo in his wallet.

But since the moment he'd heard the news of her death he hadn't looked at it. Not once. And he wasn't about to start now.

Manuel looked confused for a moment. Then a knowing expression came over his face. "You have lost someone not long ago."

Statement, not question. Christ, he didn't need this. Not now. He didn't need Manuel's intuition kicking in, he didn't need his far-flung theories about the afterlife, and he sure didn't need that look on Lisa's face that said she was listening as raptly as everyone else. The silence. Damn it, he wished every Lozano on the premises would go back to blowing the roof off.

"No," he told Manuel. "I haven't."

"It is difficult to hide, señor. Your eyes tell everything."

Manuel continued to stare at him, waiting. Then Lisa touched his arm.

"Carla?"

Dave turned, astonished that she'd spoken Carla's name. For a moment, all he could do was stand there, staring with disbelief.

"Who is Carla?" Manuel asked.

"No one," Dave said quickly. "Thanks for the hospitality, Manuel. But it's time we went to bed."

"Americans," he said, with a sad shake of his head. "They have no understanding. Death is only a transition into the next life, where your loved ones are. Dia de los Muertos is the day they come to see us again."

The thought of that sent something dark filtering through Dave's mind, something that had eaten away at him for four long years.

No. You have to stop thinking about her. You'll go crazy if you don't.

He turned back. "Do you actually believe that? That the dead come back?"

"Why should I not?" Manuel said. "Should not people who have crossed over want to visit their loved ones left behind?"

If that was true, then Carla had been watching. She'd been

watching him with Lisa, sitting with her, laughing with her, kissing her, seeing him succumb one more time to the woman he never should have touched, never should have looked at, never should have dreamed about in the dark of night for the past eleven years. The woman he'd never forgotten, even when he'd been married to Carla.

"To tell you the truth, Manuel," Dave said, "it sounds like a whole lot of silly superstition to me. But if you want to believe it, more power to you."

With that, he turned and strode away.

A few minutes later, Lisa stood in the hall outside the door of their room, her back to the wall, her eyes closed, cursing herself for opening her big mouth. The moment she'd spoken Carla's name, everything had changed. Why had she done it?

Because she could see so clearly that Dave had to be thinking about her even though he wasn't saying her name, and the silence had demanded to be filled. But if she'd had any idea that after all this time he'd still feel Carla's death so intensely, that he'd turn and hurry up the stairs, leaving her standing in that parlor as if nothing at all had happened between them, she would have kept her mouth shut.

She closed her eyes and ran her tongue over her lips. She could still taste his kiss. It had been the most incredible sensation—the fiery taste of the tequila mingling with his warm lips moving over hers in a shockingly sensual way. That he'd done it in the midst of a crowd had stunned her even more. He wanted her tonight. She was sure of it. Or, at least, he had, right up to the moment Carla had gotten in the way, coming back to haunt them like a ghost rising from the grave.

Lisa went inside the darkened room and clicked the door closed. The only illumination came from the streetlights shining through the open patio door. Dave sat on the balcony on the rattan sofa, his back to her.

She didn't know what to expect. She only knew what she wanted. With that in mind, she slipped over to the closet, opened the door, and reached into her backpack. From a zippered pocket she pulled out one of the plastic packets it held and stuffed it into her jeans pocket. Carrying condoms wherever she went was a habit she'd held over from high school, because safe was always better than sorry.

She walked across the room and leaned against the patio door frame. Swirls of the night wind of November coming down from the Sierra Madres skated across her skin, raising goose bumps on her arms and ruffling her hair.

"My, you left the party quickly," she said.

"You need sleep," Dave said, not even bothering to turn around. "You should go to bed."

Lisa felt a stab of disappointment. "Nah. I'm not really sleepy after all. And it was hot at the party. I could use a little air myself."

She moved out onto the balcony, circled the sofa, and sat down beside him. When she saw what he was holding, her heart slipped a notch or two.

His wallet, open to a photograph of Carla.

Lisa hadn't seen her since high school and light was minimal on the balcony, but still there was no mistaking the face. She was a few years older in this photo, but she looked essentially the same—blond hair, green eyes, with a soft, sensitive expression. Lisa willed him to put the photograph away, but still he stared at it. She knew any questions she asked might only inflame an already combustible situation, but not asking meant he would turn away from her completely, and that was the last thing she wanted tonight.

"How long has she been gone?" Lisa asked.

"Four years."

"I read about it afterward. Icy roads. She lost control of the car on that bridge. Wasn't that what happened?"

"Yeah. That was what happened."

"Why didn't you give her photo to Manuel?"

"I don't even know those people. Carla is none of their business."

His defensiveness sent a twinge of desperation fluttering through Lisa's stomach. *Tell me, Dave. Tell me why you can't forget her.*

Correction. Tell me how I can make *you forget her.*

To her relief, he flipped past Carla's picture, only to settle on one of a little girl about four or five years old. Lisa leaned over to get a better look. She was a pretty child, with warm blond hair and green eyes.

"Ashley?"

Dave nodded.

"She's beautiful," Lisa said.

"She's Carla. In every way."

Lisa imagined that Dave was remembering what a shining couple he and Carla had been, the very picture of perfection, blessed with a child who was a daily reinforcement of just that. In her youthful anger and jealousy, Lisa had convinced herself that Carla was nothing more than a spoiled little rich girl who was going to make his life miserable. But now she knew how wrong she'd been and just how traumatic Carla's death must have been for Dave.

She closed her eyes, cursing silently. How was it that after all this time the thought of the two of them together still sent waves of jealousy rolling through her?

Because you were in love with him. Maybe you still are. Maybe you always will be.

For the past eleven years, Dave had stayed in the back of her mind, hovering in that corner reserved for hopeless dreams that refuse to go away. And she knew if she walked away from him tonight, tomorrow she'd go back to San Antonio and spend the next eleven years wondering what might have been. She tightened her jaw subtly but resolutely.

"Downstairs," she said. "Why did you kiss me?"

He shifted uncomfortably but didn't look at her. "Peer pressure?"

"Do you really expect me to believe that?"

He was silent.

"Kissing me tonight doesn't mean you loved Carla any less."

He turned to look at her. "Is that what you think? That I feel guilty about it?"

"You don't?"

"Spare me the psychobabble. If I want analysis, I'll hire a shrink."

"Why? So you can wallow in it from now on?"

Dave's gaze turned positively glacial. "You haven't got any idea what you're talking about."

"Then why don't you enlighten me? If you're going to kiss me like that in front of a roomful of people, I think I've got a right to know what you were thinking when you did it."

"I wasn't thinking a damned thing, or I never would have done it."

"Right."

"I'd had a few beers—"

"Oh, come on."

"It wasn't a big deal, Lisa."

"A peck on the lips wouldn't have been a big deal. What you did—believe me. That was a big deal."

He didn't respond. He just shut his wallet and returned it to his pocket.

"You wanted to come back upstairs," she said softly. "And you know I did, too. So what happened to change all that?"

"I told you I'd get you out of Mexico. That's as far as anything between us is going to go."

"Why? Did you suddenly decide that I don't appeal to you after all? Now, that's a reason I'll go along with, because, you know, chemistry is just one of those things."

"That has nothing to do with it."

"Did it suddenly dawn on you that after tomorrow we'll probably never see each other again, so you figure what's the point of anything happening between us tonight? If so, that's fine, too."

"Lisa—"

"But, Dave," she said, dropping her voice, "if you wanted me before and you don't now because I spoke your dead wife's name, then you've got a problem that an entire army of shrinks couldn't possibly hope to deal with."

She held her ground, giving him a defiant stare, standing behind every word she'd said. She knew she was treading on thin ice, but maybe it was just what he needed to hear. And maybe he'd hate her forever for saying it. Either way, she had nothing to lose.

"Like I said," he told her. "You don't have any idea what you're talking about."

"I think I'm closer than you want to admit."

"I don't want to talk about this anymore."

"Maybe you need to."

"Cut it out, Lisa."

"But—"

"Will you just shut the hell up and leave me alone?"

She recoiled, feeling the jolt of his angry words lodging directly in her heart. Yes, she'd pushed him. Hard. But she wanted to know—*needed* to know—why Carla's death still had a stranglehold on him four years later. But it looked as if she was never going to find out.

"Sure, Dave," she said, rising from the sofa. "Whatever you say. And don't worry. After tomorrow, I won't be around to bother you anymore."

She brushed past him, heading for the patio door. As she came around the arm of the sofa, to her surprise, he clamped his hand around her wrist and pulled her to a halt.

"Lisa. Don't go."

It wasn't a command. Instead his voice held a hushed, pleading tone, and like some kind of invisible cord, it kept her from walking away more effectively than his grasp on her wrist ever could have. Then his grip relaxed, becoming more like a caress. He let out a long, tortured breath, then slowly, slowly pulled her back around until she was standing in front of him. The silence on the patio was broken only by the rustle of the night wind through the trees. He took her other wrist and ran both of his hands down to grasp hers, then looked up at her, his gaze solemn.

"Here's the truth. I kissed you because I wanted to. Because you looked so beautiful and we'd been sitting together all night and it seemed . . . God, Lisa." He exhaled. "Just looking at you has always done something to me I don't understand and I probably never will."

She held her breath, afraid to break whatever spell it was

that kept the longing in his voice and the desire in his eyes. "And then you wanted more than a kiss."

His gaze played over her body, easing down over her breasts to her waist, then back up to her face again. His hands tightened against hers. "I still do."

The coarse hunger she heard in his voice gave Lisa the same feeling she got in her stomach every time her plane hit a pocket of turbulence—an intense, breathless, swooping sensation that was almost painfully exhilarating. And now, when Dave pulled her between his thighs, taking her hips in his hands and burying his face against her, the feeling only intensified. He inhaled deeply, then exhaled slowly, his warm breath soaking through her shirt and burning her skin like a brand.

She heard the muffled sounds of traffic in the distance, tires rushing against asphalt, horns honking. The night air swirled through the trees, creating a whisper of leaf against leaf. Lisa sensed everything around her, but she remained strangely disconnected from all of it. All she knew, all she felt, all she wanted right now was Dave.

He tugged on her hips, easing her down until she was straddling his legs, her knees tucked beside his thighs, resting on the padded cushion of the rattan sofa. She steadied herself by placing her hands against his shoulders, and when she dared to meet his eyes again they were smoldering with want, with need. When men looked at her like that, when she could see that craving in their eyes, the subsequent rush was like a drug she needed desperately. It was a feeling like no other, that unparalleled sensation of being beautiful and desirable, of being the number one thing on a man's mind.

She knew the power of sex. She always had.

He curled his hand around the back of her neck and pulled her to his mouth, plunging his tongue inside in a deep, blistering kiss that made the one he'd given her downstairs pale in comparison. He shoved his other hand beneath her shirt and circled it around to the small of her back, his rough fingertips rasping against her skin as he pulled her closer still, his mouth burning against hers.

God, this man could kiss.

Then a sense of desperation crept in. She had no delusions that he'd suddenly fallen madly in love with her. There was a big difference between love and lust, and Dave DeMarco was experiencing a major case of lust.

He saved love for women like Carla.

No. Maybe it wouldn't be that way. Not if she made it so good for him that he forgot all about his dead wife. Made it the best sex he'd ever had in his life, so he would want to come back again and again and Carla would slip further and further from his mind. She wanted him to feel every sexual tremor like an earthquake inside him, to associate the sight of her, the feel of her, the very *smell* of her with the most incredible sensations of his life. She wanted to make sure that from this moment forward, every time he thought about sex, hers would be the face he would see.

Sorry, Carla. You can't have him. Tonight, he's mine.

She tore her lips away from his and sat up, unbuttoned his shirt, and spread it apart, stroking her hands over the rigid muscles of his chest. Then she leaned back in, trailing her lips over his jaw, his neck, feeling the roughness of a day's growth of his beard against her cheek. His hands clenched against her thighs.

"Inside," he murmured.

"No."

"Lisa—"

"Right here."

She knew how daring it felt to be outside in the night air surrounded by city lights, how outrageous, how illicit, and how much it heightened the pleasure, the excitement. Most of all, she knew beyond all doubt that his precious Carla would never have been caught dead having wild, scorching sex on a balcony.

Before he could even think about objecting again, she sat up quickly, undid a few of the buttons of her shirt, and slipped it off over her head, flinging it aside. She rested her palms on his shoulders, leaned in, and kissed him again, brushing the tips of her breasts against his bare chest.

"The balcony's secluded," she whispered. "It's dark. Trees all over the place."

"If someone sees—"

"They'll get a hell of a good show. I promise you."

chapter eleven

All at once, Dave didn't give a damn. Inside, outside, upside down—any way he could have her, that was how he wanted her. He didn't care if the whole world was watching. It was as if his mind had blanked out completely. And no wonder. With Lisa half-naked on top of him, face-to-face with him, her thighs spread, every inch of her body within touching or kissing distance—how the hell could he think about anything else?

Lisa touched her lips to his ear and whispered, "What do you want? Tell me what you want."

Good God—what *didn't* he want? "That's like giving a hungry man a smorgasbord," he said breathlessly, "and asking him to choose."

She leaned away a little. "So you're a hungry man?"

He stared back at her, feeling something more than need. More than desire. A deeper, darker, almost primitive sensation swept through him.

"Starving," he said.

She threaded her fingers through his hair and fell into him again, kissing him deeply. He closed his palms over her breasts, astonished to finally be touching what he'd only admired from a distance. God, they were beautiful, heavy and full, with hard, pointed nipples. She moaned against his lips, pressing herself against his hands, begging for more. He obliged, his gentle caresses becoming rougher as he kneaded her breasts, squeezing and releasing, his thumbs tripping back and forth over her nipples. She ripped her mouth away from his with a gasp of pleasure, tilting her head back and closing her eyes.

Bending forward, Dave held her breasts and kissed the valley between them, inhaling the scent of her. He turned his head and kissed the inner swell of one, then dragged his mouth across it until he reached her nipple. He flicked it with his tongue, then took the tender flesh into his mouth and sucked hard. She groaned with pleasure, digging her fingertips into his shoulders and grinding herself into his erection straining against his jeans. Her breathing escalated, becoming harsh and needy.

"I want you naked," she said suddenly, and before he could even think about granting her wish her hands were on his belt buckle. In seconds she had it undone and was opening the buttons of his jeans with a proficiency that astonished him. She stood up, pulling off everything south of his waist in a single swoop.

Dave was already way past caring that they might be providing an X-rated show to anyone who went to the effort to peer through a few leafy branches, particularly when Lisa stood in front of him and ripped the fly of her own jeans open with a sudden *flick flick flick flick* of the buttons. She slid her hands down inside the jeans alongside her hips and pushed them off, taking her panties with them and kicking them both aside. Suddenly she was naked in front of him, illuminated by the pale moonlight—shapely hips, slender waist, full breasts. All woman. Every single beautiful inch of her.

She glided back on top of him again, wrapping her hand around his cock, stroking it, rubbing the length of him against her. She was already hot and wet, and he wanted nothing more than to—

All at once he clutched her hands. "Condom," he muttered. "Damn it. I don't have a condom."

She leaned over, snagging the leg of her jeans she'd just ripped off. She reached inside a pocket and extracted a plastic packet.

He stared up at her with surprise. "Where'd you get that?"

"Do you really care?"

"God, no." He reached for it, but she was already ripping it open. As she rolled it down over him, moving her hands in long, smooth strokes, he dropped his head back against the sofa, his fingers tightening against her thighs in anticipation. She guided him back between her legs, and in one smooth, forceful stroke she drove down on top of him. He grasped her hips with a stifled curse, gritting his teeth against the indescribable pleasure that streaked through him. Momentarily paralyzed, he held her in place for a few seconds until he could breathe again.

"More," she whispered, her voice rough and demanding. "More. . . ."

He exhaled, easing his grip, and she rose on her knees until only the tip of him was inside her, then rode down the length of him again. She was hot and moist and tight beyond belief, and as she pumped up and down a third time, then a fourth, he caught her rhythm, guiding her with his hands. She increased her pace, clutching his shoulders to steady herself as she rocked on her knees against the worn vinyl cushion, grinding deep, taking every inch of him with every stroke. The cool night air skated across his sweat-sheened skin, but all he felt was heat. For years Lisa had moved like a shadow along the periphery of his mind, teasing him, tempting him. To have her on top of him now, naked and eager, felt like a fantasy come to life.

He opened his eyes, surprised to see her staring down at him as she thrust wildly, her red-gold hair fluttering against her forehead with every stroke. There was something so erotic about her watchful gaze, about the way she drove down on him with such focused intent, as if she was reading every move he made as a desire expressed and giving it back to him tenfold.

"God, Lisa. . . ."

"Just feel it," she murmured. "Feel it. . . ."

He dropped his head against the back of the sofa, squeezing his eyes closed again, astonished at how unbelievably fast the sensation was building inside him, like storm water pressing against a dam, threatening to burst right through. Somewhere in the back of his mind, he knew he should take control, take things slower, but the urgency was so powerful, so abrupt, so razor sharp that he couldn't have harnessed it if his life depended on it. He dug his fingers into her hips, moving her faster, as a whirlpool of blind sensation sucked him into its depths.

When the first shock wave hit him, a low groan rose from his chest. She clamped down hard around him even as she continued to thrust wildly, moving against him with ferocious intent.

"Oh, God, *Lisa*. . . ."

He ground out the words through clenched teeth, bowing his head forward, then throwing it back again as one hot, shuddering spasm after another crashed into him. They seemed to go on forever, fueled by the heat and pressure of her, by the wild, relentless way she thrust herself down on him.

As the feeling subsided, she slowed her pace, but still she moved against him, coaxing every tremor of pleasure from his body that she possibly could, until finally her movements wound down and she sagged against him, her forehead resting on his shoulder. He held her tightly, still deep inside her, immersed in the feeling of their bodies joined together.

"Should have gone slower," he said, breathing hard. "That was too fast for you. Had to be—"

She put her fingertips against his mouth, then replaced them with her lips, leaning into him with a hot, moist, lazy kiss. After a moment she started to rise, but he pulled her back, not yet ready to feel the cool mountain air dissipate the heat between them. But she persisted, rising to her feet in front of him and walking to the patio door. Stopping there, she turned back and gave him a long, slow, appraising stare. Then she disappeared into the room.

What the hell was she doing?

After a moment, Dave got a grip on his still-labored breathing, then got up and followed her inside. The sudden warmth of the room made the sweat that had beaded on his forehead trickle down his temples. He looked first at the bed. She wasn't there. Then he heard the shower running and felt a surge of disappointment.

A woman disappearing into the bathroom after sex—that had to be a bad sign. It had been too fast. He knew that now for sure. But she'd felt so good—so hot, so eager, so seemingly ready for him—that he hadn't been able to hold off for five minutes, and now all she wanted to do was wash away the experience.

Well, *shit.*

Then the bathroom door slowly opened. Lisa leaned against the door frame, her arms folded beneath her breasts. In the dim light of the hotel room he thought he saw her smile.

"Dave?"

"Yeah?"

"How do you feel about sex in the shower?"

His brain had barely comprehended that she was issuing him invitation number two of the evening before he felt an erection leaping to life all over again.

Amazing.

"Come here," she said.

He walked to the bathroom door. She pulled him inside, shut the door behind him, dousing the light at the same time and plunging them both into total darkness. She pressed him back against the closed door, circling her arms around his neck and kissing him. He wrapped his arms around her and hauled her right up next to him until the length of her body was pressed against his—firm thighs, soft breasts, hot, silky lips. She slid her hand between them, circling it around his rapidly hardening erection.

"I think you're ready for round two," she said.

"You've got my attention."

She took him by the hand, and they carefully made their way through the dark bathroom, his feet sinking into the oversize plush bathmat, and stepped blindly into the shower. Wrapped in each other's arms, they moved beneath the shower, the water washing over their bodies. Dave kissed her for a long time, their hands playing over each other in the dreamy haziness created by the hot water and the steam billowing up and the darkness surrounding them.

To his surprise, she maneuvered him around until his back was to the shower spray, then moved up behind him. "Officer?"

He blinked with surprise.

"This time you're the one under arrest," she said, her voice hot and provocative. "Put your hands against the wall."

His heart jolted hard, and for a moment all he could do was stand there, speechless.

"Oh, this is bad," she murmured, running her hands over his shoulders, down his arms, and back up again. "My suspect is resisting arrest. What do you suggest I do?"

"Well," he said, "I usually start suggesting at the top of my lungs that maybe he ought to cooperate. Lots of profanity. You know. Intimidation."

"Hmm. I'm afraid that might ruin the mood a bit." She paused. "How about if I just promise to frisk you really, really good?"

Yep, she's got you, he thought. *It's definitely in your best interest to cooperate.*

He placed his palms against the wall. Several seconds passed, and just as he was wondering what she was up to, he was treated to the incredible feeling of her warm, soft breasts slick with soapsuds, moving against his back. She rested her cheek against his back with a hum of satisfaction, then slid her hands around his hips, down to his thighs, then back up to his waist, up and down, moving inward each time. Finally she closed the hot, soapy fingers of one hand around his cock, moving them up and down in long, smooth strokes.

Jesus *Christ.*

His palms still pressed to the wall, he bowed his head as unbelievably powerful sensations rose inside him all over again. She rubbed her breasts against his back as she continued stroking him with soapy hands, making him rock-hard all over again.

After a few minutes, she moved her hands back up to his hips. "Turn around."

He turned and reached for her, but she was already slithering downward, dragging her breasts along his chest, his abdomen, and then her hands were on his thighs. He couldn't see her in the dark, but he knew she'd fallen to her knees in front of him.

She must have moved slightly, because the shower spray suddenly hit him, rinsing away the soapsuds below his waist. Then he felt her hand wrap around his cock. She stroked the length of him once, twice. On the third stroke, her mouth followed her hand.

He shuddered as her mouth closed around him, licking, sucking, tasting him, back and forth. As the water beat down on them, his hands rose almost involuntarily to cradle her head. He laced his fingers through her hair, clenching them against her scalp. With a low, harsh groan he dropped his head back against the wall. She took that as encouragement, drawing him in even deeper with an incredible fusion of lips and tongue, along with a mind-blowing suction that created a sensation unlike anything he'd ever felt before. The sound of the shower roared in his ears, the feel of her mouth and hands driving him right to the edge again. If he didn't stop her right now . . .

He grabbed her by the upper arms and hauled her to her feet. Breathing hard, he turned and pressed her to the shower wall.

"Guess I'd make a lousy cop," she said. "I didn't move fast enough with the handcuffs."

Dave leaned in and kissed her neck, feeling her pulse beating wildly in her throat, then nipped her earlobe. "I don't think you want me restrained."

In the darkness, he moved his hands to her breasts, finding them still slick with soapsuds. He squeezed them firmly, his thumbs strumming her nipples, then moved his hand down between her legs, cupping the soft flesh of her inner thigh before easing upward to meet her hot, slick cleft. She exhaled, her fingertips digging into his shoulders as he stroked her there, her hips rocking slightly, her breath coming faster.

Yes. This was what he wanted. To hear her anticipation, to feel her move against him, to sense her rising excitement. Suddenly he hated the darkness, wishing he could watch her face, wishing he could see her expression reflecting the pleasure he wanted her to feel. Then all at once she took his hand, stilling it.

"What?" he asked.

She pulled back the shower curtain with the clink of metal rings and a blast of cool air. A moment later she closed it again. He heard a small tearing sound and realized that she'd grabbed a condom. Her hand searched for him in the darkness, met his chest, then slid it down to his cock, where she rolled the condom in place. Then she circled her hands around his neck, her warm breath only a scant inch from his lips, her voice low and hoarse.

"Just fuck me."

Getting zapped with a stun gun couldn't have matched the jolt of pure lust that shot through him. When she took his cock and pressed it between her legs, he sank into her with a groan of satisfaction, astonished at how incredible it felt to be inside her again. He took her right up against the shower wall with swift, powerful strokes, engulfed in darkness, water beating down on them like a rainstorm. She curled one heel around his calf to open herself more to him and pull him in more deeply. He buried his face in the crook of her neck, trying to maintain some semblance of control, but still he was shaking, his muscles tense, his heart beating unmercifully. She was so hot. So wet. And he was so unbelievably close.

"Yes," she whispered as he pounded into her relentlessly. "Just like that. *Yes.*"

She shifted slightly to take him deeper yet, whispering in his ear the whole time, driving him right to the peak of excitement. He felt the rising pressure and froze, poised on the edge, and in the next moment an orgasm blasted through him, hitting him with the intensity of a battering ram. He thrust wildly, feeling as if he were being torn apart from the inside out. Lisa kept pace with his final strokes, driving herself against him, her breath reduced to short, hard gasps.

He clung to her as the sensations wound down, dropping his head against her shoulder, every muscle in his body falling limp with satisfaction. He slid out of her and backed against the adjacent shower wall, pulling her up against him, enveloping her in his arms as the last tremors of pleasure faded away.

"That was good," he murmured, still breathing heavily. "So good."

She pressed a kiss to his lips, then slipped out of his arms. To his surprise, he heard the jingle of shower curtain rings again as she stepped out of the shower.

What was she doing now?

When Dave thought his legs would carry him, he turned off the water, the knobs squeaking as the shower was silenced. In the darkness, he found his way out of the shower, felt for the door, and opened it just enough for the pale moonlight from the other room to light his way to a towel.

He ran the towel through his dripping hair as he walked out of the bathroom. He saw Lisa lying on her side, her elbow resting on the bed, wearing that same watchful, knowing expression she had out on the patio.

He dried off a little, then tossed the towel aside. With a huge exhalation, he lay down beside her, his hand against his chest, wondering if it was possible for his heart to burst right out of it. Turning, he saw her staring down at him, her green eyes like a pair of emeralds on fire.

"I think you're going to kill me," he told her between breaths. "Hell, I don't know. Maybe you already did."

To his surprise, she took his hand and pulled him over until he was lying on his stomach.

"What are you doing?"

She put one hand against his shoulder to keep him from rising, grabbing the lotion from the nightstand with her other one. She apologized for the floral scent, then straddled his hips. She touched him, her hands cold at first with the lotion, but they quickly warmed as she moved them over his back in long, sensual strokes. He moved his arms up to hug the pillow, sighing with satisfaction as her thumbs moved deep into the muscles along his spine.

He'd discovered tonight what he'd always suspected—this woman did nothing halfway. She poured her heart, her soul, her passion into everything, whether it was becoming a pilot, going after the bad guys, or making love with him. And it had been incredible. He'd never been with a woman who was so attuned to every move he made, reading every sigh, every groan, every involuntary clench of his muscles, making every moment wild, hot, and exciting.

And now every inch of his body felt limp with contentment, his mind pleasantly foggy, as she brought him to the other end of the spectrum, capping off total tension with total relaxation. It was as if she knew exactly what to do to wring that last bit of pleasure and satisfaction out of him until he was completely spent.

Then he thought about Carla.

He held his breath for a moment, waiting for the shot of guilt he knew was coming. But just as quickly as she'd come to mind, she shifted away again, becoming only a faint apparition in the distance that he could barely make out. He felt the strangest swell of relief, like an asthmatic who is suddenly able to breathe. Lisa had been a release, a reprieve he thought was completely beyond his grasp. For these few hours tonight, she'd made him forget. And God, if nothing else, he owed her for that.

She leaned forward and whispered in his ear, "Good?"

"Too good," he murmured. "You keep that up, and I'm liable to fall asleep."

As she continued to rub his back, he sighed deeply, thinking that there had to be another human being on earth who felt better than he did right now, but he couldn't imagine it. As the last of his energy slipped away, he closed his eyes, knowing that opening them again would be an insurmountable task. Her hands were still on him, moving, always moving, as he drifted off to sleep.

As it grew later, the light dimmed with the shifting moon, painting the room in pale monochromatic tones. Lisa leaned against the headboard, her knees drawn up to her chest and her arms tucked around her legs. Dave's steady breathing told her he'd quickly fallen into a deep sleep. He needed it. They both did. But just for now, all she wanted to do was stare at him.

His body was little more than silhouette, but even that much was impressive—strong shoulders and a broad, muscled back tapering down to his waist. He was hugging the pillow where he lay, his arms flexed, biceps bulging. She thought maybe he was the most beautiful man she'd ever seen, and she'd seen her share. That was part of the problem, of course—that she was so attracted to him and always had been, so much so that she was in danger of losing her head every time she even thought about him touching her.

She leaned her head back against the wall with a weary sigh, so tired she could barely keep her eyes open. She'd gotten so caught up in the spell of it, in the desire she'd felt for him since she was eighteen years old, that she'd have done anything to have him tonight. But that meant that tomorrow would only be that much more painful. She had no doubt that Dave would feel guilty when he thought about Carla and angry at Lisa for pushing him into betraying her memory. Neither of those things was the least bit justified, but that wouldn't stop him from feeling them just the same.

She lay down and pulled the covers over her, resisting the urge to reach out and touch him as he slept. Instead, she closed her eyes, telling herself that it was time to stop with the adolescent fantasies. Right now she saw him as some kind of knight in shining armor, but that wasn't reality. It wasn't the long haul. In truth, he was a father and a family man, with the kind of nine-to-five existence that would only tie her down.

She'd built the kind of life she'd only dreamed about as a teenager. In a world where most people went to their graves never having accomplished anything they set out to do, she could hold her head up and say that she had. And she wasn't finished yet. Not by a long shot. She still had a hundred places she wanted to go, a thousand people she wanted to meet. There was always something new beyond the next horizon, something bigger, better, and more exciting than the place she'd just left.

She and Dave were on different tracks that had intersected for a few brief moments in time, but soon they'd be going their separate ways again. It could end no other way.

chapter twelve

Adam slowly became aware of pale rays of daylight warming his face and a gentle breath of air fanning around him. He opened his eyes, but his vision was blurry. His head hurt. God, how it hurt, as if somebody were pounding on it with a hammer from the inside out.

Where was he?

He turned his head to the left, where he saw a fuzzy blob that looked like an intravenous fluid bag. It said *hospital*. But something wasn't right. The bag was hanging from something unfamiliar. A coatrack?

He blinked to clear his sight, then slowly moved his gaze to the ceiling of the room, expecting to see a blank painted surface with fluorescent lighting. Instead the ceiling vaulted upward to bare wooden rafters. And the smell. It wasn't the antiseptic odor of a hospital room but something much warmer and fresher, like outdoors. Turning, he saw that instead of heavy draperies hanging over plate glass, lace curtains fluttered at an open window.

He looked down at himself, blinking again to clear his bleary eyes. A bandage was wrapped around his chest just under his arms, with another one lower that bound his left arm to his body, immobilizing it. Looking lower still, he saw a flowered sheet pulled up to his waist. Glancing around the room, he saw an oak dresser, an overstuffed chair, a small portable television. A quilt lay folded at the foot of the bed.

Slowly it came back to him, like a movie playing inside his head, first out of focus, then slowly becoming sharper. A gunshot. Falling down a rocky hillside. Lying at the foot of that hill, feeling his life draining away.

There's your explanation. You're dead, and this is heaven.

Nothing else made any sense, except he couldn't imagine heaven needing a hospital, even one as ethereal as this. Then he rolled his head to the right and decided that his afterlife theory was making more sense all the time.

Serafina Cordero was lying on the bed next to him.

One of her hands was curled beneath her chin, her eyes closed in sleep. Dark eyelashes fanned against olive skin, with long black-as-night hair that spilled across the flowered pillowcase beneath her head. Her other hand rested against his arm, slender fingers grazing his wrist.

Sera's house. How in the hell had he gotten here?

Putting a hand to his forehead, he felt a bandage, then moved his hand enough to realize that it wound completely around his head. He tried to sit up, but pain shot through his head and chest so wildly that it took his breath away. He fell back against the pillow, groaning softly.

Sera's eyes instantly fluttered open. She rose on one elbow, her hand tightening against his arm. "Adam?"

"Damn. Thought this was heaven." He let out a tortured breath. "Too much pain for heaven."

Sera sat up quickly, her brows pulled together with worry. She moved to the edge of the bed and grabbed a blood pressure cuff from the nightstand. She crawled back to Adam, wrapped the cuff around his arm, inflated it, then dropped the stethoscope to the inside crook of his elbow.

"Sera?"

"Hush."

She listened intently, then slipped the cuff off his arm, with a gentle breath of relief. She put her hand against his cheek again, then put a thermometer in his mouth.

"No fever," she said a minute later, and he could hear the relief in her voice. "How do you feel?"

He touched his fingertips gingerly to the bandage on his forehead. "Head hurts like hell," he said in a dry, raspy voice. "And my chest."

Sera reached for a glass of water and helped him drink. His head pounded unmercifully, but the water soothed his dry throat. He settled back against the pillow with a weary sigh.

"Do you remember what happened?" Sera asked.

"Gunshot," he said. "My chest. And I hit my head. . . ." He paused as the events slowly became clearer in his mind. "I fell down a hillside. How did I get here?"

"Gabrio brought you."

"Gabrio?"

"Yes. Do you remember that?"

No. Wait. Yes, he did. He remembered a voice coming out of nowhere. Now he realized it had belonged to Gabrio. *Dr. Decker. Hey, man. Can you hear me?*

Adam blinked, shifting a little in the bed, slowly becoming more lucid. Gradually it came back to him. Gabrio had made Ivan and Enrique believe he was dead, and then he'd brought him here. The reality of that struck Adam almost as hard as the gunshot had.

Gabrio had saved his life.

"Yeah," Adam said. "I remember."

"Gabrio told me some strange things," Sera said. "Something about counterfeit drugs, and he said that it's . . ." She paused for a moment, a disbelieving look on her face. "He said that it's Robert who wants you dead?"

Adam nodded. He put his hand to his forehead. Jesus *Christ*, he had a headache. And every breath he took shot pain through his chest.

"Then it's true? And he sabotaged Lisa's plane?"

Lisa. Robert had killed her. Adam felt a swell of sorrow mingling with cold, stark anger. She'd been such a good friend. And now she was gone.

"Yes," Adam said, closing his eyes. "It was Robert. He killed Lisa."

Sera slid her hand over his. Lisa had been almost as close as family to him, and he couldn't believe she was gone.

"Gabrio told me not to go to the authorities, because they're in on it, too," Sera said. "Is that true?"

Adam nodded. "Yeah. It's true."

"I don't believe this."

He gazed at the equipment that surrounded him. "Where did all this come from?"

"I took it from the clinic. Everything I thought I'd need."

"Robert will know things are missing," Adam said.

"But he won't know I took them."

So Sera had stolen equipment from Robert's clinic and used it to keep him alive. *How about that, Robert? Do you like irony?*

"Gabrio," Adam said. "Where is he now?"

"He stayed here with you until I got back with the supplies, and then he left. He was so scared. I don't know where he is now, but he told me that as soon as that gang he runs around with finds out that he let you live, they'll kill him." She paused. "Do you think that will actually happen?"

Adam thought about Ivan and Enrique, how they'd shown up at the clinic to carry out Robert's orders without question. In their world, loyalty was everything. And the moment Gabrio showed any disloyalty, he would be their next target.

"Yes."

"But Ivan—won't he protect him?"

"Ivan's the one Gabrio needs to be afraid of."

"Surely not. His own brother?"

"His own brother."

He could tell by the look on Sera's face that the very idea of that was unfathomable. She'd always been one of those rare people who believed in the good side of humanity, no matter how much inhumanity she saw.

The dark circles under her eyes told him just how tired she must be, but still she looked so beautiful to him. She always had. The very first time he'd seen her, everything else in her midst had seemed to pale in comparison. Two years had passed since he'd first met her, and nothing had changed. He still had the feeling that he could fill entire days doing nothing but staring at her pretty face.

"I can slip you out of town," she said. "Take you to Monterrey. No one will know."

"Eventually they'll find out," Adam said, his head still

pounding. "I have to find Gabrio. If he comes with us, he'll be safe."

"The only place you should be going is to a hospital. Besides, you can't show yourself in town. If Robert finds out you're alive, he'll come after you again."

"If anyone finds out I'm alive, that kid's going to die. I'm not going to let that happen."

"But you've been shot, Adam. You need treatment."

"Where exactly is the entry wound?"

"Below your shoulder, above your heart, thank God."

"Exit wound?"

"There isn't one. The bullet is still in there. You're at high risk for infection."

"What about my head wound?"

"You have a deep laceration. You could have a concussion, or even a delayed hematoma. You know how dangerous that can be."

"That's unlikely. My speech is fine, isn't it? And I'm moving all my extremities. How are my pupils?"

"Equal and reactive."

"No neurological damage, then."

"That's hardly conclusive. God, Adam, if you could have seen the blood . . . from your head, your chest . . ."

"Do I seem disoriented?"

"No." She paused, and he could tell she was searching for ammunition. "Not now. But you've been in and out for the past twenty-four hours. Any loss of consciousness is cause for concern."

Why did she have to have a nursing degree? This would be so much easier if she were an ignorant layperson and he could just pat her on the hand and tell not to worry. But no matter how frightened she was, he wasn't moving from this house until he could talk to Gabrio. He tried to take a deep breath, only to wince at the ache in his chest. If only his head would stop pounding . . .

"I can tell you're in pain," Sera said.

"It's tolerable."

"You need a CT scan. That's the only way to know for sure the extent of your injury. And you were hypotensive because of the blood loss. Hypotensive patients with head injuries have twice the mortality rate as—"

"I told you I'm not going anywhere without Gabrio."

"But you need to see a doctor!"

"I'll stay in this room for the rest of my life before I let that kid die."

"Stop it, Adam! Just stop it!"

Her voice was hushed, but the emotion behind her words exploded into the room. She took a deep, quivering breath. "I was so afraid to sleep. I woke up every hour and took your vital signs, gave you more fluids, and put God on overtime listening to my prayers. I didn't know what the bullet had done, because you kept drifting in and out of consciousness. I was so afraid I'd wake up . . ." She paused, her voice tight with despair. "I was afraid I'd wake up and find you dead."

As tears filled her eyes, the fear and concern he saw there went straight to his heart. He remembered waking to find her hand on his arm, as if she could keep him from slipping away from her as he slept if only she kept on touching him.

"When I heard that you'd been killed in that plane crash," she went on, "I can't tell you how I felt. For two days I mourned you, Adam. I cried until there wasn't a tear left in me to shed, and I can't do it again. I can't. Please, *please* let me take you to a doctor."

The idea of her sitting in this room, crying for his memory, made him wish he could take her in his arms and hold her until she forgot every bit of that. But no matter how much pain it caused her, caused both of them, Adam could not, *would* not, put Gabrio's life at risk, even if it meant he was in danger himself.

"I know you don't understand this, but it's because you weren't there. It was the most horrific thing you can imagine." He took her hand. "Robert called Ivan and Enrique. They came to the clinic a few minutes later. Armed."

Sera turned away. "Adam, please—"

"They tied my hands, drove me out to a secluded place. Made me get out of the car—"

"Please don't tell me this!"

"Look at me, Sera."

Slowly she turned back.

"They made me get out of the car. Shoved me to the edge of a hillside, ten paces away. Gabrio asked why. Ivan said, 'Blood spatters.' Then he shot me."

Sera put her hand against her mouth, tears filling her eyes. "If Gabrio cared so much, why didn't he stop them before they shot you?"

"Disloyalty is a capital offense. Gabrio couldn't have saved me. Ivan and Enrique are animals. No conscience. But Gabrio . . . Even with all that in his life, still there's something so good in that kid that when he was faced with a decision like that, he made the right one. He could have let Ivan put another bullet in me, but he didn't, even though he knew the danger it put him in. How can I do anything less for him now?"

Sera sat there for a long time, a battle clearly raging inside her. Finally she looked up again, her voice hushed with resignation. "You can't."

She wiped her eyes with shaky fingertips, then rose from the bed. "You need to eat. I'm going to go fix you something. Then this afternoon I'll go to Esmerelda's as if I'm returning to work. Ivan is always there, and Gabrio's usually with him. I'll find a way to pull him aside and talk to him without his brother around."

Adam felt a shot of apprehension. He hated that she had to work at Esmerelda's just to make ends meet, since nobody in Santa Rios could pay her what her services as a midwife were worth. And he hated it even more when men like Ivan came through the door.

"For God's sake, watch out for Ivan," he told her. "I've seen the way he looks at you. And now that I know just how ruthless he really is—"

"If you want me to talk to Gabrio, I have to make sure

where Ivan is first. I don't want him getting in the middle of things."

Adam finally nodded. "Just be careful."

She started to leave the room, then turned back. "What if Gabrio is so afraid of Ivan that he decided to run? What if I can't find him?"

"If that's what's happened, we'll deal with it. But try to find him. Please."

She stared at him a long time. "I wish you were more self-ish, Adam. I wish that just once you'd do what's best for you and say to hell with the rest of the world. Because if only you would do that, then maybe . . ." She paused, her voice chok-ing with emotion. ". . . maybe I wouldn't love you so much."

She slipped out the bedroom door and shut it behind her. Adam closed his eyes, remembering how he'd lain at the bot-tom of that hill last night, sure he was drawing his final breaths. To his surprise, it hadn't been Ellen's face that had filled his mind. It had been Sera's. That had to mean something.

Hell, yes, it means something, you idiot. You're in love with her, too.

Until this moment, he hadn't actually allowed his thoughts to go down that road. And now that they had, it scared the hell out of him, because just about any other man on the planet could give Sera more than he could ever hope to. And the mo-ment she realized that, she'd be gone.

Dave woke to a cool breeze, and he turned to see the glass door leading to the balcony standing wide open. He rose quickly to close it, only to see his clothes and Lisa's lying in heaps on the balcony. He slipped outside, grabbed them, then came back inside. He shut the door and locked it, drawing the drapes. Turning back, he saw Lisa lying in bed, awake and staring at him.

Suddenly everything that had happened last night came back to him in a blinding rush. After they'd come back up-stairs, just being in the same room with her had brought up fresh waves of guilt he hadn't wanted to face, and he'd been thoroughly convinced that she was the last woman on earth he should be making love to. Yet he had.

And he'd never felt anything like it before.

If he wanted to stretch his motivation to the breaking point, he might have been able to blame everything that had happened last night on two beers and one oversize shot of tequila, but he had nothing to blame it on now.

He approached the bed, already feeling himself getting hard again, knowing that as long as they were in this room together he wasn't going to stop wanting her. He wasn't even going to try.

He tossed their clothes at the foot of the bed, then stretched out beside her, leaning on one elbow. He slipped his hand beneath the covers and curled it around her rib cage, but just as he leaned in to kiss her she turned away, rolled over, and sat up on the edge of the bed.

"Wow," she said, stretching a little. "Nothing like a little hot sex to really wear a girl out." She turned around and flashed him a seductive smile. "That wasn't bad, Dave. Not bad at all."

Dave blinked with surprise, her flippant tone setting him on edge. She ran her fingers through her hair, then started to get up. He took hold of her wrist.

"What's the hurry?"

She eased from his grasp. "It's getting late, and we've got places to be."

"It's not all that late."

"I told that guy we'd be there at ten-thirty. It's nine now." She stood up, grabbed her clothes off the end of the bed, then went into the bathroom and closed the door behind her.

Dave felt as if she'd slapped him.

Contrary to what his brothers thought, there had been women in the past four years. But sex had seemed mechanical and lifeless, little more than a biological act, as if his brain wouldn't allow his body to truly engage. Last night had been different. His body had been engaged on every level, alive and screaming in every way.

But to Lisa it had clearly been no big deal. Something that

had been incredible to him had been just one more roll in the hay to her. And the thought of that left him feeling . . .

Hell, he didn't know how he felt about it. All he knew was that right now, as he pictured them flying back to San Antonio and eventually parting ways, he was struck by a sense of loss he hadn't anticipated.

Great sex. That's what you're going to miss.

He had to keep reminding himself that he wasn't dealing with reality right now. Not his reality, anyway. He had a life that centered around going to work, going home, taking care of his five-year-old daughter. For better or worse, his life had taken a narrow path that was pretty much cast in stone, and he took the responsibility of it seriously.

Lisa's lifestyle couldn't be more different. Disappearing at a moment's notice. Refusing to be tied down. Scoffing at responsibility and soaring into the clouds.

The irony was almost painful. The things that attracted him to her—her passion, her independence, her free spirit—were the very things that had led her to the life she lived, a life she'd made very clear that she had no intention of giving up.

Last night she'd given him every man's dream—hot, breathless sex with no strings attached. He'd even gotten to play the bonus round, but now the game was over. If he were smart, he'd consider himself lucky and get on down the road.

chapter thirteen

Two hours later, Dave and Lisa took off from a commuter airport in Monterrey in a tiny single-engine four-passenger plane. Dave wasn't altogether thrilled about flying in an aircraft so small, but the day was bright and clear and the plane was comfortable and Lisa certainly seemed to know what she was doing. In spite of the fact that she still wore his shirt, which was several sizes too large for her, she sat with the confident bearing of a person who was born to be in a pilot's seat. As the city of Monterrey fell away beneath them and they climbed toward the clouds, he felt how much she loved to fly. Exhilaration seemed to ooze right out of her.

"This is the first time you've flown since your crash," he said. "Any problem with that?"

"Nope."

"Confidence still there?"

"Why not? It wasn't my screwup. Give me a flyable plane, and I'll keep it aloft. Give me one with water in its fuel tanks, and there's not much I can do."

"That's how they sabotaged you?"

"That's sure what it felt like. The engine cut out until I swapped the fuel tanks. It was okay for a while, then cut out again. Eventually I had no engine at all. I didn't see water on the preflight, but if they'd tinted it blue, I wouldn't have."

"That's pretty insidious."

"It's Robert Douglas, through and through." She turned to face him. "So, Dave. Ever fly in a private plane before?"

"Nope. This is a first." He looked around, then pointed to the stick beside her. "Is that the throttle?"

"Right. Push to increase power; pull back to decrease."

She showed him the various gauges—altimeter, fuel, oil pressure, heading and airspeed indicators, and about ten others he couldn't keep track of.

"And here are the flaps," she said. "They allow you to stay aloft at slower speeds for landing. And the yoke," she said, patting her hands against the thing that looked like a steering wheel, "is to bring the nose of the plane up or down. Push it forward to tip the nose down, and pull back to bring the nose up. But not too far, or you'll stall."

"Stall? What's that?"

Without a word, she eased the yoke back, tipping the nose of the plane up.

"What are you doing?" he asked.

She kept pulling back. The nose kept rising. Soon Dave felt as if they were climbing the first hill on a roller coaster, and he'd always been able to do without roller coasters.

"Lisa?"

She pulled back more. The plane climbed through a low bank of clouds. Then Dave felt a slight shudder. "Uh . . . Lisa?"

The shuddering intensified. They kept climbing. All at once an alarm went off, a deafening *booop, booop, booop* noise that Dave translated as: *We're going to die.*

"Lisa. This can't be good."

She continued to climb.

"Lisa!"

Still they were climbing, with the plane at an even sharper angle than before and the alarm still wailing. Dave held his breath, closing his fingers around the seat in a death grip. *My God. You knew she was impulsive. You didn't know she had a death wish.*

Then she pulled back the tiniest bit more, and all at once it was as if they'd hit the top of that roller coaster. There was a momentary feeling of floating. Then the plane's nose tilted down hard, and they were falling.

"Holy *shit!*" Dave clutched the door beside him, his stomach soaring right up between his ears in a nauseating rush. As the plane plummeted through the clear blue sky, he was sure he was on the verge of drawing his last breath.

"Lisa!" he shouted. "What's happening? *Lisa!*"

She reached for the throttle and pushed it forward. The plane's engine *vroomed*, and they pulled out of the dive and leveled out from the gut-wrenching drop in a huge parabolic swoop.

After a moment, they resumed flying as they had before, with everything calm and sedate and blessedly removed from the jaws of death. It took Dave a good ten-count to pry his fingers away from the door and relax the expression of sheer panic that had frozen onto his face.

He turned to Lisa. "What the hell was *that*?"

"A stall." She looked at him innocently. "You asked what one was, didn't you?"

"Did I ask you to *demonstrate* it?"

"No," she said. "That was a bonus."

"That was dangerous as hell!"

"Nope. Not dangerous at all. Well, I suppose it could be if the plane was a little too close to the ground. You've got to watch it on landing. Go too slow with the nose too high, and it's all over. At greater angles, the wing produces less lift and more drag. The more drag, the slower the speed, so the wing gives even less lift. Pretty soon you're not flying anymore."

"Hence the nosedive."

"Exactly."

Dave let out a long breath. "I don't know if you've noticed, Lisa, but I'm not exactly one to engage in thrill-seeking behavior."

She flashed him a smile, apparently thinking she was quite the humorist. "Maybe you need to expand your horizons a little."

"I just want to keep from crashing *into* the horizon."

"Not a problem. Just settle back and enjoy the ride."

"Which was exactly what I was doing before you put this thing on red alert."

"Yeah. It really got the old blood rushing, didn't it?"

There was nothing about this woman that didn't get his blood rushing. Absolutely nothing.

But now, in the aftermath of adrenaline shooting through every molecule in his body, he'd relaxed into a pleasant kind of state where his awareness felt heightened—colors seemed brighter, sounds sharper, and he swore he could smell the peach shampoo that Lisa had used this morning drifting across the cockpit. In the past couple of days, in spite of everything that had happened, or maybe because of it, he felt more alive than he had in a very long time.

"So do you do that to the doctors you fly into Santa Rios?"

"No. I figured if I scared the hell out of them they might not come back."

"So what led you to fly for a humanitarian organization, anyway?"

"Adam was the one who recruited me. He was my gynecologist, and he hit me up during my annual exam. He told me it wasn't often he got a woman with a pilot's license in a compromising position, one who just might be crazy enough to fly a handful of doctors seven hundred miles into the middle of nowhere. I thanked him for the left-handed compliment and started to get up. He grabbed my feet and told me he wasn't going to let me out of the stirrups until I said yes."

Dave grinned. "I thought I had power as a cop. Maybe I need to consider gynecology."

She smiled. "You know, I might not have let any other man live long enough to get those words out of his mouth. But Adam . . ." She shook her head. "I don't know. There was something about him. I'd always thought that all doctors were egotistical snobs, but I liked him from the beginning. These days most women would rather go to a woman gynecologist, which has hurt some of the male ones. But Adam had patients lined up around the block. And you should have seen him at the clinic. His patients loved him, and little kids hung on him like fleas on a dog." She paused. "Listen to me," she said quietly. "I'm talking about him in the past tense."

"We don't know for sure that he's dead, Lisa. We don't know what happened to him."

"Yes, we do," she said. "Robert got to him. I know he did. But I don't know how he could hurt Adam. He's one of the few people I've ever met who was really good at heart, and that *bastard* killed him. Just like he tried to kill me."

"Adam must have really been a good friend."

She glanced at him, and he was surprised to see tears welling up in her eyes. "The truth? Maybe my best friend."

Her best friend? He knew she was worried about Adam but didn't realize just how far that concern went. "You didn't tell me you were so close to him."

She swiped the back of her hand across her eyes. "I know."

"Why not?"

"I don't know," she said helplessly. "I just . . . I guess I was afraid of this."

"Of what?"

"Falling apart." She sniffed and wiped her eyes again. "I can't do this," she said, tightening her grip on the yoke. "I've got a plane to fly here."

"You and Adam," Dave said. "Were you ever . . . ?"

She glanced at him as if she didn't understand, then shook her head. "N-no. It was nothing like that. It was just . . . he was like a brother, I guess. Or how a brother should be."

"Almost like family."

"Yeah. He was. I even spent a couple of holidays with him and his sister's family in San Antonio. They were such nice people." Her eyes dropped closed. "Oh, God. I can only imagine how his sister feels right now. And she thinks he died in an accident. She needs to know the truth about that. But I guess I'm not sure exactly what the truth is."

Dave reached across the tiny cockpit and took Lisa's hand in his. She clung to it tightly.

"I'm sorry. I don't know why I'm doing this," she said.

"Because he was someone you cared about."

Lisa closed her eyes, her jaw tight, and he could tell she was trying desperately not to cry.

"You okay?"

"Yes. Of course."

Closing her eyes, she drew herself up with a deep breath,

then slowly let it out. When she opened her eyes again, her tears were under control.

"It's just a fact of life I need to accept," she told Dave, slipping her hand away from his. "People come. People go."

"Don't make light of it. You loved him."

"Yes, and sometimes I think it's just not worth it."

"Would you have traded not knowing him just to spare yourself the heartbreak of losing him?"

"I don't know. I only know how I feel now." She turned to him. "Is it worth loving somebody, even if he can be ripped away from you in the blink of an eye?"

"Yes. Of course it is."

"So is that how you felt when Carla was killed?"

Dave physically recoiled at the mention of Carla's name. "I felt a lot of things when Carla was killed. And I don't want to talk about any of it."

"Yeah, that's pretty much what you told me last night."

He felt her gaze on him, and suddenly the cockpit of this plane felt way too small.

"You must have loved her a lot," Lisa said.

Dave's jaw tightened involuntarily. "Of course I did."

"Everyone said you were the perfect couple." She paused. "I remember being so jealous of her in high school."

"You? Jealous of Carla?"

"Of course. Everybody liked her. She was pretty. She was popular. All the guys wanted girls like her." She paused. "Including you."

He stared out the windshield, his heart beating wildly, memories flooding inside him that he wished would disappear forever. "Sometimes things aren't always what they seem to be."

She gave him a sideways glance, and he could see the questioning look on her face. "What do you mean?"

"I mean that Carla and I had our problems just like everyone else."

"Like what?"

He was silent.

"You don't want to talk about it."

Yes. He did. He wanted to tell her everything about their marriage. All of it. But most of all, he wanted to tell her about the night Carla died—what he'd thought, how he'd felt, every dark, horrible detail. God, he wanted to *shout* it. But he'd never voiced any of that. Not once. To anyone. How was he supposed to explain something that he could barely acknowledge even to himself?

"Never mind," Lisa said, turning away. "It's just as well. It's really none of my business."

"Lisa—"

"No. Really. I mean, who am I, anyway? Somebody who popped into your life for a few days and is going to be popping right back out of it? Why would you want to spill your guts to me?"

"That's not it."

"Then what is it?"

What was it? Maybe it was the fact that she had no idea who she was talking to. Her image of him was so skewed that she'd probably never believe the truth. But she wasn't the only one. His friends, his family, his coworkers—not one of them understood what was inside his head. Not one.

"You think I'm a pretty nice guy, don't you?"

Lisa shrugged. "Of course you are."

"Think again."

She looked at him with surprise. "Sorry. You've lost me."

"A few days ago on the job," he said, "do you know what I did?"

"What?"

He stared straight ahead. "There was a guy sitting on a highway overpass, threatening to commit suicide. I asked him what the hell he thought he was doing sitting on that god-damned bridge, screwing up traffic and making life hell for half the cops and paramedics in the city." He paused. "Then I told him to go ahead and jump."

Lisa turned to him, blinking with surprise. "You what?"

"You heard me. I said every word of that, and more. At that moment, I didn't give a good goddamn if that man lived or died." He turned to her. "So what do you think of me now? Am I still Mr. Nice Guy?"

He could tell she was stunned, but she held her gaze steady. "Why did you say those things?"

"Because I can't stand dealing with helpless, needy people looking for attention who expect me to solve all their problems. That's why."

"You solved mine. How do you feel about that?"

The difference was so radical that he couldn't believe she was even asking that question. He saw nothing but a tremendously capable woman who had a setback but leapt right back on her feet the moment he gave her a hand up.

"You're not helpless and needy," he told her.

"I was two nights ago."

"Temporary situation. Big difference."

"How do you know the guy on the bridge wasn't going through a temporary situation?"

"I know. Believe me."

"Yeah. I guess you've seen a lot of that as a cop. So what happened? Was the guy okay?"

"Yeah. I pulled him back."

"Did he really want to kill himself?"

"Probably not."

"You've got years of experience. You knew that guy wasn't really going to do it. And you've had years of frustration, too, I'm sure, so you blew off a little steam. Quit beating yourself up about it."

"It was more than blowing off a little steam."

"Sorry. I'm going to need a little more convincing than that. Anyone who drops everything and travels seven hundred miles into the middle of nowhere to help me makes it to the top of my Nice Guy list every time."

If only she knew. If only she knew that what happened on that bridge was only a symptom of what had been eating away at him for the past four years.

No. Not four years.

Eleven years.

"Damn," Lisa said, checking her watch. "I've got to radio

U.S. Customs and let them know we're coming into the country, or I could get hit with a hell of a fine."

"You have to do that?"

"It's protocol. But it means that the customs officers will be there shortly after we land."

Good. And that was exactly what they wanted. The drugs were in Lisa's backpack in one of the rear seats of the plane. Dave wanted to have them close at hand to surrender just as soon as the plane landed. After he and Lisa told their story, there was no doubt that an investigation would ensue that would take Robert Douglas down and send him to prison for a very long time.

Thirty minutes later, Dave saw the city of San Antonio stretching out in the distance. Lisa radioed the tower at the commuter airport, and a few minutes later she was bringing the plane in. Dave looked down to realize that he'd grasped his knees so hard his knuckles had turned white.

Lisa turned to him. "Landing make you nervous?"

"Just watch where you're going, okay?"

She laughed softly.

"And none of that stall stuff."

"You sure? I could pull up a little—"

"Lisa!"

"Take it easy, Dave," she said with a smile. "Everything's under control."

He breathed deeply, gritting his teeth as the plane descended. Seconds later, she set it down on the runway so lightly that he barely felt the bump. He let out the breath he'd been holding.

"You're pretty good at that."

"Practice makes perfect."

Lisa slowed the plane, then turned it ninety degrees, and they taxied toward the terminal. Once there, she brought it to a halt. The moment she turned off the engine, Dave saw three men striding purposefully toward the plane.

"Customs agents?" he asked.

"Yeah," Lisa said, suddenly coming to attention.

"Three of them?" Dave said. "Is that normal?"

"Nope," Lisa said, her eyes wide with suspicion as they approached. "And usually they don't just hop right out here. You've got to wait a bit on them. Something's up."

One of the agents headed around the plane to Lisa's door. The other two came to Dave's.

The drugs. *Damn.* He had to get those drugs in hand before he met the agents. He quickly reached to the backseat.

"Freeze!"

Dave swung back around and looked out the passenger window, shocked as hell to be staring down the barrel of a gun.

"Step out of the plane!" the agent shouted. "Both of you!"

Holy shit. What the hell was going on here?

"Dave?" Lisa said, panic lacing her voice. "What do we do?"

"We've got no choice. Just do as they say."

"The drugs—"

"I can't get to them. They'll think I'm reaching for a weapon."

"But if they find them before we give them up—"

"Say nothing. Do you hear me? Let me handle this."

"Out of the plane *now*!" the agent shouted.

Dave unlocked his door and stepped out. The moment his feet hit the ground, the agent spun him around. "Hands on the plane!"

Dave started to pull his wallet from his hip pocket, then reminded himself that a move like that would be interpreted as a threat. He'd be facedown on the ground before he knew what hit him. Instead he held up his palms and tried to speak calmly.

"I'm a police officer. My ID is in my wallet."

"I told you to put your hands on the plane!"

He turned and rested his palms against the plane. The agent frisked him, extracted his wallet, then pulled his hands behind his back and clipped cuffs on. Looking through the windows of the plane to the other side, he could see Lisa undergoing the same treatment.

Dave turned back around. The agent flipped open Dave's wallet and stared at his badge with surprise. "You really are a cop?"

"Yes. Tolosa PD. Listen to me. There's something you need to—"

"Hey, Stevens!"

The agent turned his baffled gaze to the door of the plane, and for the first time Dave saw that while he was being frisked and cuffed the third agent had climbed inside. He'd pulled their bags from the backseat, and he was unzipping Lisa's backpack.

No. *No!*

Dave was stunned. There wasn't a way on earth that man could possibly know what it contained. No way. But any second now he was going to find out.

The magnitude of what was getting ready to happen struck Dave like a hammer blow, but there was nothing he could do to stop it. He started to shout, to say something, anything to keep the man from pulling those drugs out of the bag. But he was standing there in handcuffs. At this point, would they ever believe the truth?

A second later, the agent extracted the bag of tiny blue pills, holding them up with a small but triumphant smile.

"Bingo."

chapter fourteen

Dave spent the next few hours separated from Lisa, stuck inside a tiny interrogation room. He'd been inside plenty of rooms just like this one, but he'd had no idea what the view was like from the other side of the table. It gave him a smothering sensation, as if the room were closing in on him, growing smaller with every breath he took.

Right now he felt angry, frustrated, and humiliated. Already he'd been questioned repeatedly, and he was slowly coming to the conclusion that only a miracle was going to get them out of this one. He closed his hands into fists, then opened them again and ran his palms over his thighs, wishing he could hit something.

The customs agent didn't believe the story Dave was telling. Not one word of it. And still he didn't know how they'd known he and Lisa were carrying the drugs. It had been no random search. Those agents had come to their plane with information in hand, knowing what they were looking for. And they'd found it.

He wondered how Lisa was faring. Probably not very well. Patience and tolerance weren't her strongest characteristics. He only hoped that she was keeping her voice down and her emotions to herself and that she was telling the truth, because right now the truth was all they had.

A moment later, the customs agent came back into the room. He was an older man, balding, wearing a cheap suit that said customs agents didn't make much. But still he had a burn in his eyes, as if money was the least of what drove him to do his job.

He sat down in the chair opposite Dave, feigning a weary sigh. "Well, DeMarco, you'll be pleased to know she's letting you off the hook in there. She says you didn't know she was bringing the drugs back across the border. Of course, you've already told me otherwise."

So Lisa was trying to take the fall for him. Dave exhaled, rubbing his hand over his mouth.

"Am I confused, or is Ms. Merrick lying?" the agent asked.

"She's just trying to protect me. That's all. But neither of us is a drug counterfeiter. Robert Douglas is."

"Now, that's one point you do agree on. That Robert Douglas is the real villain here."

"Yes."

The agent sat back in his chair, tapping a pencil against his fingertips. "Yesterday an informant told border authorities to be on the lookout for you and Ms. Merrick. He suspected you would be transporting counterfeit drugs across the border."

"An informant?"

"Yes. His name is Robert Douglas."

Dave was so dumbfounded that for a moment he couldn't speak. But as he thought back over the last two days, slowly the chain of events became clear, and fury welled up inside him. Robert clearly understood a very basic principle of finger-pointing: He who accuses first wins.

That son of a bitch.

"Don't you understand what's going on here?" Dave said. "Douglas couldn't stop us from leaving town. He got worried that we'd make it across the border and tell our story, so he turned the tables on us."

"I don't know. That seems like a pretty ballsy move to me. How did he know for sure you were carrying the drugs?"

"He didn't have to know for sure. If we weren't, he was in the clear, because that meant we had no evidence that there was a counterfeiting ring at all. If we were carrying them, he could frame us. Either way, he wins."

The agent nodded thoughtfully. "That's an interesting scenario. Here's another one." He leaned forward and rested his forearms on the table. "Lisa Merrick gets herself caught up in a Mexican drug war. She wants a bigger cut, so she decides to double-cross the ringleaders of the operation and walk off with a hundred thousand dollars' worth of the stuff herself. Easy to do, since she's a pilot. She's going to fly the drugs right out of there. Unfortunately for her, they find out what she's up to and sabotage her plane."

"With a huge shipment of their drugs aboard?"

"Maybe they didn't know she had it with her at the time. Or maybe that shipment was a drop in the bucket to them and they were merely out for revenge. Those people don't take kindly to disloyalty." He sat back in his chair and folded his arms. "Somehow she manages to survive her plane going nose-first into that river. But now she's trapped. She can't show her face because the minute she does, she's a dead woman. So who does she call? You. With some big sob story about drug counterfeiting, sabotage, and attempted murder. You bite, go to Mexico, get her out, but Robert Douglas finds out she wasn't really killed in that plane crash and suspects she's up to something. He finds out that she might be going back across the border with counterfeit drugs, so he tips us off."

"That's crap. He tipped you off because he was afraid of going down himself. Can't you see that?"

The agent gave Dave yet another weary sigh, one of those that said, *I'm being very patient here, but my patience is wearing thin.* "The only person you say can back up your story is Adam Decker. Unfortunately, our information says that he was killed in the plane crash."

"I told you he was never on that plane," Dave said, his own patience wearing thin. "But by now, it's possible that Douglas has killed him, too."

"Ms. Merrick makes the same assertion. But you have absolutely no evidence of Douglas's involvement. She says she had the defibrillator that contained the drugs in the plane with her, yet she escaped the cockpit with only her backpack. No defibrillator. On the other hand, we have all the evidence in the world that you're involved. You're holding the merchandise."

"We were shot at as we left Santa Rios," Dave told the agent. "The local cops are on Douglas's payroll."

"So you said. But do you know that for sure? Or did the local cops merely spot Ms. Merrick on her way out of town and go after a member of a local drug-counterfeiting operation?"

Dave knew he was fighting a losing battle. If only they'd been able to hand over the drugs voluntarily and tell their story as they'd planned, the agents would have assumed they were telling the truth. But once the agents approached the plane, guns drawn, their theory already in place, he and Lisa hadn't stood a chance. And now, no matter what story they told, the customs agents could twist it around to fit any scenario they wanted.

"The truth is that you really don't know where Adam Decker is, do you?" the agent asked. "For all you know, he could have died in that plane crash and Ms. Merrick is feeding you a line of bullshit." He kept tapping that pencil against his fingertips until Dave wanted to rip it out of his hands. "Actually, when it gets right down to it, you don't know a damned thing about this situation outside of what she's told you. Isn't that true?"

Yes. It was. And in Dave's mind it didn't change a thing.

"What did Lisa supposedly do to make Douglas suspect her of being in the middle of a counterfeiting operation?"

"We don't know the whole story yet. But when we get a tip from a credible source, we act on it. He's a doctor running a humanitarian organization. I'd call that credible."

"And I'm a cop, for God's sake! Doesn't that count for something?"

Another sigh, accompanied by a rub to the back of the neck. Then the agent leaned forward and dropped his voice.

"Just between you and me, DeMarco, I don't think you're a drug smuggler. I think you believed her story. I think you're just one hell of a bad judge of character. In the future, you might want to think twice about the women you keep company with."

"You don't know what the hell you're talking about."

"Really?" the agent said, feigning surprise. "Tell me. How well do you know Ms. Merrick?"

"She was a friend of mine in high school."

"Have you seen her in the interim?"

"No."

"Then you're not really sure what she's been up to since graduation."

"No. Not specifically."

"Can you say for sure what she actually planned on doing with those drugs when you landed in San Antonio?"

"Yes. Turning them in to you."

"You're speculating."

"Come on! Wouldn't it be pretty stupid of her just to walk off with those drugs instead of handing them over as she said she was going to? Wouldn't I have questioned that? I'm a cop, for God's sake!"

The agent smiled knowingly. "But you're a man first, aren't you?"

"What the hell are you saying?"

"A hot little number like that could lead a man to believe just about anything, now couldn't she?"

Dave stared at him evenly, willing himself not to react, when what he really wanted to do was vault over the table and take this sarcastic asshole by the throat.

"Tell me what's going to happen now," he said, barely able to grind out the words without adding a string of profanity.

The agent looked exasperated, but this time there was no faking it. "We did a field test of the drugs. As a police officer, you're probably aware that on cursory examination we can identify only about six of the usual suspects—amphetamines, Valium, that kind of thing. So we found what we expected to find. Nothing. It'll take further testing to determine whether they contain an illegal substance, but I fully expect that to be ruled out. I think they're simply Lasotrex knockoffs, just as you and Ms. Merrick have been saying, and there's a counter-feiting operation going on." He tossed his pencil down on the table, blowing out a long breath. "Unfortunately, it's not a crime to possess look-alike drugs. You can go to your basement and make as many phony Lasotrex as you want to. It's only a crime if you choose to sell or distribute them, which is exactly what I believe Ms. Merrick intended to do. But since we have no evidence at this point to support that, we can't hold either of you."

Then the agent leaned toward Dave, a no-nonsense look on his face. "But make no mistake. There will be an investigation. And the moment that investigation implicates Ms. Merrick in a drug-counterfeiting conspiracy, which I fully expect it will, we'll be back to see her. And if it turns out that you really are part of it, we'll take you down right along with her."

The good news was that Robert apparently hadn't given the authorities any information to further implicate Dave and Lisa. But he had no doubt it was coming. Not only would Robert be covering his tracks, he'd undoubtedly be planting evidence to frame them. Once the heat was off, he could re-open business in another area and proceed as if nothing had ever happened, leaving them to take the fall.

Dave sat up straight. "I assume I'm free to go?"

"Yes. But I suggest you leave by the back door. Don't know how the press does it sometimes. They're already here asking questions about this one."

"What?"

"Hey, it's interesting news. A woman flying for a humanitarian organization supposedly dies in a plane crash, only to show up alive at a San Antonio airport with a stash of illegal drugs? Doesn't get much better than that."

Oh, that was just *great*.

Dave knew every government agency had its informants who made a buck or two on the side by tipping off reporters to any big story that happened to come through. Only now, unbelievably, he was part of one of those big stories. It would be all over town in no time. Hell, what was he saying? With cable news, it could end up all over the freaking world.

"Of course," the agent added, "your superiors will be notified of the detention, along with the fact that you're a possible suspect in a counterfeiting case. What they choose to do to you in light of that is up to them."

Dave pictured this going right up his chain of command all the way to the chief, his name being dragged through the mud. The very thought of that made him sick with humiliation.

He stood up, ready to get the hell out of there.

"One more thing." The agent came to his feet and circled the table, shoving his hands into his pants pockets. "Let me give you a little advice, DeMarco. Back away from her. As far and as fast as you can. Your attorney will be able to make a strong case for you not knowing Ms. Merrick's true motive in this situation." He paused. "Of course, if you'd like to go ahead and give me something I can use against her, anything she might have told you that could help us, I can virtually guarantee that you won't be charged."

"There's nothing to tell. Lisa is innocent. Sooner or later you're going to see that."

The agent gave Dave a sarcastic little smile of indulgence. "To tell you the truth, I think you're the one who needs to see things a little more clearly."

"What's that supposed to mean?"

"It means," the agent said, "that I'm not sure you know her as well as you think you do."

"What are you talking about?"

"I might have cut her a little more slack. Maybe even been inclined to think there was a possibility she was telling the truth." He paused. "Then we ran her priors."

Dave felt a shiver of dread. "What?"

"Eleven years ago. She was convicted of cocaine possession."

At four o'clock that afternoon, Sera parked her car in the lot behind Esmerelda's, a tidy little bar and grill whose name was a holdover from three owners ago. The proprietor now was Ario Delmiro, a large man with a booming voice and a big heart who had owned the place for a year and a half but was probably going to lose it in a matter of months if he didn't start collecting bar tabs. She hoped that didn't happen, though, because he'd always been good to her, allowing her to slip away whenever one of her mothers-to-be went into labor.

She'd stayed close by Adam all day, monitoring his vital signs, becoming more hopeful the more alert he became. But she knew that his condition could turn around quickly if he developed any complications, and she was desperate to get him to a hospital as soon as possible. He still had a bullet in his chest. And what about his head wound? Was he as stable as he was trying to make her believe? Or was he a ticking time bomb waiting to explode?

I'll stay in this room the rest of my life before I'll let that kid die.

She knew Adam meant every word of that. But every moment he stayed in Santa Rios was another moment he could be discovered, so time was not on her side. She had to find Gabrio as quickly as possible and get both him and Adam out of here.

She went in through the kitchen door and grabbed an apron. Ario saw her and came over, wiping his hands on a dish towel.

"Sera! Thank God you're back! Full house out there. I need you. Feeling better now?"

She'd felt bad lying to Ario about being sick so she could stay with Adam, especially since several of his other employees routinely feigned sickness for no other reason except that they didn't feel like coming in.

"A little," she said. "But I'm missing those tips, you know. Had to get myself back in here."

She slid out the swinging door into the bar and immediately spotted Ivan sitting with a couple of the usual suspects—Enrique Flores and Juan Atilano. They were all good-for-nothing men who spent their afternoons and evenings drinking and playing cards, charging themselves up for late night mayhem. Unfortunately, she didn't see Gabrio with them.

She edged up next to Gloria, one of the other waitresses, and told her she'd take over Ivan's table. Gloria practically kissed her. The big tips they left rarely compensated for their sexual come-ons, and Gloria had clearly had enough of their wandering hands for one shift.

Sera went over to Ivan's table with an offhand hello and an

offer to bring them another round. Ivan gave her a protracted stare, shifting his eyes up and down, a lecherous smile seeping over his lips. He was one of those men who looked at a woman with one thing on his mind and one thing only. That little up-and-down glance was designed to intimidate her and at the same time indicate his considerable sexual prowess. Or so he thought.

"Where you been?" Ivan asked. "Haven't seen you around here in a couple of days."

She picked up the empty beer bottles from the table. "I've been sick."

"Well," he said, slinking his hand around the back of her thigh. "You're looking pretty good now."

Sera eased away from him, fighting the disgust that swelled inside her.

"Come on, now," Ivan said, his voice low. "You'll like what I've got to offer."

"I'm a busy woman," Sera said. "No time for fun, you know?"

Ivan took a sip of his beer. "You don't know what you're missing."

No. Sera knew exactly what she was missing. And she intended to keep on missing it.

She emptied an ashtray. "So where's your kid brother? He's usually here with you."

"Funny thing. He's been sick, too. Flu or something. Hasn't left the house in a couple of days."

He didn't run. Thank God. "So he's at home?"

"Yeah. He's at home."

Sera felt a surge of optimism. This was better than she could have hoped for. She knew Ivan's pattern. He'd spend a couple more hours drinking and maybe playing a few hands of poker, then head out for whatever evening activities he and his buddies had planned. If she left right now, she could slip over to their house and talk to Gabrio before Ivan even thought about returning home.

"Hey, Ivan," Enrique said. "She sure seems interested in your kid brother. Think maybe she's looking for a real man?"

Enrique and Juan laughed, and Ivan glared at them.

"A woman throws you over for your baby brother," Juan said, shaking his head. "Pitiful, man. That's really pitiful."

The men laughed again. Ivan sat back in his chair with a scowl, gripping his beer bottle with white-knuckled intensity. He slid his hand along the back of Sera's thigh again, but this time his fingers were spread, holding her in a bruising grip.

"So what's the deal?" Ivan said. "Do you like boys, or do you like men?"

"I was just concerned that Gabrio was sick. Are you taking care of him?"

"I told you. It's just a bug. What's there to do? Stand around and watch him throw up?"

"I suppose you're right." She extricated herself from Ivan's grip. "I'll bring you another round."

She could feel Ivan's gaze boring into her as she walked away, but she wouldn't be around much longer to have to deal with him. After she brought them their drinks she slipped into the kitchen and found Ario.

"I'm so sorry," she said, putting on a pained expression at the same time she was pulling off her apron. "I thought I could handle working today. But, Ario, I feel lousy. Really lousy. I'm afraid I'm still just too sick."

His face fell. "No! Sera! We're so busy! I need you out there!"

"I really am sorry," she said, grabbing her purse and heading for the back door. "Really. I hate to leave you like this, but I'm sure I'll be fine again by tomorrow. I'll see you then, okay?"

She hated lying to him, but she had no choice. Over his protests, she slipped out the back door and headed for her car.

In minutes, she'd reached Gabrio's house—a tiny run-down cinder-block structure in a neighborhood nice people would take great pains to avoid. She parked out front and stepped up to the porch.

She knocked. Waited.

Nothing.

She knocked again. *Please be home. . . . Please. . . .*

She listened for any movement inside the house. She heard nothing.

When she knocked for the third time, she came to the ominous realization that this wasn't going to be as simple as she'd hoped. Gabrio's car was here, but he wasn't answering the door.

Peering through the window, she saw the interior of the dilapidated little house. The television was on. An ashtray on the coffee table held the butt of a cigarette, still smoldering. Gabrio was definitely home, but he was nowhere to be seen. Sera looked through the doorway into the kitchen, then craned her neck around and managed to see part of the way down the hallway leading to the bedrooms. Nothing.

She believed that Gabrio might be sick, but she doubted that the flu had anything to do with it. She remembered the crushing fear that had been in his eyes when he'd brought Adam to her—the look of a person who's in the middle of something dark and hideous and doesn't know how to get out of it. Any sickness he was experiencing right now was probably the result of guilt and horror all meshed together until it had incapacitated him. He wouldn't answer the door because he was afraid Adam was dead. Or that he was still alive. Maybe both.

She banged on the door again. "Gabrio! Please answer the door! Please! I have to talk to you!"

She tried the door. It was locked. She knocked on it again, then took one more look through the window.

Gabrio was peering through the doorway leading to the hall.

As he came into the living room and walked slowly to the front door, her heart leapt with hope. The lock clicked, and he opened the door a crack. His face was tight and drawn, with dark circles under his eyes, and when he spoke his voice was coarse and raspy.

"What do you want?"

"Let me in, Gabrio. Please. I need to talk to you."

He swallowed hard. "Adam's dead, isn't he?"

"No! He's alive. For now, he's okay. But I need to get him to a hospital in Monterrey. We want you to come with us."

Gabrio blinked with surprise. "Come with you?"

"I know you're afraid of your brother. You should be. Once it comes out that Adam is alive, he'll hurt you. You have to get out of here."

"No. My brother won't hurt me."

"When you brought Adam to me, you said he would."

"No," he said sharply. "I shouldn't have said that. My brother would never hurt me. Never."

"Then you've told him you saved Adam's life?"

Gabrio's jaw trembled. "N-no. Not yet."

"If you're so sure he'll protect you, then why haven't you told him?"

Tears gathered in his eyes. He tried to push the door closed, but she put her hand against it.

"Gabrio. Please listen to me. Adam refuses to leave unless you come with us."

"No. It's a trick of some kind. You want me to give my brother up for what he did. That's why you're here, isn't it?"

"No! I just want you to leave with us! That's all! We just want you to be safe!"

"I told you Ivan shot him, and now you want to make him pay for it. But I'm not telling anyone else what happened, no matter what! I'm not giving my brother up!"

Gabrio slammed the door and locked it. Sera pounded on it again. "Gabrio, please!"

"Go away!"

"Gabrio!"

She heard his footsteps fade away as he disappeared into the hall again. She turned and leaned against the door, frustration running wild inside her. She had no choice but to go home and tell Adam that she'd failed. And that meant that he would refuse to leave town and get medical attention, which meant he was still in danger.

This nightmare was never going to end.

Sera got into her car. Ten minutes later, she pulled up to her house and went inside. She heard the low hum of the television in her bedroom upstairs. She came into the room to find

Adam propped up against the headboard, a look of hopeful expectation on his face.

He muted the television. "Did you talk to him?"

She came over and sat down on the bed next to him. "Yes. He refuses to come with us."

Adam looked at her incredulously. "But he knows he might be killed as soon as I show myself!"

"He thinks we want him to come with us so we can force him to testify against his brother. And he refuses to do that."

"Are you kidding? He ought to be telling the whole damned world what his brother did. And he ought to be running from him as fast as he can."

"Adam, you've seen this before. I know you have. Kids always refuse to tell doctors what their abusive parents have done to them. All they want to do is go back home. It's the only life they know, no matter how horrible it is. Gabrio is no different. No matter how much he knows in his heart that his brother will hurt him, he can't admit it. And he can't conceive of anyone wanting to help him, because nobody has ever given a damn about him before."

Adam shook his head. "He's so scared. The poor kid is so scared that he's not thinking straight."

"Yes. I know. I don't want him hurt any more than you do, but right now he's so lost and confused that we might never get through to him."

"We have to think of another way."

Sera sighed heavily. "There may not be another way."

"God, Sera, how in the hell did this happen? He's going to die, and I can't do anything about it."

Sera was silent. She had no idea what to say.

Adam nodded toward the television. "I was watching the news. You'll be pleased to know my memorial service is scheduled for Thursday morning in San Antonio." A look of anguish crossed his face. "My sister. I wish I could tell her I'm alive, but I don't dare. Not yet. God, I can't even imagine how she feels right now."

She slid her hand over his arm. "Adam, I don't want Gabrio

hurt any more than you do, but the time may come, very soon, when you'll have to think about leaving him behind."

"I can't."

"You may not have a choice."

Adam shook his head in frustration. Then his gaze drifted toward the television, and his eyes suddenly widened. "Sera. Look."

She turned, shocked to see a familiar face on the screen.

Lisa Merrick.

Adam fumbled for the remote and turned up the sound.

". . . pilot for a humanitarian organization who was presumed to have died in a plane crash in central Mexico two days ago surfaced alive and well today, only to be arrested in San Antonio on suspicion of drug smuggling. . . ."

Adam stared at the screen with an expression of shocked disbelief. "My God. It's Lisa. She's alive."

chapter fifteen

By the time Lisa arrived at her apartment, it was nearly five o'clock. She'd never spent a more horrendous three hours in her entire life—three long, unbearable hours filled with accusations she'd had to endure, anger she'd had to swallow, and anxiety she'd felt at the thought that Dave was being questioned at the same time she was, with the same accusations being thrown at him as were being thrown at her.

And Robert Douglas was the one who'd tipped off the customs agents.

The very idea that he'd have the audacity to turn the tables on them so completely flabbergasted her. But it hadn't taken long for her surprise to turn to anger. He may have won this battle, but somehow, someway, she was going to make certain he lost the war.

Right now, though, she had a king-size headache and her mind felt muddled, just as it had felt for the past three hours. Out of desperation that Dave not be dragged down with her, she'd told those agents over and over that he had nothing to do with it, that she alone had knowledge of the drugs in her backpack. But they clearly didn't believe her. And it was probably because Dave was in there telling the truth. But then, had she really expected him to do anything else?

They told her he was going to be released, just as she was, but she was terrified to see him. She couldn't bear the look that was sure to be on his face, the one that said, *All I did was try to help you, and this is what I get?*

If he was smart, he was on his way to San Antonio International right now and before the day was out he'd be back in

Tolosa where he belonged. She wished she'd never called him that night, wished he'd never come to Santa Rios, wished she was still sitting at that abandoned mining camp, injured and delirious, even if it meant dying there. Anything but having him facing a prison sentence because of her.

She'd taken a cab from the airport to Blue Diamond Aviation, where she'd managed to pick up her car without running into anyone she knew. They'd hear soon enough that she was alive. They'd also hear she'd been detained on drug charges, and she certainly didn't want to talk to anyone about that.

She strode up the sidewalk leading to her apartment, and as she approached her front door she turned and saw somebody sitting on the porch railing. Her heart skipped wildly.

Dave.

He just sat there, his arms folded and his eyes narrowed, his angry expression sending an avalanche of anxiety plundering through her. He rose slowly. She started to unlock her apartment door, then thought better of it. She turned and faced him, her back to the door.

He approached her, his gait slow and threatening. "Open the door."

"Why are you here?"

"We have some talking to do."

She felt a jolt of apprehension. "About what?"

He inched closer, his jaw tight with anger. "I've got something to say to you, Lisa, and I can't guarantee it won't be at the top of my lungs. So unless you want your neighbors to wander out here to find out what all the commotion's about, you'd better open the door."

With every word he spoke, Lisa felt the weight of guilt press against her until she could barely breathe. She turned, her hands shaking, and opened the door. She went inside and headed straight for the kitchen. She heard Dave close and lock the door and drop his bag beside it, then heard his footsteps behind her. She tossed her backpack onto the kitchen table. When she turned back, his expression had become positively glacial.

"Tell me about your drug conviction."

Lisa felt as if the floor had fallen out from beneath her feet. She would have done anything—anything—to keep him from finding out about that, but apparently the customs officials had filled him in.

"It doesn't matter now," she told him.

His eyes widened. "Doesn't matter? What do you mean, it doesn't matter? Did you think you could just hand those drugs over to the customs agents and accuse Robert of counterfeiting without them finding out you'd been convicted of a drug offense?"

She blinked. "What?"

"What's the first thing they do when somebody blows a whistle? They check out the whistle-blower! Even if you hadn't been accused of the crime yourself, the minute they found out you had a drug conviction any credibility you had while trying to take Robert down would have been shot to hell. And now that you've been accused," he said, glaring at her, "let's just say that they're not the least bit inclined to believe anything you say."

She raised her chin, her voice quivering. "So they told me."

"I want to know what happened. Tell me how in the hell you got convicted of cocaine possession. And by God, you'd better tell me the truth."

"I suppose all you want is the facts."

"That's a damned good start."

"Fine. I was at my brother's apartment. The police stormed the place. Lenny was caught dealing for the fourth time, which meant he bought a fifteen-year prison sentence. They found five grams of cocaine in my purse. I was convicted of possession and got probation."

"Were you using cocaine?"

"Would you believe me if I told you no?"

"To tell you the truth, right now I don't know what to believe."

She glared at him. "Then nothing I say will make any difference, will it?"

"Lisa," he said, his voice escalating, "if you want me to

believe you were innocent of those charges, you'd better start talking!"

"I don't give a damn *what* you believe!"

He stared at her in silence, his face tight with anger. "Fine. Just forget it. I shouldn't have come here in the first place. There's a seven-thirty flight to Dallas. I intend to be on it."

He started out of the kitchen, and suddenly Lisa couldn't bear the thought of it ending this way between them. He'd been like a lifeline to her, a lifeline she was watching slip right out of her grasp.

"Dave. Wait."

He stopped and turned back, his face fixed in a harsh frown. She shouldn't have to defend herself against accusations that weren't true. Damn it, she just shouldn't have to. But she didn't want Dave walking out of here thinking she was guilty of anything.

"It happened the summer after our high school graduation," she said. "I wanted out of Tolosa, but I had almost no money and nowhere to go. So I took a chance and called Lenny in San Antonio. He told me I could stay with him as long as I wanted to."

"I'm listening."

"I figured if I could stay with him, I could save more money and be able to take flying lessons sooner." She paused. "And Lenny was my brother. I hadn't seen him in years. All of a sudden we were together again, and we were actually talking. I remember feeling so excited that my life had finally taken a turn for the better."

"So what happened?"

Lisa closed her eyes. It was a memory she had no desire to dredge up. "The day after I moved in, guess who showed up? The police. They decided it was a good time to raid a drug dealer."

Dave stared at her for several seconds, his angry gaze faltering. "Was it true? He was still dealing drugs?"

"Oh, yeah. Big-time."

"So you were caught up in it, too?"

"Yeah. And my brother, who'd been oh, so nice to me,

didn't think twice about stuffing five grams of coke into my purse to get rid of it, then swearing it wasn't his. That was the least of what he had hidden around his apartment."

"He took you down with him?"

"Yes. Even when he could have told them I had nothing to do with it, he didn't. I was lucky I was charged only with possession. But do you want to know the bad part? I actually thought that he'd changed and that somehow, someway, I could have an actual relationship with my brother. Can you imagine anyone being that stupid?"

Dave just stood there, stunned. As tears filled Lisa's eyes, he imagined her going to Lenny's house and the glimmer of hope she must have felt when it looked as if she had at least one family member who was going to act like family. Instead, he'd handed her yet one more reason never to trust anyone again as long as she lived.

"I knew what he was," she went on. "I *knew*. But what did I do? I walked right into his life like some kind of fool and ended up getting taken down right along with him." Her jaw trembled. "Maybe you did the same thing."

"What?"

"If you hadn't come to help me, you wouldn't be in this mess. Instead, you're taking the fall right along with me." She wiped her eyes, swallowing her tears. "You need to go home, Dave. Go home to your family where you belong."

Common sense told him she was right, but something far more powerful was keeping him from walking out the door. Every step of the way, this situation had grown more chaotic, and he'd gotten dragged into it right along with her. Further association with her could only hurt him in the eyes of the law. He should be on his way home to Tolosa by now, to a life that didn't get him personally involved in crap like drug convictions, attempted murder, and women who couldn't seem to stay out of harm's way. The only problem was that he felt an overwhelming need to be the one to keep her out of harm's way.

"I can't stand this, Dave," she said, her voice faltering. "I can't stand knowing that you might be facing a prison sentence when all you did was try to help me. I can't *stand* it!"

She turned away, her hand over her mouth, as if she was trying desperately to keep from crying. He reached out and touched her shoulder. She shuddered away from him.

"Don't. *Please* don't."

"Lisa—"

She spun back around. "Damn it, Dave! Will you just cut your losses and get out of here?"

Suddenly the telephone rang. They both turned to stare at it, and after a few seconds Lisa took a deep breath, swept her hair away from her forehead with a rake of her fingers, then picked up the phone and said hello. A moment later she froze, her eyes widening. She slid her hand against her throat, stumbled a few steps to the kitchen table, and collapsed on a chair, wearing a look of shock and disbelief. "Wh-what did you say?"

When Dave heard the tremor in her voice, he came to attention. "Lisa? What is it?"

She turned her tearful gaze up to meet his. "Adam is alive."

For the next ten minutes Lisa spoke to the person on the other end of the phone, her voice tight with emotion. Dave sat down beside her and listened to half a conversation that told him that while Adam Decker was alive, something was still terribly wrong. Finally, after a promise to call back, Lisa hung up the phone and sat back in her chair, looking completely overwhelmed.

"Who were you talking to?" Dave asked.

"Serafina Cordero. She's the one who's taking care of Adam."

"Did you talk to him, too?"

"For just a minute. My God. He's alive. Adam really is alive." She shook her head slowly with disbelief, tears filling her eyes again. She smiled briefly, then placed her hand against her chest, taking a deep breath. "He's alive. I just can't believe it."

"Tell me what's going on."

She sighed with weary relief. "I barely know where to start."

Little by little, she filled him in on the whole story, telling him that by the grace of a sixteen-year-old kid with a conscience Adam had survived the execution Robert had ordered. But now he refused to leave Santa Rios.

"What you're telling me," Dave said, "is that no matter what condition Adam is in, he won't leave without Gabrio?"

"Yes," Lisa said. "And Sera hasn't been able to convince him to come with them. But the clock's ticking. He still has a bullet in his chest, and she's afraid his head wound is worse than it appears to be. They won't know the extent of that until he has a CT scan. And every minute he's down there is another minute that Robert might find out he's still alive and come after him again."

Dave let out a long breath. He'd seen no-win situations before, but this one topped them all.

"I have to help them," Lisa said. "I have to get Adam to a doctor. And I have to talk to Gabrio. God, can you imagine how scared he must be right now?"

"Yeah, but what can you do from here?" Dave said.

A gleam of determination entered her eyes. "Nothing. That's why I'm flying back down there."

"You're flying—?" Dave shook his head. "No. It's not safe for you down there. If Robert or Ivan sees you, they'll kill you."

"They don't have to know I'm there," Lisa said. "I can fly down and help Sera talk Gabrio into coming along. I always knew he was a good kid, in spite of where he came from. What he did for Adam proves that. And he loved it when I took him up in my plane. He didn't admit it, but I could tell he did. He'll listen to me. I know he will."

"Surely if he thought his brother would kill him, he'd want out of there. He'd be grasping at straws. Looking for anyone to help him."

"It's the logic of the abused. No matter how impossible it seems, you always hold out hope." She paused. "You know. That your brother might not be as bad as you think he is."

Lisa's gaze never faltered, driving home her point, and he realized just how right she was.

"So you're going down there," he said.

"Yes. And if you're thinking of trying to stop me—"

"I'm not going to stop you." He let out a heavy sigh. "I'm going with you."

She turned away. "No. You need to go home. You have a family to think about, a daughter—"

"Do you really think I'd leave you at a time like this?"

"I don't want to hurt you any more than I already have. I have a drug conviction—"

"You were innocent. I know that now."

"You're taking my word for that."

"Yes. And that's good enough for me."

"I can't guarantee what we'll find down there. What will happen. We managed to get out of there once. Our luck just might run out."

He stroked a finger through the hair along her temple. She looked back at him.

"I'm not letting you go alone."

"But—"

"Do you want me to come?"

She stared at him plaintively, then looked away. "I can manage without you."

"I didn't ask you that. I asked you if you wanted me to come."

She opened her mouth to speak, then closed it again. Her rigid expression slowly melted into acceptance. "Yes. Of course I want you to come."

Dave shook his head slowly. "Why is that so hard for you to say? Didn't I tell you once that if you ever needed me I'd be there?"

"You fulfilled that promise already."

"Did I say anything about it being a onetime deal?"

"No."

"Okay, then. Think of it as a perpetual coupon you can cash in anytime you want to."

He tucked his hand behind her neck, pulled her toward

him, and kissed her on the forehead. "I'll help you get Adam and Gabrio out of there. I promise."

She nodded.

"Do you have access to a plane?"

"Yes. Blue Diamond has seven in the fleet. At least a couple of them should be available."

"Will they let you take a plane if they happened to see the news and know what happened at the airport?"

"Probably not. That's why we're not going to ask."

"So we're moving into theft now?"

"Technically, no. I have the keys and the authorization to fly any of them. The owner might not want me to under these circumstances, but I think it's best if we don't ask permission."

Dave checked his watch. "How soon can we get out of here?"

"Sunset is coming up fast. I can't land in Santa Rios in the dark, particularly since using the airstrip would attract too much attention even if it were lit. We don't want Robert knowing we're even in the country. We'll have to wait until dawn."

"How long is the flight to Santa Rios?"

"Three hours."

Dave nodded. "Okay then. You'd better let Sera know what we're planning to do."

Lisa phoned Sera back and told her they'd be there by ten o'clock in the morning, that she was bringing a friend to help, and that they'd be landing in the long, flat valley behind her farmhouse. And Lisa assured her that somehow, someway, she'd get all of them out of there.

She hung up the phone. "It's a go. We'll fly out at dawn."

"If we can get Gabrio to come with us, what about getting him into the U.S.?"

"Adam says he has a friend who's an immigration lawyer. He can get Gabrio a nonimmigrant visa very quickly and then do whatever needs to be done to keep him in the country later."

"Good," Dave said, then frowned. "Where did you say we were landing?"

"There's some farmland at the back of Sera's property that's plowed under this time of year. Nice and flat. Secluded. With luck, I can put a plane down there."

"Luck? How much luck are we talking about needing?"

Lisa smiled. "Are you asking the odds of us walking away from a landing like that?"

"Uh . . . yeah."

"Less than a hundred percent."

Dave closed his eyes.

"But more than zero."

He shook his head.

"Don't worry," she said. "I'm thinking probably a whole lot more than zero."

"Okay. I did notice that you seem to fly as well as you shoot."

"I fly *way* better than I shoot."

"Then I'm in good hands."

Her smile faded, and they stared at each other a long time. "Dave? Why are you doing this?"

"What? Putting my life in your hands?"

"No," she said. "Letting me put my life in yours."

Suddenly he felt the same way now as he had in high school when he'd stood in that shop and looked at a girl who was so strong and so capable in so many ways, then discovered that she was more vulnerable than he ever would have imagined.

"You're in a bad situation right now," he said.

"Yes."

"Yet you haven't said a word about bringing Adam up here so he can tell the true story about the drugs and clear our names. All you've talked about is going down there because you love him and because you know exactly what that poor kid is facing. And you're determined to help them both."

"Yes," she whispered.

"So I'm determined to help you."

She closed her eyes with a gentle sigh. "It's dangerous."

"Yes. But I can't stand to see you take the fall for something you didn't do." He drew closer, his arm brushing against hers.

"And I can't stand to see you cry." He glanced at her lips, so soft and full, thinking how incredible it felt to kiss her. "And every time I look at you, something happens to me that I can't explain. It's attraction. It's admiration. It's this strange out-of-breath feeling I get when I even think about touching you."

"Then don't think about it," she said.

"What?"

"Just do it."

chapter sixteen

Dave slid his hand along Lisa's neck, pulled her toward him, and kissed her. She leaned into him, wrapping her arms around his neck, and God, he couldn't believe how good it felt. That he was suddenly touching her again made everything they'd done last night come back to him, reminding him of just how much he wanted her. How much he'd always wanted her.

Good *God*, he had no business doing this. Not in the middle of this terrible situation when their emotions were high and their resistance was low. He kept telling himself that, even as he swiveled around and pulled her into his lap, dragging her right up next to him until her breasts were pressed against his chest. And still he kissed her, feeling her hot, moist tongue twining with his. He moved his hand up and down her leg, shifting it slowly inward, wishing he could get these damned jeans off her and put his hand against the warm, silky skin of her thighs instead of denim.

In lieu of that, he slid his hand beneath her shirt and settled it against her waist. When his cold hand met her warm skin, she gasped a little, her fingers tightening against his shoulder. He paused until her flesh warmed his, then moved his hand upward to close over her breast. He gave it a gentle squeeze, then teased his thumb over her tight, hard nipple. She reacted instantly, shifting against him, grinding her thigh against his erection, a moan of pleasure humming against his mouth. Her hands were moving, always moving, her fingers massaging the tight muscles of his neck, her palm pressing against his chest, her thumb stroking his jaw. A hundred different sensations bombarded him all at once. He'd never been with a woman like Lisa—so hot, so responsive, so instantly ready for anything he could imagine. He was about five seconds away from standing up, sweeping her into his arms, and carrying her off to bed when suddenly she tore her lips away from his.

"I want you," she said breathlessly. "Right now."

He stood up immediately, hauling her to her feet alongside him. "Bed."

"I said *right now*."

She sat down on the tabletop, grabbed him by the shirt collar, and pulled him right between her knees, kissing him hard and deep as she moved her fingers down the buttons of his shirt with lightning speed, then yanked the shirttail out of his jeans. She took the shirt off, tugging hard to pull the still-buttoned cuffs over his hands, then flung it aside and ran her hands up and down his arms from shoulder to elbow, a hungry look in her eyes.

"I have to touch you," she said, her voice low and coarse, moving her lips so close he could feel her hot breath against his chest. "I have to. Everywhere."

She reached for his belt buckle, ripped it open, then gave the fly of his jeans the same treatment. He'd barely kicked everything off before she was dragging him back again. When she took his cock in her hands, stroking it back and forth, he closed his eyes, loving the feel of her hands on him, moving so expertly, pressing hard enough to excite the hell out of him and then so gently he wanted to beg her for more. She knew what made him crazy, and she never hesitated to do it.

She lay back on the table. He pulled her jeans and panties off, and as he was tossing them aside she drew her feet up and rested her heels against the edge of the table. He moved between her bent knees and placed his palms on the table on either side of her, sliding his cock between her legs, feeling a jolt of pure lust when he found her already hot and wet. He stared down at her, his breath coming faster.

"This is insane."

"No," she said. "*This* is insane."

She took hold of the sides of the shirt she wore and yanked hard. Buttons scattered, skating across the table and plinking onto the kitchen floor. She shoved the fabric away, then slowly, sensuously dragged her hands down over her breasts, her abdomen, her thighs, then traced the same path back up again, before finally crossing her arms over her head against the tabletop and giving him a smoldering look.

"I guess I owe you for a shirt," she said.

"I don't give a damn about the shirt."

"Touch me."

As he skimmed his hands over her body, her eyes drifted closed. He pressed his hands to her breasts, alternately squeezing and releasing, circling his palms around them and teasing his fingertips over her nipples. She closed her eyes with a soft sigh of pleasure, writhing gently beneath his touch.

His fingers spread wide, he moved his hands along her waist, her hips, the tops of her thighs. Pressing her legs farther apart, he eased his hands along the tender skin of her inner thigh.

Yes. There. That smooth, perfect skin he'd been dying to touch. Cradling her legs in his arms, he lowered his head and kissed his way along the warm, soft flesh, then dragged his lips along the junction between her thigh and pelvis. But the moment he touched his tongue to her clit, her hands shot out and grasped his.

"What?" he asked.

She felt blindly for her backpack, which was still on the table, and unzipped one of the pockets. She pulled out a condom, put the plastic package between her teeth and ripped it open. Sitting up, she rolled it down over him with a few quick strokes.

"Are you always this prepared?" he asked. *Just how many men have you slept with?*

"I never leave home without them," she said. *More than you can count. Does that make you think twice?*

"Before now, I don't care who you've been with," he told her. "But from here on out, I'm going to."

The words rolled through his mind and right out his mouth before he ever realized he'd said them. Lisa froze. They stared at each other, breathing hard, his words hovering in the air between them. He lifted his hand and traced his fingertips over her cheek. Instantly she caught his hand in hers, then pulled him toward her, her voice harsh and needy.

"Just fuck me," she whispered.

Those words sent the same thousand-volt shock shooting through him as they had in Monterrey, every nerve in his body coming alive with anticipation. She lay back on the table, pulling him along with her. Falling forward, he slapped his palms against the table and plunged into her with a single forceful stroke. She threw her head back with a strangled whimper and clutched his biceps, then rocked toward him in a silent plea to continue.

He began to move inside her, his pace increasing tenfold in a matter of seconds, quickly becoming a hard, furious rhythm. She rose to meet every stroke as he plunged into her again and again, the table quivering beneath them. He squeezed his eyes closed, blood pulsing wildly through his veins, his breath coming in harsh gasps.

He couldn't get enough air. Couldn't get enough. The room seemed to swim around him until finally it fell away altogether and he was aware of nothing on earth but Lisa spread out on the table beneath him, taking his body into hers.

For a moment he opened his eyes, and he saw her staring up at him, her eyes endless pools of emerald green, as if studying every nuance of his movements, every shift of his gaze, the slightest contraction of his muscles. He closed his eyes again, fighting the release he knew was only moments away. He wanted to know . . . needed to know . . .

"Lisa . . . ?"

He could barely say her name for the tension in his throat, for the overpowering sensation of her hot, tight sheath surrounding him. But he didn't know if she was with him—

"Now," she told him. *"Now!"*

She dug her fingers into his shoulders and arched against him, her inner muscles tightening around him. That was all it took to send a climax slamming into him, ripping a deep growl from his throat and pummeling him with one nerve-shattering pulse after another. With every muscle taut and every nerve alive, he rode out the last shuddering sensations with deep, grinding thrusts before finally falling to his forearms over her, his head bowed, completely spent. He dropped his forehead between her breasts, trying desperately to drag in a good, solid breath.

"That," he said, "was incredible."

Still breathing hard herself, Lisa ran her palms over his shoulders, then stroked her fingers through his hair. "Just incredible?"

He laughed a little, sending just enough oxygen back to his brain that he could function again. He rose and took her hand, pulling her to a sitting position. She kissed him again, hard and deep, then dragged her hands along his chest.

"Let's get a shower."

Shower. God, if she had anything in mind like last night, he knew that this time she probably *would* kill him.

She very nearly did.

By the time they finally collapsed in bed, he was completely exhausted. It was only seven o'clock, but considering they needed to fly out of here at dawn, sleeping now would do them both a world of good.

He felt as if he'd had selective amnesia for the past hour and a half, the situation they were in disappearing from his mind altogether. But as they lay in bed now it all started to come back to him, and he knew there was something he had to do. Something he should have already done.

"I'm sure my brothers have heard what happened by now," Dave told Lisa, rising from the bed. "I'd better give Alex a call and tell him what's going on. I'll be back in soon."

She nodded and closed her eyes with a weary sigh. Her cheeks were still flushed pink from the hot shower, her reddish-gold hair still tangled and damp. At that moment, he was sure he'd never seen a more beautiful woman.

He should be going home. He knew that. But he couldn't fight it. He couldn't fight the all-consuming attraction he felt to this passionate, excessive, exhilarating woman who was little more than a hundred and twenty pounds of adrenaline rush, a woman who would fit into his life, and his daughter's life, like a leopard fits into a petting zoo.

Maybe in the light of day he'd go back to denying it, but right now, as he stared down at her, he knew the real reason he'd made her that promise all those years ago. Because he thought that someday, no matter which way life led him, if Lisa took him up on his promise, he'd have to fulfill it. One tie, one link, one tiny thread that had continued to connect them all these years.

And here they were together again.

Lisa lay awake in her bedroom, staring into the darkness. She knew why Dave had gone to the kitchen to make that phone call, even though there was a phone right beside him on the nightstand. Because he didn't want to have that conversation in front of her, the one where he had to justify to Alex what had happened and why he wasn't coming home. She had no idea what he would tell his brother. She was only glad he was staying. And that was exactly what she'd been afraid of. Wanting him too much.

Every moment she was with Dave was heaven and hell all rolled into one, the glorious feeling of being in the arms of a man who had lived in her heart for eleven long years, a man she'd practically been obsessed with, combined with a feeling of apprehension that sooner or later the ax had to fall. He had a life to return to in Tolosa, a child to think about, and undoubtedly there was a woman in his future who'd be the perfect wife for him and mother for his daughter.

Every time I look at you, something happens to me that I can't explain. It's attraction. It's admiration. It's this strange out-of-breath feeling I get when I even think about touching you.

She didn't know what that meant, except that sex did crazy things to men. Made them do crazy things, say crazy things. For the sake of great sex, politicians became reckless, rulers abdicated thrones, international spies spilled state secrets.

Before now, I don't care who you've been with, he'd told her. *But from here on out I'm going to.*

And some men turned possessive in the heat of the moment and said things they didn't really mean.

Just always make it good for him. Make him want you so much that he can't stop thinking about you, and maybe he'll be yours forever.

Good Lord. What was she thinking? *Forever?*

That was so irrational. The very idea of her sitting in Tolosa, Texas, playing soccer mom and baking cookies was so foreign that she almost couldn't imagine it. And no reality existed where Dave would forget his family and his job and climb into the clouds with her, leaving her free to fly at a moment's notice but still be there whenever she wanted him.

Even as she was beginning to realize just how much she wanted him, she wanted her independence more. She had the life she'd always dreamed of, and no matter where this led, she had no intention of giving that up for anything.

Or anyone.

Dave sat down in one of Lisa's kitchen chairs, drumming his fingertips on the table, waiting for Alex to come on the line. Finally he heard his brother's voice.

"Hello?"

"Alex. It's me."

"Dave? Where are you?"

"San Antonio."

"What in the hell is going on there? Tell me there's been some mistake. Tell me you weren't picked up on drug charges."

Dave steeled himself against the accusation in his brother's voice. "You heard."

"Hell, yes, I heard!"

"Take it easy, Alex. They haven't charged us yet."

"But you were arrested for carrying counterfeit drugs! What the hell was that all about?"

Dave told him the whole story, from the time he found Lisa in Santa Rios, to being chased out of town, to the moment they were picked up at the airport in San Antonio.

"Good God!" Alex said. "You mean to tell me that you were chased out of town by the police? You could be dead right now in some unmarked grave outside of Santa Rios."

"It didn't happen that way, Alex. I'm just fine."

"No, damn it, you're not fine, or you wouldn't be in the middle of all this! You need to come home!"

"Not yet. We're going back down to Mexico."

"You're *what*?"

Dave knew his brother had plenty more reprimands to heap all over him, but Alex kept quiet long enough for Dave to tell him about Adam and Gabrio and what was happening in Santa Rios.

"Okay," Alex said. "I agree. Bad situation. But what the hell are you doing getting mixed up in it?"

"If I can get Adam Decker up here, he can back up our story and clear both of our names. But that's the least of it. He's in danger down there. If Robert Douglas finds him before we can get him out of there, he's a dead man."

"Jesus," Alex said. "What a fucking mess."

"I'm going down there. It's the only way."

There was a long silence. He pictured his brother on the other end of the phone, pacing up and down.

"Okay," Alex said finally. "If the guy can clear your name, by all means get him out of there. But you know what? You never should have gotten mixed up in this situation to start with. For God's sake—you've got a daughter to think about!"

"Don't lay that guilt trip on me," Dave said hotly. "Don't you do it."

"I know what Lisa was like in high school. News reports say she already has one drug conviction."

"That was a false conviction. Her brother set her up."

"Right. They're all innocent, aren't they?"

"I know what it sounds like, Alex. But Lisa hasn't done a damned thing wrong, then or now, and I don't want her taking the fall for it."

"Damn it, Dave, what's the deal with her, anyway? Why the hell did she call you in the first place? I know you knew her in high school. That was a long time ago, yet the minute she's in trouble, your name pops up on her radar. Why you?"

He paused. "We were friends."

"It's more than that. I asked you before, and I'm asking you now. What went on between you two back then?"

Dave was silent.

"Just how personal are things between you and Lisa?"

"That's none of your business."

"So it is personal."

Dave let out a breath of disgust. "Yeah, Alex, it's personal. Is there anything else you'd like to know?"

"No. I've got a pretty clear picture now."

"Of what? Of your brother thinking with his dick instead of his head? Is that it?"

"Hell, I don't know what it is! All I know is that Lisa Merrick is bad news. You've got to ask yourself how she gets herself into messes like this. You don't want a woman like her. She'll only cause you one hell of a lot of trouble."

Dave felt a surge of anger, flaring up from a place that had smoldered inside him for a very long time. As if Alex were the ultimate authority on what he wanted? As if he or the rest of the family knew anything about him at all?

Alex sighed heavily. "Look, Dave. I know it's been hard on you these past few years. But you got through it, because you've always had your head on straight. Everybody counts on that. So when you go off the deep end like this, we've got to wonder why."

You got through it. You can get through anything.

They just didn't know. His family, his friends—nobody. They had no idea just how he *hadn't* gotten through it, how Carla's death still ate away at him and always would. His family always expected that he'd find another woman just like their glowing image of her, who'd be the perfect mother, the perfect wife, and then he'd settle down and play house all over again.

They thought they knew what he wanted. They didn't know a goddamned thing.

"It's just like you said, Alex. I'm the guy with his head on straight. So get off my back. I know what I'm doing."

"I'll tell you what you've been doing. You've been risking your life for a woman you never should have been messing with in the first place."

"Let's get something straight here. I didn't call to ask your opinion, and I'm sure as hell not asking your permission. I just called to tell you I'm going to Mexico. I don't know how long I'll be gone. Just watch Ashley for me until I get back. I've got to go."

As he was hanging up, he heard Alex's voice. "Dave— wait."

He pulled the phone back to his ear, gripping it tightly and dropping his forehead to his hand in frustration. There was a long silence.

"I don't like this," Alex said finally. "If I told you anything else, you'd know I was lying." He let out a long breath of resignation. "But I know you, Dave. So I know that somehow you must be doing the right thing, even if I sure as hell can't see it."

"It is the right thing, Alex. Trust me on that, will you?"

"Yeah. Just be careful. I don't want to have to explain to Ashley why her daddy went to Mexico and never came home."

Dave listened for reproach in Alex's tone but didn't hear a bit of it. All he heard was concern.

"You guys take care of her for me."

"You know we will."

"I'm staying at Lisa's apartment tonight, and then we're flying out tomorrow at dawn. You can't tell anyone where I'm going or what I'm doing. I don't want anyone even knowing we're in Mexico, and I sure don't want anyone knowing that Adam Decker is alive until we can get him out of there."

"I hear you. Just keep me posted, will you? Let me know what's going on?"

"Yeah. I will.

"If you need any help, call me."

"I will."

Dave hung up the phone, knowing that his brother was as pissed off at him as he could possibly be, yet at the same time he'd go to the mat for him if things got tough. Lisa had been right.

No matter how bad the situation was, his family was on his side. But nobody was there to be on Lisa's side.

Nobody but him.

Lisa opened her eyes when she heard Dave come back into her bedroom. He pulled back the covers and slid beneath them, falling to his back and settling his head on the pillow, his arm resting against his forehead.

"Did you talk to Alex?" she asked him.

"Yeah. I talked to him."

"Had he already heard?"

"Oh, yeah. News travels fast in the Tolosa Police Department."

"Did you tell him you're innocent? That it was my fault you were caught up in this situation?"

"I told him the whole story. Then I told him I was going back down to Mexico."

"What did he say to that?"

"He's not happy about me leaving my daughter."

"Understandable."

"He's not happy about me getting into another potentially dangerous situation."

"Also understandable."

Dave was silent.

"What else?" Lisa asked.

"Nothing."

"It's me, isn't it?"

"What?"

"He knew who I was in high school, and he thinks a man like you shouldn't be hanging around with a woman like me, desperate situation or not."

"No. He doesn't think that."

"You're lying."

Dave let out a breath of frustration.

"Well, you can tell Alex he doesn't have a thing to worry about. I mean, a little hot sex between friends hardly translates to a ring and a wedding date, now does it?"

Dave turned slowly to face her. "Is that all this is to you, Lisa? Hot sex between friends?"

He looked at her without blinking, and in the dim light of the bedroom his eyes looked dark as coal. Finally she tore her gaze away. She arranged the sheets and blankets mindlessly, then settled back against the pillow again, never meeting his eyes.

"Come on, Dave. Let's face it. I'm not Carla. I could never be anything like Carla."

He looked at her with surprise. "Is that what you think? That I want you to be like Carla?"

"That's the kind of woman you want, isn't it?"

"Don't do that," he said sharply.

"What?"

"Don't tell me what I want. For God's sake, Lisa, the whole damned world thinks they know what I want, and I'm sick to death of it."

He exhaled sharply, staring at the ceiling. She could see the accelerated rise and fall of his chest, as if he was taking angry breaths, but she didn't know why.

Yes, she did. She'd mentioned Carla again.

Lisa said nothing for a long time, letting the silence settle the air between them. Finally she turned to him and spoke quietly.

"Then what do you want?"

A minute passed, maybe more. Finally he let out a heavy sigh, then slowly turned to her, his face a sparse silhouette in the dim moonlight. Rising on one elbow, he moved in close and spoke softly.

"I want you to be exactly who you are," he said. "I want you to do outrageous, spontaneous things. I want you to keep me on my toes. I want you to take charge of your own life. I want you to be tough and resilient and think nothing about standing up to the devil himself."

He stroked his hand through her hair, slowly, thoughtfully. "But when you hit those places in your life when you just can't handle things yourself, I want you to come to me."

The sincerity in his voice and the burning look in his eyes took her breath away. All she could do was stare at him, a sudden surge of awareness sweeping through her, the most secure feeling that with Dave in her life it wasn't all up to her anymore.

As he slid back down to his pillow, taking her hand in his, it struck her that she'd never actually slept with a man in her own bed. If she went to his house, she could make a quick escape afterward so there was none of that morning-after awkwardness. But there would be no awkwardness tomorrow morning. They'd rise at dawn, and once more Dave would do everything he could to help her.

What the future would bring, she had no idea. But for now, this was exactly where she wanted him to be.

chapter seventeen

Until Adam heard Lisa's voice on the telephone, he hadn't allowed himself to believe that she really was alive. They'd survived. Both of them had actually survived. And if anyone could persuade Gabrio to come with them, it was Lisa. Never in his life had Adam met anyone as strong-willed, as decisive, as determined as she was. He smiled to himself. If she was driving toward a goal, God help any person who got in her way.

For the first time since he woke in Sera's bed, his headache had begun to subside, which was a good indicator against the possibility of ongoing complications. His muscles were still stiff and achy, but his bruises from the fall down that hillside had begun to fade to pale purple and yellow rather than black and blue. Pain still shot through his bullet wound every time he moved, but so far there was no evidence of infection.

He sat up and eased his legs over the side of the bed with a soft groan. He paused a moment for the little stars dancing in his head to disappear, then rose and took the two impossibly long steps to Sera's overstuffed chair. He sank into it gently, his muscles first crying out in pain, then relaxing against the new surface. Sera would object—strenuously—but damn, it felt good to be out of that bed.

It was nearing nine o'clock. Looking out the window, he saw the barn in the distance, lit by flood lamps, where Sera kept her two Shetland ponies. They were all that was left from what had once been a farm full of livestock. More like house pets than horses, they trailed after her like a pair of puppies looking for attention. She'd gone outside to feed them, and he

watched her now as she opened the corral and slipped inside
The dappled ponies approached her immediately, sniffing her
pockets. She pulled out a carrot, broke off pieces of it, and fed
it to them on the flat of her hand.

Adam had been at Sera's house many times over the past
few years, and more than once he'd gone out to the barn with
her to feed the ponies. One night in particular, he remembered standing in the corral with her near dusk, listening to
the crickets chirping and the swish of the ponies' tails as they
swept away flies. She mentioned that when she eventually
moved back to the U.S. she was going to bring the ponies with
her. He told her that she'd better get ready to pay one hell of a
big pet deposit.

She'd laughed a little, then turned to face him. In that moment, something shifted between them. They stared at each
other a long time. Too long. She dropped her lashes for a moment, and when she looked back up at him again something
had entered her eyes that hadn't been there before. A knowing
expression. A flicker of desire.

An invitation.

He'd never in his life wanted to kiss a woman more.

Instead, he'd turned away, saying something about the
ponies or the weather. . . . Hell, he didn't remember what he'd
said. But from that moment on, he'd stopped looking at her as
a colleague or even a friend. That was the moment he started
looking at her as a woman.

He watched out the window as Sera went into the barn, and
a moment later she emerged with buckets full of grain. She
set them down on the ground and the ponies attacked them.
With a last pat for each of them, she headed back to the house.

He heard her come back inside, then her footsteps on the
stairs. The shower ran for a while, then fell silent. A few minutes later, she came to the door of the bedroom wearing a robe
and slippers. Her eyes widened.

"Adam! What are you doing up?"

She hurried into the room, closed the window and pulled
the curtains, then turned to face him. "Back to bed."

"I'm sick of that bed."

"It's where you belong. Right now."

"Damn, you're bossy."

She raised an eyebrow. "I'm in charge here, Doctor, not you. Give me your hand."

She helped him back into bed, then gently pulled the covers up to his waist. She sat down beside him, tucking the covers around him. "How are you feeling?"

"I'm fine."

"Headache?"

"Actually, it's a little better."

She took his vital signs and found them to be normal, then checked his pupils. "That was a nasty contusion. There's still the chance of delayed hematoma. You could have a slow intracranial bleed as we speak."

"Yes, I could. But we're going to be out of here tomorrow. I'll have a CT scan the minute we hit Monterrey."

"Do you really think Gabrio will listen to Lisa?"

"She's our best shot," Adam said. "As long as he lets her in the door."

"That's where Lisa's friend comes in. He's a cop. She says he'll find a way into that house."

"So who is this man she's bringing with her, anyway?"

"I have no idea. She says he's just a friend."

"Must be a good one," Adam said. "She calls him in the middle of the night, and he drops everything and comes seven hundred miles into Mexico to help her. Is there something she's not telling us?"

"I guess we'll find out." Sera sighed. "Tell me this is going to be over with soon."

"You sound as if you want to get rid of me. Have I been such a bad houseguest?"

Sera smiled softly. "I've wanted you in my bed, Adam. I just wish it were under different circumstances."

Adam shook his head. Was there anything this woman thought that she didn't say? "That's what I like about you, Sera. I never have to wonder what you're thinking."

"But I have to wonder constantly what you're thinking." She paused. "How do you feel about me?"

Loaded question. And one he didn't want to answer.

"You know how I feel about you. I think you're smar you're beautiful—"

"You know what I mean."

He turned away. "This isn't a good time to talk about this.

"No, it's the very best time. You can't walk away from me.

"You're taking advantage of my condition."

"Yes, I am."

"Come on, Sera. I'm practically old enough to be you father."

"So that's how you think of me? Like a daughter?"

Not a chance. If he thought about a daughter the way h thought about Sera, they'd haul him off to jail.

"I think you know better than that," he told her.

"Then don't tell me it's an age thing between us, becaus I'll know you're lying."

Adam was silent.

"You never told me why you're going to Chicago."

"To take a new job. You know that."

"No. I mean, why are you taking a new job?"

"It's a good opportunity."

"Right. Chief of staff." She shook her head. "Sorry. I jus can't see it."

"You don't think I can handle it?"

"Oh, you can handle it, all right. I just think you'll be miserable. How many babies do you suppose you'll be able to deliver while you're shoveling through a mountain o paperwork?"

None. Thank God.

"It's a small hospital," he said, "but it's growing, so a lot o prestige will eventually be associated with the position. In a few years—"

"You don't care about prestige."

He stopped short, letting out a breath of frustration.

"You do, however, care about your patients, your friends your family." She paused. "And unless I'm mistaken, you also care about me."

What could he say to that? The worst thing he could do was

try to deny it. She'd see in a heartbeat just how big a liar he really was.

"I know I'm pushing here, Adam. But I don't have the luxury of mincing words. Time isn't on my side."

"Sera—"

"Tell me you don't love me."

He looked away. *Stop it, Sera. Please don't do this to me. Please don't make me lie to you.*

"Say it, Adam. Say you don't love me and I'll never bring it up again."

He started to say it. The words were on the very tip of his tongue, poised to come out of his mouth. But he was tired of lying. Tired of lying to himself, tired of lying to her. So damned tired of denying what he'd felt for her all this time that he just couldn't do it anymore. Words tumbled out of his mouth that had been bottled up for two long years.

"Of course I love you," he said. "How the hell could I not love you? You're an incredible woman, so much so that sometimes it's all I can do to keep my hands off you, to keep from telling the whole world that I'm in love with you, to keep from stopping people on the street and telling them—"

"Why didn't you *say* something?"

"Because you need another man, Sera. One who can give you what I can't."

"You have everything I want, Adam. Don't you know that? You're the most caring, compassionate man I know. You have a kind word for everyone. You're lying here, wounded and in pain, refusing to get help for yourself for the sake of somebody else. It's why I love you."

He turned away. "You don't know everything about me."

"Of course not. That's what a lifetime together is for."

A lifetime together. She was killing him. Word by word, she was killing him. If only she knew how desperately he wanted that. And how impossible it was for him even to think about.

"Sera? Do you remember what you said to me the very first time I met you? About the reason you became a midwife?"

"What?"

"You told me that watching a man and his wife holding that new baby, knowing it was something they created together, was the most beautiful thing in the world."

"It is," she said. "I meant every word of that."

"I believe you." He paused. "Sera, if you knew at this moment that you would go through your entire life and never get pregnant, never have a child of your own, how would you feel?"

"I will have a child of my own."

"Answer the question."

"I suppose . . . I suppose I'd be devastated."

"Yes. Of course you would. Wanting something so close to your heart and knowing you'll never have it is hell. You want to have children."

"Yes. Of course I do. Don't you?"

"Did I ever tell you that?"

She blinked with surprise. "Well, no, but I assumed—"

"You shouldn't have."

"Adam, you're hardly too old to have children."

"That has nothing to do with it."

"But you love children. I don't understand—"

"I know you don't. And I can't explain it to you. Just know that I'm way past being able to think about that."

She stared at him a long time, her eyes narrowing thoughtfully. "There's something else."

"Something else?"

"Something you're not telling me."

"I don't know what else there is to say."

"Plenty," she said softly. "I can see it in your eyes."

"It's getting late. I'm a sick man, remember? I need my rest."

"You've never told me about your wife."

Adam froze, stabbed by pain that was as raw and real as it had been three years ago. He turned away from Sera's sharp gaze, wishing she'd stop probing into things that were best left alone.

"You never talk about her," Sera went on. "Who she was,

how she died. I asked Lisa about her once, but she said I should talk to you. I suppose I should have long before now."

"Sera—"

"You and your wife never had children. Why not?"

Adam's pulse kicked hard, and in seconds his heart was racing. Looking down, he saw his hands had tightened into fists and he didn't even realize he'd done it. He consciously relaxed them, only to realize his palms were sweating.

"We almost did," he said quietly.

"I don't understand."

Just tell her, damn it. After all this time can't you at least say it without falling apart?

"My wife died when she was seven months pregnant."

For several seconds, all Sera did was stare at him, her lips parted in a small, silent gasp. Then slowly she slid her hand to her throat, tears welling up in her eyes.

"Oh, Adam," she whispered. "I'm sorry. So sorry. I had no idea."

Her compassion only fueled his misery. He couldn't look at her. He couldn't stand to see the empathy on her face that reflected the pain in her heart.

"To lose both a wife and a child," she murmured. "The pain you must have felt . . . I can't even imagine. . . ."

"Please, Sera," he said. "Please don't. I can't take this."

He couldn't. He couldn't stand the flood of memories that came rushing back to him, the incessant echoing of Ellen's voice inside his head, the overwhelming helplessness and despair that he knew he might never overcome. And he certainly couldn't deal with it in front of Sera.

"Please leave," he implored her, refusing to meet her eyes anymore. "Right now. *Please.*"

But still she sat there. After a moment, he felt her hand against his cheek. "Adam . . ."

He turned back to see a single tear coursing down her face. Her own burning desire to have a child was reflected in the pain she felt for him, and that only tormented him more.

She eased closer to him, so close that her long dark hair fell along his forearm. She rested her other hand against his thigh, but it wasn't until he felt her breath against his lips that he realized what she intended to do.

"Sera—"

"No," she whispered. "I have to. . . ."

She pressed her lips to his in a tender kiss, her other hand stroking his thigh in the faintest of caresses, as if she was driven to touch him and afraid of hurting him all at the same time. That gentle touch was enticing beyond measure. He knew he should be pulling away, but he'd wanted to kiss her for such a long time, a thousand times over, and he found himself leaning into her, tilting his head and closing his mouth over hers.

It was wrong. He knew it was wrong, but he hadn't kissed a woman in three long years, and the feeling overpowered him. But not just because he was kissing a woman. It was because he was kissing Sera, who was more special to him than anything else in his life. Pain still pounded at his head, but he didn't feel it. Memories circled the periphery of his mind but stayed at bay. His heart was still racing, but his despair had shifted to euphoria, his anxiety to exhilaration. For a few blessed moments, he felt nothing but Sera's kiss and the love she was pouring into him.

She finally leaned away from him, her beautiful brown eyes still glistening with tears. She backed away slowly and stood up, and he thought she was going to say good night and walk out of the room. Instead, she pulled down the covers on the other side of the bed.

She opened her robe and pushed it off her shoulders, letting it fall to the floor. She wore a long, filmy blue nightgown that seemed to shimmer in the dim lamplight, skimming along her hips and breasts. He'd never seen anything more beautiful in his life, and he couldn't tear his gaze away.

"What are you doing?" he asked.

She slid into bed beside him. "Sleeping with you."

"Sera . . ."

"I don't want to leave you." She paused, staring at him with a soft, plaintive expression that went straight to his heart. "Please tell me you want me to stay."

As she waited for his answer, all he could think about was how much he wanted her there, now and forever. He wanted her beside him all the days and nights of his life. That wasn't possible, could never be possible, but just for tonight he wanted to feel the warmth of her body next to his, smell her soft floral perfume, hear her gentle breathing.

And think about things that could never be.

"Yes," he whispered. "Stay."

She settled her head on the pillow beside him with a tender sigh, her hand finding his arm and stroking it softly. He closed his eyes, trying to commit the way he felt right now to memory—a memory he hoped would last a lifetime.

"Do you remember a time," Sera said softly, "when you first came to Santa Rios, when a woman who was in labor came to my house? She was single. She'd had no prenatal care at all and I thought she might be in premature labor, so I called you and asked you to come over. Do you remember her?"

He thought back. "Yes. I remember."

"She was so scared. She had no friends or relatives. She was crying. Screaming in pain. I couldn't calm her down. And then you arrived."

Sera shifted a little, tucking her arm beneath her pillow.

"You went into the room and sat down on the bed beside her. You took her hand and spoke to her in a voice that was so soft and compelling that she stopped crying. Then you brushed her hair away from her forehead, put your hand against her cheek and told her that you knew she was scared and you knew how much it hurt, but there was nothing to be afraid of because you were going to be there to help her through every minute of it. And then . . ." Sera slid her hand down and closed it over his, squeezing gently. "Then you took a tissue and wiped the tears off her face." She sighed softly. "That was the moment."

"The moment?"

"The moment I fell in love with you."

Adam felt a rush of longing so powerful he thought it might tear him apart. That she'd had those thoughts all this time astonished him. He knew just how much he was drawn to her, but he'd never imagined to what extent she'd felt the same about him.

"Someday soon you'll want to try again," Sera said. "You'll want to reach for the happiness you lost that day."

"No. That'll never happen. Please don't think it will."

"Time heals," she said. "The day will come when you're ready to love again, when you're ready to think about having another child." She paused. "I want to be there on that day."

He couldn't say anything. Nothing. Words simply wouldn't come. To want so badly what she'd described and know it could never be was the most painful thing on earth.

"Sweet dreams," she whispered.

If only she knew. If only she knew that closing his eyes brought dreams that haunted him, far from the sweet ones she'd wished for him. Loving him came with an even greater price than she realized, and he knew in his heart that it was one she would never want to pay.

The sun had barely crept over the horizon the next morning when Dave and Lisa took off in a single-engine six-passenger plane from Blue Diamond Aviation. Dave still wasn't the happiest small-plane passenger in the world, but this one was bigger than the last one they'd flown in, and he'd come to realize that Lisa knew precisely what she was doing. And it was definitely the best way to make it to and from Santa Rios in as little time as possible.

"Damn, it's cold in here," Lisa said. "I need to tell my boss to do something about this heater. Will you grab my jacket out of my bag?"

Dave handed her the jacket, and she slipped it on. The look fit her exactly—jeans, T-shirt, denim jacket, boots, a fresh, clean face devoid of makeup, and short reddish-blond hair going every which way, as if she had far better things to do than spend hours in front of a mirror. She sat with the confident bearing of a person who looked as if she was born to be in a pilot's seat.

Dave peered out the windshield. "So what's the weather like between here and there?"

She smiled. "What's the matter, Dave? Still sweating the small-plane experience?"

He shrugged. "Just wondering." "The weather." She tapped her finger against the yoke. "Well, let's see. I guess there is that torrential rainstorm over Brownsville. I suppose we ought to watch out for that."

He whipped around to face her. "You're flying into a rainstorm?"

"And I suppose we'll have to skirt that massive electrical storm east of Monterrey."

"What?"

"Don't worry!" she said with a wave of her hand. "Those will seem like nothing once that category five hurricane swings north from the Yucatán Peninsula and smacks into Santa Rios."

Dave stared at her dumbly for a moment, then slowly closed his eyes, shaking his head. Once his heart rate returned to normal, he gave her a deadpan stare. "How about we just take a roundabout route over the Bermuda Triangle?"

Her eyes lit up with excitement. "You know, I've never flown through there before. Sounds like fun."

He wondered if there was anything about his profession that would rattle *her*. A hundred-mile-an-hour police chase? Pulling assorted body parts from a ten-car pileup? Disarming a crack addict carrying an automatic weapon and enough ammo to start World War III? Drinking the coffee at the station house? Surely there was at least one thing that would get to her, and once he found out what it was he intended to find a way to terrorize her with it.

"Where did you learn to give your passengers such a hard time? Do they teach you that in flight school?"

"God, no. When I took lessons, I had to toe the line. Behave myself. Speak when spoken to. Might as well have been in the military."

"Did you get your pilot's license in San Antonio?"

"Yeah. After Lenny was arrested, I managed to stay in his

apartment through the rest of the month because it was paid up. I got a job at a crummy little diner. I hated that place, except for one thing."

"What's that?"

"It was right across the street from the airfield."

"Ah. Good planning."

"Good fortune. They were looking for a waitress. But you know, I worked my ass off in that place. No matter how many times I had to smile when I didn't want to, dodge butt pinches from dirty old men, and soak my feet at the end of a double shift, still I did it. I was making a lot in tips, and I knew it wouldn't be long before I had the money for flying lessons. But they came in a way I didn't expect."

"How's that?"

"One day an older woman sat down at the counter. She had steel-gray hair. A body like a battering ram. And I could tell by the look on her face that she took no crap from anyone. One of the other waitresses told me she was Marge Watkins, the owner of Blue Diamond Aviation. I remember going into the kitchen, thinking fast, trying to get my nerve up to talk to her before she walked out. Then I went back out to the counter."

"What did you say to her?"

"I asked her for a job."

"Just like that?"

"Yeah. Shocked the hell out of her, I think, but she just stared at me, saying nothing. I told her quickly that I didn't care what I did there, as long as I was employed. She asked me why I wanted to work for her. I took a deep breath and told her that someday I wanted to learn how to fly."

"What did she say to that?"

"She just laid her fork down, sat back in her chair, folded her arms, and asked me what in the hell made me think I could ever learn how to fly a plane."

Dave raised his eyebrows. "Wow. Tough old broad."

"Oh, yeah. And I was shaking like crazy, but I wasn't about to let her see that. I raised my chin, glared at her, and asked her what in the hell made her think I couldn't."

Dave smiled. "What did she do then?"

"Nothing. She just sat there staring at me. I felt so humiliated that I wanted to crawl under the counter. But then she reached into her wallet, pulled out a business card, and told me to come see her in the morning."

"She gave you a job?"

"Yes. I was so excited. Less so when I found out some of the things she had in mind, but excited just the same. She had me filing, answering phones, washing planes, cleaning oil stains off the pavement, making coffee. I swear if a toilet needed cleaning she handed me a scrub brush. She was loud, brassy, and intimidating, and I was terrified of her. I hoped that she'd take pity on me and let me have a little time in the air before I actually had the money to do it. But no. Until I had money on the table, I stayed on the ground.

"Eventually I went through ground school. Then came my first day in the air. I showed up and looked around for one of the regular instructors. But guess who was waiting for me? Marge. God, I was terrified."

"So how was it?"

Lisa sighed softly. "There were so many days when I hated that woman. She was so blunt and demanding that I felt totally inadequate. But then I'd see her nod a little, as if she approved of something, or she'd toss off a comment as she was walking away that told me that maybe I wasn't the worst student in the history of aviation. She never let up on me, never let me do anything half-assed, and she sure as hell didn't take any attitude. Then one day I turned around, and I was a pilot. And a damned good one at that. Looking back, I have her to thank for it."

"Does she still run Blue Diamond?"

"No. She died only a few years after I got my pilot's license. She was diagnosed with cancer, and within a couple of months she was dead." She paused. "Then the most amazing thing happened."

"Oh?"

"The day after her funeral, her attorney contacted me. It seemed that she'd left me something in her will."

"What was that?"

"A 1964 Piper Cherokee."

Dave's eyebrows flew up. "She left you a plane?"

"Yes. I was stunned. I just stood there in the attorney's office, staring at the keys. I think I ended up crying. I don't really remember. Then the attorney handed me a note she'd written to me."

Lisa leaned into the backseat, reached into her backpack, and grabbed her wallet. She opened it and reached into one of the pockets, extracting a folded, water-crinkled piece of paper and handing it to Dave. He opened it carefully and read:

I thought I loved flying more than anyone on earth. Then I met you. Marge.

Only a few words. But they explained everything.

"So where is that plane now?" Dave asked.

"At the bottom of the Mercado River."

As Lisa slipped the note back into her wallet, Dave noticed her eyes glistening. He sat back in his seat, thinking that for somebody who swore she needed nobody she'd sure had a few good people in her life to help her along the way.

An hour later, they approached Santa Rios. When Lisa swung wide around the town to bring the plane in from the south, dropping lower and lower over the field where she intended to put it down, Dave started feeling queasy all over again. It was one thing to have a nonlethal landing on a nice, smooth runway. It was another thing to put a plane down in a bumpy field. It wasn't as if his life flashed before his eyes, but he was definitely thinking about the extra life insurance he'd taken out last year and wishing he'd doubled the amount.

"Lighten up, Dave," Lisa said. "This is no big deal."

"I'm fine."

"You're clawing the seat. That's hell on the upholstery."

Dave yanked his hands away and stuck them in his lap, but still they were sweating. When the plane finally touched down, though, she was right. Nice and smooth. Piece of cake.

She taxied the plane to the edge of the field and parked it

behind a grove of trees, where it would be invisible from the dirt road that ran alongside the field a quarter mile in the distance.

"Any chance of somebody spotting the plane?" Dave asked.

"Nope. The next nearest farmhouse is five miles south of here."

They got out, grabbed their bags, and started the half-mile hike toward Sera's farmhouse in the distance.

"You say Sera's a midwife?" Dave asked.

"Yeah."

"So what's the connection between her and Adam?"

"That's the connection. Or at least, that's how it started out. He's an obstetrician. They bonded over babies. Actually, she's in love with him, but he pretends she's not. And he pretends he's not in love with her."

"That's an awful lot of pretending going on."

"Adam lost his wife three years ago, and he just hasn't gotten over it. I still don't know why he was moving to Chicago, where he'd never be able to see Sera again. I tried to suggest that those plans might be a little misguided on his part, but he turned deaf on me." She trudged on. "But you know, sometimes people are brought together over desperate situations."

Yeah, Dave thought. *Sometimes they are.*

A few minutes later, they went through a gate that led from the field into the barn area. A corral adjoining the barn contained two dappled gray ponies, who stuck their noses through the fence looking for attention.

Dave and Lisa reached the farmhouse. As they circled around to the front and climbed the steps to the porch, Sera came to the door, a pretty Hispanic woman who gave Lisa a heartfelt hug.

"I'm so glad you're here," Sera said. "I don't know what I'd have done without you."

"How is Adam doing?"

"He's good. I'm still worried, but for now, he's okay."

Lisa introduced Dave, and Sera gave him the same kind of hug she'd given Lisa.

"Thank you for coming, too," she said. "I don't even know who you are, but sometimes I think God sends angels, you know?"

Dave smiled. "Can't say as I've ever been called one of those."

"I have a feeling I'm going to be elevating you to sainthood before all this is over. Come with me."

She led them up a wide oak staircase to the second floor, then down the hall to a bedroom. Lisa stepped into the room.

"Adam," she said, the word rushing out on a huge breath of relief. She hurried to the man's bedside, then stopped suddenly. "I'm just dying to give you a great big hug. But if you've survived this far, I don't want to rock the boat."

"Ask my nurse if it's all right."

Lisa turned to Sera, who smiled at her. "That's just the kind of medicine he needs."

Lisa sat down on the bed and hugged Adam, gently but with the kind of sincerity people reserve only for those who mean the most to them. Adam returned her hug with equal enthusiasm. They seemed like two very good friends tied to each other with a family kind of closeness. No wonder the news of his death had shaken her up so much.

"Adam, this is Dave DeMarco. He's going to help us find Gabrio and get all of us out of here."

Dave approached Adam and shook his hand. "Lisa was pretty relieved to find out you were alive."

"The feeling was mutual, believe me," Adam said.

Dave turned to Sera. "Where does Gabrio live?"

"A small house on the east side of town. Ivan said he's been sick for a couple days and has been staying home. I think he's been sick ever since the night Adam was shot."

"Lisa and I will go talk to him."

"He may not even answer the door."

"I'll break in if I have to."

"That's going to scare the poor kid to death," Sera said.

"I'll take it as easy as I can. One way or the other, I guarantee you I'll get Lisa inside." He turned to Adam. "But if he still refuses to leave with us, that's all we can do. If I put him on that plane with us against his will, that's kidnapping, and that's a line I refuse to cross."

Adam sighed, then nodded. "Okay. I can't ask for more than that."

"We need to verify a time when he's there and his brother isn't," Dave said. "I want Ivan out of the mix."

"I can drive by their house this afternoon," Sera said. "If Gabrio's car is there and Ivan's isn't, it probably means that Ivan is at Esmerelda's, the bar where I work. He comes in there almost every day. I can keep an eye on him until you talk to Gabrio."

"Good. That'll work."

"What about another vehicle?" Lisa asked. "We're going to need two."

"I still have my father's old car out in the barn," Sera said. "It's not much, but it'll get you there."

"Is there gas in it?"

"Should be. I drive it every once in a while and I filled it up recently."

Adam turned to Sera. "What if Ivan decides he wants to leave the bar before you get back here with Gabrio?"

"I'll persuade him to stay," Sera said.

"Watch yourself," Adam said. "Please."

"I'll be fine."

He reached out to her. "Come here."

She sat down beside him. He took her hand. "I know you can take care of yourself, but that doesn't stop me from worrying about you. Just please be careful."

She traced her fingertips over his cheek. "I will."

Dave gave Lisa a subtle but distinct "it seems you were right" look.

"What time do you go to work?" Dave asked Sera.

"Four o'clock."

"We'll plan on moving out then."

chapter eighteen

Gabrio sat on his kitchen floor, leaning against the wall, a sense of dread closing over him until he could barely breathe. As the wall clock ticked off the seconds, he looked around the room, thinking how shabby this house was compared to the house in the U.S. that he'd lived in when his mother had been alive. He remembered it being clean and neat, with the smell of dinner cooking—something good and hot and filling. In this house there were layers of dust and grime, the musty odor of leaking pipes and mold, and he couldn't remember when dinner had been more than something eaten fast just to keep body and soul together.

He rested his head against the wall behind him and closed his eyes. He hadn't thought to turn off the television in the other room, and the voices lulled his already sleepy mind. He felt dizzy and light-headed, and he couldn't make himself think straight no matter how hard he tried.

God, he was tired. So tired.

It was only a matter of time. Sera would get Adam to a hospital if she hadn't already, and sooner or later everyone would find out he wasn't dead after all. And then all hell would break loose. He was surprised it hadn't already.

Just tell Ivan. Tell him what you did.

After all, it would be better, wouldn't it, to tell his brother what had happened before word got back that Adam was alive? That way Ivan would have a heads-up in dealing with the other men and be ready to protect him. And he would protect him, wouldn't he?

Gabrio had tried to make himself believe that. Tried with

all his might. But he knew better. He'd seen what Ivan and the others did to guys who fucked up. He'd *seen* it. It would make no difference that he and Ivan were bound by blood, because he knew his brother had loyalties stronger than that.

Gabrio had a thought about running, but what would be the point? No matter where he went, they'd find him. And where would he go even if he wanted to leave? He had no friends anyplace else and no family. What was in this town and in this house was all he had.

From the floor beside him he picked up the gun. He brushed the cool barrel against the side of his head, resting it there, wondering if that was best. Then he put the barrel in his mouth, the metal clicking against his teeth. He removed it again and stared at it, wishing he'd never even touched a gun before, wishing he lived someplace where they weren't a cold, hard fact of life. And death.

He put the barrel of the gun against his temple again, stroking it through rivulets of sweat. He wondered if he'd see his mother. Oh, Jesus, he hoped so. If he did it right, it might hurt for a second, but then all the pain would disappear and he'd see nothing but light. He closed his eyes and wrapped his finger around the trigger, his hand trembling, and gritted his teeth. He only hoped that suicide really wasn't a mortal sin and that God would have mercy on him.

Dave steered the old Buick down the alley behind the street where Gabrio lived, thinking that there had to be a neighborhood in Tolosa as crappy as this one, but he didn't think he'd ever seen it. The houses were cinder block, most of them unpainted, their overgrown yards scattered with junk.

Just after four o'clock, Sera had phoned back to her house from Esmerelda's to tell them that she'd driven by Gabrio's house and found his car there and that Ivan, true to form, was at the bar drinking himself into oblivion. She promised she'd find a way to keep him there until they called to tell her the coast was clear. Dave intended to make quick work of this. Get in, get out, and do everything he could in between to make sure the kid left with them.

"That's the house," Lisa said.

Dave brought the car to a halt in the alley behind the house Lisa indicated, killing the engine.

"We're going in the back?" she asked.

"Less conspicuous. I still don't want anyone knowing we're back in town. Do you think he'll come to the door if he sees it's you?"

"I can't say for sure. If he doesn't, what's Plan B?"

"I'm breaking in. Door, window, whatever."

They got out of the car and made their way through the backyard.

"You go to the door," Dave told Lisa. "I'll stand to one side until you can get him to open it. Then we'll both go in."

Lisa nodded. When they reached the house, Dave turned around and stood with his back against the outside wall of the house. As Lisa reached up to knock on the door, she peered through threadbare curtains into the kitchen and gasped.

"Dave! He's got a gun!"

"What?"

"At his own head! He's going to shoot himself!"

Lisa cleared out of the way as Dave raced to the door. He tried it first, found it locked, then stepped back and gave it a hard kick. The lock cracked and the door flew open, smacking against the wall. Gabrio was sitting on the kitchen floor, and he immediately swung the gun up and pointed it at Dave.

"Who the fuck are you?" he shouted. "Get out!"

Lisa stepped quickly into the house. Gabrio looked at her, blinking hard, as if he couldn't quite believe his eyes.

"What are you doing here?" he said. "Why aren't you in jail? The drugs. I thought—"

"Calm down, Gabrio," Lisa said. "We're here to help you. This is Dave. He's a friend of mine."

Gabrio whipped around to Dave. "What the hell do you want?"

"Gabrio," Dave said. "We know you were the one who saved Adam's life, so we know you won't shoot us. So just drop the gun, okay?"

Gabrio's eyes shifted back and forth between them. Shaking, he lowered the gun. Dave thought they were in the clear. Then Gabrio raised the gun again and pressed it against his own temple.

Lisa gasped and started toward him.

"Stop!" Gabrio shouted.

Dave grabbed Lisa's arm and pulled her to a halt.

"Don't come any closer, or I'm pulling the trigger! I swear to God I am!"

Dave held up his palms, meeting the kid's eyes, keeping his expression neutral. "We hear you, Gabrio. Just take it easy, okay?"

"Leave me alone!"

Dave stood there for a moment, stock-still, waiting for the silence to settle the air between them. Then slowly he lowered his palms.

"Gabrio? Tell me why you're doing this."

"Because my life is shit, that's why!"

"Why is your life shit?"

"Because I've fucked up everything! I was the one who told Ivan that they found the drugs. And then they sabotaged Lisa's plane, they shot Adam, and now Ivan said Lisa's been arrested because she had the drugs . . . oh, *God.*"

His voice was hoarse with anguish. He closed his eyes for a moment, and Dave moved closer. Gabrio's eyes sprang open again. "Man, I told you to get the fuck away from me!"

Dave had a real bad feeling about this. The kid wasn't blowing smoke. Before they got here, he'd been sitting alone, clearly agitated, clearly thinking about killing himself. He looked as if he hadn't slept in a week. He was confused, disoriented. If Dave didn't play his cards right, Gabrio was going to end up dead.

"Doesn't matter," Gabrio went on, his grip tightening and releasing and tightening on the gun. "I'm dead either way. Ivan told me to do something, and I didn't do it. Once he and the other guys find out—"

"That's why we want you to come with us," Lisa said.

"Come with you?"

"Back to the U.S. If you come with us, they can't hurt you."

Gabrio gave her a choked laugh. "Oh, yeah? You think they won't find me? Wherever I go?" He pressed the gun harder against his temple, his eyes alight with fear. "I've seen what they do to guys who fuck up. I've *seen* it!"

"So this is better?" Lisa said. "Hanging around here and waiting for them to come after you?"

"Shut up! Just shut up and leave me alone!"

Lisa started to say something else, but Dave put a hand against her arm, warning her to tone it down. The kid wasn't thinking straight. He was confused. Restless. Edgy. All he could see right now was the terrible chain of events he'd set off by passing along that information and the ultimate horror that his own brother might be the one to make him pay for it.

A sense of calm came over Dave. It was the strangest feeling but one he recognized well. His nerves were taut, on-edge, but his mind was fully engaged in the moment, working to take control of the situation.

"Gabrio," Dave said evenly, "I think we need to talk about a few things."

"I told you to leave me alone!"

"I'm afraid I can't do that. See, if I turn around and walk out of here, you might pull that trigger. And I'm not going to let that happen."

"Why the hell not? What's it to you?"

"I know we don't know each other. But Adam told us all about how you saved his life. Do you know what they call men who do things like that?"

"What?"

"Heroes."

Gabrio blinked, still gripping the gun so tightly that his knuckles whitened. "Hero? *Shit.* I've fucked up everything. I told them that Lisa and Adam found the drugs. If I hadn't done that—"

"Did you know that Robert Douglas was going to try to kill them?"

"No! I swear to God I didn't know that!"

"Okay. So do you think just passing on information when

you have no idea that it's going to hurt somebody means you deserve to die?"

The kid's eyes shifted back and forth, his breathing shallow and irregular. "That's not the only thing."

"I know. You're afraid of your brother and his friends. You figure killing yourself beats them coming after you. And you're afraid that your brother wouldn't protect you against them."

The kid swallowed hard, and Dave could see the anguish in his eyes at the very thought of that. But he had to get Gabrio thinking straight. Thinking logically.

"Gabrio," Dave said, "who shot Adam?"

"I'm not going to tell you that!"

"We know. We know exactly what happened. It was Ivan. And Enrique was there, too. Isn't that right?"

Gabrio just stared at him, his jaw tight, his breathing labored.

"Who sabotaged Lisa's plane? Was it Ivan and Enrique?"

"I'm not telling you a damned thing!"

"Did you know that Ivan put the local cops on to us and they tried to kill us as we were leaving Santa Rios?"

He could tell by the look on Gabrio's face that the kid hadn't heard that. His jaw began to tremble. *"Shit."*

"If they're the ones doing all the bad stuff, why should you be the one to die for it?"

Gabrio blinked quickly, as if processing that thought for the first time. The tension was slowly leaving his body, his muscles becoming limp. He was easing into agreement, into resignation, and that was just what Dave was looking for. But still Gabrio wasn't lowering the gun, and Dave knew that until he took the threat away anything could happen.

"Okay," he told the kid. "You know you haven't done anything worth dying for. So what else is there, Gabrio? Is there another reason that you want to kill yourself?"

Gabrio stared at him for a long time, tears filling his eyes. His voice became a plaintive whisper. "Because I want to see my mother again."

Dave felt as if the floor had just fallen out from under his feet. Oh, Jesus, this poor kid really did have nobody in this life, so he was looking ahead to the next one, hoping for something better. Dave had to get him out of this situation. Out of this town. Out of this fucking *country*.

"When did your mother die?" he asked.

"I was ten."

"Tell me about her."

Gabrio shrugged, his arm starting to tremble from the weight of the gun. "I—I don't remember much."

"But you loved her."

He nodded.

"My mother died when I was just a kid, too. She had cancer. I don't remember much about her, either, but still it was hard growing up, you know? But I want you to think about something. As much as your mother would like to see you, too, do you think she'd want it to happen like this?"

Gabrio blinked again, his respirations becoming slower. More measured. "No."

Dave held out his hand. "Then why don't you give me the gun?"

Gabrio stared at Dave a long time, sweat trickling down his forehead. Finally he eased the gun away from his temple, revealing a deep red mark where he'd pressed the weapon so hard against it. He lowered the gun to the floor beside him.

Dave resisted the urge to pounce on it, instead moving forward slowly, leaning over and sliding it from Gabrio's grasp with a small, silent breath of relief. The kid pulled his knees up and rested his elbows on them, then dropped his head to his hands, his shoulders jerking with sobs.

Dave turned to see Lisa staring at Gabrio, her body tense, as if she was feeling every shiver of emotion the poor kid felt.

"How could Ivan do those things?" Gabrio said, tears choking his voice. "How?"

"I know how you feel," Lisa said. "It hurts. You feel betrayed. I know—"

"No! You don't know! Goddamn it, he's my *brother*!"

To Dave's surprise, Lisa eased forward and sat down beside Gabrio on the floor. After a moment, she slipped her arm around his shoulders. He tried to shrug away from her, but she persisted, leaning in close to him and speaking quietly.

"Gabrio, listen to me. Sometimes you've got to cut loose. You've got to admit that everything you came from is crap and there's something better out there for you."

"Better? Yeah, right."

"I told you already. We want you to come back to the U.S. with us. Adam has a friend who will help you get a visa."

Gabrio looked up. "A visa?"

"Yes. What Sera told you is the truth. Adam wants you out of here. He knew if anyone found out he was alive you'd be in danger, so he refused to leave without you. You saved his life, and now he wants to save yours. We all do. That was why Sera came to talk to you yesterday, and it's why we're here now. For you. We want you to come with us."

Gabrio looked at Lisa with total disbelief. Clearly the kid couldn't imagine a scenario under which anyone would take his welfare into consideration. Ever.

He wiped his face on the shoulder of his shirt, then shook his head. "Ivan could still find me. And if he does . . ."

"He won't even know where you are," Lisa said. "But even if he tries to come to the U.S., he's going to have to go through us to get to you. And we're not going to let him do that."

Dave could only imagine how scared this kid must be. And now Lisa was telling him there was a way out. His posture said he didn't believe her, but his eyes were silently praying she was telling him the truth.

"I—I can take care of myself," Gabrio said weakly.

"I know you can. Most of the time. But sometimes when things get bad, everybody needs a little help."

The kid was calmer now but still so confused, so lost. He looked up at Dave. "What's going to happen to Ivan?"

"Probably nothing," Dave said. "His crimes were committed here. He's a Mexican citizen. He's got local law enforcement on his side. Even if what he did comes out, he'll probably never be prosecuted."

Gabrio took a deep, shuddering breath. "I know he should pay for what he's done, but . . ."

"But you don't want to be the one to make that happen," Lisa said.

"That's right. I'm not giving my brother up. No matter what. I'm not telling anyone anything he's done. You can't make me do that."

"You won't have to," Lisa said. "You won't have to say anything against your brother. I promise you. Okay?"

"He's not always bad," Gabrio said. "I know it seems like he is, but he's not. Not always."

"I know," Lisa told him.

"Maybe someday he'll stop."

"Maybe he will."

He bowed his head again, his eyes closed, still torn between the only existence he'd ever known, no matter how shitty it was, and the unknown of going with them. Lisa stayed right next to him, doing everything she could to transmit a sense of hope into the kid. Finally he swallowed hard and turned to look at her.

"Where are we going exactly?"

Dave breathed a sigh of relief. *We.* The kid had made his decision.

"Monterrey first," Lisa said, "so we can get Adam to a hospital and get your paperwork in order so you can enter the U.S. Then San Antonio."

Gabrio responded with a deep, anxious breath.

"I know it scares you to go to a new place," Lisa said. "And it scares you to trust anyone. But this time it's okay. I promise you it's okay."

"Will you be there?"

Lisa nodded. "Yeah. I'll be there."

Dave took a step forward. "We need to leave as soon as possible. So if there's something you want to take with you, grab it now."

Gabrio ground the heels of his hands into his eyes, then swept them across his shirtsleeve, glancing up at Dave as if he couldn't bear the thought of another man seeing him in tears. Finally he got up from the floor and headed down the hall toward a bedroom.

Dave gave Lisa a hand up, and she sank into a kitchen chair with a breath of relief. "God, Dave," she said softly. "I was so afraid he was going to pull that trigger. I'm so glad you were here. I couldn't have talked that gun out of his hand. No way. You were so calm. You said just the right things."

Dave sat down next to her. "So did you."

"I know exactly how he feels. Exactly. He feel so alone. Like there's nobody on earth who cares if he lives or dies. And it's not fair, really, because it's nothing more than an accident of birth."

Dave nodded. They sat in silence, the wall clock ticking away the seconds. Then Lisa turned to him, her voice fading to a near whisper. "Do you remember when you were talking to your daughter the other night on the phone, when she was watching *Cinderella* with John and his wife?"

"Yeah?"

"Do you know I've never even seen *Cinderella*? Or *Bambi*, or *Snow White*, or *Mary Poppins*. . . ." She looked at Dave, tears clouding her eyes. "Please don't think you're spoiling Ashley with all that stuff. Please, please don't. A kid needs those things so much. . . ."

Dave slipped his arm around Lisa and hugged her close, knowing that from now on he was going to look at his life, and his daughter's life, in a whole new light.

"Even after all that's happened, he still doesn't want to do anything to hurt his brother," Dave said. "Can you believe that?"

"Yeah," Lisa said. "I can believe it."

Dave thought about how she'd held out hope about her own brother to the point of traveling hundreds of miles to San Antonio on the off chance that he'd taken a turn for the better. If anybody could understand how Gabrio felt, it was her. And she promised she'd be there to help him when they got to San Antonio, a promise he knew beyond all doubt that she would keep.

I don't want to depend on anyone, and I don't want anyone depending on me.

Dave hadn't bought that when Lisa said it two nights ago in Monterrey, and he sure wasn't buying it now.

Gabrio returned a few minutes later carrying a tattered canvas bag.

"Anything else?" Dave asked.

The kid glanced helplessly around the filthy little house, then reached up and rubbed a crucifix he wore between his thumb and forefinger. Finally he shook his head.

Dave stood up. "Then let's go."

chapter nineteen

Sera picked up a tray of drinks off the bar, wishing she knew what was happening at Gabrio's house. Forty-five minutes had passed since she'd phoned Dave to tell him Ivan was here. It would take ten minutes for them to get from her house to Gabrio's. What in the world was happening?

She glanced over to Ivan's table, where he, Juan, and Enrique sat drinking as usual. So far, so good.

The bartender had slipped away for a moment, so she ducked behind the bar, made a couple of drinks to fill an order, and put them on a tray. Coming back around, she scooped up the tray to take it to one of the tables.

"Sera."

She turned back, shocked to see who was standing behind her.

Robert Douglas.

At nearly six-foot-two, he towered over her, staring down at her with dark eyes that had once seemed merely unapproachable. Knowing what she knew now, they seemed cruel and merciless.

What did he want?

Calm down. He comes in here all the time. Nothing new about that.

She set the tray of drinks back down on the bar, hoping he couldn't see her hands shaking. "Hello, Robert."

He settled onto a bar stool. "I just wanted to let you know that I've got a charter flight coming down tomorrow afternoon to take me back to San Antonio for Adam's memorial service on Thursday morning. I know the two of you were close. I thought maybe you'd like to come along."

You bastard. The words beat at her mind, clawing to get out. He was playing it straight down the line, as if he weren't the one who'd ordered Adam's execution, as if he weren't the one who had sabotaged Lisa's plane, as if he weren't the one who had caused this terrible chain of events that just might end up with a young boy getting killed. Of course he'd show up for the memorial service. People would question it if he didn't. And he would stand there with a pious look on his face, listening to one person after another saying wonderful things about Adam, a man whose shoes Robert wasn't fit to lick.

"I'm sorry," she said. "I wish I could, but I've been sick for the past few days and missed work. I really shouldn't miss any more. But if you'll extend my condolences to his family I'd appreciate it."

"I will." He shook his head sadly. "Adam's death was such a shame. He was a good friend."

Sera swallowed the anger that boiled into her throat, warning herself to say very little. The last thing she needed was to tip off Robert that she knew more about this situation than she should.

"Yes," she agreed. "I'm going to miss him."

"Did you see the news report about Lisa Merrick?"

Sera's heart beat frantically. "Uh . . . yes. I did. It said she survived the plane crash that killed Adam. And that she was smuggling drugs. I can't imagine that she would do such a thing."

"I'm afraid it's true," Robert said. "Of course, no one believes Adam had anything to do with it. He was just flying back with her on a regular run when she also happened to be carrying contraband. He was nothing but an innocent bystander who got caught up in a drug war."

Your drug war, you bastard. "They said she was arrested trying to smuggle something on a plane into the U.S. Is that true?"

"Yes." Robert shook his head sadly. "Some people do things that the rest of us will never understand."

To her surprise, he reached out and covered her hand with his where it lay against the bar, giving her a smile that didn't quite reach his eyes. "If you'd like to reconsider attending the service, I can arrange a hotel room for you for tomorrow night and then fly you back down here after the service on Thursday. Are you sure you won't come with me?"

His hand tightened against hers, and Sera thought she was going to be sick. "No, Robert," she said, extracting her hand from beneath his. "As I said, I have obligations here."

"I understand. I'll be flying out at four o'clock tomorrow. If you change your mind, you know where to find me."

With that, he tossed a few hundred pesos on the bar and walked out the door. She hated him with every ounce of her being. If he never got what was coming to him in this world, she prayed he'd get it in the next one.

She picked up the tray of drinks again. When she turned, she saw Ivan rising from the table where he'd been sitting with Juan and Enrique, tossing down money at the same time.

No, no, no!

She set the drinks back down on the bar and hurried over as nonchalantly as she could, pretending to be clearing the table behind where he'd been sitting.

"Leaving so soon, Ivan?"

"Yeah. I'm done."

Sera felt a jolt of panic. "Why, I don't think that's possible. There's still alcohol behind that bar."

"Got lots to do." He paused, eyeing her up and down. "Unless you'd like to pull up a chair and join me."

The very thought revolted Sera. "Now, Ivan, you know I'm working. Ario doesn't like us messing around on the job."

"Now, you know I'm one of Ario's best customers. Do you really think he's going to mess with me?"

Sera couldn't think of anything to say. Absolutely nothing. If she didn't sit down with him, he was liable to walk right out that door.

"Uh . . . sure," she said. "I'll sit for a minute. Just let me get this round of drinks to some other customers."

Without so much as a backward glance to Juan and Enrique, Ivan moved to a table for two along the wall, where he slumped down in one of the chairs. Sera took the drinks to the customers who had ordered them, moving as slowly as she could, praying every moment that the phone would ring.

Nothing.

Finally, when she couldn't put it off any longer, she sat down beside Ivan. He leaned toward her, moving so close she could smell the alcohol on his breath. She hated the way his eyes narrowed when he drank, with a lethal expression that set her nerves on edge.

"I like that nice, big farmhouse of yours," he said. "We could have a really good time there. Maybe even tonight." He paused. "Maybe even now."

"What? You're not even going to buy me a drink first?"

A thin smile came across his lips as he clearly saw himself leaping the first hurdle. He had no idea that very soon he'd be landing on the other side facedown in the dirt.

"Sure," he said. "Whatever you say."

"Sera!" Ario called out. "Phone for you."

Sera's heart leapt with hope. She started to rise from her chair, but Ivan wrapped his fingers around her wrist. "Tell Ario to take a message."

"I can't. It could be one of my pregnant mothers with a problem. I have to answer."

He tightened his grip. "We were just starting to have a good time."

"Small delay," she said, staring him directly in the eye. "That's all."

Slowly he released her, then leveled a gaze at her. "Come right back."

"Sure, Ivan."

Sera slipped away from the table and hurried into the kitchen. She grabbed the phone. "Hello?"

"Sera. It's Lisa. We're back at your house, and everything's fine. Gabrio is here. He's coming with us."

"Oh, thank God," she said. "Thank God." Sera breathed deeply, feeling as if the concrete block that had been pressing against her chest for the past two days had finally lifted.

"Is Ivan still there?" Lisa asked.

"Yes. And I'm leaving right now."

Sera hung up the phone and glanced back out to the bar, where Ivan sat sprawled in his chair waiting for her return, clearly on his way to becoming a monumental drunk. She slipped out the back door and hurried to her car, thinking that if there was any justice in this world, he'd drink himself to death.

When Adam heard the front door open downstairs, he sat up suddenly, praying to God that everything had turned out okay. A few minutes later, he heard footsteps on the stairs and Lisa appeared at the doorway.

"Gabrio?" he said.

"Downstairs. He's coming with us."

Adam exhaled with relief. "I knew you could do it, Lisa. I knew you could. Thank you."

Lisa came into the room and sat down in the chair beside Adam. "I've got to tell you, though. He's pretty freaked out right now."

"What do you mean?"

"When Dave and I got there, he had a gun to his head."

Adam just stared at her, blinking with disbelief. "He was going to kill himself?"

"I can't say for sure that he would have done it. But he was really shook up. Dave had to talk the gun out of his hand."

"But why would he want to kill himself?"

"Because he's the one who informed on us. That led to Robert trying to kill us, so he thinks he's the cause of everything. And with the possibility of his brother coming after him . . ." Lisa sighed. "He thought it was his only way out."

"Is he all right now?"

"He's still a little shaky. Not thinking too clearly. But he's made the decision to come with us."

"Thank God. Send him up here, will you? I want to talk to him."

Lisa patted Adam on the arm and stood up. "Sure. I'll go get him."

A few minutes later, Adam heard footsteps on the stairs. Gabrio appeared at the doorway. Hollow half circles darkened the area below his eyes, eyes that radiated a wariness so ingrained that Adam wondered if it would ever go away.

"Come in," Adam said.

Still the kid stood there, uneasiness shouting from every muscle in his body. His gaze went to the bandage on Adam's head. Gabrio rolled his eyes heavenward for a moment, his chest heaving with a harsh breath.

"Oh, man. I'm so sorry about what happened. I should have stopped them. I should have—"

"No. You couldn't have."

"I should have done something. Anything but let them . . ." Tears filled his eyes. "Anything but let them shoot you."

"Come here," Adam said.

Gabrio paused, his lips tight, and even from across the room Adam could see him trembling. Slowly he walked toward the bed.

Adam sat up and swung his legs over the edge of the bed. "Sit down for a minute, okay?"

Gabrio looked down at the overstuffed chair.

"It's okay," Adam said. "Just sit."

The kid sat down, his elbows on his knees and his hands clasped in front of him, refusing to meet Adam's eyes.

"Listen to me," Adam said. "You couldn't have stopped them. If you'd tried to, you would have gotten both of us killed. You did exactly what you should have."

The kid just stared at his lap, shaking his head slowly.

"Gabrio."

Slowly he looked up.

"It was one of the bravest things I've ever seen any man do," Adam said. "You saved my life. I'll never be able to repay you for that."

Adam held out his hand. Gabrio looked down at it, as if he hadn't the faintest idea what to do. Adam continued to hold his hand out until finally Gabrio reached out hesitantly and shook it.

"I'm sorry for what Ivan did," Gabrio said, his voice quivering.

"You're not your brother. You don't have to apologize for anything he's done."

Gabrio nodded a little, falling silent.

Adam could tell Gabrio still didn't fully believe anything he was being told and years might pass before he found the capacity to trust anyone. But even though he had a long road ahead of him, at least the worst was over. At least now he'd have a chance at a decent life, and Adam was going to do everything he could to make sure he got one.

Sera parked her car in front of her house and got out, blinking against the late afternoon sun streaming through the windshield. Hurrying inside, she found Lisa and Dave waiting in her living room.

"Where's Gabrio?" she asked.

"Upstairs with Adam," Lisa said.

Sera was overcome by a flood of emotion, so grateful for what they'd done that she could hardly put it into words. "Thank you. Both of you. I don't know what I'd have done without you." Her eyes filled with tears. She put her arms around Lisa and gave her a hug, then did the same to Dave.

"No doubt about it," she told him, sniffing a little. "I'll be putting in your application for sainthood the minute we get to San Antonio."

He smiled. "I'd have settled for angel wings."

Lisa stole a glance at Dave, and Sera could tell that her contention that he was just a friend wasn't even close to the truth. There was something so real, so telling, in Lisa's gaze—admiration, attraction, appreciation, all those things that signaled just how much this man meant to her.

Friends, maybe. But that certainly wasn't all.

"Okay," Dave said. "We need to get out of here." He turned to Lisa. "Take one of the cars, drive out, and get the plane ready to take off. I'll get everyone packed up here. By the time we get there, you'll have the plane ready and we can leave." He turned to Sera. "Do you have your things together?"

Sera nodded. "Everything's packed and sitting by the back door."

"Do you have some extra blankets we could bring along?" Lisa asked. "The heater in this plane isn't the best, and Adam needs to stay warm."

"I'll get them right now." Sera walked to the stairs, then turned back suddenly. "Oh! The ponies! If I'm going to be gone for a while, I need to turn them out to pasture."

Dave held up his palm. "You get the blankets. I'll turn the ponies out."

"There's a twenty-acre pasture with a stock pond to the west of the barn. They can stay there for the time being."

"Okay. Then meet me at the back door and we'll load up."

Sera nodded. As Dave and Lisa went to the back door, Sera went up the stairs into one of her guest bedrooms and fished through a closet to find two blankets they could take along, grabbing an extra pillow at the same time.

She came back down the stairs and had almost reached the bottom when she heard a knock on her front door. She jerked to a halt, her hand tightening on the banister.

Three more loud raps.

Who could that be?

She prayed it wasn't a woman in labor. She couldn't deal with that now.

Trotting down the final two stairs, she spilled the blankets and pillow onto the sofa, then walked toward the front door, stopping first to peer through the curtains to the porch.

Ivan.

A chill of fear swept through her. She knew he'd be angry that she'd left, but she never for a moment imagined that he'd follow her to her house. What if he saw Adam or Gabrio? Or even Dave and Lisa? What would he do?

He'll go away. Just say nothing, and he'll go away.

He beat on the door again.

Sera squeezed her eyes closed, willing him to leave. For a moment, she heard nothing. Then she saw the doorknob turn.

She gasped softly, unable to remember if she'd locked the door or not. She felt a call for help rising in her chest, but she stifled it immediately. It would only bring Gabrio down the stairs, and if Ivan happened to get inside she had no idea what he might do if he saw his brother here. She stood there, immobilized by panic, watching as the knob twisted ninety degrees. Then the door clattered in its frame.

Yes. Thank God. It's locked.

Relief gushed through her. A few moments passed. Then she heard something rattling around in the lock.

What was he doing?

Seconds ticked by. The knob turned again. This time, the door opened, and Ivan stepped into the house. Sera's heart slammed against her chest.

Their gazes met, and a drunken, malevolent expression spread across his face. "You ran out on me. Not a smart thing to do."

She raised her chin and spoke sharply. "That door was locked."

He gave her a mocking laugh. "You think a lock keeps me out?" He clicked his pocketknife shut and slid it back into his pocket, then shut the door.

"I think you'd better leave," Sera said.

"Oh, yeah? Is that what you think? How about if I tell you I'm not interested in what you think?" His gaze slid all the way down her body and back up again. "You got a couple other things I'm interested in, though."

You have to get him out of here. Now.

"We had plans," he said, moving toward her like a wolf edging toward its prey. "Remember?"

Sera was silent.

He took one threatening step after another, backing her against the sofa. "So you want to tell me why you walked out on me?"

"I'm sorry, Ivan," she said with as much of a conciliatory tone as she could manage. "I guess I'm still not feeling well. Maybe another time."

"No," he said sharply. "Not another time. Now."

When he came closer still and pressed himself against her, she felt something hard at his waist beneath his jacket.

A gun. He's got a gun.

It was all Sera could do to remain calm, to try to think, to find a way to get this man out of her house before he had the opportunity to use that gun.

Then Ivan looked to one side, his eyes narrowing with confusion. "What the hell is that?"

Sera turned to where he was looking, and dread shuddered through her. Gabrio's bag was sitting on the floor beside the sofa.

"That's my brother's," Ivan said.

"What are you talking about?"

"My brother's bag!" Ivan said. "What the fuck is he doing here?"

"He's not here. That's not his bag."

"You think I don't know what it looks like?" Ivan glared at her. "A little young for you, isn't he?"

"Ivan, I'm telling you he's not here."

Ivan turned immediately and strode into the kitchen. "Gabrio! Where are you? Get the hell out here!"

Ivan came back out of the kitchen and headed up the stairs. Sera raced after him. She grabbed him by the arm and pulled him around. "Ivan! Stop!"

He yanked his arm from her grip and took the stairs two at a time. He hit the second floor landing and strode down the hall, screaming for Gabrio. Sera raced back through the living room, searching frantically for something to use as a weapon. Anything. Anything that would stop Ivan from going into that bedroom.

When Gabrio heard the muffled shouts of a man downstairs, he snapped his head around, listening. But it wasn't until footsteps pounded up the stairs and the shouting became more distinct that he realized whose voice it was, and a cold, ugly fear rose inside him.

"It's Ivan," he said to Adam. "Oh, Jesus. My brother is here!"

Adam sat up suddenly. "Are you sure?"

"Yes! It's him!"

"Gabrio! Get out of here! *Now!*"

But it was too late. A second later Ivan stormed into the room. He stopped short, staring at Adam, then swung his gaze around to Gabrio. A look of utter confusion entered his eyes.

"What the fuck is going on here?"

Gabrio heard the drunken slur in his brother's voice, that tone he'd heard so many times right before a slap to the side of his head or a backhand across the face. But those things were nothing. Nothing compared to what Ivan was going to do to him now. And what he was going to do to Adam. To everyone.

"He was alive," Gabrio said. "I couldn't let you shoot him again! Ivan, please! It's not right to do this. Can't you see that?"

Ivan's expression leapt into red-hot rage. "What the hell you talking about? You had a job to do, and you didn't do it!"

Slowly he reached beneath his coat and pulled out a gun.

"Oh, Jesus, Ivan! Don't do this! *Please* don't do this!"

Ivan looked at Gabrio, his eyes cold. "I'll deal with you in a minute."

He raised his gun and pointed it directly at Adam. In that instant, Sera burst into the room behind Ivan, swinging a fireplace poker in a wide arc. She caught him in the upper arm at the same moment he pulled the trigger. A shot exploded, sailing harmlessly into the wall in an explosion of plaster. Ivan stumbled sideways and fell to his knees.

Gabrio dived at his brother, knocking him to his back and climbing on top of him. Ivan still had the gun clenched in his fist. He smacked Gabrio on the side of the head with it. Gabrio recoiled, but he was so filled with fury, so filled with hate, so filled with disgust for everything his brother was that the pain didn't even register. Ivan outweighed him by a good thirty pounds, but it didn't matter. He grabbed his brother's wrist and smacked his hand that held the gun against the floor, once, twice, until finally the weapon came loose. Gabrio grabbed it, backed away, and scrambled to his feet, pointing it at Ivan.

Ivan stood, stumbling a little, holding his palms up. "Hey, man, what the hell is this?" He gave Gabrio a shaky smile. "You're going to shoot me? Is that it?"

"Take one step, and I will. Swear to God, Ivan. I will."

Ivan laughed, but it sounded hollow. "No, you won't. I'm your brother. You won't shoot me."

Gabrio's mind felt dark and sluggish, every horrible second passing like an hour. His hands were shaking so hard he could barely hold the weapon.

"Give me the gun, kid," Ivan said.

"Why?" Gabrio shouted. "So you can kill somebody else?"

"What do you think you're doing, holding a gun on your own brother?" Ivan said, anger edging his voice. "Huh, Gabrio? What the hell is that?"

"I have to stop you!"

"Give me the gun," Ivan said sharply, holding out his hand. "Now!"

"No!" His hands shook wildly. "I'm not giving it to you!"

"I said give me the goddamned gun!"

His face twisted with anger, Ivan strode toward Gabrio, his hand out, as if he intended to rip the gun right out of his brother's grasp.

Gabrio pulled the trigger.

The shot seemed to echo a thousand times over in the tiny bedroom. The force of the bullet knocked Ivan backward, his hands flying into the air. He hit the floor on his back, a starburst of blood staining his shirt.

And then he was still.

Gabrio's mouth dropped open, and for several seconds all he could do was stare down at his brother's body, his gaze going first to the bloodstain on Ivan's chest, then traveling upward to his eyes—dark, glassy eyes staring straight into death.

He's dead. You killed your own brother.

Shaking violently, Gabrio dropped his hand to his side,

then relaxed his fingers. As the gun clattered to the floor, he fell to his knees beside it, bowing his head, sobs welling up in his throat as anguish overtook him.

This couldn't be happening. It couldn't.

He felt Sera kneel beside him. She put her arm around his shoulders, and he started to cry. He couldn't help it. She was talking, saying over and over that it was okay, that he hadn't had any choice, but Ivan was his brother, his *brother*. . . .

A few moments later, Gabrio heard footsteps coming up the stairs and Dave and Lisa burst through the bedroom door.

"We heard shots," Lisa said. Then she glanced down at the floor, a look of horror spreading over her face. "Oh, my God. What happened?"

"I shot him," Gabrio said, his voice strangled with sobs. "He was going to kill Adam. I had to do something. I *had* to. . . ."

Dave knelt beside Ivan. Put his fingers on his neck. He looked up at Lisa and shook his head, confirming what Gabrio already knew.

He's dead. He really is dead. Oh, God. . . .

Gabrio heard Sera telling Dave and Lisa what had happened in a hushed, anxious voice but barely comprehended the words. He felt like he was going to throw up, and he couldn't stop crying. Then Lisa knelt next to him, pulling him into her arms and holding him tightly, saying the same things Sera had.

Dave asked Sera for an old sheet, and he spread it over Ivan's body. Then he turned to Gabrio.

"I'm sorry," he said softly. "I'm so sorry this had to happen."

Through tear-filled eyes, Gabrio looked up at Dave, wondering why he wasn't happy that Ivan was dead. Instead, his face was filled with sadness. Then Gabrio looked at Lisa, at Sera, at Adam. He couldn't believe they were looking at him the same way Dave was, with sorrow that somebody was dead, even if it was Ivan, a person who'd only made their lives hell. And then he thought back to how he'd told these people that he wasn't going to say anything against Ivan about the terrible things he'd done.

He bowed his head again, feeling so stupid for that now. So damned stupid. They had to think he was so dumb for being loyal to somebody so awful, even if he was his brother.

And they were right.

Gabrio hated everything that had led to this. He hated his brother for being a criminal, he hated that Ivan had tried to murder people, and he hated Robert Douglas for being the one who had ordered him to kill.

His head still pounding with misery, Gabrio looked at Lisa. "Robert Douglas. He told Ivan to kill people. Is he going to pay for what he's done?"

Lisa glanced up at Dave, sighing a little. "I don't know. Adam can back up Dave and me and get us off the hook, but by now Robert is on to us. He'll have covered his tracks. We may never be able to tie him to the counterfeiting network. And if we can't do that, prosecuting him for anything else . . ." She sighed. "I just don't know."

Gabrio swallowed his tears. "If I told you where they're making the drugs, would that help?"

chapter twenty

Dave stood motionless along with everyone else in the room, staring at Gabrio as if he'd handed them the key to the whole puzzle. And maybe he had.

"Where?" Dave said.

"There's an abandoned mining camp a couple of miles outside town. That's where they're doing it."

Dave exchanged glances with Lisa. She looked as surprised as he was. "It can't be."

"I'm not lying. Swear to God."

"We've been there recently. We didn't see an indication of anything going on. Where exactly are they operating?"

"There's a big building back in the trees where they used to keep a bunch of mining equipment. That's the place."

Dave didn't remember seeing any building like that, but the area had been heavily wooded. And he'd certainly had no reason to be looking there for the counterfeiting operation.

"There's machinery in that building to do the counterfeiting?" Dave asked.

"Yeah," Gabrio said. "I don't know how they do it, exactly, but the stuff is there."

"But what about electricity?" Dave asked. "Surely they'd need something to—"

"Diesel generators."

This was beginning to make an awful lot of sense to Dave. "Are there records inside that building? Documents that will implicate Robert?"

"Files, I think. Don't know what's in them."

"We were so close to it," Lisa said to Dave. "Why didn't we see people out there?"

"By that time, Robert had probably suspended production, worried over what had happened. He was holding off gearing back up again until the heat was off."

"Dave," Lisa said. "If we can get those records . . ."

"We can take him down."

For a long time they didn't speak, the possibilities crackling in the air between them.

"But we have to get Adam and Gabrio out of here first," Lisa said.

"No," Adam said. "You stay here. Get the evidence. We'll go to Monterrey by car."

"You're injured," Sera said. "If the road is rough—"

"It's not a bad road between here and there," Adam said. "And it's more predictable than turbulence on a plane."

"Are you sure you'll be okay?" Dave asked.

"Positive."

Dave turned to Sera. "How much gas do you have in your car?"

"I filled up yesterday."

He turned to Adam. "Okay then. Here's what we'll do. Sera can drive you and Gabrio into Monterrey. Get to a hospital so they can check you out, and then start the wheels in motion to get Gabrio out of the country. Lisa and I will stay here, and as soon as it gets dark tonight we'll check out the mining camp, find the evidence we need to nail Robert, then fly back to the U.S. Then the minute he crosses the border, they can get him on the drug charges."

"We're not even completely sure he's still down here, are we?" Lisa asked.

"Yes, we are," Sera said. "He came into Esmerelda's when I was there this afternoon."

"He did?" Adam said.

"Yes. He told me he'd ordered a charter flight to arrive here tomorrow afternoon to take him back to San Antonio. He invited me to go with him."

Adam's eyes narrowed. "What for?"

"He said he knew how close you and I had been, and he asked if I'd like to go with him to attend your memorial service on Thursday morning."

"Bastard." Adam's jaw tightened with anger. "I know what he wants. If you went with him, before the day was out he'd be after you just like he is every other woman in this town. And he has the nerve to attend my memorial service when he's the one who tried to kill me?"

He turned to Dave and Lisa. "Get him. Whatever it takes."

Ten minutes later, Dave and Lisa helped Adam into the backseat that Sera had carefully prepared with pillows and blankets to make him as comfortable as possible. Leaving Sera with him, they went back up the porch steps again to grab her bags that were just inside the kitchen door.

"Hey, man."

Dave turned at the sound of Gabrio's voice. He stood on the back porch, his hands thrust inside his pockets.

"My brother," he said. "What are you doing with him?"

Dave didn't really want to think about that yet, but the kid had a right to know what was going to happen. "I'll have to bury him. Someplace remote where nobody will find him. I'm sorry about that, Gabrio, but I just can't risk—"

"I know. It's okay."

Still he stood there, staring at Dave.

"What is it?" Dave asked.

Gabrio let out a shaky breath. "I—I know what he's done and everything, but can you say something? You know, after you do it? We're Catholic, or at least my mother was. . . ."

Right now Dave didn't feel the least bit inclined toward any kind of mercy for Ivan Ramirez, but he felt a tremendous sense of loyalty to Gabrio.

"Sure I will. Anything in particular?"

"There's that one verse," he said. "Something about 'the Lord is my shepherd.' Do you know that one?"

"Yeah. I know that one."

"That'd be okay."

Dave nodded. "Time for you to get on the road."

Dave and Lisa grabbed Sera's bags and took them to the car. Sera got out of the backseat and slid behind the wheel, and Gabrio got into the passenger seat.

Before shutting Sera's door, Dave leaned in to talk to everyone. "Adam, you and Gabrio stay out of sight on the way out of town. Sera, don't stop for anything. Just move on through. And, Adam, make sure whoever you talk to about a visa for Gabrio keeps it confidential. I don't want Robert tipped off until we can get out to that mining camp and see what's there."

Adam nodded. "Thank you both for everything."

"Just be careful. And call us the minute you hit Monterrey so we'll know you're safe."

Dave stepped back and stood next to Lisa as Sera closed the door. She started the car, and Dave and Lisa watched as they drove away. With the sun low on the horizon, nightfall would be coming soon.

"Thank God we got them out of here," Lisa said, then turned to Dave. "When should we head out to the mining camp?"

"We'll wait until dark. Might as well have all the cover we can get."

An hour and a half later, Dave and Lisa drove up the pot-holed road leading to the mining camp. Dave stayed alert for anyone in the area, but it seemed as deserted as the night he'd come here to rescue Lisa. A half moon lit the sky, dimming periodically as clouds passed over it.

They passed the bunkhouse, then kept on moving up the road, peering through the trees until they saw the structure Gabrio had talked about. Dave swung the car around to the back of the building where it couldn't be seen from the road.

They got out of the car. The night held just a hint of warmth, but the air was perfectly still and painfully quiet. Every step they took through fallen leaves seemed sharp and magnified, every whispered word a shout.

On first glance the building looked as deserted as the bunkhouse, but when they got out of the car Dave saw a pair of diesel generators beside the building, just as Gabrio had indicated.

The door was padlocked. Dave took out a crowbar, and after a considerable amount of effort he finally managed to break through the lock.

"Anybody who comes out here is going to know this place was broken into," Lisa said.

"Can't be helped. Hopefully we'll have Robert nailed before he realizes anyone's been checking him out."

They went inside, shining flashlights around to check out the building. While the exterior looked decades old, the interior had been cleaned up considerably. Dave saw something that looked like a large mixing vat, along with a piece of machinery that appeared to contain molds for the pills. Creating counterfeit drugs was an astonishingly simple process. The chemical content of the pills was irrelevant, and counterfeiters hardly worried about the environmental conditions surrounding the manufacture of their product.

In the rear of the building Dave saw a door that looked as if it led to an office. He handed Lisa his gun. "Keep watch at the window. I don't want anyone walking in here unexpectedly. I'll see what I can find in the office."

Lisa nodded, and Dave went into the office, shining a flashlight around the perimeter until he located two file cabinets. He opened the drawers and scanned the contents, pulling out one file after another. Some of them didn't seem to pertain to anything concerning the drugs, unless he just wasn't seeing the connection. Some appeared to be production reports, which might help prove the magnitude of the operation but not who was involved. But when he came upon a folder containing a list of names, he knew he'd found something they could use.

He stuffed the lists back inside the file, tucked it under his arm, and shut the drawer. He came out of the office.

"Find anything?" Lisa asked.

"I think I struck gold."

He opened the file folder and Lisa shined the flashlight on it.

"See these names?" he said. "Looks to me like they belong to pharmaceutical sales reps who are peddling legitimate products along with the counterfeit one. Every one of them is associated with a city, a territory, and a list of pharmacies."

"Do you see Robert's name anywhere?"

"No, but unless I miss my guess, this list could lead us right to one of the sales reps, who just might be willing to give Robert up in exchange for immunity. And look at this."

He flipped a couple of pages, then pointed. "It looks as if the network spreads throughout Texas, running all the way from San Antonio to Dallas, then east to the Louisiana border."

"Right through Tolosa?"

"Exactly. If I can fax these documents to Alex, he can help us out on that end. Find somebody who's willing to talk."

"That's perfect."

"Any idea where there's a fax machine in this town?"

"Sure. At the clinic."

"Any other place?"

"I have no idea. Santa Rios isn't exactly the business hub of central Mexico."

"Then we need to get into the clinic."

"I have a key. But isn't that a little dangerous?"

"Would Robert have any reason to be there this late?"

"I can't see why. But the apartment building where he stays is right next door."

"As long as we're careful, we should be able to get in and get out without anyone knowing it. Five minutes, max."

They left the mining camp with the file folders, and a few minutes later Dave parked the car a block away in the alley that ran behind the clinic. Keeping an eye on the apartments next door, they approached the building, finding it completely dark. Lisa put a key in the lock and let them in. Dave flicked on a flashlight, holding it toward the floor, and they went into the small administrative office and found the fax machine.

"Wait a minute," Lisa said. "If Robert sees phone records with a call to Tolosa—"

"He'll probably never even notice. And even if he does, I

doubt he'll put two and two together." Dave glanced over his shoulder. "If Robert were to come here, would he enter through the front door or the back?"

"The back."

"Keep watch for me."

Lisa went to the window and peered through the blinds to the apartment building next door.

"Everything's quiet," she told Dave.

"Good. This'll only take a minute."

Dave picked up the phone and dialed Alex's house. His brother came on the line.

"Alex. It's me."

"Dave! Where are you?"

"No questions. Just shut up and listen. I'm deadly fucking serious here."

Dave's voice stopped his brother short. "I'm listening."

"Give me your fax number. Home."

Alex gave it to him, and Dave wrote it down.

"I'm sending you some documents. Very important, very confidential. I'm going to call you back the moment I send them to make sure you got them, then call you later and explain."

"Okay. I'll be waiting."

Dave hung up the phone, dialed the number he'd written down, and pushed the send button. He held his breath as the speaker in the fax machine blared out the number dialing, then the ring.

"Damn, that's loud," he whispered. "Are we okay out there?"

"Nobody in sight."

Now, if only this machine didn't glitch and Alex's machine picked up . . .

Dave watched and waited. Finally the machine caught the first page and pulled it through with a soft mechanical grinding noise, and then the others after that. *Damn*. Did it always take this long for a fax machine to suck up a document and send it?

Finally the machine beeped, signaling that the transmission was complete.

Dave picked up the phone, called Alex back and verified that he had the documents and that he could read them clearly, then hung up. Dave quickly grabbed the sheets he'd faxed and stuffed them into the file folder.

"Done," he said. "Let's get out of here."

They hurried out of the room, closing the office door behind them. Dave followed Lisa out of the clinic. Watching the apartment building carefully, they hurried to the car and backed out of the alley. Ten minutes later, they were back at Sera's house. Dave phoned Alex.

"Tell me what I'm looking at," Alex said.

"Distribution records of the pharmaceutical drug ring based out of Santa Rios. Names associated with pharmacies all over Texas and New Mexico. Look near the bottom of the fourth page. The network goes through Dallas all the way to Tyler and Tolosa."

"So who do you think the names are beside the pharmacies?"

"Maybe the pharmacists themselves, but I'm betting they're sales reps acting as middlemen. You'll be able to find out quickly enough. The pharmacies may not even know they're getting counterfeit product. They're buying the drugs in good faith and selling them as if they're the real thing."

"You could be right," Alex said.

"Can you find out for sure who these people are? Lean on a few of them for me and find somebody who'll talk? We know Robert Douglas is at the heart of the operation, but we need somebody who's willing to testify to that, or lead us to somebody who can."

"I'll see what I can do. So where is Douglas right now?"

"In Santa Rios. But we've found out that he's flying out tomorrow afternoon so he can be at Adam Decker's memorial service in San Antonio on Thursday morning."

"Give me the number where you are."

Dave gave him Sera's phone number.

"I'll start first thing in the morning," Alex said. "When are you coming back?"

"As soon as I know for sure that you've got somebody

who'll talk and no more evidence is necessary. We can be back in a matter of a few hours."

"Okay. I'll do what I can."

"How is Ashley? Does she miss me?"

"Miss you? Hell, no. When is there time to miss you? John bought her a pony, and tomorrow they're taking her to Disney World. He nixed the college education thing, though. He figures that's your responsibility."

"John's a smart-ass."

Alex's voice became serious. "Of course she misses you. So be careful."

"I hear you. You just get me that informant and everything's going to be fine. Get back to me as soon as you can."

"Consider it done."

"Give Ashley a kiss for me."

"Consider that done, too."

Dave hung up the phone and turned to Lisa.

"So what now?" she asked.

"We wait."

Adam lay in the backseat of the car, staring out the window into the night sky, wishing the clouds would pass. A bright moon would help. Stars. Some kind of light. They'd been traveling over two hours, the miles speeding away beneath them, but still they weren't moving fast enough.

He looked over at Gabrio asleep in the front seat, then turned his gaze to Sera. He tried to picture her face in his mind, but other thoughts crept in, and the longer he lay in the darkness, the more completely the barren landscape invaded his consciousness.

Sleep. Just sleep. That's all you have to do. Then when you wake up, you'll be there. People. City lights. And then you'll be fine.

But with every mile that passed away his nerves felt more taut, his mind jumbled and dark. A sense of déjà vu rose inside him that made his stomach turn over.

He heard Ellen's voice, soft but desperate: *Adam. Something's wrong.*

He'd heard those words a thousand times inside his head in the past three years, ten thousand times, and now he heard them louder than ever. They seemed to latch on to one corner of his mind, then balloon up inside him until they drove every other thought away. No matter what he did, he heard every tortured breath, every gasp of pain, every agonized sound of Ellen's cries unleashed inside his head.

Adam, help me! Please help me!

And then the most horrifying thought of all swept through his mind. He saw not Ellen's terrified face but Sera's, crying in pain, begging with him, pleading with him. . . .

A strangled gasp tore from his throat. "Sera, stop the car."

She whipped around. "What?"

He sat up, his head pounding. "I said stop!"

Sera wheeled the car to the shoulder of the road and put it in park, the engine still running. Leaping out of the car, she yanked open the back door. She climbed in and knelt down beside him, her face filled with panic. "Adam, what is it?"

He squeezed his eyes closed, trying desperately to get a grip on himself. He took several deep breaths, hating the fear and despair that had taken hold of him one more time.

"I can't lie in the backseat of this car. Not on this road. Not in the dark."

"What's the matter?"

He couldn't tell her. He couldn't say it. God, the last thing he wanted to do on this barren stretch of road was tell her why his heart was pounding and his mouth was dry and his mind just wouldn't forget.

Hold it together. You have to hold it together.

"It's just . . . I just need to sit up front."

"You need to lie down."

"No! Damn it, I need to get out of here!"

Sera recoiled. Gabrio looked over the backseat, his face startled. *You're scaring him. You're scaring that poor kid to death, and that's the last thing on earth he needs right now.*

Adam held up his palm. "I'm sorry," he said, hoarseness clogging his voice. "I just . . . I'm fine. I just need to switch with you, Gabrio. Okay? Can you sit back here and let me sit up there?"

The kid swallowed hard. "Yeah. Sure."

Sera helped Adam out of the car. As Gabrio slid into the backseat, Adam got into the passenger seat, wincing with pain as he sat down. Sera closed the door behind him, then circled the car to get back into the driver's seat.

As she pulled the car back out onto the highway, Adam looked to the road ahead, at the headlights slashing through the darkness and dissipating into nothingness. He felt as if they were driving straight into hell.

"How much farther?" he asked.

"We'll be there within the hour."

He nodded, then turned on the radio. Music would help. Noise. Distraction. He leaned his head gently against the back of the seat.

"Adam?" she whispered. "Are you all right?"

Out of the corner of his eye he saw her turn to him with that sweet expression of love and concern that went straight to his heart.

"Don't worry, Sera. I'll be fine. Really. Just get me to Monterrey, and everything will be fine."

But he wasn't completely sure of that. He just didn't know. Sometimes he thought he'd reached the point where he was sure it wasn't going to bother him anymore, and then something like this would happen and he'd fall apart all over again.

It was never going to end.

Never.

chapter twenty-one

Lisa came out the back door of Sera's house and sat down on the porch swing beside Dave. She handed him a beer, then popped the top on one herself. They swung gently, watching Sera's ponies in the pasture to the east of the barn. The moon had risen to a small half circle of pale amber high in the sky, and warm night air swirled around them, the temperature a good ten degrees higher than normal for this time of year.

"I had my hopes up," Lisa said. "Sera had all the ingredients for margaritas. Unfortunately, I couldn't find any tequila."

"Beer's fine."

"Actually, I was kind of hoping for something stronger."

Dave nodded. "Hell of a day, huh?"

"I've said that every day for the past four days. Is there any end to this?"

"Yes. Alex will call tomorrow and tell us he's got an informant, which means that when Robert crosses the border again he's toast."

"Will Alex be able to pull it off?"

"If anybody can, he can. Once he gets his teeth into something, he doesn't let go."

"Especially if he's helping his brother."

Dave smiled a little. "Yeah."

"You've got a good family, don't you?"

He nodded. "The best."

"You're a lucky man."

Dave turned to Lisa. "Just because you struck out on one family doesn't mean you can't start one of your own."

"It's the kind of life that works for you," she said. "But not for me."

"You need to think twice about that."

"We've talked about this, Dave. I know where I'm going. And that's not it."

Dave nodded and took a sip of beer, staring out into the night. "Have you thought about where this is going?"

"Where what is going?"

"The situation between the two of us."

"Situation?"

"If you hadn't noticed, we've been relatively unable to keep our hands off each other for the past few days."

She turned away. "Just think of it as one extended adrenaline rush. Once that goes away, the rest will go away, too."

"I don't think so."

"Come on, Dave. You and I both know this is a short-term thing. Let's not go looking for any deep meaning here, okay?"

"You mean let's keep it hot and mindless and try really hard not to think about it?"

"I haven't met a man yet who objected to that."

"You've met one now."

For some reason, Lisa suddenly felt hot. Uncomfortable. Still Dave's eyes were on her, probing and insistent, and she countered by replacing the frown she wore with a seductive smile. "So you don't want to have hot sex with me on the back porch?"

"No, I don't." He leaned in, kissed her gently on the lips and whispered, "I'd rather make love to you in the bedroom."

The sensual way the words rolled right off his tongue sent warm shivers down Lisa's spine. For maybe the first time in her life, she sat within kissing distance of a man and had no idea what to say.

Dave set his beer down, then stood up and held out his hand.

"What?" she asked.

"Come with me."

"But—"

"Don't argue."

She opened her mouth to say something. Nothing came

out. Her heart had started to thump a little harder right about the time he kissed her, and it was really gearing up now.

She set her beer down, took his hand, and he led her into the house. But as they walked through the living room she had a sudden uneasy closed-in feeling, as if a touch of claustrophobia had swept over her. When they passed the sofa she stopped him suddenly, circled her arms around his neck, and kissed him deeply.

"Sofas are nice," she whispered against his lips, stroking the back of his neck with her fingertips. "You can do all kinds of things on a sofa."

"Yes. I suppose you can."

He reached up, disengaged her hands from around his neck, and led her up the stairs. Halfway to the second floor, she turned him around and rose to the same step where he stood, inching closer and splaying her palms over his chest. "Ever had sex on a staircase?"

"Can't say that I have."

"It's . . . interesting."

"I'll take your word for that."

He took her hand and continued up the stairs, dragging her right along behind him. They reached the landing and started down the hall.

"Dave—"

"The hall has hardwood floors," he said. "That would be painful."

"There's a rug—"

"Wool. I'm allergic."

"The bathroom—"

"I've already showered today."

He led her into Sera's guest bedroom. The lamp was switched on low, bathing the room in a warm yellow glow. To her surprise, he walked over to where his bag rested on the floor, knelt down, unzipped it, and pulled something out. With a flick of his wrist he tossed a handful of condoms onto the bed.

Lisa stared at them, swallowing hard. "Optimistic, aren't you?"

"I was a Boy Scout."

He took her hand again and pulled her around to face him. He buried his fingers in her hair, pulled her to him, and kissed her deeply. Slowly. Sensually. Moving with the speed of grass growing.

Faster. Faster. Come on. Let's go!

She reached for his shirt buttons. He put his hands against hers, stilled them, then returned them to her sides. She countered by grabbing his belt buckle. He took her hands again, held them at her sides, then inched so close that she had to take a step backward. She bumped into the wall, then looked up to find him staring at her intently. Just the sight of those dark, watchful eyes focused solely on her made her heart leap wildly.

"You know, Lisa, you've given me a hell of a ride over the past couple of days."

She curled her lips into a seductive smile. "Why, thank you. Glad you enjoyed it."

"Trouble is, you didn't come along for the ride, did you?"

She frowned. "What are you talking about?"

"You know what I'm talking about."

She swallowed hard and turned away. "Of course I did."

He took her chin in his hand and turned her back. The moment she met his eyes, she looked away again.

"My God," Dave said. "I'm right."

She slipped away from him, putting some much-needed distance between them, then turned back with a defiant expression. "Well, so what?" She made a scoffing noise. "Men. *Jeez*. Their egos are so fragile. They come all unglued if they think they haven't—"

"This has nothing to do with my fragile ego. It's hard to give somebody something when she refuses to take it."

"It's not important."

He inched close to her again, tucked his hand behind her neck, pulled her toward him, and kissed the spot just beneath her left ear. Warm shivers spread all the way to her toes.

"Tell me, Lisa. Have you ever felt the thing that you're so absolutely sure is unimportant to you?"

"Of course I have."

"With a man?"

She pulled away again. "Will you stop asking stupid questions?"

"Sure. Just as soon as I think you're telling me the truth."

"Please. You're acting like I'm some silly little virgin who doesn't know the meaning of the word *sex*."

"Nope. I can pretty much attest to the fact that you're not one of those. I just think that up to now it's been all give and no take."

"Come on, Dave. Do I strike you as somebody who wouldn't insist on having *everything* I thought I had coming to me?"

"You'd have to want it first."

"And what woman in her right mind wouldn't?"

"One who can't bear the thought of not being in control of every single aspect of her life."

"So now I'm a control freak."

"You said it yourself. That's one reason you like to fly."

"But that doesn't mean I can't *ever* let go."

"Prove it."

"What?"

"Lie down."

"What?"

"Do as I tell you to. Lie down on the bed."

She had no idea what he was going for, but at least being on the bed meant they were that much closer to getting down to business.

She sat on one side of the bed, and Dave pressed her gently down to her back. Then, to her surprise, he took her wrists and lifted her hands over her head until her fingertips brushed the vertical spindles of the headboard.

"Take hold of these," he said, wrapping her fingers around them, "and don't let go."

Her eyes flew open wide, and she jerked her hands away. "Are you crazy?"

Slowly, deliberately, he took her by the wrists again, then wrapped her fingers around the spindles. She snatched her hands away again. "Will you cut it out?"

He sighed, shaking his head. Standing up, he walked over to the draperies, reached for something behind them, and gave it a hard yank. When he turned around, she saw a cord dangling from his hand. He closed his fingers around it and ran it through his palm a couple of times. Lisa's heart jolted as if a thousand-watt current had shot right through it.

"You wouldn't."

"Try me."

She sat up. "This is silly."

He strode back across the room, every step he took feeling to Lisa as if a gale-force wind were blowing her down to her back all over again. She stared up at him, swallowing hard.

"What's it going to be, Lisa? My way?" He nodded down at the cord. "Or this way?"

"Well, now," she said, trying to keep her voice light. "You've never struck me as the kinky type."

"Nothing kinky about it. It's simply a battle I intend to win."

Her breath was coming faster. She couldn't seem to control it. No matter how hard she concentrated, still she was breathing faster. He sat down on the bed beside her, rested his palm against her hip, leaned in, and kissed her neck.

"What if I scream?" she said.

His breath tickled her ear. "The damsel in distress thing really isn't your style."

"Maybe not, but I'm betting it's effective."

He eased his lips along the column of her throat. "Nah, I don't think you'll scream. See, there's this little matter of keeping our presence here a secret. This is not the time to draw attention to ourselves."

"We're out in the middle of nowhere."

"Then screaming won't do you any good, will it?"

He moved his lips over her collarbone, his voice humming against her, sending shivers all the way to her toes.

"Forget screaming," she said. "I've got a pair of knees, and I'm not afraid to use them."

He stood up quickly, grabbed the bedspread, and pulled it hard around her legs. Still standing, he put his knee down on top of it, until her legs were trapped like a butterfly inside a cocoon. She squirmed against him.

"I'm tougher than I look," she warned. "You might have a fight on your hands."

"A fight?" he said, raising an eyebrow. "Now, I do love a good fight."

"No way. You're one of the good guys, Dave. Calm, cool, and sensible."

"Maybe not."

"Oh, really? That's the Dave I know. What's changed?"

"You came back into my life." He stared down at her, his expression charged with emotion. "And that changed everything."

Lisa felt a fundamental shift at that moment, as if that gale-force wind had whipped around and smacked her flat on her back all over again. A few minutes ago he'd asked her where this was going between them. She still had no answer for that, but she had the most uncanny feeling that she was on the verge of finding out.

With her legs still wrapped tightly in the covers, Dave sat down beside her, made a slipknot in the cord, then reached for her wrist. She yanked it away.

"Oh, all *right*." She circled her fingers around the spindles of the headboard, which gave her the most heart-thumping feeling of having her body completely exposed.

"Now," he said, "no matter what happens, do *not* let go."

"If I do?"

"It's back to Plan A. And God only knows when I'll let you go then."

She believed him. Every word. She flexed her fingers against the spindles, telling herself that it was no big deal, really. That she could let go anytime she wanted to.

"This is really dumb," she told him.

"But no problem for you, right?"

"Of course not. Well, aside from the fact that the man I'm sleeping with appears to have some deep-seated bondage fantasies he's just dying to play out. I admit I find that a little distressing."

With a tiny smile, he rose and slowly pulled the bedspread away from her, his gaze trained on her body the whole time.

"The light," she said. "Turn out the light."

"Oh, no," he said, tossing the covers into a heap on the floor. "I've got a really nice view here. Why would I want to mess it up?"

Her heart quickened as she waited for him to touch her, kiss her, or do whatever he had in mind that she couldn't fathom. Instead he went to Sera's dresser and thumbed through the drawers.

"What the hell are you doing?" she asked.

"New rule," he told her, still fishing through the drawer. "I don't mind you talking. But reprimanding isn't allowed."

He'd gone off the deep end. That was the only explanation. Most people got dysentery when they drank Mexican water. Dave turned into a sexual deviant.

"Ah. Here we go." He closed the drawer and turned around, and she was surprised to see him holding a pair of scissors.

"What do you intend to do with those?" she asked.

He sat down beside her, opened the jaws of the scissors, and slid them over the hem of her shirt.

"What are you *doing*?" she said, squirming away from him. "You'll ruin my shirt!"

"I've got no choice. See, you can't let go of that headboard."

"I don't believe this."

"Don't worry. I'll buy you a new shirt. Maybe a couple of new ones. Of course, I'll be the one picking them out." He paused, staring at her. "And you know, now that I think about it . . ."

He placed the scissors on the bed next to her, then hooked his finger into the scoop neck of her T-shirt and slowly pulled it down until it met her cleavage, his finger teasing her skin lightly all the way down. "I think it should be a little lower here."

He considered that for a moment, then passed both hands slowly but firmly over her breasts, pulling the fabric snug against them. "And maybe a little tighter here."

Lisa quivered at his touch, her nipples tightening in the wake of his hands. He held the fabric taut and stared down at her.

"Dave. Come on. This is silly."

"Don't interrupt. I've got a nice fantasy going here."

As he mulled that over for an eon or so, her nipples grew more erect with each passing second. He was going to stare at them forever. Boldly. Blatantly. And for some reason, that made her feel hot as hell and more exposed than if she were naked.

"I think," he said, in that maddening contemplative voice, "that I'm going to slip into that store dressing room with you when you're wearing one of those tight little low-cut shirts."

"Men aren't allowed."

"I'll bribe the salesgirl." He slid his hands along the sides of her rib cage until they reached her waist. "I'm going to turn you around to face the mirror." He slipped his fingertips beneath the hem of her shirt, meeting bare skin. "Then I'm going to stand behind you, put my arms around you, and slide that stretchy little shirt up until I get a really good look at what's under it."

He moved his hands up, taking her shirt along with it. It tripped over her nipples before finally gliding away to reveal her breasts. Lisa's heart leapt.

"You're going to buy me shirts just so you can take them off me?"

"Mmm. It sounds even better when you say it."

Dave stared down at her with total appreciation, his gaze lingering. And lingering. And *lingering*.

"Dave?"

"Sorry. I was just thinking what a beautiful sight this would be in a three-way mirror."

Lisa felt a sharp tingle between her legs. She flexed her hands against the spindles, her back arching almost involuntarily, desperately wanting him to do *something* besides stare at her.

Touch me. Please. Your hands. Your mouth. Anything. Everything.

Slowly he lowered his head.

Yes. Yes!

He placed a gentle kiss between her breasts. She waited, waited. . . .

He rose again, pulling the shirt back down to her waist.

"Wh-what are you doing?" she asked, a little breathless.

He picked up the scissors.

Yes. Cut it off. Get rid of it. And do it quickly.

She closed her eyes as he parted the scissors at the hem of her shirt again, but *quickly* didn't appear to be a word in his vocabulary this evening. He cut as if he had all night to do it, forcing Lisa to endure the steady *snip, snip, snip* of the scissors as they slit her shirt, along with the feeling of the cold, hard steel inching its way along the skin from her navel to her neck.

Dave reached for the neckline of the shirt and gave it a final clip, then performed the same slow, maddening cutting action along both sleeves. Finally he laid the scissors down, grasped the shirt, and pulled it away from her body. Tossing the tattered remains aside, he stared at her naked breasts. Just stared, long and hard, until Lisa thought she was going to go crazy.

"Now it's your turn," she told him, flexing her fingers against the spindles.

"Excuse me?"

"Your shirt. Off."

He looked at her admonishingly. "I'm sorry, Lisa. You're in no position to demand anything."

"Okay then, how about I reach up there and rip it off you?"

"That would require you to let go of that headboard, and I told you already . . . I wouldn't advise that."

He curled his hand around her rib cage, kissing the upper swell of her breast once, twice, moving at such a leisurely pace that she wanted to scream at him to get on with it. He moved up to kiss the base of her throat, then the side of her neck.

"But if you'd like to ask instead of demand," he said, "I'll take your request under consideration."

"Now I'm an *impolite* control freak?"

He gave her a tiny knowing smile. Tightening his hand along her rib cage, he flicked his tongue against her earlobe, then nipped it gently. Suddenly her jeans felt way too tight, way too confining. She could actually feel the area between her legs growing hot and swollen. And damn it, if it took a private consultation with Miss Manners she was determined to get him out of that shirt.

She turned her head and whispered against his cheek, "I'd like it very much if you took your shirt off."

He backed away and stood up, unbuttoning his shirt and taking it off, and not getting in any hurry at all to do it. Finally he tossed it down, and one word formed in her mind: *wow.* She could live to be a thousand and never get enough of looking at him. And touching him. Which she was dying to do right now.

"I can do all sorts of things with my hands," she told him, easing her voice down into the provocative range. "You might be interested in some of them."

"Thank you for your input. I'll take that under advisement."

He circled around to the foot of the bed. His gaze traveled the length of her body, from her feet to her head and all the way back down. That staring again.

"Dave, I'm starting to feel a little silly here. Can we get on with it?"

He shook his head sadly. "You're an impatient person, Lisa. A minor character flaw, but a flaw just the same. You need to work on that."

She exhaled with frustration. *Right.* And he seemed to be more than willing to give her all the "hands-off" training she needed.

Finally he took hold of her ankles, and after a lengthy caress he pushed them apart. He rested his knee on the bed between her thighs, dropped a palm on either side of her hips and leaned over her, the muscles of his shoulders and arms standing out in sharp relief. He pressed a kiss just above her navel, sending a thrilling little shudder shooting right up her spine. Rising again, he unfastened the buttons of her jeans, stopping after each one to tease a fingertip over any newly bared skin.

Yes. Now we're getting down to it.

Once the last button was undone, he slid his hands all the way from her hips to her calves, finally catching the legs of her jeans near her ankles and pulling.

"Maybe you'd better help a little," he said. "Which is *not* permission to let go."

"Then how . . ."

He waited patiently.

"Oh, for heaven's sake."

As he pulled, she lifted her hips, squirming left and right. His tiny smile said he was enjoying the show, and his sudden inability to pull a pair of jeans off a woman said he was creating the show on purpose. Finally he pulled just enough that they skimmed over her hips and down her legs. He tossed them aside, then eased her panties down over her hips, her thighs, her calves, and finally past her feet. And a glacier could have thawed in the time it took him to do it.

She was naked. He wasn't. That wasn't the order she generally strove for. But at least they were making progress.

Come on, baby. Let's rock.

To her surprise, he walked to the door of the bedroom.

"Hey! Where are you going?"

"I'll only be a minute." He pointed an admonishing finger. "And remember what happens if you let go."

He left the room, and she heard his footsteps on the stairs. What in the hell was he doing?

This was completely insane.

Get up. Take control of this outrageous situation. Get him naked and get on with it.

Then she glanced down at the drapery cord still lying on the mattress beside her.

Better stay put.

A minute later, she heard his footsteps coming back up the stairs. He came into the room holding a large bowl. What in the hell was he doing?

He sat down on the bed beside her again, setting the bowl on the nightstand. He reached into it, and what he extracted made her heart go crazy.

A lime.

Dave grabbed a knife from the bowl and flicked through the lime, separating it into two halves.

Lisa's eyes widened. "Oh, you have *got* to be joking."

"Those Lozanos. Gotta hand it to them. They really know how to kick a party up to the next level."

"Dave, no. This is insane. I'm going to let go. I swear—"

The first frigid drop hit right at the hollow of her throat. If he'd released a lit match on her, she couldn't have felt it more. Even though the lime juice was cold, it seemed to sizzle against her skin, and she had to clamp her mouth shut to keep from gasping.

"You're out of your mind," she said between clenched teeth. "You know that, don't you? You're completely out of your mind."

He ignored her, squeezing the lime half until it dripped into the hollow of her throat, then moving it to either collarbone, down to her breastbone, and circling her nipples, letting each drop fall slowly and singularly. He blazed a path of lime juice down her stomach, into her navel, as she watched with rapt disbelief. She had no idea just how intense a Chinese lime juice torture could be.

Then he moved lower, and she nearly gasped when she realized how far he intended to take this.

She immediately pressed her thighs together. He countered by teasing his fingertips in a tickling motion along the crevice between her thigh and pelvis. As she twisted away from him, her legs fell open, and he took the opportunity to squeeze the remainder of the juice of the lime half right between her legs.

"You play dirty."

That smile again.

Then he reached into the bowl again and produced a salt-shaker.

Not in her wildest dreams had she imagined that she'd be

making like a head-to-toe tequila shot tonight, or that the slightest sprinkle of salt along the same path as the lime juice could make her practically jump out of her skin.

"I'm taking it easy on the salt," he said, shaking lightly. "Gotta watch the old blood pressure."

Which meant he intended to taste every bit of it, and the thought of that made Lisa's heart rate shoot through the roof.

"Don't tell me you found the tequila," she said.

"Not a drop in the house," he said, eyeing her body from head to toe. "But I have a feeling that in just a minute I won't give a damn about that."

He set the saltshaker down and stood up, and she finally got at least one wish she'd made tonight. He stripped completely, and she saw to her immense relief that he appeared to be as ready as she was to *get on with this*.

But still he was in no hurry.

He began by licking at the hollow of her throat, his tongue moving gently against her, waking up nerve endings she didn't even know she had. Then he teased his tongue over her collarbone in a slow, sensuous back-and-forth motion. She wanted to scream. Centuries turned more quickly than this man was moving.

Edging downward, he circled his tongue around her right nipple, then sucked it into his mouth, taking the salt and the lime juice in an intense pulling motion that sent fiery hot tremors radiating right down between her legs.

"I love the way you taste," Dave said, his lips humming against her breast. "And the salt and lime juice aren't bad, either."

He moved to her other breast, giving it the same treatment, licking and sucking the salt and lime away, every movement of his lips and tongue so slow and sensual that she almost couldn't endure it. Then he moved along her breastbone, working his way down to her navel, stopping periodically to swirl his tongue in tiny circles or reach out the tip of it to capture a stray drop of lime juice. Lisa had never felt anything like it in her life. He was concentrating every bit of his attention on one tiny part of her body at a time, elevating the sensitivity of that particular part until she wanted to scream.

"Dave?" she said breathlessly.

"Uh-huh?"

"You've got to stop this."

He responded by streaking his tongue over her abdomen. She stiffened, sure he was going to move lower still. Instead, he stopped and stood up.

"Now," she said on a harsh breath. "I want you inside me. Right *now*."

He came around to the foot of the bed, where he gently pressed her legs apart. He stared down at her for a long time, devouring her with his eyes, his intense gaze making her heart rate soar. She lifted her hips, encouraging him to plunge right inside her. Instead, he began to stroke her legs with his fingertips.

No, no, no!

"Dave—*now*."

"Hush."

"But I want you to—"

"What you want is not the issue here. I'm far more interested in what you need."

He passed his thumbs over the creases between her thighs and pelvis, causing salt to scrape gently against her skin. Dipping his head, he ran his lips across her, then followed with his tongue, easing toward the very center of her.

Oh, God, oh, God, oh, God. . . .

Exposing her clit with his thumbs, he teased his tongue in a half circle around it on the continued pretense of finishing off the lime juice and salt. She couldn't breathe for the anticipation she felt, and when he finally flicked his tongue against the most sensitive part of her a flash of unbearable sensation streaked through her. She gasped and twisted hard to one side.

"Easy, baby," he said, holding her hips until she stilled. "You act as if the men you've been with have never done this before."

"They haven't."

"Only because you wouldn't let them. Fortunately, I don't have to ask."

He lowered his head again, this time closing his mouth over her with a soft sucking motion of his lips and tongue that made her squirm all over again, but he held her in place, and after a moment the sharp stabs of sensation melted into something warm and pleasurable. He splayed his palm against her abdomen to hold her steady, then swept two fingers of his other hand over her moist opening. With his mouth still against her, he slid his fingers deep inside her, then stroked them back and forth at the same time his tongue moved in an incredible rhythmic motion that did away with all pretense of salt and lime juice removal. Every move now was focused only on making her crazy with need, driving her from feeling warm and pleasurable right into hot and passionate.

"Dave . . . oh, God. . . ."

With no voluntary thought at all, she began to flex her hips in sync with his movements. She was used to control, demanded control, but now she had no control at all. He was propelling her right into a realm where she wasn't thinking straight, where everything seemed hot and hazy and unsure. She tried to focus, tried to think, but all at once it felt as if she'd flown into a bank of clouds and couldn't get her bearings. Her breath was coming so fast she felt dizzy and lightheaded, shifting her perception until the pleasure seemed distorted, her heart racing with uneasiness instead. With every stroke of his tongue and fingers, one more fragment of her carefully constructed sense of control slipped away, until she felt as if she were falling, as if her plane had stalled and she was plummeting toward earth, only this time there was nothing she could do to pull out of the dive.

"No!"

She pulled away from the headboard, sat up, and grasped Dave's shoulders, breathing hard, her eyes squeezed closed. "Stop. Please stop. *Please.*"

Dave leaned away with a regretful sigh, shaking his head. "Now you've done it."

He rose, came around the bed, and sat down beside her. He picked up the cord.

"Dave," she said, her breath coming in ragged spurts. "No. You're not actually going to—"

"I don't make idle threats."

He took hold of her wrists and slid the looped cord loosely over them. When she tried to pull away, he gave her a warning stare.

"Now, Lisa, while you're a woman I'd generally think twice about messing with, you and I both know that the outcome here is hardly in question."

She couldn't believe it. He actually intended to tie her up.

"I'm a very patient man," he said in a firm but even voice. "But before this night is out, I *will* get my way."

She still felt so hot and swollen between her legs, her whole body trembling with the need she felt desperate to deny. As she sat there, her chest still heaving, he wound the cord around her wrists in a figure eight motion, and some force she couldn't fathom kept her from pulling away. Then he eased her down to her back again, held her bound wrists over her head, and secured them to the headboard spindles. With a final tug on the cord, he leaned in and teased his lips against her ear.

"I've got you now. I can do anything I want to, and there's not a damned thing you can do about it."

Her heart hammered her chest, beating with the frantic pace of a hummingbird's wings. She tried to concentrate on the incredible level of sexual excitement he'd brought her to, but she couldn't. She couldn't fight the feeling that washed over her with her wrists bound, the terrible sense that she was caught. Trapped. Completely at the mercy of another human being. With her control completely stripped away, her apprehension quickly turned to panic.

She pulled on the cord that bound her wrists, desperate to free herself, desperate to get away, desperate to—

Wait.

She froze, breathing hard.

Pulled again.

With next to no effort, she could have slipped right out of the cord that held her.

She snapped her gaze up to meet Dave's and found him staring down at her, waiting for her next words. Just staring at her, his dark eyes solemn and sincere.

Trust me, he was telling her. *Just let me love you.*

As the depth of his understanding suddenly became clear, her world seemed to tilt into an entirely new dimension. He was trying to give her something that went right to the heart of the relationship between a man and a woman, a connection she needed so much. And more important, he was giving her the pretense to accept it, if that was what she needed.

He was right. So right. He couldn't give her anything if she refused to take it. With a desperation that drenched her very soul, she wanted all he had to give her, no matter how much she had to open herself up to get it.

"You seem to have forgotten where you were," she said, her voice quivering.

"Do you remember?"

"You were touching me." She swallowed hard. "With your tongue."

A faint smile crossed his lips. "Now, how in the world could I have forgotten that?"

As he rested his hands against her thighs, she let her legs fall to either side. But when he pressed his mouth to her again, the feeling was so intense that she couldn't help shivering beneath his hands.

"Just relax, baby," he told her. "Relax. . . ."

His voice was hypnotic, his hot breath skating across her. She closed her eyes and gave herself to him completely, allowing him to touch her, tease her, to send her on an upward spiral all over again. The tension he created slowly pulled her tighter and tighter, like an arrow on a bow, quivering with the need to be released. Soon her breath became short, sharp gasps, her mind so far beyond reason that she couldn't have managed a single coherent thought. It was as if she were climbing through that cloud bank again, only this time she was focused on the clear blue sky she knew was beyond it and wanting it more than anything.

He paused for a moment, and she instantly arched up to meet him again. "No! Don't stop! *Please* don't stop! Oh, God, Dave . . . *don't stop*!"

Words of sheer desire tumbled from her lips in a spontaneous rush. He pressed his mouth to her again, and somewhere deep inside her something caught fire. Flared.

Exploded.

She cried out his name, shuddering wildly, as wave after wave of incredible sensation slammed into her. He clamped down hard on her hips, holding her steady, compelling her body to accept every bit of pleasure that he could possibly wring from it. Still she gripped the spindles of the headboard, her eyes squeezed shut, overwhelmed by the feeling that she'd burst through those clouds into a sun so brilliant it couldn't possibly be real.

She sensed him grabbing one of the condoms, ripping it open, and before she could even breathe again, before the sensations had faded away, he rose above her, moved between her legs, and plunged inside her in one deep, possessive thrust, intensifying the climax still pulsing through her. He fell to his forearms, his dark gaze locked onto hers, transfixing her with the burning desire that filled his eyes.

"Do you feel how much I want you?" he said, his voice a harsh whisper. "Do you?"

"Yes," she said, barely able to speak. *"Yes."*

"Hold on to me, baby. Put your arms around me."

She twisted her wrists wildly, pulling loose from her bonds, then wrapped her arms around him. Oh, *God*, it felt so good to finally touch him, to hold him like this. As he moved inside her with hard, forceful strokes, she clutched him tightly, her fingertips digging into the muscles of his back and shoulders, bruising him, she knew, but she couldn't stop. She had the most glorious sensation of him filling her, not just her body but her heart, her mind, her deepest needs. Unbelievably, instead of her climax fading away, she felt that place inside her spark again, deep ripples of heat swelling through her. An act that always generated a raw, unfinished sensation for her felt on the verge of being full and complete, and she wanted it more than anything.

She rose to meet every stroke, begging him with every breath to bring them both together to that glittering moment of release. The same foggy sensations clouded her mind as before, the same spasms radiated deep inside her, all of it expanding and multiplying with every furious thrust.

"Oh, God . . . Lisa . . . *yes*. . . ." A groan rose in his throat, a deep, rasping sound of pleasure that seemed to quiver through his entire body. "Come with me, baby. . . . Come with me. . . ."

He'd barely gotten the words out when she drew in a deep, gasping breath. It was happening again. She couldn't believe it.

Oh, *God,* she was coming again.

She cried out as the sensations swept through her, deep, concentrated spasms that seemed to go on forever. They locked every nerve and muscle in their grip, bubbling up from someplace inside her that had never been touched before. And Dave was right there with her, holding her so tightly, drawing himself deeply inside her as the last waves of pleasure washed over them both.

Breathing hard, he lay against her, every muscle taut, his face buried against her neck. "Yes," he murmured. "Every time, just like that. That's how it's going to be from now on."

"Oh, God," she said suddenly, shifting beneath him. He rolled to one side. She sat up suddenly, barely able to breathe, the sheer power of it making her tremulous and unsteady. "Oh, my God."

He sat up with her, wrapping his arm around her waist from behind and settling his chin in the crook of her neck. She tried to shudder from his grip.

"Take it easy, baby," he said.

"It was too much," she said, "too much. . . ." Suddenly she felt swamped with emotion, the pounding of her heart erratic and unchecked. And tears were streaming down her face. Tears? Why in the hell was she crying?

"Just relax," he said. "Lie back down."

She thought about how she'd screamed, begged, been totally out of control, and suddenly she felt embarrassed. She refused to look at him. "No. I can't. I acted . . . a little crazy. . . ."

"And I loved it," he murmured. "All of it."

She swept her tears away with the back of her hand and started to get up. He pulled her back down again.

"I'm still a little salty," she said. "I—I need a shower."

"No. I know what you need," he said, wrapping his arm around her again. "What you've needed for a very long time. And I'm going to give it to you until you wonder where your next breath is coming from."

His words made her satisfied body shudder to life all over again, even as she felt as if she had to get out of there right *now*.

"You don't understand," she said.

He sighed softly. "Yes, I do." He backed off a little, his voice quiet and measured. "You need space right now. You need to pull yourself together, to feel as if you're in control again. And most of all," he said, "you need to convince yourself that this didn't mean anything to you, just in case it doesn't mean anything to me. Is that right?"

She turned to him, astonished that he'd just put voice to the feeling she always had when she was with a man. That feeling of putting herself into somebody else's hands. That feeling that somebody else controlled even a moment of her life.

That feeling that if she gave her heart along with her body, the joke would be on her.

"Yes," she said softly.

"Then go."

She expected to see anger on his face, but all she saw was compassion. For several seconds she just sat there, staring at him until finally he held out his hand. She took it, and he eased her down next to him, pulling her back into his arms again. He held her gently, running his hand along her thigh in deep, calming strokes.

"It's like claustrophobia," she said. "I get this breathless feeling, like I've got to get away."

"Is that how you feel right now?"

Slowly her breathing was returning to normal, her heart rate calming. She felt heavy, relaxed, and as content as she'd ever been in her life, knowing now that the invisible cords that bound her to Dave were more powerful than any physical ones could ever be.

"No," she said on a sigh. "I feel good. So good."

"Then I don't want you running away from me every time we make love. And I won't have you giving me a really nice backrub and putting me to sleep, either."

She smiled a little. "So no more backrubs."

"Well, maybe after you've come three or four times. But by then it'll be a moot point, because you'll be the one who's asleep." He slid his hand along her neck and kissed her hair, her temple, then pulled her close again. Her eyes began to get heavy, and she knew exactly what Dave had meant. Any moment now she was going to be asleep.

Then she heard the phone ring.

She blinked her eyes open. "Sera?"

"Let's hope so." Dave rose from the bed. She started to throw back the covers, but he put his hand on her shoulder. "Just stay here," he told her. "I'll get it."

He went into Sera's bedroom to answer the phone while Lisa waited in bed. He returned a few minutes later.

"That was Sera," he told her. "They're at Hospital San Juan in Monterrey. Adam's having some tests right now, but they made it there just fine."

"Thank God."

"I told them what we found out here, and she's going to pass it on to Adam."

"Good. He'll be so happy to hear it."

Dave climbed back into bed, and immediately Lisa curled up next to him with a sigh of relief and contentment rolled into one. His body was so warm next to hers, so inviting, and she was tempted to think that somehow it could be like this forever.

She'd been right all along. She'd never stopped loving him. She loved the man who'd told her that day eleven years ago that there wasn't anything on earth she couldn't do if she wanted it badly enough. She loved the man who'd come to Mexico on a cryptic phone conversation just because she was in trouble. She loved the man who lay with her now, who understood more about her than any man ever had before. But where did they go from here?

I don't want you running away from me every time we make love.

How many more times could there possibly be?

I want you to be exactly who you are.

Fine for now. But what about the long haul? Was he actually thinking about the possibility of there being one? If so, he was closing his eyes to reality. He had a daughter, a family—the kind of staid, settled, conventional life she knew would eventually suffocate her.

But as she closed her eyes and hovered in that nebulous world between sleeping and waking, those impossible images began to play through her mind. And Dave was standing in the midst of it all, opening his arms to her, inviting her to be part of it. And suddenly she wasn't suffocating. She was breathing deeply, drawing it all in—feeling as if she was taking huge, endless, invigorating breaths for the first time in her life.

chapter twenty-two

Sera followed the nurse across the busy emergency room of Hospital San Jose, through a pair of metal doors, and into the patient area. She'd spent the past hour and a half waiting for Adam to be examined and tests to be run, practically tapping her fingernails right down to the quick on the arm of the chair where she sat.

The nurse swept back a curtain. Sera eased up to Adam's bedside, and the nurse shut the curtain again. The moment Sera's eyes met Adam's, he smiled at her, and her heart melted.

"How are you doing?" she asked.

"I'm fine."

"What did the doctors say?"

"X-rays defined the position of the bullet. They're coming soon to take me for a short surgical procedure to remove it and debride the wound. I might have limited use of my shoulder and arm for a while, but they tell me that with physical therapy eventually I'll be good as new."

"Thank God. And the CT scan?"

"Normal. It seems I have a brain and it's in fine working order."

Sera breathed a sigh of relief. "Then you really are going to be all right."

"Thanks to you and Gabrio, yes. Where is he?"

"Asleep on a sofa in the waiting room. He's still so tired. I told him I'd get him a hotel room, but he doesn't want to leave. I think he's still a little scared."

"He's got a right to be. He's been through a lot. Did you talk to Dave and Lisa?"

"Yes. And they have some good news."

When Sera related everything that Dave had told her, Adam's face brightened. "So it's possible they can find somebody who'll blow the whistle on Robert?"

"Yes."

"That," Adam said, "really makes my day."

Sera eased closer, taking his hand. "I was so worried about you. I still am."

She studied his face for a long time, trying to see beyond the unconcerned expression he wore. Clearly there was something hiding beneath it. Finally he gave her a sigh of resignation. "You want to know about what happened in the car."

"Only if you want to talk about it."

He looked away, and for a moment she thought he was going to say no. Then he tugged on her hand. "Sit down."

She sat down on the edge of the bed, waiting. "This is hard for me to say, Sera. I don't talk about it. To anyone."

"You can talk about it to me," she said softly. "You know that."

Finally he turned his gaze to meet hers. "I told you my wife died when she was seven months pregnant."

"Yes."

"It happened on a road just like the one we were driving on. A dark, deserted highway in west Texas."

"A car accident?"

"No. Something worse."

His expression became tight and strained. He stared down at the sheets as he spoke, his hand tightening against hers.

"It was about nine o'clock at night. We were driving along when all of the sudden Ellen told me she felt strange. That something was wrong. I told her that she was fine, that she was just uncomfortable from being in the car for a couple of hours. But she kept telling me something didn't feel right. Then all at once, she doubled over. Cried out. By the time I pulled over to the side of the road, she was already bleeding."

Sera's heart quickened. "She was having a miscarriage?"

"Placental abruption. And from the blood that was there . . ." He swallowed hard. "From the blood that was there, I knew it had to be a complete separation of the placenta from the uterine wall. But the mortality rate even with an abruption that severe is usually low." He let out a shaky breath. "Unless you're sixty miles away from the nearest hospital and you can't stop the bleeding."

Sera closed her eyes. "Oh, no."

"Ellen looked down. Saw the blood. She started crying. Screaming in pain. I can still hear her voice, over and over in my head. All I could do was phone ahead to the hospital, drive a hundred miles an hour on that godforsaken road, and pray. Ellen kept crying and screaming and pleading with me to help her, to do something to save our baby. But for all my training, all my experience, there was nothing I could do. And after a while—" He stopped short, his voice faltering. "She wasn't screaming anymore."

"Oh, Adam. . . ."

"I barely remember coming into town," he said, his voice trembling. "It's like . . . I don't know. Like a nightmare that I just remember bits and pieces of. I drove to the doors of the emergency room, and they came out and took her inside. I sat out in the waiting room. Every minute seemed like an eternity. And then the ER doctor came out." Adam's face contorted, his jaw tightening. "He told me that my wife and child were dead."

Sera's heart twisted with anguish, tears welling up in her eyes. She felt as if she was suffering every terrible moment right along with him.

"Ellen and I had tried for years to have a child. She had some problems that made conceiving difficult and we thought it was never going to happen. Then, when she was forty-one and we'd begun to look into adoption, we found out she was pregnant." He closed his eyes. "I can't tell you how I felt. The only thing missing from my life was the chance to be a father. It was our last chance." He paused. "My last chance."

She shook her head. "No, Adam. It wasn't your last chance."

"Sera—"

"I know you love me. And I want to have a child more than anything. And now that I know you do, too—"

"No. I don't."

"Please, Adam," she said, desperation creeping into her voice. "You can't give up. I know how horrible it must have been for you. I know how much it hurt. But part of the healing is knowing that you haven't lost that kind of life forever. You can have it again."

"No, Sera. I can't."

"But—"

"There's more."

She froze. "What?"

"The night Ellen died," he said. "I fell apart. I just . . . I just lost it."

"Of course you did," she said. "Any man would."

"No. You don't understand. I fell apart completely. Completely. I was—" He looked away, as if he'd do anything not to say the words. "I was institutionalized for almost a month."

Sera stared at him in silence as the magnitude of his words sank in. Institutionalized? God, how distraught must he have been?

To think of the grief he must have felt staggered her. The only reality he'd had that night was one where his wife and baby were dead, and he just couldn't face it. To avoid the pain of losing them, he'd lost himself.

"I missed their funeral because I was so sedated that I barely knew who I was," he said. "I think there was a time when my family wondered if I'd ever make it out of that place. I suppose it's a miracle I ever did." He paused, a faraway look in his eyes. "But still, in the dark of night sometimes, driving down a road like the one we drove down tonight, it's as if it's happening all over again. I experience the same pain I felt then, the same horror, the same helpless feeling that I can't do a damned thing to save the woman I love and the baby she's carrying."

"So that's why . . ."

"Yes. That's why you thought you had a lunatic in the car."

"No. Don't say that. I just knew something was hurting you. That's all."

"I just can't shake it, Sera. Maybe I never will."

"But you went back to practicing medicine. Delivering babies."

"As long as it was somebody else, I could deal with it. And after a while, my family encouraged me to see other women. To start a new life. I thought I could. Eventually. But then days turned to weeks, and a few years passed. I was getting older, and I finally realized that the window was closing." He stared at Sera, his eyes filled with a sadness beyond measure. "And then you came along. So young, your whole life ahead of you, and wanting a baby of your own more than anything in the world. How in the hell was I supposed to deal with that?"

"But, Adam, the odds of anything that terrible ever happening again—"

"No. Don't tell me you're young and healthy, so chances are you won't have any problems. I know that. Don't tell me that the way I feel is irrational, because I know that, too. Don't tell me that love will get us through it, because if that were true, Ellen would be alive today."

"It's only been a few years. Time heals. It won't be long before you'll feel differently, and—"

"No! Why do you think I fell apart out there? Because I can't handle it!"

"Not alone, maybe. But I love you, Adam, and I know that together we can—"

Adam yanked his hand away from her. "Don't you know how much this is killing me? If you loved me as much as you say you do, you wouldn't be doing this to me!"

Sera recoiled at his sudden outburst. Adam took several harsh breaths. He closed his eyes, sadness washing over his face, his voice becoming a painful whisper.

"God, Sera, I'm sorry."

"No. Please don't apologize."

"I just want you to listen to me. To understand." He opened his eyes again and fixed his gaze on hers. "When we were on the road coming here, I thought about Ellen. About how she'd cried and screamed and begged me to help her. And then . . ." He hesitated. "Then I imagined it was you."

When a fresh flood of anguish filled his eyes, Sera could feel her dream shattering—her dream of getting pregnant with Adam's baby, living those months of anticipation together, sharing the joy of childbirth. Still, the grief he'd suffered and the pain he'd lived with all this time only made her love him more. It only made her that much more desperate to be the light at the end of that long, dark tunnel he'd been walking in for so long.

"Of course I want to have a baby," she told him. "But there are other ways. We can adopt a child, can't we?"

"Don't you remember what I asked you a few days ago?"

"What?"

"I asked how you would feel if you knew you were going to go through your entire life and never get pregnant, never have a child of your own. You told me you would be devastated."

"Disappointed. That was what I meant."

"You said what you meant."

"Losing you. That's what would devastate me."

He shook his head slowly. "My problems aren't magically going to go away. You saw what happened earlier this evening. Just how fit am I to be a father under any circumstances? Or a husband, for that matter?"

"I can't believe you're even saying that."

"If we were to get married, a year would pass, then two, and sooner or later you'd come to resent me. You'd think about the old man you married and all his hang-ups and wish to God you'd made another choice. And if that ever happened, I couldn't bear it."

"But nothing else matters to me without you!"

He looked at her so tenderly that her heart nearly broke. "Find another man, Sera. One who will love you and cherish you and give you the family you want. And sometime in the future, the day will come that you'll realize it was the right decision. And instead of resenting me for the rest of your life, you'll thank me."

Tears filled her eyes. "No. That's not what I want. Please, Adam, *please*. . . ."

"I love you enough to let you go, Sera. You've got to do the same for me."

She bowed her head and began to cry. He reached out and stroked her hair, and she took his hand, kissed his palm, then clutched his hand with both of hers. She knew now that he was never going to allow her to love him through this terrible situation.

He was going to tell her good-bye.

At eight-thirty the next morning, Dave climbed the steps to Sera's back porch, kicked dirt off his boots, then came through the door to find Lisa in the kitchen making a pot of coffee. She was barefoot, hair still damp from the shower, wearing a T-shirt and jeans. He sat down at the table and pulled off his boots.

"You took care of it," she said.

Dave let out a weary breath. "Yeah."

"You should have woken me," she said. "I could have helped."

"No need. It's done."

Lisa sighed. "Thank you."

"Considering everything Gabrio did for us, it was the least I could do for him."

She came closer and stared down at Dave. "You even said the Bible verse, didn't you?"

"Yeah," he said. "But it's been a while. I imagine I screwed it up a little."

"But you said it anyway." Lisa kissed him gently on the lips. "You're a good man, Dave. You know that?"

As he stared up at Lisa, Dave thought about how they'd made love last night and how he'd seen right inside her to the vulnerable woman she tried so hard to hide. There was suddenly so much more involved in the way he felt about her that he couldn't begin to sort it all out. All he wanted to do when this whole mess was over was drag her right back to Tolosa with him and insist she stay forever.

But that was impossible. Hadn't she said it? Repeatedly? She didn't want a family, she didn't want responsibility, she didn't want anything tying her down, and in her mind everything about his life would do just that. A sudden image sprang to mind of him keeping her under lock and key like a bird in a cage to make sure she didn't fly away.

"I need to get a shower," he said.

"Coffee will be ready when you get out."

He went upstairs and showered, but when he came out of the bathroom ten minutes later he was surprised to find Lisa upstairs, tucked into bed. Wearing nothing.

He smiled down at her. "Coffee?"

"I decided it would only keep us awake."

Dave slid into bed beside her, pulling her into his arms and making love to her, slowly, tenderly, taking his time, making sure she felt every gentle touch, every whispered word. She opened herself to him in every way a woman could, then gave it back to him in ways he'd only dreamed about. For the next few hours he felt as if they were two people insulated from the rest of the world, connecting to each other in the most intimate way possible.

Afterward, Dave rose to one elbow and stared down at her. Her cheeks were flushed, her eyes glowing. In the late morning light pouring through the bedroom curtains she looked radiant. He brushed his fingers through her hair in a languid caress.

"Now, this doesn't mean I never want to get wild on a kitchen table again," he said. "You know that, don't you?"

She smiled. "Yeah. I know that. Balconies are nice, too."

"Don't forget the shower."

"Anywhere you say," she told him. "Anytime you say."

He lay back down and wrapped her in his arms. As they dozed off, Dave made a mental note to hold her to that promise.

Two hours later, Lisa opened her eyes, squinting against the noontime sunlight streaming through the window. Turning over, she glanced at the clock.

"Dave," she said. "It's nearly noon."

After a moment, Dave sat up in bed. "I'd better check the answering machine to make sure we didn't sleep right through a call from Alex." Yawning, he rose from the bed, went to Sera's room, then returned a moment later. "Nothing."

"How long do you think it'll be before we hear from him?" Lisa asked.

"I have no idea. It could take him a while to pin down an informant."

Lisa sat up in bed and stretched. Glancing out the window, she saw the barn in the distance. "The ponies have wandered back up here. Suppose we ought to feed them?"

"Sera said they'd be okay on pasture alone. But they probably wouldn't mind a little grain."

"Let's go down there. I've never petted a pony before."

"Never?"

Lisa slid out from beneath the covers. "My childhood wasn't exactly privileged, remember?" She dug through her bag and pulled out a pair of panties. "Ashley, on the other hand, is probably riding one in your backyard as we speak."

"What?"

Lisa put on the panties, then wiggled into a pair of jeans. "You told John to buy her one, didn't you?"

Dave sighed with disgust. "It'd be just like John to actually do it. Just to piss me off."

"There's nothing a kid likes better than a pony." She stopped and stared at him. "Aren't you going to get dressed?"

Dave smiled, clearly admiring the fact that she still had nothing on from the waist up. "I'm just watching the show."

Lisa rolled her eyes. "If you don't get dressed, I'm dragging you down to the barn naked."

"Hmm. A naked man, a domineering woman, and a pair of ponies. Didn't I see that in a porn movie once?"

"I wouldn't know. I only watch chick flicks."

He grinned. She gave him an admonishing look, then tossed his bag to the bed. "Move it."

He pulled out a change of clothes. "Actually, Ashley's

afraid of dogs, so I don't know how she'd do with something as big as a pony."

"Nah. Ponies are different. All little girls like horses."

No. Ponies weren't different. Not to Ashley. Everything loomed bigger and more frightening to her than to the average kid.

"Last week a kid smacked her with a swing at school," Dave said, pulling on a pair of jeans. "She sat down in the corner of the playground and cried."

"Was she hurt?"

"No. Not really."

Lisa slid her arms into a T-shirt. She tugged it down over her head, then swept her fingers through her hair. "Well, I'd cry, too, if somebody hit me with a swing."

"No, you wouldn't. You'd tell him if he ever messed with you again, you'd put the swing where the sun don't shine."

Lisa smiled. "Sure. Now I would. But when I was five?"

"I'm betting even then."

"I'm the exception, Dave. Not the rule."

Dave shrugged into a shirt. Instead of buttoning it, though, he paused, a brooding expression on his face. "Ashley's really timid most of the time. Even clingy. She just can't handle things, you know? And the older she gets . . ."

"She's just a little girl. A lot of little girls are timid."

"You weren't."

"I didn't have that luxury. Ashley does. She has a father who'll keep her safe."

"What if I can't?"

"What are you talking about?"

"I see her mother in her. I'm afraid that she's going to be like Carla. And if she is . . ."

His voice trailed off. Lisa had no idea what he was trying to say. She stood there for a moment, confused, then started tucking her shirt into her jeans. "So what if she's a little shy like Carla was? You're a good father. I know you are. Why do you worry so much?"

He sat down on the end of the bed, and for a moment he seemed lost in thought. "Carla was more than just a little shy."

Lisa buttoned her jeans. "What do you mean?"

"She was dependent. Needy. Helpless."

Shocked by his words, Lisa froze for a moment, then walked over and sat down on the bed next to him. "What are you talking about?"

He exhaled, closing his eyes. "Day in and day out, she clung to me as if I was only one step away from walking out the door."

"I don't understand. Why would she think that?"

"Insecurity." He paused, then turned his gaze to meet hers. "And because she knew what happened between us."

Lisa recoiled. "She what?"

"That day in the shop. She knew."

Lisa was horrified. "But how? I never told her, Dave. I swear to God I didn't."

"I know you didn't."

"Then how—"

"I did."

For the count of three, Lisa stared at him with total disbelief. "You *what*?"

"I told myself that if she was going to marry me, she should know everything about me. No secrets. So I told her."

"But why? I never would have said a word. She never would have found out."

"I know. I told myself that I was just trying to be honest with her. But I think . . ." He was silent for a moment. "I think I was trying to drive her away. Deep down, I was hoping she'd call off the wedding."

Lisa couldn't have been more shocked if he'd slapped her. "You didn't want to marry her?"

"No. At the time I didn't really realize why. But somehow I knew. Deep down, I knew it wasn't right."

"What did she say when you told her what happened between us?"

"She made excuses for me. Told me it was your fault, not mine, and that she knew I'd never do anything like that again."

"She wasn't angry?"

"Sure she was. At you. It was my fault, and she was angry at you. No matter what I told her, she just kept taking up for me." He rubbed his hand over the back of his neck. "Finally I made a decision. If she wasn't going to call it off, I was."

"You told Carla you didn't want to marry her?"

"Yes."

"What happened?"

"As soon as I said it, she started to cry. She told me over and over how much she needed me, and said if I walked away from her then, she couldn't go on living." He paused, then turned to Lisa, a strange light in his eyes. "Then she told me she knew where her father kept his gun."

Lisa's mouth dropped open. "Oh, God. She didn't."

"I was stunned. I couldn't believe I'd driven her to something like that. I apologized. I told her that of course we'd get married, and I promised that I'd always be faithful to her so she'd never have to feel that way again. And I never told another soul what happened."

"But, Dave, you should have. Don't you know that? You should have told somebody what she was doing to you!"

"I was just a kid, Lisa! What was I supposed to do? I was terrified to say anything. I thought if I humiliated Carla by telling someone that I'd even thought about calling off the wedding, she'd kill herself."

It was as if a curtain had fallen away, exposing as a lie something Lisa had accepted as truth all these years, and she just couldn't believe it. Dave and Carla had seemed like the couple on top of a wedding cake, pristine and perfect, their lives scripted right out of a storybook. Sure, all married couples had their ups and downs, but the fact that there had been a dark side to Carla and Dave's relationship astonished her.

"After we were married, things were fine for a while," Dave said. "Then the insecurity started all over again. If I worked late, she'd quiz me, wondering where I'd been. If she found a receipt from a restaurant she didn't recognize, she gave me the third degree about that, too. At the same time, she had no life of her own. I was it. She rarely left the house. I started to see that something more was wrong than just a little bit of insecurity. But she kept telling me that I was all she needed, that I was everything to her. Then she did it again."

"What?"

"I had to stay late at work one night. When I got home, she accused me of cheating on her. I denied it. She said she knew I was lying, and she threatened to kill herself again. I had to take my guns out of the house, because I believed she might actually do it."

"But you didn't tell anyone?"

"She said if I ever said anything to anyone, I'd come home and find her dead."

Lisa slid her hand to her throat. "Oh, Dave. . . ."

He closed his eyes as dark memories seemed to fill his mind. "I begged her to see somebody. A doctor. A psychologist. Somebody. But she wouldn't even admit she had a problem. She kept saying that I was all she needed. But pretty soon it was happening all the time. Every time I'd work late, or was gone from home longer than she anticipated, she'd accuse me of sleeping around. Then the tears would start, followed by the threats."

"God, Dave. How did you deal with that?"

"Not very well. Particularly when Ashley came along. I couldn't imagine her growing up around a mother like that. Carla loved her. She really did. But how can you be a good mother when you're barely able to deal with your own life?"

He dropped his head to his hands, rubbing his temples with his fingertips, and Lisa could see how badly he'd wanted to run away from all of it. How lonely he'd felt. And how he must have lain awake at night sometimes wishing he were anyplace else on earth.

"Sometimes when Carla was yelling at me, crying, threatening to kill herself, I just couldn't take it. I'd have these flashes, these split second thoughts, when . . ." His voice became a raw whisper. "When I wished she'd just go ahead and do it."

Lisa was shocked. "No. You didn't really feel that way."

"Yes. I did. Sometimes it was right there on the tip of my tongue. I wanted so badly to say it. I wanted to tell her just to do it, to get it over with so I wouldn't have to deal with her problems anymore."

Lisa slid her hand against his shoulder. "I can't believe that you really wanted her to kill herself. You didn't want that."

"I don't know what I wanted. But I'm telling you, Lisa, the night her car went off that bridge . . ." He choked a little on the words, as if they'd been buried for so long that speaking them was an almost insurmountable task. "I remember the moment I got the news. The strangest feeling swept over me for a few seconds. It felt like . . . relief. I needed a way out of that prison. That night, I got it."

As he buried his head in his hands again, she could feel the guilt rising off him like smoke from a smoldering fire. Then she thought about the man on the bridge last week who'd threatened suicide. No wonder Dave had snapped. The echo of Carla in his mind must have been deafening.

"You've felt guilty ever since that night," Lisa said.

"Wouldn't you? God, Lisa, just saying it makes me sound like some heartless son of a bitch who wanted his sick wife dead."

"No. You just wanted out of an intolerable situation that wasn't your fault in the first place. Why should you feel guilty about that?"

He looked up at her. "Maybe it was my fault."

"What?"

"I don't know. I kept thinking that if only I'd loved her more, if only I'd made a bigger commitment to her, things would have been different."

"How much more could you have committed? You married her, and you promised to be a faithful husband. And you were."

"Yes. But my heart wasn't with her. She knew that. From the moment I told her about you, she knew it."

"But, Dave, there was nothing between us! It was just a kiss. We got caught up in an emotional situation. That's all. It didn't mean a thing!"

"It didn't?"

"Of course not!"

Dave turned slowly to face her, fixing his gaze on hers. "The day I married Carla, when I came out of the church, I saw you across the street."

Lisa looked back at him in shocked silence, suddenly feeling as if he'd discovered some deep, dark secret of hers she'd never intended to tell. She wished she could lie. She wished she could tell him that he must have been mistaken. Or if she'd been there, it had to have been some kind of coincidence. But she couldn't.

Instead she gave him a dismissive shrug. "So you want to know why I hung around waiting for you to come out of that church? Well, maybe it was because I was a dumb, misguided eighteen-year-old girl who thought she was in love with you." She laughed, but it came out sounding harsh and strained. "Imagine that."

"I did. All the time."

Lisa stared at him wordlessly, unable to believe what he was telling her.

"I cared about you, Lisa. Far more than you ever knew."

He slid his hand over Lisa's where it rested against her thigh, and just that tiny touch telegraphed every bit of the despair he must have felt back then, coupled with the feelings he'd had for her that he'd been forced to deny.

"Lisa? Do you know what the definition of hell is?"

"What?"

"Taking your new wife on a honeymoon and wishing she was somebody else."

Lisa's heart was suddenly beating rapid-fire. How could she have known? How could she have known that while she was walking away from the church that day he'd desperately wanted to walk away with her?

With a hand against her shoulder, Dave pressed her gently back on the bed, then eased down on one elbow beside her. He brushed a lock of hair away from her forehead, then trailed his fingertips down her cheek.

"Sometimes after a particularly bad day," he said quietly, "I'd lie awake in bed, and I'd see your face in my mind. You were so independent, so passionate, in every word you spoke, every move you made. And I thought, God, to have a woman like that . . . what a relief that would be."

He kissed her gently, and she inhaled the feel of his lips against hers. She couldn't believe what he was telling her. Couldn't believe it.

"That night in Monterrey," he said, "you were right. I felt guilty, but not because I was having feelings for a woman other than my wife. I felt guilty having feelings for the woman I never forgot, even when I was married to Carla. Because of the way I felt about you, I came into that marriage only half-way, and she always knew it. Wanting you again made me feel as if I was betraying her one more time."

"How does it feel now?" Lisa whispered.

He stared at her a long time, his thumb skimming back and forth along her cheek. "Like I'm getting a second chance and I'd better not screw it up."

He kissed her again and she melted into the bed, feeling as if every dream she'd ever had was coming to life. For these few moments, she put their differences out of her mind and saw only the connection between them—a connection that had lasted over the miles and over the years to come back now stronger than ever.

"Ever since Carla's death," Dave said, "I've wanted to run from anyone who needed anything from me. It made me feel trapped. Closed in. I think it was a knee-jerk reaction to getting dragged down into somebody else's problems for so many years and not being able to do anything to help her."

"No. Carla took advantage of you. Don't let the resentment you feel because of that make you forget the wonderful gift you've got."

"Gift?"

"It's part of who you are, Dave. Taking care of things. Being there for people. I felt it all those years ago, and I feel it even stronger now. You've just got to realize you're helping people out of caring and not out of obligation."

"I won't lie to you, Lisa. When you called me, it really blindsided me. I'd tried so hard to put you out of my mind that having anything to do with you felt like betrayal all over again. If I hadn't made you that promise . . . I don't know. I might never have come."

"Are you sorry you did?"

"God, no. I want to help you any way I can."

"Because you feel obligated?"

"No," he said. "I told you before. I'm here because I care about you."

He stroked her hair, staring down at her with such warmth that for the first time she finally allowed herself to see the truth in every word.

"And once you're on your feet again," he said, "you won't just walk. You'll run. If you happen to stumble, I can be there with a hand up. You'll never be reaching for me just to drag me down. That's what I've got to have, Lisa. What I need a woman to be."

What I need a woman to be. The words sent shivers down her spine, and as he leaned in to kiss her again Lisa knew in her heart that there were things that would always keep them apart, but just for now she wanted to pretend that dreams really did come true.

Then she heard the phone ring, and her heart jumped. Dave got up, and Lisa followed him to the phone in Sera's bedroom. Dave picked it up, waiting until the person on the other end of the line spoke first.

"Alex," Dave said finally. "I hope you've got some good news."

chapter twenty-three

"I found a sales rep who spilled everything," Alex said. "We've got our witness."

Dave breathed a sigh of relief. Alex was good at his job. For fear of feeding his already expansive ego, Dave had to watch telling him that too often. But damn, he was good.

"So he's going to testify against Robert?"

"Yes. A little immunity from prosecution goes a long way."

"Good. That's good." Dave checked the clock beside the bed, then talked to his brother again. "Okay, Alex. It's one o'clock. Robert should be on his way to San Antonio right now. Do you have customs officials in place at the airport to grab him?"

There was a moment of silence. "No. That's the bad news."

"What?"

"We checked with the charter companies in San Antonio first thing this morning and found the one he'd contacted, just to ensure that we knew exactly when he was coming in. Right before the pilot was due to fly out, Robert called and canceled."

Dave felt a stab of apprehension. "You mean he's still down here?"

"Evidently. I thought that was fishy, so I started checking into his bank accounts. Sometime late this morning he moved virtually every monetary asset that he could out of his U.S. accounts into Mexican banks."

"He knows somebody's on to him?"

"It seems so."

"But how?"

"I don't know. But it means he may never come back across the border."

"But if he never comes back to the U.S.—"

"He'll never be prosecuted. Extradition from Mexico is almost unheard of. There are serial killers from the U.S. sipping margaritas in Tijuana as we speak."

Dave felt righteous anger explode inside him. "Do you mean to tell me he's going to get away with this?"

"Unless he chooses to come back across the border, our hands are tied."

Dave just sat there, paralyzed with disbelief. This couldn't be happening. They had evidence tied up with a nice, neat bow sitting back in the U.S., and it wasn't going to do them a damned bit of good.

"There must be some way to deal with this," Dave said.

"No. There's nothing you can do. Cut your losses and get out of there."

Dave turned to look at Lisa, knowing she'd gotten the gist of the problem. She met Dave's gaze with an expression of pleading, of hope, waiting for him to tell her that somehow this was going to be all right. That somehow they were going to take down the man who'd tried to kill her.

That somehow he was going to make right for her what had gone so wrong.

Dave thought about how she'd spent her whole childhood living with parents who didn't give a damn about her, who'd forced her to become harsh and wary, who'd taken the joy right out of her life. Then she'd dealt with her low-life brother and faced a drug conviction she was innocent of. Now she faced circumstances she couldn't control that threatened to tear her life apart one more time. Call it a streak of hellacious bad luck, karma gone wild, or anything else you wanted to, but the fact remained that it wasn't fair, it wasn't right, and, by God, this time it wasn't going to happen.

"Alex," he said. "We're coming back today."

"Good."

"And Robert's coming with us."

"What?"

"I'll call you later and let you know when we'll be there."

"Dave, listen to me. That son of a bitch has a multimillion-dollar operation going. He's already proven he'll kill to protect it. I want you out of there *now*."

"I told you I'm bringing him in."

"Dave? Let it go, Dave. *Dave!*"

He hung up the phone over his brother's protests, then turned to Lisa. "We're getting out of here today. But we're not leaving alone. Robert is going to be on that plane with us."

"What are you talking about?"

"We're taking him back across the border."

"He's not going to like that."

"I hadn't planned on asking his permission."

The phone rang again. "It's Alex calling back," Dave said. "Let it go."

Ten rings later, the phone fell silent.

"Let me get this straight," Lisa said. "You're planning on grabbing him, putting him on the plane, and flying him back to San Antonio."

"Yes. Where we'll have customs officials waiting for him."

"That's kidnapping."

"I'd prefer to think of it as a police escort. But before we can grab him, first we need to find him. If he really is pulling completely out of the U.S., the clinic is history, so I doubt he's there. Do you know the number at his apartment?"

Lisa told him. Dave dialed, then handed her the phone. "Just listen. If someone comes on the line you recognize as Robert, hang up."

She listened a moment, then flicked her finger over the disconnect button. "He's there."

"With no other doctors down here, will he be alone in the building?"

"Yes."

"Then we should be able to grab him with no problem."

Dave strode back to the guest bedroom, Lisa taking two steps to keep up with every one of his. He buttoned his shirt and tucked it in, then grabbed a gun from his bag.

"Dave? Are you sure you want to do this?"

A sense of righteous anger surged through him all over again. "Robert tried to kill you. Then he tried to frame you for a crime you didn't commit, and now he thinks he's gotten away with all of it. I'm not going to let that happen."

He slid the gun into his jeans at the small of his back, then put on his jacket.

"Messing with you was a big mistake on his part, Lisa. Because now that means he's going to have to deal with me."

They went downstairs, and Dave phoned Alex back to tell him what they'd decided to do. Even though the phone was against Dave's ear, Lisa could still hear the expletives pouring out of his brother's mouth. It took Dave a good three or four minutes to calm Alex down long enough to hear their plan. Eventually he relented, and from Dave's side of the conversation she could tell that Alex was going to arrange to have customs officials at the San Antonio airport three hours from now to make an arrest.

"He sounds real happy about this," Lisa said as Dave hung up the phone.

"That's just Alex. He has to fly off for a little while. Eventually he winds down enough that you can reason with him."

"Kind of volatile for a cop, isn't he?"

"Oh, he's not like that on the job. Only with family."

"People he cares about."

"Exactly." Dave shook his head. "He yells because he loves us. Show me the logic in that."

"You know the logic in that."

Dave tucked his hand behind Lisa's neck. "Yeah," he said softly. "I do." He pulled her forward and kissed her, then rose from the kitchen chair. "Let's get going. The sooner we're in the air and out of here, the better I'm going to like it." He started toward the door, then turned back. "Better bring a blanket."

Lisa slumped with disgust. "So I get to ride in the backseat again?"

"Now is not the time for Robert to find out you're back in town."

They left the house and got into the car, with Lisa tucked against the floorboard of the backseat. It wasn't long before Dave pulled the car into the alley that ran behind the apartment building and killed the engine.

"Okay," he said. "We're there."

Lisa rose from the backseat.

"Have you got the plan straight?" he asked her.

"No problem."

"He won't be expecting anything, so it'll be easy to get the drop on him. But I still want you to stay on your toes."

"I will."

"The longer we're here, the more chance we have of being spotted. So we can't mess around. Get in, grab him, get out."

"Gotcha."

"Okay. Let's move."

They got out of the car and moved along the side of the building opposite the side where Robert's apartment was. They walked into the courtyard and slipped quietly through the front door of the building, letting it close silently behind them.

Lisa pointed to the door of Robert's apartment, then positioned herself farther down the hall, just as Dave had told her to do. Dave went to the opposite side of the door and pressed his back to the wall beside it. Lisa nodded, and he reached up and rapped on it three times.

A long time passed, and Lisa was beginning to think Robert wasn't going to answer. Then she heard footsteps inside the apartment and the door swung wide open.

"Hi there, Robert," she called out. "Nice day, isn't it?"

Robert stepped out into the hall, turning immediately to stare at her. She couldn't help enjoying the look of utter surprise on his face and how that surprise turned to shock when Dave moved up behind him, wrapped his arm around his throat, and jammed the barrel of his gun beneath Robert's right ear.

Dave shoved the man back into the apartment. "Facedown on the floor!" she heard Dave shout. *"Now!"*

By the time Lisa made it to the apartment door, Dave had

Robert on the ground, his knee pressed into his back, the barrel of his gun against the man's neck.

"What the fuck is going on here?" Robert shouted, his face twisted with anger.

Dave pulled a length of rope from his pocket with his free hand so he could secure Robert's hands behind his back. "We're taking you for a plane ride. There are some customs officers in San Antonio who can't wait to meet you."

All at once, Lisa heard a noise behind them. She spun around and recoiled with shock. A young Mexican woman stood in the bedroom doorway. She was naked except for a sheet wrapped around her. She wore a look of sheer terror.

She held a gun.

"¡Párese!" the woman shouted. "¡Déjalo!"

In the span of a single second, Lisa realized what they'd walked into. Robert kept a gun around the house, and now his girlfriend of the moment was pointing it at Dave, telling him to leave Robert alone.

"Drop it!" Dave said.

Robert squirmed beneath him. "¡Pégalo!"

"No!" Dave shouted. "Don't shoot! Drop the gun!"

"¡Diji pégalo, ahorita!" Robert shouted.

With Robert screaming at her to shoot, the woman raised the weapon and squeezed her eyes closed. Lisa turned away in a reflex action, and a second later a shot exploded. She heard a ceramic crash. As the woman ran screaming for the door, Lisa started to turn back, only to see Dave's gun lying on the floor.

She dived for it, slapping her hand against it at the same time Robert rose to his knees. She brought the weapon around, but he lunged for her, knocking her to the floor. He clamped his hand onto her wrist, then slammed it down, dislodging the gun. He picked it up, rose to his feet, and backed away, breathing hard, first pointing the weapon at her, then quickly swinging it around to look for Dave.

Dave. *Oh, God.*

For the first time, Lisa saw him lying on his back on the

floor. It looked as if he'd dragged down a lamp when he fell. It was lying in pieces beside him. His head was bleeding.

He wasn't moving.

"Dave!" Lisa shouted.

"Well, look at that," Robert said, visibly relaxing. "Not only is she a good lay, it looks like she's a pretty good shot, too."

Lisa wheeled around to face him. "You son of a *bitch*!"

"Yeah, but now I'm the son of the bitch in charge."

Lisa looked back at Dave, her heart racing. He still wasn't moving. How badly was he hurt?

Please let him still be alive.

"Dave DeMarco, right?" Robert said. "The cop who was picked up with you in San Antonio?" He glanced at Dave lying on the floor. "Looks as if he should have left well enough alone."

"Why didn't you go to Adam's memorial service?"

"A few of my players turned up missing. Ivan Ramirez. His brother, Gabrio. Smelled fishy. I made a few phone calls. Still don't know what happened to them. But guess what I did find out? Somebody in my network talked. Damned if I'm going back across the border now. But that doesn't really break my heart." He gave her a malicious smile. "Life's pretty good down here."

Lisa glared at him, so filled with hate for what this man had done that it was all she could do not to go for his throat. If only Dave would move. Get up. Something. *Anything* to tell her he was still alive.

Robert walked over to where Dave lay slumped on the floor, training his gun on him the whole time. Blood covered the side of his head, and he lay still as death.

"A head wound," Robert said. "She's an even better shot than I thought." He turned back to Lisa. "One down, one to go."

The anguish Lisa felt almost incapacitated her. This couldn't be happening. It couldn't. She had a flash of Dave's family, his daughter, and all the people in his life who loved him, who would eventually find out that he'd died like this. And it was her fault. It was all her fault for dragging him down here in the first place. Tears welled up in her eyes, and she put her hand against her mouth to stifle her sobs. She loved him. God, how she loved him, and she may have gotten him killed.

Robert put a foot against Dave's shoulder and gave him a hard nudge. Nothing.

Oh, God. It's true. He's dead.

Then Robert turned to walk away, and something happened that shocked the holy hell out of her. Dave sat up suddenly, spun around on one hip, and smacked his leg against Robert's ankles, knocking him right off his feet. Robert came down hard on the floor. Dave climbed on top of him, clamping his hand down on Robert's throat at the same time he used his knee to trap the man's arm that held the gun. With a single hard yank, Dave took the gun from Robert's grasp and jammed the barrel against the side of his neck. Robert choked and gagged for breath, but Dave didn't let up.

"Don't move, you asshole, or I swear to God I'm pulling the trigger." He glanced at Lisa. "Grab the rope."

Lisa just stood there, stunned. Blood dripped from the side of Dave's head onto his shoulder, yet he was acting as if he hadn't even been shot.

"The rope, Lisa! Move it!"

She retrieved the rope from the floor and brought it to Dave. He turned Robert over, handed Lisa the gun, then yanked the man's arms behind him.

"Dave!" she said. "You're bleeding! The bullet—"

"I wasn't hit. She got the lamp."

"But the blood—"

"The lamp exploded and knocked me backward. A piece of it sliced my head open. By the time I realized what was happening, Robert already had the gun. I figured it would be in our best interest if I stayed down."

She couldn't believe it. It was just a scalp wound? All that blood, but he was okay? "Oh, God," she said, swiping the tears out of her eyes, almost collapsing with relief. "I thought you were dead."

"No way," he said. "This bastard's going back across the border if I have to climb off my deathbed to drag him there."

Dave finished tying Robert's hands, then took the gun back from Lisa. She hurried to the bathroom, found a hand towel, and when she brought it back out Dave already had Robert on his feet. She tried to press the towel against Dave's head, but he shrugged it off.

"Just bring it along. We need to get him out of here."

Then Lisa heard something outside, and she could tell Dave heard it, too.

"Sirens?" she said.

"Shit. His girlfriend probably called the cops. Let's go!"

But when he took hold of Robert to drag him out the door, the man tried to wrestle away. "Fuck you! I'm not going anywhere!"

Dave shoved him three steps forward and slammed him against the wall, pressing the barrel of his gun against the side of his head.

"Now, Robert," he said, restrained fury filling his voice, "you and I both know that down here there aren't any rules. I could kill you, get back on that plane, return to the U.S., and nobody would even know I'd been here, and even if they did, I doubt they'd give a shit. The only reason you're still alive is because I'm still hanging on to one tiny thread of humanity where you're concerned. It snaps, you're a dead man. You got that?"

Robert's eyes widened just enough that Dave knew the man was finally taking him seriously. He shoved Robert out the apartment door, through the courtyard, then around the edge of the building to the alley, where he pushed him into the backseat of the car.

"Are you sure you're okay to drive?" Lisa asked Dave.

"I'm fine." Dave slammed the back door. They leapt into their seats, pulling their seat belts across them. Dave started the engine, shoved the car into gear, and burned rubber.

"How fast can you get that plane off the ground?" Dave asked.

"We can hop in, start the engine, and go. You get us there, and I'll put us into the air in a hurry."

They approached an intersection. Dave sped right through the stop sign, but when Lisa looked down the intersecting street she saw a sheriff's car a block away, coming toward them.

"I think they've seen us," Lisa said. "Let's move!"

A few seconds later, the police car skidded around the corner to follow them, lights flashing and siren blaring. Dave gunned it through town, steering wildly around any cars that got in his way, at the same time laying on his horn to warn anyone who was even thinking about crossing the street.

"Gee, Dave," Lisa said, her eyes wide and her back plastered against the seat. "You're getting pretty good at this."

"Practice makes perfect. How are we doing back there?"

Lisa looked over her shoulder. "They're still there, but they're not gaining on us."

Soon they approached the outskirts of town. Dave maneuvered through the last stop sign, then hit the gas hard. Nothing but open road lay ahead of them. If they could reach the dirt road that ran to the west of Sera's property and turn onto it without being seen, they were home free.

Lisa looked over her shoulder. "Looks like they've fallen back. We may just make it."

The road was filled with curves, which Dave negotiated with as much speed as he possibly could and still keep all four tires on the ground. Lisa kept looking over her shoulder, but no police car came into sight. Then they came around a bend, and Lisa recoiled.

"Dave! Look out!"

Dave slammed on the brakes and veered hard to the right, but not in time to keep from crashing into the back fender of a police car that was turned sideways in the road. The impact spun it out of the way and smacked Lisa and Dave hard against their seat belts. Dave wheeled their car back to the center of the road and hit the gas again.

"Looks like they radioed ahead to another unit," Dave said. "You okay?"

"Yeah. You?"

"I'm fine."

Peering out the windshield, Lisa saw the left front end of their car mangled beyond description. "Oh, boy. Is that a problem?"

"We're still moving. I'm taking that as a good sign. What's going on behind us?"

Lisa looked over her shoulder. "They're turning around."

"Yeah?"

"And coming after us."

"Shit."

"There's our turnoff!" Lisa said, pointing down the road.

Dave hit the brakes, tires squealing, then made the ninety-degree turn onto the dirt road. He hit the gas again, kicking up a cloud of dust behind them.

"Are they still on our tail?" Dave asked.

"I don't know. It's hard to see." She paused, staring hard, trying to make out a car in the midst of all the dust. Nothing . . . nothing . . .

"Damn it!" she said as the front end of the police car came into view. "They're still coming! We need more of a lead, or we're never going to make it."

"I'm going to slow down," Dave said. "Let them get closer."

"What?"

Dave slapped his gun into Lisa's hand. "Do your thing, baby."

Lisa had spent hours at the shooting range in San Antonio preparing for the worst, but never in her wildest dreams had she imagined that it would pay off like this.

She took the gun and turned around, glancing down at Robert huddled in the backseat. "Better keep your head down, Robert, or it's liable to get blown off."

With that, she blasted out the back window of the car with a single shot so she could see more clearly. Then she zeroed in on her target.

"Are you close enough to hit something?" Dave asked her.

"Drop back a little more, just to make sure."

Dave eased off on the accelerator. When the car behind

them came into range, Lisa squeezed off two shots in quick succession. A moment later, the police car slid sideways, careened off the road, and slammed into a wooden fence. She turned back around and slumped in the passenger seat.

Dave blew out a breath of relief. "Damn, you're good."

"Still think I ought to stick to chick flicks?"

"God, no. If I catch you watching a chick flick, I'm taking away your Blockbuster card."

Lisa pointed ahead. "Okay. There's the gate leading into the field."

"Hang on."

Dave smacked his foot onto the brake, swung the car around ninety degrees, then hit the gas again, crashing right through the rickety gate in a loud crunch of wood on metal. As they sped away from it, Lisa looked out the back window in amazement. The gate was kindling. She turned to Dave.

"Now who's been watching too many action-adventure movies?"

"There's something to be said for the direct approach."

Lisa glanced out the back window again. "Damn it!

"What?"

"They're coming on foot! If they get within shooting range, we're going to be in trouble."

Dave sped across the quarter-mile expanse of field, bumping along the furrows. It seemed to take forever before they reached the grove of trees where the plane was hidden. Dave brought the car to a fishtailing halt, killed the engine, and they leapt out. As he was hauling Robert out of the backseat, Lisa was pulling out her keys and opening the door to the cargo compartment. But as soon as Dave shoved Robert toward it, he started to fight back.

Dave slammed Robert up against the side of the plane, smacking his head against it, then shoved him toward the compartment again. Still he balked, and Lisa knew that with a man his size, conventional methods weren't going to cut it.

She stepped forward and grabbed Robert by the arm. Spinning him around, she took him by the shoulders and kneed him right in the groin. As he doubled over and gagged in pain, together she and Dave shoved him inside the cargo compartment, then slammed the door and locked it behind him.

"The direct approach," Lisa said breathlessly. "*God,* that felt good."

She'd barely said the words when a shot exploded and a bullet pinged against the plane.

"Let's get out of here!" Dave shouted.

Lisa circled the plane, climbed onto the wing, and opened the pilot's door. Three more shots went off. She fell into her seat and closed the door behind her. A few seconds later, Dave did the same.

She started the engine. Breathing hard, she gave it some throttle, and the plane started forward, more bullets slamming into it. She swung it around ninety degrees, then accelerated across the field. Looking out the window, she saw the men take aim again.

"Get down!" she shouted.

They both ducked. One bullet hit the nose of the plane, another the rear fuselage. Lisa checked her ground speed, then slowly pulled back on the yoke, and they were airborne. She heard more gunfire, but no bullets hit the plane. They rose into the sky, leaving the gunmen behind.

"Have they hit anything that might bring us down?" Dave asked.

"We're flying. I'm taking that as a good sign."

As the landscape fell away beneath them, the engine hummed evenly and nothing seemed amiss. Lisa scanned her gauges. "Fuel is staying level, so I'm assuming it's not pouring out. Everything else looks good."

She circled the plane around to head back north. Below them she saw the men with guns and their wrecked car. She imagined just how pissed they must be, and she felt a rush of pure exhilaration.

"We did it, Dave. Look at them down there. Bet they're cussing up a storm!"

The vindication she felt at that moment was satisfying beyond description. Robert was going to pay for every horrible thing he'd done, and they were going to have the joy of watching it happen. Adam and Gabrio were safe. She and Dave were on this plane together, alive and well, making their way back to the U.S. Life just didn't get any better than this.

Well, there was one *tiny* problem.

"I guess I'm going to have a little trouble explaining the condition of this plane to the owner," she said. "Suppose I can convince him that bullet holes give it character?"

When Dave didn't respond, she turned to look at him. His head was resting against the back of the seat, and he was staring straight ahead.

"Dave?"

He closed his eyes, clenching his teeth, and for the first time she realized how pale he was. Then she looked down at his seat, and what she saw made her heart lurch.

It was soaked with blood.

"Sorry, baby," he said. "This time it's for real."

chapter twenty-four

Every bit of Lisa's elation fled, replaced by a horrible sense of dread. Dave had taken a bullet. And enough blood coated the seat for her to know that it was far more than a flesh wound.

"Let me see it," she said.

He slowly moved his hand, revealing a bullet hole in the side of his thigh. When she saw how quickly the blood seeped out she thought she was going to be sick. She paused for a few seconds, taking a deep, steadying breath.

Stay calm. You can't help him unless you stay calm.

She set the trim to maintain correct altitude, then let go of the yoke. She had to get something over the wound. Stop the bleeding. But she'd left the towel behind, and they certainly hadn't taken the time to stop and get their bags out of the car. Glancing around the plane, she saw nothing else that she could use to hold against the wound.

"Your shirt," she told Dave. "Take off your shirt."

The moment he removed his hand from the wound again, even more blood came out. Lisa pressed her palm hard against his thigh, and he sucked in a breath of pain.

"I know it hurts. I know. But I have to hold something against it. Get your shirt off."

He unbuttoned his shirt, then gritted his teeth and leaned forward, slipping out of it. She placed his hand against the wound again to help slow the flow of blood.

"Hold on tight to it, okay?"

She poked a key through the fabric of the shirt, then ripped away a piece of it, folding it into a pack.

"There you go messing up one of my shirts again," Dave said. "Pretty soon I'm not going to have a damned thing left to wear."

"God, Dave. Please don't cut up. Not now."

"Take it easy, Lisa. It's going to be okay." He glanced at the yoke. "Shouldn't somebody be flying this thing?"

"I've got it under control. Move your hand."

He eased his hand away, and she quickly pressed the pack against the wound.

"Hold that," she told Dave, putting his palm back against it. She tore the shirt into strips.

"Can you lift your leg?" she asked.

He raised his leg as best he could, and she slipped the strips beneath it, circling his thigh and making a knot just above the wound to tie the pack in place. Blood was already soaking through it. She pressed her palm hard against it, and Dave gritted his teeth.

"I'm sorry," she said. "But I have to hold it tight."

"I know. It's okay."

With his head against the back of the seat, he rolled it to the left to look at her. "Guess this'll teach me not to mess around getting into the plane next time, huh?" He smiled a little, but she could see the pain in his eyes.

"Dave, I'm so sorry. I never should have gotten you into this."

"No. It was my decision. I was the one who wanted to go after Robert."

"But I never should have let you. You'd already done so much for me. To put your life at risk like this—"

"Again. My choice. And everything's going to be all right. We haven't come this far for things to fall apart now. Just get us to San Antonio, okay?"

"No. We're landing in Brownsville. It's only an hour away. I wish I could put down before then, but there's nothing between here and there but open country. I'll make sure they have an ambulance waiting."

"What about Robert?"

"I'll ask the controller in Brownsville to contact customs

agents in San Antonio and tell them what's happening. They can arrange to have agents in Brownsville waiting to pick him up." She paused. "And I'll have them call Alex. He needs to know what's happening."

Dave looked for a moment as if he wanted to object. Then he glanced down at the blood seeping through the bandage on his leg and simply nodded. That was her first indication that he really did know what a dangerous situation he was in, and her own apprehension took a quantum leap.

Lisa radioed ahead and explained the situation. As she was asking them to contact Alex, she started to imagine what it would be like if she had to tell Dave's family that the worst had happened. They already thought he was crazy for having anything to do with her. If she ended up getting him killed . . . oh, God, how was she ever going to deal with that?

Even though Dave was losing blood, for the first ten minutes or so he seemed alert. But by the half-hour mark he started to get groggy. And no matter how hard she held the pack against his leg, blood continued to seep out, eventually dripping to the floor below.

She kept talking to him, even though his responses grew more sparse. Her fingers ached from pressing them so hard against his wound, but she wasn't going to let up. Not for one second. With the blood he was losing even with the pressure, she couldn't imagine what it would be like if she let go.

So she wasn't letting go.

"How are you doing?" she asked.

"I'm okay," he said with a weak smile. "Just thinking about tequila shots."

So was she. That and every other moment of the past few days that had brought them so close together. After everything that had happened between them, the very idea that she could lose him now was inconceivable.

As the minutes ticked by, Dave's respirations grew faster and more shallow and his eyes began to glaze over. Looking down, Lisa saw blood covering the floor beneath his seat, and she had to fight the ache of hopelessness that began to eat away at her.

Then she saw it. Far on the horizon, Brownsville was coming into view.

"Dave! We're almost there. Hold on, okay? We're almost there."

He nodded almost imperceptibly, slowly blinking his eyes. She was losing him.

"Hey, Dave," she said, trying to keep her voice light. "What do you suppose Arnold and Bruce and Sylvester would do in a situation like this? They'd probably think it was no big deal. I mean, this is a piece of cake compared to hanging off helicopters and getting hit by an explosion at the top of a skyscraper, right?"

"Yeah," he said weakly. Then he rolled his head around to look at her. "But the difference is that they go home at the end of the day . . ." He took a breath. "No matter how many times they've been shot."

"So will you."

There was a long silence.

"Maybe," he said.

Looking over, she saw his eyes growing heavy, and his face was deathly pale.

"No," she said suddenly. "Not maybe. Don't you *dare* say maybe. I can see Brownsville. We'll be down in just a few minutes. I know you can hold on for a few more minutes."

He sighed weakly. "Lisa?"

"Don't talk, Dave. Save your strength. We'll be on the ground in no time."

"If things go wrong, tell Ashley I love her. And my family, too."

"Dave, stop it!" she said. "You're going to make it. You can tell them yourself!"

"Promise me."

"Dave—"

"Promise."

She swallowed hard, fighting the sobs that choked her throat. "I promise."

"Something else."

"Yes?"

"Promise me that no matter what happens, you won't blame yourself for this."

She clenched her teeth, willing herself not to cry. Of course she was going to blame herself. Now and through the rest of eternity.

"Lisa. Promise me."

She blinked hard to keep the tears away. "I promise."

He nodded a little. "You know what?"

"What?"

"This morning," he said, his voice fading, "when we were talking, I don't think I ever got around to what I was really trying to say."

"What's that?"

He said the words softly, almost inaudibly. "I love you."

Lisa felt a rush of pure joy at the same time her heart was breaking. After all this time, to hear him say those words . . .

Then his eyes drifted closed.

"Dave?"

He didn't respond.

"Dave!"

Tears filled her eyes, clouding her vision. *No.* She had to see to land. She had to see clearly so she could bring this damned thing down in a perfect three-point landing, because that was all she could do for him now. Give him a soft landing and get him into that ambulance.

She made contact with the tower again, and they told her an ambulance was ready and waiting on the runway. She swung around for her final approach, then brought the plane down as gently as she could. Off to one side she could see an ambulance shifting into gear to meet her.

She brought the plane to a halt, killed the engine, then turned to Dave again, continuing to put pressure against his wound until the paramedics could arrive. She put her other hand against his bloodstained cheek, then dropped it down to his shoulder. Sliding it down his arm, she took his hand in hers.

"I love you, too," she whispered. She knew he couldn't hear her. But she had to say it anyway, just in case.

Just in case she never got another chance.

The ambulance screeched to a halt. Two paramedics got out and rolled a stretcher up to the plane. They climbed up on the wing and opened the door.

"There's a bullet wound in his thigh," Lisa said. "He's lost a lot of blood."

"How long has he been unconscious?"

"Only a few minutes."

"Head wound, too?"

"Just a laceration," Lisa said.

"Okay. Let's get him out of here."

Soon they had Dave out of the plane and strapped to a gurney. They wheeled him quickly back to the ambulance and loaded him on board. Lisa circled the ambulance to get into the passenger seat.

"Hey!"

She turned back to see two men approaching, flashing badges. "Are you Lisa Merrick?"

"Yes?"

"Where's our drug counterfeiter?"

They were customs agents. She'd forgotten all about Robert. She lobbed her keys to one of them. "The cargo compartment. He's all yours."

She got into the vehicle and slammed the door behind her, then turned around to look through a small window into the back of the ambulance. A paramedic was already hooking Dave up to needles and tubes and God knew what else. His eyes were still closed. He wasn't moving. And he was pale. So pale.

She'd done all she could. She only prayed it was enough.

For Lisa, the next hour was hell on earth.

They arrived at the emergency room, and the paramedics took Dave inside. All she knew at that point was that he was alive. Nothing else.

She paced the floor, then sat down in a waiting room chair for exactly three minutes before getting up to pace some more. If only somebody would *tell* her something.

The emergency room was a busy place, but she felt strangely disconnected from all of it. Nurses and staff bustled around the area. A mother patted a coughing baby on the back. Children tussled with each other over a Happy Meal toy. An old lady read a tabloid newspaper. It seemed so surreal that life could be going on normally out here while Dave might be in there dying.

I love you.

She couldn't forget the elation she'd felt when she heard him say those three words. Still, it was something that was almost impossible for her to accept. So she wasn't going to accept it. Not yet. Not until everything was back to normal. It was even possible that he might not remember saying those words to her.

Or her saying those words to him.

"Lisa Merrick?"

Lisa spun around and came to her feet. "Yes?"

A man approached her wearing hospital scrubs. A doctor. She couldn't read his face, but she could tell he had news, and her stomach tightened with anticipation.

"How is he?" she said.

"It was touch and go there for a while, but we got him stabilized. They're taking him up for surgery to remove the bullet and repair the damage."

Lisa put her hand against her chest. "Then he's going to be all right?"

"Yes. Depending on how much damage the bullet did, he could have a bit of a recovery period. But otherwise, he's going to be just fine."

Every one of Lisa's muscles went weak, and suddenly she felt light-headed. Her knees buckled a little, and the doctor caught her by the shoulders and lowered her to a chair.

"Are you all right?"

Lord, she was falling apart. But finally it was the good kind of falling apart, the kind that occurs when something wonderful happens, like winning a $10 million lottery.

Or finding out that the man you love is going to live.

"Yes," she said. "Oh, yes. I'm okay. Believe me. I'm just a little overwhelmed."

"Would you like some water?"

"No. I'm fine. Really. Can I see him?"

"I'm sorry, but they've already taken him up. When you're feeling better, you can go up to the waiting room on the third floor. They'll let you know when he's out of surgery."

"Thank you."

The doctor rose to leave, then turned back. "Oh. I almost forgot. He wanted me to tell you something."

"Yes?"

"He said, 'The movie's never over until the hero gets the girl.' Do you know what he means by that?"

"Yes," she said with a smile. "I know."

Four hours later, Dave slowly opened his eyes, blinking until his sight cleared. He felt groggy, and it was a moment before he realized where he was. In a hospital room. Hooked up to an IV. And enough pain was shooting through his leg to remind him of the surgery he'd had.

Between then and now, all he remembered was a few lucid moments in the recovery room before the pain medication had knocked him out all over again. He remembered looking up to see Lisa standing next to his bed, the worry on her face finally replaced with relief, looking more beautiful than he'd ever seen her before. She'd held his hand, stroked his arm, and in minutes he'd fallen asleep again.

He turned over a little, wincing at the pain in his leg, and what he saw replaced his frown with a smile. Lisa sat in a chair beside his bed, her elbow on the arm, her chin resting in her hand, asleep. As if she sensed him watching her, her eyes fluttered open, and she sat up slowly.

"Hi there," he said. "Taking a little nap?"

She smiled, her eyes droopy. "More like a big nap."

"How long have you been there?"

She stretched a little, then checked her watch. "I don't know. I've lost track. Four hours? Five?"

He held out his hand. She rose from her chair, came to the bed, and sat down next to him.

"How are you feeling?" she asked.

"Alive. Not much else matters."

"I was so worried about you."

"I know. But everything's okay now."

She brushed the hair off his forehead, then trailed her fingertips along his cheek before letting her hand rest in her lap again. Her face fell into a frown. "I'm sorry," she said on a shaky breath. "I'm so sorry this happened."

"No apologies. It's over now."

"If you hadn't made it . . ." She bowed her head, and he could see her trying not to cry.

"Come here, baby." He tugged on her hand, coaxing her to lie down next to him.

She sniffed a little. "No, Dave. Your leg—"

"It's okay. My bad leg's on the other side, along with all those tubes and things."

"But this is a hospital."

"Do you see any signs posted? You know—a man and a woman in a hospital bed, with a big red slash through them?"

She smiled a little, and he eased her down next to him, wrapping his arm around her. She rested her head on his shoulder, and he sighed with satisfaction. "That's much better."

"Yes," she said, relaxing against him. "Much, much better."

"Okay. Here's another place to add to the balcony and the shower. A hospital bed."

"You're in no condition for hot sex."

"You're right. I'm incapacitated. I'd be totally at your mercy."

"Are you trying to turn me on?"

"Is it working?"

"Yes."

"Then I'm trying."

Suddenly the door opened and a quick glance told Dave that the DeMarco contingent had arrived. Lisa instantly leapt up and moved away from him to sit on the edge of the bed.

Too late. Judging from the looks on his brothers' faces, they'd both gotten an eyeful.

Alex strode into the room first, walking right up to Dave's bed, looking, as usual, as if he was ready to take command of any situation that needed commanding.

"We were stuck at Love Field," he said. "They had a fucking security lockdown thirty minutes before our flight was supposed to leave. We called ahead to the hospital, and all some idiot here could tell us was that you were in surgery."

"Nice to see you, too, Alex."

"Are you all right?"

"Yeah. I'm fine."

"You don't look fine."

"Thanks, big brother. I appreciate that. Got flowers for me, too?"

"Leg wound?"

"Thigh. The bullet's out. I'm okay."

"Hell of a lot of blood vessels there. Christ, you could be dead right now. Any permanent damage?"

"The doctors say no."

Alex let out a harsh breath. "Good *God*, you had us worried. For a while there we had no idea what was going on."

"Will you lighten up? I told you I'm fine."

"I talked to the customs agents in Brownsville. They've got the guy locked up. What the hell happened down there?"

"I'll tell you all about it later." Dave turned to Lisa. "Alex, John, this is—"

"Lisa Merrick," Alex said, his expression of relief slowly morphing into a stoic glare. "You're the one."

She blinked with surprise. "What?"

"You're the one who called Dave in the middle of the night and dragged him to Mexico. Got him arrested on drug charges. And now he ends up getting shot?"

Dave felt a flash of foreboding. "Alex—"

"What the hell happened down there to make my brother end up in a fucking hospital?"

Lisa's eyes widened. "W-we had a little trouble on our way out of Santa Rios."

"A little trouble?" He pointed at Dave. "You call this a little trouble? Dave goes down there to help you and this is what he gets?"

"Alex!"

"Look at what you've done! You almost got him killed!"

Lisa opened her mouth, but no words came out. She got up from the bed.

"Lisa, don't!" Dave held out his hand. "Come back!"

"No, Dave. No. I've . . . I've got to get out of here."

Dave reached for her, but she slipped away, then side-stepped Alex and John.

"Lisa!" Dave shouted. *"Lisa!"*

She yanked open the door and left the room, closing it behind her.

Dave whipped around to face Alex. "What in the *hell* was that all about?"

"You're lying here with a bullet wound, and you have to ask me that?"

"Go *get* her!" Dave shouted.

"No! I told you before. She's bad news! You don't want—"

"Alex," Dave said, his eyes narrowing dangerously, "don't you ever again, in this lifetime or the next, try to tell me what I want, because you don't have a fucking clue. Do you understand?"

Alex held up his palm. "Look, Dave. I know you've been through a lot here. You're just not thinking straight, you know?"

"I'm not *thinking straight*? What kind of patronizing ass-hole of a thing is that to say?"

"I'm just trying to show you how misguided—"

"Alex!" John said.

Alex whipped around. "What?"

"Was your head up your ass when we walked into this room?"

"What?"

"Haven't you been listening? Can't you see he's in love with her?"

Alex blinked with surprise. "Huh?"

John made a scoffing noise. "Jeez. I thought I was a moron

about this kind of thing. Looks like you've got me beat by a mile."

Alex turned back to Dave. "In love?"

Dave pointed at the door. "Alex, I'm warning you. If you don't go out there and bring her back in here right now, I'm getting out of this bed and tearing you in half. Now *go!*"

chapter twenty-five

Lisa sat in a waiting room chair, her stomach tied in knots, Alex's words still echoing through her mind. It was as if he'd verbalized all the recriminations she'd been heaping on herself for the past several hours, and she just hadn't been able to stand it.

She heard footsteps. Looking up, she saw Alex coming down the hall, and her heart suddenly hammered her chest. *No.* She couldn't hear any more. She just couldn't. She rose from her chair.

"Lisa!"

As she started to walk away, he jogged after her, catching her arm. "Lisa. Wait. Don't go."

She spun around and yanked her arm loose, staring at him hotly. "What do you want?"

"Dave wants you to come back."

"Hard to do with his badass brother blocking the door."

"I'm sorry," he said, clearly choking on the words. "I'm sorry I said those things to you."

"No, you're not. You're just sorry you pissed Dave off."

Alex shoved his hands into his pockets and looked away. "Yeah, I'm not too happy about that, either."

"Cut out the phony apologies. Dave's not here. Go ahead. Tell me what you really think of me."

Alex let out a disgusted sigh, looking at the floor, at the window, at the wall, anywhere but at Lisa. "Oh, hell, I don't know! I don't even know you! All I know is that Dave went to help you and ended up almost getting killed. What would you think if you were me?"

"I don't know," she said, her voice escalating. "I don't know what I'd think! All I can tell you is that the most horrendous moments of my life were spent on that plane, praying to God I could get him to a hospital fast enough to save his life. Dave has done things for me—" She felt herself choking up, and she swallowed her tears. "He's been there for me in ways you can't possibly imagine, and if I could go back and take that bullet for him I'd do it in a second, because there isn't anything—*anything*—I wouldn't do for him!"

Lisa crossed her arms and looked away, hating the feeling of trying to defend herself one more time. Would there be a time in her life when she didn't have to do that? Ever?

They stood there a long time, seemingly at an impasse. Lisa knew the only thing that kept either of them from walking away was the tenuous connection they shared because of the one person they both loved.

Alex drew in a long breath and let it out slowly. "I watch out for my family, Lisa. Sometimes . . . Sometimes I get a little carried away. I'm sorry." He paused. "And I mean that."

Lisa tried like hell to stay mad at him, but she couldn't. The very idea that he cared so much for Dave, even if he expressed it all wrong, was something that made her heart turn to mush.

"Look," Alex said. "I know right now that you'd just as soon spit on me as look at me, but still I'm asking you. . . ." He held out his hands. "Have a little pity, will you? If you don't go back into that room, there's no telling what Dave's going to do to me. I've had my nose broken once. I don't care to have it broken again."

Lisa rubbed the back of her neck, looking down the hall leading to Dave's room. An elevator pinged, and she heard the sound of a gurney being rolled down the tile hallway.

"It seems he's in love with you," Alex said.

Lisa turned back. "He told you that?"

"No. John told me that. It appears to be obvious to everyone but me."

Lisa felt a swirl of longing that she instantly shoved aside.

"Here's some good news for you, Alex. Dave isn't really in love with me. He just thinks he is."

Alex shook his head. "No. Now, you're wrong about that."

"What?"

"Dave doesn't just think anything. He knows. He's been that way since he was a kid. He's calm, sensible, and the vast majority of the time . . ." Alex sighed. "He's right."

No. This situation had been unique. Explosive. Emotional. And once everyday life encroached again, things could easily change.

"Go back to him," Alex said. "He wants you there. And that means I want you there."

In that moment, Lisa realized that Alex didn't have to completely understand why Dave was doing something to support the fact that he was doing it. And she thought maybe that was the most loving thing of all.

Together they turned and walked back down the hall. She came into Dave's room. He gave her a look of relief and held out his hand. "Come here."

She walked back to his bedside. He tugged on her hand, easing her down to sit next to him.

"You two," Dave said, pointing to his brothers. "Out."

"We'll call the rest of the family," John said. "Let them know what's going on. We'll be back in a little while."

They left the room, and as soon as the door closed behind them Dave turned to Lisa. "Did he apologize?"

"Yes."

"Did he mean it?"

"Yes. I think he did."

"He damned well better have."

But it didn't matter what Alex had said or whether he was sincere or not. Lisa still couldn't help feeling self-conscious, as if she'd gotten stuck in the middle of someplace she just didn't belong.

"I told you how Alex flies off sometimes," Dave said. "But he always comes to his senses."

"He was just defending you. You should be glad about that."

"I might be, if I wasn't on the verge of decking him."

No matter how much Dave went on, still she could see just how much he and his brothers loved one another. She could sense it in every move they made, every word they spoke. And it made her feel even more like an outsider looking in.

"I want you to come back to Tolosa with me," Dave said.

Her heart was suddenly beating rapid-fire. "What?"

"We have to see where we go from here. We can't do that when we're four hundred miles apart."

"But I can't . . . I can't just leave my job—"

"There are aviation companies in Tolosa."

"Yes. I could work anywhere. But it's not just that—"

"Then what is it?"

Dave didn't know what he was doing. He was acting on emotion, just as he had been these past several days. And she'd been doing the same thing. No matter what terms she and Alex might have come to, she was never going to forget that look he'd given her earlier. The look that said: *What in the hell have you done to him? Get out. You don't belong here.* She was just so afraid that sooner or later Dave was going to come to that same conclusion.

"You need somebody . . ." She turned away. "Somebody who can be a mother for Ashley."

"Yeah. We are a package deal."

"Okay," she said on a shaky breath. "Let's talk about that. I don't clean house worth a damn. I don't cook. I don't even know how to bake cookies unless I slice them off a roll, and even then I usually burn them. I don't know how to braid hair. Little girls like Ashley have to have their hair braided, right?"

"It's not terribly hard to learn."

"Symbolism, Dave. Go with me here, will you?" She let out a harsh breath. "Don't you get it? All that stuff isn't me."

"It could be."

"Well, maybe I don't want it to be. If we keep on with this, I'm afraid that someday you're going to want more from me than I'm willing to give. And then where will we be? Parenthood ties you down. Do I have to tell you that? And for that matter, so does marriage. I don't want anything to keep me from flying. It's everything I ever dreamed of."

Dave looked at her with a knowing expression, as if he could see right inside her. "Is it really everything you've ever dreamed of?"

Lisa froze. Of course it was. It had been the number one goal in her life, the thing she loved more than anything else.

But suddenly she knew it wasn't enough.

Flying wasn't everything she'd ever dreamed of. For a long time she'd told herself it was, but that wasn't true. Not even close. In the past week, she'd realized that there were other hopes and dreams inside her that she'd refused to acknowledge because she was so afraid of their never coming true.

"You need to fly," Dave said. "I know that. But when you come down to earth again, you need a place to come home to, where there's somebody waiting for you." He squeezed her hand. "Somebody who loves you."

Lisa couldn't believe what was happening here. They weren't in the middle of a desperate situation. Dave wasn't hanging in the balance between life and death. He wasn't in a state where blood loss was making him loopy.

This was the real thing. He loved her.

All at once she realized that being in that cockpit wasn't freedom. It was safe, yes. She had complete control there, and nobody on earth could hurt her. But what a lonely, barren existence, when she had nothing else. She'd never kept it in perspective for what it was—an exciting profession that she enjoyed beyond measure. Instead, she'd made flying her life when it was really the place where she'd gone to run from life. Dave was right. What good did it do to go up in the clouds when there was nothing for her when she came back to earth?

But could she ever be the woman he needed? His daughter needed? No matter how much she wanted to be, the question was: Could she?

"What I told you a minute ago," she said. "It wasn't quite true."

"What's that?"

Her voice started to tremble. "I told you that if we kept on like this, someday you'd expect more out of me than I was willing to give you. That wasn't true. Not even close." She took a deep breath, tears filling her eyes. She looked away for a moment, hoping she wasn't going to cry.

"I'm willing to give you everything, Dave. My whole life. Everything. I love you. I've loved you for so long I don't remember a time when I didn't." She paused. "I'm just so afraid that everything I've got to give you won't be enough."

He pulled her into his arms. "Oh, baby, you have no idea how wrong you are about that."

"Are you sure?"

"A minute ago I told you that I wanted you to come to Tolosa because I wanted to see where we go from here. Actually, I already know where we go from here." He leaned away and took her face in his hands. "I want you to marry me."

Lisa just stared at him. "Y-You don't know what you're saying."

"I know quite well what I'm saying. I was shot in the leg, not in the head."

"This is so sudden—"

"Is it really?" His voice softened. "I've loved you for a very long time, Lisa. And you feel the same about me."

She stared into those dark eyes, and suddenly she couldn't speak anything but the truth. "Yes."

"Then you'll marry me?"

Lisa closed her eyes, suddenly feeling as if she were soaring straight up into the clouds. She opened her mouth to respond, but she felt so overwhelmed by it all that she couldn't speak.

"Just say it, Lisa. Say the word I want to hear."

He stared at her expectantly, but his gaze said he knew without a doubt what her answer was going to be.

She did, too.

"Yes," she whispered. *"Yes."*

He smiled at her, a broad, radiant smile that took her breath away. "When will you come to Tolosa?"

"Oh, God, I don't know. . . ."

"One week?"

"That's fast."

"Not fast enough," Dave said.

"I suppose I'll meet the rest of your family then."

"Yes."

"And Ashley."

"Yes."

She took a deep, shaky breath. "Is it possible to be ecstatic and terrified all at the same time?"

He smiled. "You'll be fine, Lisa. Trust me. You'll be just fine."

chapter twenty-six

The next evening, Adam lay on one of the double beds in a Monterrey hotel room, his head propped up on a pillow, staring into the darkness. He'd flipped out the light at ten-thirty, but now, forty-five minutes later, he still lay awake. Gabrio was sprawled on his stomach on the other bed. He'd probably fallen asleep the minute his head hit the pillow.

At least one of them could sleep.

Not that it didn't feel good to be out of the hospital. Adam's wound still ached after the surgery and he'd have to wear a sling for a couple of weeks, but eventually he'd be good as new. Dave and Lisa had made it out of Mexico with Robert in tow. It had been touch and go, but they were safe and Robert was in jail. Adam's attorney friend assured him he'd have a nonimmigrant visa for Gabrio by tomorrow afternoon, and then the two of them would be flying back to San Antonio. Everything was taken care of, but still Adam felt restless. Edgy.

All he could think about was saying good-bye to Sera.

Because she'd insisted on staying in Monterrey until she saw him safely onto the plane, she was in the room next door, undoubtedly asleep by now. After tomorrow, he might never see her again.

"Hey, man. You still awake?"

Adam was surprised to hear Gabrio's voice in the darkness.

"Yeah," Adam said. "You, too?"

In the dim moonlight he saw the kid turn over, then tuck his arm behind his head. "What time are we flying out tomorrow?"

"Four-thirty."

"Never been on a big plane like that before."

"You've flown with Lisa, so a commercial plane will be no problem."

"Yeah. That's what I figured."

The kid sounded tense, but Adam didn't think it had anything to do with the plane ride. Gabrio's life had been turned upside down in the past week, and tomorrow he'd be faced with yet one more unfamiliar situation. In the end, he was going to have a life far better than the one he'd left, but it was still going to take some getting used to.

"I guess you're probably a little uptight about going to live in a new place," Adam said.

There was a long silence. "Maybe a little."

"My family will meet us at the airport. It'll be a little strange at first, I know. But everything's going to be okay."

"Yeah. I know." He paused. "I just wish Sera was coming with us."

Adam closed his eyes. *So do I.*

Even though he was doing the right thing, for some reason it still felt wrong. But how could it be wrong to want her to have the best life possible, even if it meant that he couldn't be part of it?

When they were at the hospital, Sera had seen a job posting for an obstetrical nurse. She'd talked to the supervisor and gotten the job, which meant she'd be moving to Monterrey very soon. He was glad, at least, that she wouldn't be returning to live in Santa Rios. She'd be taking a job she was going to love, and she'd be living in a big city, where she'd have the opportunity to meet a lot of other people.

To meet a lot of other men.

"She has her new job here," Adam said.

"Couldn't she get a job in San Antonio?"

"She could, I guess. She's just not going to."

"Why not?"

Adam sighed. "It's complicated."

No. Actually, it's very simple. You can't let go of the past long enough to give her what she wants. What she needs. What she deserves.

Down the hall Adam heard the muffled sound of an elevator bell as it reached their floor, the soft *whoosh* of the doors as they opened. Then silence again. And he couldn't stand it.

Every moment that ticked away brought him closer to that good-bye tomorrow, and the very thought of it made him sick. Someday, maybe very soon, Sera was going to meet another man who would realize what an incredible woman she was, a man who would lay the world at her feet.

A man who would have the family with her that could have been his.

"She's pretty," Gabrio said.

"Uh-huh."

"Nice."

"Yeah. I know."

"Do you love her?"

The kid might as well have shot him right in the heart. The answer was yes. More than ever. Distance wasn't going to change that. Neither was time. The world could pass away to dust, and still he was going to love her. And the longer he lay there, the more intolerable the thought of life without her became.

"Yeah. I love her."

"So why isn't she coming with us?"

"I know this is hard to understand," Adam said, "but sometimes there are a lot of other things to consider besides love."

"Like what?"

All at once, Adam didn't have an answer to that question.

He lay there motionless, trying to conjure up some kind of response, but he couldn't. It was as if the reasons he was walking away from Sera, the ones that had been carved in granite, were suddenly scribbled in sand. And with every moment that passed the words seemed to shift, to fade, until finally a mental wind came and blew them away altogether. Suddenly he couldn't think of a single thing to take into consideration *but* love.

"Does she love you?" Gabrio asked.

"Yeah. She does."

"But she wants to stay here?"

"No. Not exactly. She—"

She wants to marry you. To have a family. To follow you wherever you go. To love you for the rest of your life.

"She wants to come with me," Adam said, a note of awe in his voice, as if it had taken until that moment for the magnitude of it to finally hit him.

"And you're not letting her?" Gabrio shook his head. "Don't take this wrong, man. But you must be crazy or something."

Adam realized that for the first time in ages he was lying awake in the dark, unable to sleep, but not because he couldn't banish the traumatic thoughts that had consumed his life for the past three years. He was lying awake because he loved Sera so much that he couldn't stop thinking about her. The only trauma he was obsessed with now was the thought of never seeing her again.

Under any other circumstances, he'd never be presumptuous enough to tell her that she didn't know her own mind, that she couldn't make her own decisions, that she didn't know what was good for her and what wasn't. So why was he telling her that now?

He closed his eyes and pictured Sera.

Then he pictured his life without her.

He tossed back the covers and sat up on the edge of the bed. Gabrio was right. He must be crazy. In the room next door was a beautiful young woman he should be thanking God for instead of pushing away.

He flipped on the lamp, groaning a little at the pain in his shoulder.

"Something wrong?" Gabrio asked, blinking against the bright light.

"Yeah," Adam said. "Something's wrong. But it won't be for much longer."

He rose from the bed, wearing nothing but the bottoms to the pair of pajamas that Sera had bought for him while he was in the hospital.

"Where are you going?" Gabrio asked.

"To Sera's room."

"Oh, yeah?"

"I might not be back for a little while. Will you be all right here by yourself?"

"Sure."

Adam started toward the door, then turned back. "Actually, I—"

"What?"

Oh, hell. This was probably a really bad example to set for a kid, but what else could he do? "I . . . uh . . . I might not be back until morning."

Gabrio rose on one elbow. "Does this mean Sera's going with us to San Antonio?"

"It's up to her. I just hope to God she hasn't changed her mind."

"Then make it good, man. This is not the time to mess up."

With a furtive smile, Adam left the room, closing the door behind him. He couldn't have imagined a time in his life when he'd be taking advice on romance from a sixteen-year-old kid, but there it was. And it was pretty good advice at that.

He went to the room next door and knocked gently. After a moment, the door opened slightly and Sera peered out, a worried expression on her face.

"Adam? What is it? Is something the matter?"

Without a word, he pushed the door open and came inside, closing it behind him. He turned, and in the dim lamplight he got a good look at Sera and his mouth went dry.

She was wearing a blue nightgown, the same one she'd had on in the bedroom at her house. He remembered how she'd slid her robe off her shoulders, revealing that blue fabric clinging to every beautiful curve of her body. He hadn't been able to take his eyes off her then, and he couldn't take his eyes off her now.

"God," he murmured, staring down at her.

"Adam? What's the matter?"

"Sera, I . . ."

But words wouldn't come. Not one. He had so much to say that it got all tangled up in his mind. Instead, he slowly raised his hand to her shoulder and hooked his thumb beneath the narrow strap of her nightgown. He pushed it aside, watching as it fell against her upper arm. Leaning in, he kissed the spot where it had been.

"Adam?"

Sera's voice was almost a whisper, filled with surprise and confusion. He wanted to tell her why he was here, needed to tell her, but he couldn't stop touching her. He moved his lips up to her neck, kissing her there, savoring her smooth skin, her soft scent. Beneath his lips he felt the flutter at the pulse point in her neck, a pulse that seemed to escalate with every breath she took.

"Adam? What are you doing?"

"If you don't want this," he murmured, "say so now."

"Of course I want it. I've thought about it . . . dreamed about it. . . ."

Thank God.

He caught the back of her neck in his hand and drew her lips to his. He kissed her boldly, with no hesitation, parting her lips with his, tenderly but insistently delving his tongue inside her mouth. He moved his hand up to lace his fingers through her sleek dark hair, feeling it fall in ripples against the back of his hand. This was it. This was the way he'd wanted to kiss her so many times before, as if he couldn't wait to make love to her. She tasted so warm, so sweet—

"No," she said breathlessly, pulling away. "You can't do this to me."

"What?"

"You can't do this now and then walk away tomorrow. I can't take that, Adam. I can't."

"You won't have to." He wrapped his hand around the small of her back, easing her up next to him again. "Yes, I'm walking away tomorrow. But you're walking away with me."

She blinked up at him. "What?"

"I was a fool, Sera. I couldn't see what was right in front of me. I love you, and I don't want to spend one more moment of my life without you."

She looked at him with disbelief. "I don't understand. Yesterday you said there was no future for us. You wanted me to find another man—"

"No. Don't say that. Please don't say that. I can't even stand the sound of it."

"They were your words."

"And you'll never hear them again. Do you love me?"

"You know I do."

"Then tell me you'll come with me to San Antonio."

She stared at him as if she still didn't believe what was happening. "You want me to come with you? Are you sure?"

"I've never been more sure of anything in my life."

Tears filled her eyes. "Of course I'll come with you. It's all I ever wanted."

Relief washed over him. Thank God. Thank God he hadn't pushed her away so hard that she never wanted to come back.

"What about Chicago?" she asked him.

"Forget Chicago."

"You're not going?"

The truth of the situation was suddenly so clear to him that he couldn't believe he hadn't seen it before. He didn't want to go to Chicago. In taking that job, he hadn't been getting on with his life. He'd been running from it.

"No. I'm staying in San Antonio."

"You are?"

"You were right. I don't give a damn about an administrative job. I do give a damn about my patients, my friends, my family . . ." He kissed her gently. ". . . and you." He curled his hand around her neck, easing closer to her. "I want to make love to you, Sera. Right now."

She eased away from him. "I-I can't."

"No," he said, gently pulling her back. "Please don't tell me that." He expelled a breath of frustration. "I know I've been unsure about a lot of things over these past few days. But not anymore. You don't ever have to doubt me again."

"It's not that."

"Then what is it?"

"I haven't got anything with me. No birth control. No condoms. Nothing."

"It doesn't matter."

"I could get pregnant."

"God, I hope so."

Sera blinked with surprise. "I don't understand."

"I want to have a baby."

She looked at him incredulously. "But I know how you feel about that. I can't ask you to—"

"You don't have to ask. It's what I want. What we both want. And just as soon as nature cooperates, it's going to happen."

"Are you sure, Adam? Are you sure you can deal with that?"

"Yes. But probably not very well. I'll worry the whole time. I'll probably lose a lot of sleep and God knows what else. I'm not out of the woods yet where all that's concerned. All I know is that I've found the path to take me there." He slid his hand along her cheek. "It's you, Sera. And the very thought of letting you go . . ." His took a deep breath, trying to keep his voice from choking up. "I finally realized that for all the fear I've felt for the past three years, nothing compared to that."

Tears brimmed in her eyes. "I thought I'd lost you. I thought—"

"No. You never have to worry about that again."

She nestled closer, so soft and warm and inviting, and he held her tightly, secure in the fact that everything was finally going to be all right. He thought about the hundreds of times in the past two years when he'd dreamed about making love to her, and he couldn't believe that tonight that dream was going to come true.

"What about Gabrio?" Sera said suddenly. "Is he all right by himself? What did you tell him?"

"That I might be gone all night."

"You told him that?"

"Yes."

"But if you stay here, he's going to know—"

"He's going to know exactly what's happening. He's made it through some terrible things in his life. I think he can handle a little evidence that two people love each other."

Adam reached up to slide her other strap off her shoulder. "This is a beautiful nightgown," he said, then kissed the place where the strap had been. He moved his lips up close to her ear. "Will you show me what's underneath it?"

A few moments later, the shimmery blue fabric lay puddled on the floor. Staring at Sera in awe, he slowly reached out, dragged his fingertips from her collarbone to her chest, around the outer swell of her breast, then eased his hand down to take hers. He pulled her toward him, and she responded by circling her arms around his neck and giving him a long, thorough, sensuous kiss that answered every bit of the desperate need that had been buried inside him for so long. But with one hand incapacitated he couldn't touch her the way he wanted to and love her the way he'd dreamed about since the day he'd met her.

"Damned sling," he murmured against her lips. "I may have made a promise I can't keep."

"Where there's a will, there's a way," she said. "Is there a will?"

"God, yes."

"Then I'll show you a way."

They eased over to the bed, where Sera kept her promise. She found a way. She was everything he'd always dreamed she would be—soft and gentle and beautiful beyond his wildest dreams. And he discovered with astonishment that there was little room in his mind now for the fear and anxiety that had consumed his life for three long years. Instead, it was filled with thoughts of the woman who was bringing him out of the darkness and making his life whole again. The woman who was going to give him the family he'd wanted so much.

The woman he was going to love forever.

chapter twenty-seven

Lisa pulled her car up to the curb in front of the tidy brick house, and it was just as she'd imagined it would be—shutters on the windows, shrubs out front, and a pot of flowers by the door. A child's bicycle stood on the front sidewalk. Crayon drawings of a pumpkin and a ghost decorated one of the bedroom windows, apparently left over from Halloween. Occasional gusts of November breeze relieved two maple trees of the last of their fall leaves.

Just the sight of all that made Lisa's nerves skitter. It looked sweet and snug and homey—exactly the kind of place she never imagined she would belong. The deep, calming breath she took didn't calm her in the least.

It was now or never. And never wasn't an option.

She got out of the car. As she was closing the door, for the first time she glanced to the park across the street, where she saw an overgrown softball field with a mangled backstop. A game was in progress, but the World Series it wasn't.

She recognized Alex and John, along with a couple of women who might have been their wives. Populating the rest of the field was an eclectic assortment of people who were probably aunts and uncles and cousins, along with several kids. Even a few senior citizens stood in the outfield wearing baseball gloves.

Then she saw Dave. Even with his healing injury, he was in the thick of it, standing behind the catcher and acting as umpire. He looked as if he belonged there, dead center in the heart of a great big extended family.

Somebody hit the ball. A little girl on third ran toward

home as fast as her little legs could carry her. She hit home plate, stomping on it with both feet at once, then ran to Dave. He leaned over and gave her a hug, planting a big kiss right on her cheek.

Ashley.

The attack of nerves Lisa had when she approached the house had suddenly magnified tenfold. Then Dave happened to look in her direction. He froze, staring, then started to walk toward her.

As he strode across the field, still limping a little, her heart leapt into her throat. He stepped off the curb and crossed the street. When he circled around her car, she couldn't read his expression, and suddenly all kinds of terrible thoughts crossed her mind.

Maybe he's changed his mind.

Maybe he's had second thoughts.

Maybe he's going to tell you he doesn't want you here after all.

Without missing a beat, he swept her into his arms, dropped his lips to hers, and kissed her, and all the *maybes* flew right out of her mind.

She had the sense that his entire family was watching, but she couldn't have stopped him if she'd wanted to. Not when he was kissing her as if he were standing in the middle of a bunch of tequila-loving partyholics in a Monterrey hotel and the Cowboys had just declared victory.

When he finally pulled away, a quick glance toward the ball diamond told her that she'd been right. Every member of the DeMarco family had stopped playing and had turned to watch them, their jaws dropping right down to the dirt.

"Dave," she said a little breathlessly, "your whole family saw that."

He glanced over his shoulder. "Oh, yeah. They're nosy." He sighed. "I'm afraid you'll have to get used to that."

"And your brothers. They're coming this way."

"One more thing you're going to have to get used to."

"Hey, Lisa," Alex said as they approached. "It's about time you showed up. Dave's been waiting. And not too patiently."

"Alex? You want to shut up?"

"Not particularly." He turned back to Lisa. "Do you play softball?"

Lisa glanced toward the ball diamond. "No. I watch the Rangers a lot, but . . . no. I've never played."

Alex grinned. "No problem. You can be on my team. Learn from the master. Dave here would be lucky to make it in Little League."

Dave turned to Lisa. "Alex is a legend in his own mind."

"Hey!" Alex said. "Who still holds the home run record at Tolosa South, huh?"

"Reliving his high school glory days," John said, shaking his head sadly. "Is that pitiful or what?"

"Jealousy is an ugly thing, John." Alex turned to Lisa. "So you two move it, will you? We've got a game to play."

Alex and John turned and trotted back toward the ball diamond.

"Hey, you guys!" Dave called out. "Send Ashley over here, will you?"

As they nodded and continued on, Lisa felt a rush of apprehension. Dave took one look at her face, and his brows pulled together with concern.

"Hey," he said gently. "What's the matter?"

"I don't know if I can do this."

"Lisa? You want to be here, don't you?"

"Yes," she said, closing her eyes. "You know I do. More than anything. But I'm so afraid of screwing it up."

"You won't screw anything up. Trust me."

A few moments later, she looked over to see Ashley on the other side of the street. Dave checked the traffic in both directions, then motioned her across. Lisa remembered seeing her photo when they were at the hotel in Monterrey, but it didn't do her justice. Lisa didn't think she'd ever seen a more beautiful child in her life. Or maybe she was already becoming biased and didn't even realize it.

"Ashley," Dave said. "This is Lisa."

The girl looked up at her shyly, and suddenly Lisa felt her mouth go dry. She had not one clue what to say to her.

"Lisa flies planes," Dave said. "I bet she could take you up in one sometime."

Ashley glanced up at Lisa. "A real plane?"

"Uh-huh," Lisa said. "Would you like to go flying with me? It's fun."

Ashley shrugged.

Silence.

"That's a pretty braid you have in your hair," Lisa said.

Ashley pulled it over her shoulder and tugged on it self-consciously.

"Do you know how to braid?" Lisa asked.

"I braid my Barbie's hair."

"Do you think sometime you could show me how?"

Ashley peered up at her. "You don't know how?"

Lisa's heart jolted. "Uh . . . no. But you can show me, right?"

Ashley shrugged. "I guess."

Silence.

"My hair's really short," Lisa said, sweeping her hand through it. "Guess we won't be braiding it, huh?"

Ashley just stared at her.

"Maybe I'll grow it longer. How do you think that would look?"

Silence. And Lisa couldn't think of one more thing on earth to say.

"Hey, sweetie," Dave said, "why don't you go back to the game? Tell everybody we'll be there in a minute."

She gave Lisa one last wary glance, then turned and trotted off, her long braid bouncing against her back.

"Well," Lisa said, her throat tight. "That went well."

"Don't worry. You know Ashley's just shy, particularly around people she doesn't know." He smiled. "But at least we know now that we have the braiding thing under control."

"Please, Dave. Don't tease me about this."

He pulled her into his arms. "I can't promise you it'll be easy," he said softly. "I can only promise you it'll be worth it."

"It scares me to death."

"It shouldn't. You're exactly what she needs. You're going to be so good for her."

She looked away. "I hope so."

He tucked his finger beneath her chin and coaxed it back. "There's only one thing you have to do, and everything with Ashley will fall into place."

"What's that?"

"Love her father."

Tears filled Lisa's eyes all over again. "I do. More than her father will ever know."

In that moment, she knew in her heart that no matter how shaky everything felt, it was going to be all right. She'd trusted Dave with her life, and she wasn't going to stop trusting him now.

epilogue

Lisa pulled her car into Dave's driveway, killed the engine, and sat in blessed silence for a moment. She'd spent the past two days flying a group of rowdy beer company executives to an island in the Bahamas for a two-day blowout, and she was quite certain that if she heard one more round of "Ninety-nine Bottles of Beer on the Wall" she was going to go completely off her rocker. About the time the third guy lost his lunch on the return trip, she decided it was time to back off on the charter schedule so she could stay in town more often, which was where she wanted to be more and more. After all, in a few weeks she would be a married woman. And a mother.

As soon as she'd arrived in Tolosa she'd applied with an aviation company, and on the strength of her references from Blue Diamond in San Antonio they hired her immediately. It fulfilled everything she'd ever wanted to do as a pilot, but strangely, she found that every moment she was in the clouds she was looking forward to getting back to earth.

She took an apartment midway between Dave's house and the airfield. She spent her days flying, and when she was in town she spent her evenings with Dave and Ashley. Dave never rushed her, never took more than she was willing to give. And that made her want to give him everything.

She unlocked the front door of the house and went inside. Dave's car was out front, but he wasn't in the living room. She checked the kitchen and didn't find him there, either.

Then she went into his bedroom, surprised to find him propped up on pillows, leaning against the headboard of his bed. On the nightstand sat a plate of fudge beside a big bowl of popcorn. She looked at the television. A movie was on pause.

Cinderella?

The entire scenario could lead to one conclusion only. The man she loved was a dreadful liar.

"See, I told you!" she said, pointing an accusing finger at Dave. "I told you that you spoil Ashley just as much as John and Renee do!"

"Oh, yeah?"

"Yeah." Lisa looked around the room. "Where is she?"

"With John and Renee."

Lisa blinked with confusion. "So what's all this?"

Dave gave her a warm, inviting smile and patted the bed beside him. "Come here, little girl."

She stared at him, but it was at least ten seconds before his meaning struck her. When it did, all the breath left her body.

She walked slowly to the bed and climbed up next to him. He fluffed the pillows behind her back, then slipped his arm around her and pulled her close. He put the plate of fudge beside her and the bowl of popcorn right into her lap. He handed her the remote.

"You can replay the good parts all you want to."

Lisa stared at the remote hanging loosely in her hand. No matter how hard she gritted her teeth, her jaw started to tremble and tears filled her eyes. She blinked, and a couple of them ran down her face.

"Now, we still have some rules," Dave said admonishingly. "No tears in the popcorn."

She sat up suddenly, dropped the remote and slid her arms around his neck, hugging him fiercely, her face buried against his shoulder. And she cried. God, how she cried, because she loved him so much that if she didn't she was going to burst with it.

"And if you're a very good girl," Dave said, "tomorrow I'll take you clothes shopping."

Lisa laughed through her tears and melted against him, then turned to stare into those deep, dark eyes, remembering a time when she'd prayed that a thousand more tomorrows would be filled with the sight of him. The fact that she was going to have ten thousand more was beyond her comprehension.

Dave held her, rocking her gently, enclosing her in a shelter of warmth and caring for the first time in her life. He was giving her the family she'd never had and the love she would cherish forever.

In the end, it was everything she'd ever dreamed of.

Letting her go would be a crime . . .

I GOT YOU, BABE

by Jane Graves

On the run for a robbery she didn't commit, Renee Esterhaus is stuck in the middle of Texas with a broken car and a sadistic bounty hunter hot on her trail. Desperate for a way out, Renee decides to make a promise she never intends to keep—offer the first man she meets a night of unforgettable pleasure in return for a ride. A night to remember, all right, since the handsome guy turns out to be a cop with a pair of handcuffs and zero tolerance for sweet-talking criminals.

John DeMarco was supposed to be on vacation, far away from the lowlifes he endured on a daily basis. Even with his guard down, he doesn't expect to be duped—especially by a beautiful blonde con artist whose claims of innocence and tempting curves are nearly impossible to resist. Renee is not a woman he can trust . . . so why does he feel himself falling in love?

Published by Ivy Books
Available wherever books are sold

She's easy on the eyes and . . .

WILD AT HEART

by Jane Graves

When private investigator Valerie Parker tails a cheating wife late one night, it's business as usual—until the woman is murdered and the man she's with becomes the prime suspect. Val gets an even bigger shock when she discovers the suspect's identity: He's Alex DeMarco, an old flame she swore she'd never speak to again.

As a cop, Alex knows better than to ignore his instincts, but for some reason he offers a strange woman a ride home anyway. When she turns up dead and he comes face-to-face with Val Parker, his problems are only beginning. As they work together to clear his name and to protect Val's life, Alex finds himself drawn once again to the wild, impetuous woman from his past—even as the shocking secret behind the murder threatens to tear them apart forever.

Published by Ivy Books
Available wherever books are sold

Subscribe to the new Pillow Talk e-newsletter—and receive all these fabulous online features directly in your e-mail inbox:

♥ Exclusive essays and other features by major romance writers like Linda Howard, Kristin Hannah, Julie Garwood, and Suzanne Brockmann

♥ Exciting behind-the-scenes news from our romance editors

♥ Special offers, including contests to win signed romance books and other prizes

♥ Author tour information, and monthly announcements about the newest books on sale

♥ A Pillow Talk readers forum, featuring feedback from romance fans...like you!

Two easy ways to subscribe:
Go to **www.ballantinebooks.com/PillowTalk**
or send a blank e-mail to
join-PillowTalk@list.randomhouse.com.

Pillow Talk—
the romance e-newsletter brought to you by
Ballantine Books